Praise for Anna Durand's Books

"I have enjoyed this whole series, but Emery and Rory [from *Scandalous in a Kilt*] have stolen my heart and are now my favorites!"
The Romance Reviews

"An enthralling story. [...] I highly recommend the writing of Ms. Durand and *Wicked in a Kilt*, but be warned you will find yourself addicted and want your own Hot Scot."
Coffee Time Romance & More

"Anna Durand's sizzling romance novel, [*Wicked in a Kilt*], is a compelling and well-written tale about second chances at romance. [...] Durand has the gift for writing steamy hot prose that's authentic and in good taste."
Readers' Favorite

"*Dangerous in a Kilt* by Anna Durand delivered! [...] It was the journey, characters, and smoking hot sex scenes that kept me turning the pages."
The Romance Reviews

"There's a huge hero's and heroine's journey [in *Dangerous in a Kilt*] that I quite enjoyed, not to mention the hot sex, and again, not to mention the sweet seduction of the Scotsman who pulls out all the stops to get Erica to love him."
Manic Readers

"[*Fired Up* is] quite the hot romance story with a real plot and well-developed characters. [...] I loved the fact that Mel and Adam were friends before they were lovers, as it made their romance feel much more real."
Readers' Favorite

"Action from page one [of *The Mortal Falls*] keeps you on the edge of your seat for this romantic adventure trip. I enjoyed the story line, the teasing build up before the fantastic sex scenes, and the characters!"
Romance Authors That Rock

Other Books by Anna Durand

DANGEROUS
in a Kilt

Hot Scots, Book One

ANNA DURAND

DANGEROUS IN A KILT

ISBN: 978-1-934631-75-1 (paperback)
ISBN: 978-1-934631-76-8 (EPUB ebook)
ISBN: 978-1-934631-77-5 (Kindle ebook)
ISBN: 978-1-934631-99-7 (audiobook)
Library of Congress Control Number: 2016952974

Manufactured in the United States.

Jacobsville Books
www.JacobsvilleBooks.com

Publisher's Cataloging-in-Publication Data
provided by Five Rainbows Cataloging Services

Names: Durand, Anna.
Title: Dangerous in a kilt / Anna Durand.
Description: Lake Linden, MI : Jacobsville Books, 2016. | Series: Hot Scots, bk. 1.
Identifiers: LCCN 2016952974 | ISBN 978-1-934631-75-1 (paperback) | ISBN 978-1-934631-76-8 (EPUB ebook) | ISBN 978-1-934631-77-5 (Kindle ebook) | ISBN 978-1-934631-99-7 (audiobook)
Subjects: LCSH: Man-woman relationships--Fiction. | Scots--Fiction. | Chicago (Ill.)--Fiction. | Romance fiction. | BISAC: FICTION / Romance / Contemporary. | FICTION / Romance / Romantic Comedy. | GSAFD: Love stories.
Classification: LCC PS3604.U724 D36 2016 (print) | LCC PS3604.U724 (ebook) | DDC 813/.6--dc23.

Chapter One

Streaks of violet, crimson, and sapphire bounced off me from lights suspended from the ceiling, while the pulsating beat of electronic music resonated through my bar stool. I swiped through my phone's touch screen until I located the entry in my calendar—"8:00 PM: Date with Cliff @ Dance Ardor." Yep, there it was. The clock in the corner of the screen told me the time was now 8:30 PM.

I balanced atop a skyscraper stool, wearing a sort-of-new dress with my brand-new stiletto heels dangling high off the floor, and all for nothing. The jerk had stood me up.

Located smack dab in Chicago's trendy West Loop district, Dance Ardor was an underground club notorious for its...uninhibited atmosphere. According to my online research, this club was the place to go if you wanted a wild night to remember.

I glanced over my shoulder, past the dance floor and the tables arrayed around it, to a wall half the height of the vaulted ceiling. From my vantage, I couldn't see the purple-curtained private booths behind the wall, but the club's website assured me they existed. This was my last hurrah. I wanted more than dinner and flowers tonight.

A man in a hip-hugging tartan kilt strolled past, accompanied by a woman draped in a matching plaid that crisscrossed her breasts and wrapped her hips mini-skirt style. Yep, I got stood up on Midsummer Kilt Night at a raunchy club. Lucky me.

I shoved my phone back in my purse. For all I knew, Cliff was here watching me. My skin crawled at the idea. Though my dating profile included a photo, his hadn't. But when a girl trolled a dating site dedicated to semi-anonymous flings, she had to accept the unknown. The thrill I'd enjoyed when I scheduled this date had long since dissolved into unease. *Ditch the worry, remember the mantra.* I smoothed my dress, sitting up straight, and mentally recited my mantra. *Take a risk, have an adventure, be wild.*

This could be my last chance. No longer a boring accountant, I'd transformed into Erica Teague, wild woman. *Ugh.* Wild? That was one thing no one had ever called me. I scratched the back of my hand, chewing the inside of my cheek. I could do this. Really, I could.

Out on the dance floor, couples writhed in fervid hunger, grinding their bodies against each other yet keeping their eyes shut, each lost in a different world. My problem in a nutshell. I allowed my partner to hypnotize me while he pulled moves I couldn't see with my blinded eyes. Presley Cichon tricked me, sure, but I enabled him.

Yanking my phone out, I checked the time again—8:36. I clapped the phone down on the bar. My stool quivered from the abrupt motion. Just my luck, I picked a stool with a wobbly leg.

The song changed. Unnatural instruments screeched and thumped a tuneless rhythm. I rubbed my temples. Maybe the club hadn't been such a good idea after all.

A drunk guy stumbled into me, knocking my stool off kilter. I seized the edge of the bar.

"Sorry," the guy slurred. His bleary gaze swept over my body. His tongue poked out to moisten his lips. "Whoa, yer hot. But I like bigger tits on my honeys."

I hugged my bare arms. *Addendum to the mantra—take a risk, but not with a drunk.*

The bartender shooed away my admirer, flashing me an apologetic smile. My shoulders rose and fell on a sigh. "Could I get an apricot brandy?"

"Sure thing."

A moment later, the bartender plunked a snifter in front of me. I wrapped my hands around the pear-shaped glass. The drunk guy had moved on, his arm locked around a buxom brunette in a designer mini dress with a psychedelic, bright-pink pattern. It draped over her slender figure, an elegant and outrageously expensive garment. Despite the zilch I knew about designer clothes, even I recognized the couture pedigree of her outfit.

My shoulders slumped as my gaze fell to the cherry red dress I wore, which I'd bought yesterday. It was vintage, meaning bought at Goodwill, and its pedigree was more discount outlet than haute couture. Safety pins concealed in the fabric converted a modest neckline into a sexy plunge that highlighted my cleavage. The safety-pinned hem flounced around the tops of my knees when I stood but sitting down it rode up to reveal a wanton swathe of my thighs.

I swigged my brandy. A flash of fruity sweetness raced over my tongue, chased by a tangy burn. Why was I waiting for a man who didn't have the courtesy to call and cancel? *Enough of this.* I leaped off the stool onto my five-inch heels and tottered, mirroring my stool's motion. What the hell had I been thinking, wearing stilettos for the first time in my life?

Strong hands grasped my upper arms. "Easy there."

I craned my neck to behold my would-be savior. My heart thudded.

A giant of a man peered down into my eyes, his body towering several inches above me. *Whoa, mama.* The heels elevated my five-four to five-ten, which must've made him well over six feet tall. Thick muscles in his impossibly broad shoulders flexed as he maintained his hold on me. The lights glistened on his short, dark hair, casting it in unearthly hues. The sensation of his fingers on my skin and the proximity of his body flooded me with heat and my mouth watered at the sight of acres of hard, defined muscles straining his skintight black T-shirt. His powerful thighs vanished under a kilt, its plaid woven in pastel shades of green and blue with orange lines threaded through them. The blue in the fabric echoed his pale eyes, which studied me with electrifying interest. Black combat boots covered his feet but somehow, combined with his angular features, they lent him a rugged appeal.

I raked my gaze over his body, drinking in every inch of him until our gazes intersected.

Recognition lit his face. "It's you. Erica."

"And it's you." Who the hell was he? The guy seemed to know me but— Ohhhh. This must be Cliff. I shook off his hands, whipped out my phone, and tapped the clock on its screen, tipping it so he could see. "It's eight thirty-nine."

His full lips quirked. "Quite the timekeeper, eh?"

That deep voice, spiced with an enticing Scottish brogue, flowed over the words like warm molasses. *Forget his yummy accent. You're a wild woman and wild women don't wait around for late-comers.* I shook off his hands. "I've been here for thirty-nine minutes. Doesn't that mean anything to you?"

"Not really." His attentive gaze browsed over me. "Except your bum's oot the windae."

He was speaking gibberish. Great, I'd arranged a sex date with a lunatic.

"Buckled, are you?"

I spread my arms. "Do you see any buckles or belts on this dress?"

He chuckled—with no derision, simply amusement. "I meant are you drunk, lass?"

"Me?" I snorted, waving a dismissive hand. "No. Never."

Besides, I'd had just one sip of brandy.

He leaned in to stare straight into my eyes. His glacial blue irises sparkled in the light glinting off them. I caught a whiff of his rich, dark cologne and underneath, an earthy spice all his own. My senses came alive at the exotic scent of him, and the flecks of darker blue in those striking eyes mesmerized me. I swallowed. Hard.

"Your eyes look all right," he announced, and pulled away.

"What?"

"Pupils get dilated when a person's drunk. Yours look normal and your breath is fine, so I'm assuming you aren't buckled after all."

"Gee, thanks. Why—"

"Let me buy you a drink." He gestured to the bartender. "In the name of neighborliness and all."

Neighborliness? A totally nutso part of me, "buckled" on hormones, urged me to forget any and all flaws this hot Scot might reveal. *Take a risk.* I'd already enacted that part of the mantra, by asking out a guy I met online. Next, I needed to engage in an adventure, aka one night of mind-blowing sex as a send-off before my freedom was snatched away from me. Part three urged me to be wild whenever the opportunity arose.

And arise it had. In the form of one tantalizing man in a kilt.

Danger, danger, a warning siren screamed in my brain. I smashed the blasted thing to shreds. It was a remnant of the old me, the boring, organized accountant who never had any real fun.

Cliff picked up my half-empty glass and swished the liquid inside. He scrunched his nose in mock disgust. "Brandy? That's a bairn's drink." He deposited the glass on the bar. "You're in a club. Have a real drink with me."

Be wild. I leaned against the bar, shoulders rolled back, and flicked my hair. "Sure. What did you have in mind?"

Chapter Two

C liff smiled, and all my inhibitions melted into a puddle at my feet. Screw global warming. A smile that sizzling could annihilate the arctic ice sheet in two seconds flat.

The music crescendoed just as Cliff rattled off our order to the bartender. I couldn't catch what he said. Then the music wound down to segue into a quieter song with a lulling melody. I rocked my hips to the tempo of the music, my shoulders swaying too, the fabric of my dress rushing over my skin like a lover's touch.

Cliff's lips parted, his eyes devouring my movements and glazing over with…desire. For me? I lifted a hand to my throat, feeling my pulse racing beneath my skin.

The bartender brought us two small glasses, each holding a mere inch of amber liquid. Cliff downed his in one gulp.

I lifted the glass to my lips. It felt cool against my skin. I inhaled the pungent, earthy aroma. What the hell. I sucked in a breath and tossed back the drink. Fire seared my throat. I sputtered, coughed, wheezed, but the fire burned in my gut now. Slippery warmth flared through my veins. My legs wilted, but I locked my knees to stay upright. My thoughts fuzzed, every worry fading into the background. *Me like this.*

"Another," I shouted to the bartender. Within seconds, I snatched my next glass of amber ecstasy, tossed it back, and slapped my glass on the bar. "Another."

Cliff waved the bartender away. "The lady's done for the night."

The bartender, halfway to us, wandered away.

I frowned at my date. "What'd you do that for?"

He plucked the glass from my hand. "Don't drink much, do you?"

"So?"

Cliff grasped my upper arms, his skin hot on mine. "Best take it easy then. Whiskey's potent and one glass has clearly done a number on you."

"I drank whiskey?"

"Aye, and that's whisky spelled the Scottish way, without the E." Humor glimmered in his eyes and dimpled his cheeks. "You Americans don't know how to spell."

"Well, you Scots don't know how to pronounce anything." Numbed by the booze, I slanted toward him and pitched my head back to see his face. "Are you a Highlander?"

"Matter of fact, I am."

"Got a big sword?"

He captured my chin with his thumb and forefinger, bending his head. His mouth hovered deliciously close to mine. His voice dripped with sensuality. "Matter of fact, I do."

My attention flicked down to his kilt. "Don't see it."

"Maybe I'll show you later. At home."

An idea of what his "sword" might look like flashed through my mind, igniting an ember deep down. I swung my gaze up. "What do Highlanders wear under their kilts?"

Oh shit. Had I said that out loud?

His breath whispered over my lips, tickling me down to my core. "I think the whisky's getting to you."

"Feel fine." To prove my point, I twirled on my high heels without teetering. The glow of the whisky was fading, too soon. I longed for another shot of it, to drown my warning siren in its fiery depths. More than whisky, I thirsted for...Cliff.

I scuffled backward a step and bumped into the bar. How on earth could I want a man I didn't know, a man I met over the Internet? A man named Cliff. Really? My body hummed for a guy named Cliff. Well, I came here for a one-nighter. Might as well take the Highlander by the sword.

Cliff braced one elbow on the bar, crossed his ankles, and roved his eyes over my body. My skin tingled wherever his gaze flitted over me. *Have an adventure. Be wild.* I sidled up to the bar in front of him. Thanks to his cocked hip, his kilt had shifted and tightened over a bulge underneath the fabric. An impulse exploded through me, the need to slide my hand under the kilt and grasp him was almost irresistible.

A blush scorched my cheeks.

Come on, do something. I hoisted up onto my tiptoes and tilted my chin up. Our mouths were a hair's breadth apart.

"Sure ye didn't have a pint or two before I got here?" His voice quavered ever so slightly, and his pupils had dilated, though I doubted from the whisky. This gorgeous man wanted me.

My pulse rocketed into the stratosphere. My breaths quickened. *Seize the moment.*

His mouth was wide, his lips full and a dusky pink. I grazed my teeth over my bottom lip. What would this man taste like? Whisky, for sure. But what else? I burned to know, to experience his lips, his tongue—

Cliff bent toward me, just a touch, his eyes glossy.

My stomach fluttered. *Now or never, wild woman.* I leaned in, hoisting my heels up off the floor. My breasts skimmed his chest, and oh my, even that faint touch had me struggling for air.

His hands settled on my elbows, his fingers splayed over my bare skin. "Erica, you are exquisite, like a rare orchid plucked from a field of heather."

The blaring music, the odor of sweaty bodies, the clinking of glasses...All of it vanished. Enveloped in our own bubble, we edged closer to each other. His eyes blazed, my heart pounded. Closer. His chin brushed mine. Closer.

I pressed my lips to a stranger's. The lush softness of his mouth yielded to mine, the seductive hint of whisky teased my senses. I exhaled a soft moan.

He went rigid. I know he stopped breathing, because his breaths no longer tickled my skin. I flattened a hand on his hard chest and explored the lines of his muscles through his shirt. My every heartbeat resounded in my ears, my every nerve awakened. I molded my mouth to his, my breasts grazing his chest. Tight muscles slackened throughout his body and then, at last, his lips softened.

My mouth went dry. What was I doing?

Being wild. Shedding my skin. Transforming into a woman who embraced freedom and life with everything she had.

I slipped my tongue between his lips. His breath hitched, but his teeth blocked me from stealing deeper inside.

A resigned groan rumbled through his chest. He took charge of the kiss, his lips raking over mine, his jaw relaxing. I flung my arms around his neck, my heels well off the floor, my body suspended from his. He nibbled at my lower lip with a gentle playfulness, then sucked it into his mouth for a heartbeat before claiming my mouth again. My nipples peaked, sensitized in an instant. I plowed my hand into his silky hair, hauling him in for a tongue-thrusting kiss, more intoxicating than any alcohol. His velvety strokes explored my mouth, and I plunged my tongue deeper, deeper, deeper. The bump under his kilt swelled.

He pulled away, lips parted, eyes hooded.

Panting, I gaped at him.

Cliff curved an arm around my waist and drew me snug against his aroused body. His accent thickened, his voice raspy. "Are ye sure ye know what yer doing, lass?"

Hot man, hot mess, danger ahead.

My stomach lurched. I shook my head, my hair flinging around my face, and staggered backward. I lifted my hand to my mouth, swore I spotted dark stains on my fingertips, and scrubbed them on my dress. A memory flickered before my eyes, of a stern policeman squashing my fingers into an ink pad and pressing them onto a card one by one. After three weeks, no traces of ink remained, except in my mind. If Cliff knew the truth about me, he'd run. *Stupid, stupid mantra.*

Cliff reached for my hand. "Erica, are ye all right?"

Too much, all too much. I bolted.

My heart hammered. The music and the lights blurred into a surreal movie playing out around me as I hurtled through the doors and out into the night. By the time I slammed my car door and twisted the key in the ignition, I was shaking from head to toe. One night of hot sex. What on earth had I been thinking? One fact consoled me.

At least I'd never have to see Cliff again.

Chapter Three

The next morning, I woke with a headache cinched across my forehead—not from a hangover, because I hadn't drunk enough for that, but from gritting my teeth all night while I slept. Memories of last night besieged me. Cliff's hot body. His soft, supple lips. The brief taste I'd stolen when he opened his mouth to me. I'd wanted so much more. So naturally, I freaked out and ran away.

I flopped onto my back, arms crossed over my eyes, and cursed myself. My satin nightie caught under my butt, stretching tight over my breasts. I wriggled to free the fabric. Sunlight streamed through the crack between the blackout curtains on the window and leaked through the gap between my arms. I squashed my arms together to block the glare.

Somewhere in the middle of my mostly sleepless night, I'd figured out why I bolted. The game plan had been solid, but my resolve wavered. One night with a stranger, one incredible fantasy brought to life, sounded good. I'd craved it out of desperation I might never get the chance again. Faced with the reality of giving myself to a man I knew only from his brief profile on a dating site, the real me reared her head. I was no man-eater, prowling raunchy clubs for fresh meat. I couldn't go through with it. But oh, I had enjoyed that kiss. Maybe I succeeded after all in being wild.

Claws clicked on the wood floor, accompanied by panting. A weight landed on the bed, depressing the mattress at my feet and bouncing me. I dropped my arms to my sides. My golden retriever, Casey, wagged his tail. It thumped on the blanket.

After a self-pitying moan, I heaved my torso off the bed to lean over and pat my companion on the head. "Morning, Casey-wasey."

He lunged forward to slap a wet kiss on my mouth. I spluttered and wiped my mouth, then shoved the dog off the bed. "No tongue, remember? I'm not that kind of girl."

Not for canines, anyway. I'd thrust my tongue into Cliff's mouth without hesitation and permitted him to plunder mine in return. A hot shiver rippled through me as I flashed back to my body plastered to his and the faint pressure of something stirring under his kilt. *Stop thinking about him.*

A tiny thread of regret came loose inside me. Poor Cliff. I wound him up and left him hanging. Maybe I'd send him one last message and apologize for fleeing.

Casey rested his chin on the bed's edge, tail wagging, and whimpered.

"I know, I know, it's breakfast time." I swung my legs over the edge and my feet struck the chilly wood floor. With a yawn, I launched myself off the bed.

Twenty minutes later, I'd consumed two bowlfuls of chocolate Cheerios and downed a mug of steaming-hot green tea. Casey settled for chicken gizzards in addition to his dry dog food. Mmm, I loved the stench of raw gizzards in the morning. Refreshed, in spite of the chicken parts, I clasped Casey's collar around his neck, clipped the leash onto it, and pulled the front door open.

I yelped. My heart thrashed against my ribs.

Cliff smiled. "Morning, neighbor."

Stonewashed blue jeans hugged his hips and another tight T-shirt, this time jade green, stretched over his chiseled chest. The leash fell from my hand.

Casey flung his front paws onto Cliff's thighs. The man I'd kissed last night scratched my dog behind the ears. Casey, ebullient at the attention, licked Cliff's arm.

My fantasy Highlander's smile faltered. "Aren't you happy to see me?"

Happy? Seriously? I snagged Casey's collar and dragged him away from Cliff. "Are you stalking me?"

"Stalking?" He scratched his cheek. "I thought to follow you last night to make sure you were all right, but you took off so bloody fast. Might not believe it, but I am an honorable man."

A panicked laugh hiccupped out of me. "Honorable? Stalking is a crime, buddy."

My terrifying guard dog hopped up and down on his front feet, his tongue lolling.

"Erica." Cliff raised his hands, palms out. "I'm trying to be friendly."

"Go creep out some other random girl you hunted down online." I pushed Casey out of the doorway with my foot and pulled the door halfway closed. "Leave me alone, Cliff."

I slammed the door. Casey whined.

"Forget it." I wagged a finger at him. "Stalkers bad. Dog bite stalkers. Got it? No licking."

My Highlander's voice resounded through the door. "Who the bloody hell is Cliff?"

A chill trickled through me. I stared at the door, unable to budge a muscle. How could he not know his own name? The truth reeled through me and the room spun once. I never spoke his name last night. When a stranger acted like he knew me, I'd assumed he was Cliff. But if the Highlander wasn't Cliff, then who in heaven's name was he?

One way to find out. I fastened the security chain and eased the door open a few inches.

The Scot lifted one brow. "Cliff?"

"Who are you?"

He offered me his hand. "Lachlan MacTaggart. I moved in next door yesterday. House-sitting for my friend, Gil Friedman, as an excuse for a holiday in America. Gil told me about you—your name and how much he and his new bride like you."

I stared at his hand, blinking slowly. He claimed to know Gil, so...I clasped his hand. Warm fingers closed around mine in a firm grip. I managed to say, "Erica Teague. But you know that already."

"Pleasure to meet you, Erica. Officially."

"Uh-huh." His hand lingered on mine, his thumb dancing over my knuckles. The feathery touch sizzled through my whole body. I withdrew my hand and folded my arms over my chest. "How did you know what I looked like?"

"I arrived yesterday while you were out. When you came home, you set about tending to your rose bushes."

Not my rose bushes. Mom would kill me if I let them wither. This guy did not need to know the details of my living arrangements. "The roses were here when I moved in."

"You care for them with such tenderness, it's wonderful to watch." Lachlan gave me a guilty smile. "Suppose I did stalk you, by accident. I truly am sorry about last night, though."

"Wasn't your fault." Hey, why was I consoling this guy? "How do I know you're really house-sitting for Gil and Jayne?"

"Call him. He's at my place in Scotland and he's got his mobile. Said you knew the number."

Gil had given me his cell number in case of emergency and I gave him mine for the same reason. Despite three years of living next to him, I couldn't say we were besties, but he and Jayne had invited me over for dinner on occasion and I'd cooked for them too. Gil helped me clean up the mess when a storm knocked a tree branch down in my yard and he ran three blocks to catch Casey when the dopey dog took off after a big truck. He and Jayne were the closest thing I had to friends.

"Call Gil," Lachlan said. "And if you want me, I'll be next door."

He strode down the steps and across the adjoining yards to Gil's house. If I wanted him? I wouldn't. No way. My gaze was riveted to his taut ass, accentuated by those second-skin jeans, as the muscles shifted with each of his long strides. The door to Gil's house clicked shut behind Lachlan. I stood there for a moment, one hand on the doorknob, gazing out through the gap between the frame and door.

With a wistful sigh, I pried myself away from the view and shut the door. Wistful Erica, that I was. Wimpy Erica too. But wild and wanton Erica? *Last night you were.*

I grabbed my phone to call Gil. He answered on the fifth ring, sounding way too cheerful for my time zone. While I talked to him, I made coffee. I reserved java for emergencies, and this morning I definitely needed a serious caffeine boost.

"Erica, hey." He gave a surprised little laugh. "Imagine hearing from you. Did my pipes explode or something?"

"Wouldn't your house guest take care of that?"

"Oh." At least he had the gentlemanliness to sound chagrined. "You met Lachlan."

Met. Kissed. Accused of stalking. "Yeah. He, uh, stopped by to say hello. Why didn't you let me know you'd have a house sitter while you're gone?"

"Plum forgot. Lachlan called a week ago saying he wanted a break from Scotland, and me and Jayne had talked about getting a house sitter anyway, so...We decided to turn my business trip into the start of a Scottish honeymoon. We switched houses. Jayne and me are at Lachlan's apartment in Edinburgh this week, then we're heading up to his place in the Highlands. It's stone gorgeous up there."

I felt my brows tighten, crinkling my nose. "How long is Lachlan staying here?"

"Four weeks."

Twenty-eight days living next to the only man I'd ever kissed without even knowing his name. And he wanted to be *friendly.* "Is Lachlan married or involved with anybody?"

Gil chortled. "Do I detect a crush?"

"No." I slapped the coffee pod into the single-serve machine and snapped the lid shut. "How do I know the guy living there is really Lachlan? Maybe you should send me a photo of him."

"Cripes, Erica, you are so paranoid." I heard shuffling and then he said, "I'm e-mailing a photo of me and Lachlan. Satisfied?"

Not in the slightest. The mere mention of the Scot's name had my lips burning with a desire to finish what I started last night. "Yes, I'm satisfied. Thank you." I twirled a lock of hair around my finger. "So, does he have a significant other?"

The volume of Gil's laughter overtaxed my receiver's speaker. "You like him, don't you?"

"No." Damn. That came out a little petulant and a lot unconvincing. "I like to know my neighbors, that's all."

"Well..." He coughed. "If you want to know more about Lachlan, better ask Lachlan."

Uh-oh, wife alert. I grunted as I grabbed a mug from the cabinet. "Thanks for the info. And for the head's up about your house sitter."

"He's a good guy, Erica. Relax." Gil's voice took on a conspiratorial tone. "Bake some of those yummy brownies of yours and take them over to Lachlan. A housewarming gift. He'll love it."

"Housewarming?" I thumped my mug on the counter. "Are you selling him your house?"

"No, I just thought—" He blew out a breath. "Man, you are so suspicious. I love you, kid, but you have got to learn to let people in. All's I'm saying is, make a friend."

"You're my friend." I slid the mug into the coffee maker.

"Erica." He drew my name out with exasperation. "You need more friends than me and Jayne."

Grumbling, I drummed my fingers on the counter. The coffee maker drip-dripped with all the speed of a glacier traversing a continent.

"Come on," Gil chided. "Go over there and practice your social skills. I already told Lachlan you're a real sweetie and you've got a big heart to match your big mouth."

"Excuse me? I do not have a big mouth."

"No, of course not," he said with no sincerity whatsoever.

"I can't believe you told Lachlan I have a big mouth."

Gil tried but failed to restrain a chuckle. "Like he wouldn't figure it out on his own."

"Remind me to never let you write an online dating profile for me."

"Relax, your big mouth is one of your best qualities." Gil gave a long-suffering sigh. "Just give Lachlan a chance. He's a good guy. Besides, you're stuck living next door to him for a month."

I focused on the coffee slowly amassing in my mug. My new neighbor was a scorching Highlander the sight of whom drove me to lose control and lose my mind. Why me?

"You'll do it, right?" Gil asked. "You'll be nice to Lachlan? Cuz frankly, he could use a friend too."

"Why?" I didn't worry about the suspicion in my voice. I had a right to it. "What's wrong with him?"

"Ask Lachlan." A pause, and then Gil added, "He's not a criminal or a pervert. You'll like him, sweetie, so get your butt over there and be as charming as I know you can be. Toodles."

He hung up. Since when did Gil Friedman say toodles?

I had no choice. Like it or not, my almost one-night stand ate, drank, and slept twenty feet away from my quiet sanctuary in suburbia. Maybe I could get away with pretending last night never happened, but I disliked inviting elephants into my home. They tended to trash the furniture.

Gil assured me Lachlan wasn't a criminal. That made one of us.

Casey scampered up to me, his leash still dangling from his collar, and hopped on his front feet.

"Jeez," I whined. "Can I have my coffee before you start pestering me to be nice to Lachlan?"

The dog chuffed his dissent.

A knock resounded from the front door. Mug in hand, I marched to the door and drew it open. My throat constricted. An icy spike rammed straight into my heart. I stammered but couldn't form words.

Presley Cichon smirked. "Hey, babe. Miss me?"

Chapter Four

et the hell off my property." *And out of my life.* I clacked my coffee mug down onto the table beside the door. Dark liquid sloshed out. I shielded myself with the door, glaring at Presley through a narrow gap. My legs quivered, and I locked my knees for support. My mouth was suddenly parched. "I dumped you, remember? Or have you developed early onset Alzheimer's?"

A sick part of me wished he had, the part hungry for vengeance or at least some kind of punishment.

He leaned against the house where the bedroom jutted out alongside the door and hooked a thumb in the pocket of his gray slacks. His coppery brown eyes undressed me with a covetous sweep over my body, then sharpened on my face. The bastard had no right to be so good-looking.

When he angled his head, the sunlight sparked on green flecks in his irises. "I missed you, babe. Is that a crime?"

My jaw clenched. Breaths hissed out my nostrils. "Actually, it kind of is. We're involved in litigation, in case you forgot."

Presley ran a hand through sandy locks that curled around the nape of his neck. His lips curved in a boyish smile, the kind most women swooned over, the kind I had once swooned over—but no more. He cocked his head. "Come on, I'm not a witness or anything. We aren't breaking any laws by talking."

I ground my teeth. "After what you did, you've got a lot of nerve showing your face here. We are not friends."

He sauntered two steps closer. I lifted my chin to meet his gaze. Damned if I'd give him the pleasure of seeing me cringe. Presley tapped a finger on my chin. "No, sugar, we're not friends. We're way more." He stroked his finger up my jawline. "This is all a big misunderstanding. Let me in so we can talk."

Disgust slithered through me and I shook off his touch. "You're a sleaze, Presley. I can't believe I ever slept with you."

Behind me, Casey growled softly.

"Come on, babe." He settled one hand on the frame and the other on the door, exerting a slight pressure. "Let's kiss and make up."

The musky scent of his cologne choked me. Despite my thundering heartbeat and the faint quiver in my hands, I kept my voice fierce. "You set me up. And now, what, you want to get back together? You're insane."

He clucked his tongue. "Set you up? Sweet thing, all the evidence points to you and nobody else, which the DA told you when you tried to feed him your cock-and-bull story about me conspiring against you. But I forgive you."

My brain screeched to a halt. Chill morning air, tainted with his cologne, seeped into my gaping mouth. *He* forgave *me*? Once, I'd been gullible enough to swallow whatever he told me, but since then I'd gone on a bullshit-free diet.

"We had a good thing once," Presley said, his tone steamy as a summer day in the tropics. "And you need somebody to stand by you through this ordeal. I can be what you need, Erica, you know I can."

His voice exuded heroin-laced honey, an enticing blend that used to tempt me. During our...What should I call it? "Relationship" didn't fit. During our *affair*, Presley's sweet words and sensual ways had drugged me with a high so intense I abandoned all reason. Today, I couldn't believe I'd wasted five months with him, or that I'd trusted him so much I ignored the warning signs. *Can I use your computer, Erica? Mine's glitching again and these clients are gonna rip me a new one if I don't get this work done.* I stifled a disgusted groan at the memory. What had I said in response? Oh yeah, I remembered. *Sure, Pres, here's my password.* My rational brain told me I couldn't have known what he was really up to, but I still hated myself for not figuring it out.

Presley's fingers coiled around mine, joining our hands. His felt cold, his grip a little too firm. "What do you say, babe?"

I wrenched my hand free. "What do you really want?"

"To talk, like I said."

"Screw you, *babe*." I tried to shut the door, but he jammed his foot in the way. Casey snarled and started barking. A door banged shut somewhere outside. I pushed on the door as Presley shoved back, the door inching in and out like a seesaw tipped up on its side. Push, pull, push, pull. The door inched inward, despite my arms burning from the exertion.

Presley threw his whole weight into the door, banging it into my chin. I choked back a cry as pain radiated through my jaw.

"Quit it!" I kicked at his foot. "Stop or I'll call—"

"The police?" He threw his head back and laughed. "You're so funny. Who do you think they'll believe? A filthy little thief, or the Harvard-educated, prized son of the Cichon dynasty?"

"Get away, you twisted son of a bitch!"

I yanked the door inward, knocking him off balance, and then slammed it shut on his foot. He howled, his face contorted in agony. Stumbling backward, he shouted a string of the most vulgar curses I'd ever heard. Casey darted outside and latched onto Presley's calf. I seized Casey's collar, dragging him back into the house.

An imposing figure vaulted across the concrete walkway to whomp down beside Presley. Lachlan zeroed in on me. "Need a hand?"

"Thanks, but this creep was just leaving." I glowered at Presley, though my lower lip trembled. He scrambled to his feet, scowling at Lachlan.

Though Lachlan's posture remained casual, his gaze hardened on Presley and his tone dropped to a dangerously soft volume. "Your visit is over, laddie. Take yourself away from here."

Presley stepped back from the door, nose high, lips tightened into a smirk. "Or what? You'll torture me to death with bagpipe music?"

A muscle in Lachlan's jaw twitched. "I don't take kindly to scunners who try to force their way into a lady's home."

The "scunner" in question flicked his middle finger at Lachlan.

"Okay-okay," I said, and rushed forward to plant myself between the two men. "Let's end this right now. You two walloping each other won't solve anything."

Lachlan arched one eyebrow at me. "Sure you don't want me to give him a right skelping with a caber?"

"A caper?" Presley sniggered. "Ooooh, hitting me with pickled garnish sounds real scary."

My Highlander aimed a deadly smile at my scumbag ex. "A caber's a very large wooden pole. Best know what yer on about before ye start bumping yer gums, laddie."

Presley's forehead wrinkled. He cast me a sidelong glance. "Where'd you find this jerk-wad?"

"He's my new neighbor." A pleasant tingle shivered down my spine. I shook it off and jabbed a finger in the direction of Presley's canary yellow Alfa Romeo, parked at the curb. "You have no place in my life anymore. Go."

The cretin ground his teeth, lips working, his gaze nailed to Lachlan. Then he hunched his shoulders and trudged toward the car. As he jerked open the driver's door, he called to Lachlan, "How ya like my ride, Scotch Tape?"

Lachlan beamed a wide smile at him. "Quite nice, I must say. Shame I had to leave my Aston Martin back at Inverness, but I've got pictures if you'd like to see."

Presley dove into the car and yanked the door shut. The vehicle rocked. The Alfa Romeo's engine roared to life. Tires squealed as he tore off down the street. Across the way, Mrs. Abernathy froze in the middle of watering her geraniums and cast me a befuddled look. I shrugged, waving.

Lachlan sighed. "A right scunner, that one, but a coward at heart."

"He's a lying, cheating asshole too." With the incident over, the adrenaline rushed out of me, ushering in a cold wave. A shudder radiated out into my whole body, rattling my teeth.

Lachlan touched my arm. "You're shaking. Let me help you inside."

"I'm fine." I sank into those blue eyes and suddenly everything seemed less awful. My quivering even subsided. *How strange.* "Thank you, Lachlan. I'm grateful for your help with Presley."

"That'd be the lying, cheating asshole."

"Yeah." With him standing so close, every time I inhaled I got a dose of his masculine scent. I envisioned him in that kilt, shirtless this time and wielding a massive sword. Oh, and a caber slung over one shoulder while he threatened to skelp an army of people who'd wronged me. I shivered. If only he were *my* Highlander.

Lachlan slid his hand down my arm to take my hand. He sandwiched it between his big palms. "Is there someone I could call for you? A relative or friend or—someone."

"I'm fine, I swear." I should've pulled my hand away, but it felt too good to have his hands around mine. If he'd tried to hug me, I would've let him. To be wrapped in those arms…I pulled my hand free. I was doing it again, letting a man lull me into trusting him. "I appreciate your concern, but I have to go."

Casey bounded out the open door to hurl his furry body at Lachlan, who wrapped his arms around my dog, muttering things I couldn't make out. When Lachlan rose, Casey trotted to me and sat down like the best-trained dog in the world. I scratched his head. "You're not fooling anybody. Sit and stay, my ass." Though I struggled not to spiral down into Lachlan's eyes, those pale blue irises lured me in again. My voice turned breathy. *Rats.* "Thank you. Again."

He shrugged. "I cannot abide bullies. Heard a right rammy going on over here and came to offer my assistance. In the name of neighborliness, of course."

I realized I was twirling a lock of my hair and clamped my hand at my nape. He smiled. Might as well have fired a hormone missile straight at my nether regions. Heat erupted in my belly, racing down to places that should not be heating up, not here, not now. Not ever again. I'd been on the verge of escaping into the house, but clearly, I was the same old Erica. Might as well have strapped a flashing neon sign to my chest that said, *Gullible hussy, free for the taking, queue forms at left.*

"Um…" I floundered for words, my brain addled by the sight of him and by *that* smile. "I could've handled Presley on my own, but I appreciate the save."

"Anytime, lass, anytime. But you can stop thanking me, three times is plenty."

His words rolled over me, warm and sweet and full of promise. *No, you moron, he is not hitting on you.* Right. I had to get it straight. He rushed over here out of common courtesy and chivalry toward a woman he perceived to be in danger. Nothing more.

Lachlan moved toward Gil's house. After a couple steps, he paused to glance back at me. "If you want me—"

"I know where you live." I scratched my neck. "Didn't mean that in a creepy way, like I'm planning a home invasion."

His gaze flickered down to my breasts, his expression darkening, and then he looked straight into my eyes. "Invade anytime. I'm certain I can take you."

In seconds, he was gone. The front door of Gil's house clicked shut behind him. I wandered back into my house, reclaiming my coffee mug. Why had Presley wanted into the house so badly? He'd been a jackass of the first order when all hell broke loose in my life, and when I realized he was responsible for the melee, I chucked him with the garbage, where he belonged. Now he expected I'd admit him into my home? His actions baffled me, but I knew one thing for certain. He did not want to get back together with me. His motives struck me as far from amorous.

Scuffling into the kitchen, I climbed onto a stool at the oak-wood island. Casey laid down at the stool's base, chin on the floor. I folded my hands around the mug and rubbed my thumbs on the warm, smooth surface. Lachlan had galloped to my rescue, a knight without a steed, ready to defend my honor and my life. Would he have "skelped" Presley with a big wooden pole? Or his fists?

Guilt trickled through me at the warm rush I got from imagining just such a scenario. Presley Cichon deserved a beating. I'd fantasized about running him down with my car or hiring a hitman to take him out, but the spectacle of Lachlan MacTaggart issuing quiet threats pleased me even more. Every woman wanted a knight in shining armor, whether she admitted it or not. Maybe it was in our DNA to wish for a savior.

Lachlan. Strong, sexy Lachlan. I itched to turn my head, or even just my eyes, to peek out the window. From the kitchen, I could look across the breakfast nook, out the bay window and straight into the side window of Gil's living room. Lachlan might be there now, stripping off his shirt and donning his kilt, about to practice his swordsmanship. My gaze flitted in that direction. *No, no, no.* I commanded my eyes to face straight ahead, with nothing more enticing to look at than the refrigerator. *Lachlan.* His name whispered to me like a siren's song.

Helpless to resist, I spun on my stool to face Gil's house.

The living room was empty. Darn. No salacious spying for me today. But thanks to his tantalizing offer, I could see him if I wanted. His voice rumbled in my mind. *If you want me...*

It was rude of me not to welcome him to the neighborhood. I'd take Gil's advice, bake my signature brownies, and present them to my new neighbor as a housewarming gift. Nothing more.

Before heading into the kitchen, I checked my e-mail. Two messages awaited, one from my mom, the other from my erstwhile sex date, Cliff. My finger on the mouse button, I prepared to click to open his message. Did I want to know what he had to say? I clicked twice. The message, forwarded from the dating site, opened onscreen. It read, "Sorry. Resched?"

No explanation. No groveling for my forgiveness. He couldn't even be bothered to type out whole sentences. Like I'd reschedule with this guy. I punched the keys to spell out, "Thanks, but I met someone else. I'm sure you will too."

Since I had met Lachlan, my blow-off was technically true. I sent the message and switched to my mom's e-mail.

"Greetings from Florida," it began. "Hot and sticky here, as usual. Dad forgot to charge the cell phone again, so I'm getting in touch the old-fashioned way. Ha-ha." My parents, like me and a lot of other people these days, relied on a cell phone as their sole telephone. Landlines were so passé. Of course, you had to remember to charge your phone. Her message continued, "Are you okay? We haven't heard from you in over a week. If you're sad about Presley, don't be. I never liked him, and you deserve so much better, honey. Call us soon. We miss you. Don't let your bosses work you too hard. Love, Mom."

My vision blurred as tears threatened to flow. I inhaled a shaky breath and willed the tears away. I was lying to my parents. They thought I still worked at Cichon, D'Addio & Rothenberg, the premier accounting firm in Chicago, owned by the richest family in the city—Presley's family. How could I tell them the truth? *Hi Mom, how's it going? I'm charged with felony* *theft because my ex-lover planted evidence on my work computer implicating me in the embezzlement of $250,000 from the firm's clients. I'm looking at four to fifteen years in prison. Say hi to Dad for me.*

I covered my face with my hands. I had to forget about all this or I'd crack. Dropping my hands, I let my gaze wander back to Lachlan's window. What better way to wash away my sorrows than baking for my sexy neighbor?

After typing out a quick reply to my mom, assuring her I was not dead and I'd call soon, I set to work whipping up the brownies. I kept envisioning Lachlan's hard body and his killer smile. I relived our kiss in my mind and my lips tingled from the memory. *Lachlan*, the siren crooned—and I succumbed.

Chapter Five

askets of pink petunias hung at either side of the door, a touch added by Gil's girlfriend—
now wife—Jayne. Beside me, Casey whimpered, swished his tail,
and panted. I patted his head and murmured, "Yeah, we're both
excited. But we need to play it cool, okay?"

The pooch hopped on his front feet.

I rolled my eyes. "You're a hopeless case."

Maybe I was too. My belly fluttered, and for some weird reason, I kept
licking my lips. *Suck it up and do this, woman. Neighborliness, remember?* I
smoothed my T-shirt, wiped the sweat from my palms on my jeans, and
rapped on the door. I'd spent twenty minutes applying makeup and curling
my hair, for reasons I couldn't fathom. War paint, that's what it was. If I
looked impressive enough, then maybe Lachlan would think twice about
messing with me.

I rolled my eyes at myself. Sure, that was the reason.

The door swung inward. He looked as mouth-wateringly good this time
as when he'd confronted Presley. With one hand on the door, he cocked his
hip. Just like he'd done last night. It had a similar effect too, straining his
jeans across his groin instead of a kilt. I gulped, but the lump stayed lodged
in my throat.

To his credit, he stared at my eyes instead of my breasts. "You want me, then?"

No sarcasm or innuendo. Just an honest question.

Shoulders back, I slanted my head back to look at him. "I talked to Gil.
He sent me a photo of you and him together, so I know you're who you say
you are." I pointed at the bag hooked over my shoulder. The rectangular
baking dish pooched out the bag's sides. "Besides, I brought you a house-

warming slash thanks-for-scaring-the-bejesus-out-of-my-ex gift."

He ducked his head just enough to peek at me through thick, dark lashes. His laughter crinkled the skin around his eyes and dimpled his cheeks. "You checked me out, eh? Suppose after last night, I can't blame you for being suspicious. And I must admit, it's rather endearing." His gaze darted to the bag before settling on my eyes again. "You owe me no gifts for lending a hand, but I'll accept it as a housewarming present."

"Deal." I bit my lip. "May I come in?"

"Of course."

Casey, unable to contain his glee any longer, jumped up to plant his paws on Lachlan's stomach. The Highlander knelt to scratch the dog's ears. My canine companion chuffed with joy. If Lachlan whispered into my ears while petting me with those powerful, deft hands, I'd make plenty of noise too. *Cut that out this instant.* I couldn't start anything anyway, with incarceration looming ahead of me.

Lachlan rose and rolled back his muscular shoulders. "Your dog seems to like me."

"His name is Casey, and he's easier than a drunk hooker. He gets just as excited about the mailman and the squirrel in the backyard."

"Careful, with words like those I might get to thinking you fancy me."

"Then you're easier than Casey. Unfortunately, I'm no longer in the market for romance."

"You did kiss me last night."

"I—well—" My cheeks flamed hot enough to fry eggs. I fixated on the door jamb and rocked back on my heels. "Do you want the damn brownies or what?"

"You are a difficult one, aren't you?" I couldn't help glancing at him, and my stomach did a stupid little flip-flop. He winked. "I love a challenge."

"Oh please." I shook my head. "I'd have you fleeing back to Scotland in a week, tops."

He swung the door wide, sweeping an arm in a come-in gesture. Casey tumbled over the threshold first. As I shuffled past Lachlan, he slipped the bag from my shoulder. "A gentleman never permits a lady to carry a heavy load."

"It's brownies, not iron ore."

He shut the door. "Indulge me."

Another ridiculous flip-flop in my stomach. "Fine. But if you try to carry me, I'll bite you."

"An intriguing offer."

His lips split in a bright, heart-melting smile. My whole body relaxed and warmed as if I'd slipped into a hot tub—or taken a Xanax. I skimmed my fingers over my lips, recalling our kiss.

What on earth was I doing? This man eviscerated my self-control, like Presley had done to me before. Reasserting that control was the only sensible strategy here. I straightened, cleared my throat, and shoved my hands in my jeans pockets. "It wasn't an offer."

"I know." His lips sealed together, still curved at the corners. He dipped his head to mine. "Thank you for the sweets, Erica."

Oh, the way he said my name, with that brogue and a hint of sensuality, made me visualize all sorts of outrageously carnal acts. What was it with me and this man? I'd snapped. Like a space shuttle cut loose from its tether to the space station, with all thrusters malfunctioning, I was cast adrift in outer space with dwindling oxygen. But when Lachlan MacTaggart spoke my name, I drew in a deep draft of fresh air. This was ridiculous. I dealt in tabulations, not inexplicable lust. Numbers never lied. Except when Presley Cichon got his greedy little fingers on them.

Casey and I trailed Lachlan into Gil's living room, stepping down three stairs into the sunken space. The L-shaped sofa featured overstuffed cushions, as did the pair of armchairs positioned across from the sofa, separated from it by a glass coffee table. Sunshine streamed through the glass doors that overlooked the backyard. The light glittered in Lachlan's eyes and kissed his skin with a golden hue.

I plopped down on the sofa. Casey pounced onto the cushion beside me.

"Casey!" I tried to push him off, but the dog simply cuddled in deeper. I flashed Lachlan a sheepish look. "I am so sorry. I let him lie on my sofa and I don't usually take him to other people's houses."

"Let the pup have his fun." Lachlan, seated in an armchair, gave me a wicked smirk. "Besides, it's not my sofa."

"Gil didn't demand a security deposit?"

"We're friends. He trusts me." Lachlan settled back into his chair and braced one ankle atop the opposite knee. "Glad as I am to see you, I had the impression you wanted nothing to do with me."

I could do nothing except gaze into the crystal-clear blue eyes locked on me. The intensity of his focus fired a charge through my body. "I thought we should clear the air."

"You mean talk about last night."

I nodded. My stomach churned, and electricity buzzed over my skin, but I could do this. I had to. Living next to this man for a month without clearing the air would suffocate me. "I've never done anything like that in my life. I didn't intend for it to happen, and it most definitely will not happen again."

"So, you won't be molesting me here in the den." He waggled his eyebrows.

The fire flared in my cheeks again. I dipped my head to count the threads in the woven rug under my feet.

"That was a stupid joke," Lachlan said. "I apologize, never meant to embarrass you."

"I humiliated myself quite well." I dared to look up at him. "You must think I'm a total slut."

He canted his head and studied me. "May I ask what you were doing in the club?"

"I had a date. He stood me up."

"The infamous Cliff."

"Yes." I clasped my hands on my lap. "When you showed up and knew my name, I assumed you were him."

"That does explain your obsession with the time." One corner of his mouth angled downward as his eyes narrowed. "Did you have any idea what sort of club it was?"

"Yes. I've heard the rumors." Staring at the rug, I gripped the sofa's edge. "People go there to find casual sex partners."

"Aye." He rumbled out a noise, half sigh and half growl. "You don't belong in that place, Erica."

I rolled my eyes up to study him. "Why were you there?"

He squirmed, his features crimping. "I wanted what the club has to offer."

An altogether different image flashed in my mind this time, of Lachlan picking up a blonde in a slinky tube dress, taking her into one of the private booths and—

I flopped back against the sofa and hugged myself.

Wincing, Lachlan scratched his own ear the way he'd scratched Casey's. "It was a mistake. After you left, and I couldn't catch up to you, I went back into the club. Couldn't do it, though."

"Why not?" *I don't care, I don't care, I don't care.* Aw hell, who was I kidding? I was dying to hear the answer.

"It's simple." He bent forward to trace a fingertip over the coffee table in slow figure-eights, his attention riveted to the movements. "None of those women measured up to you."

Time seemed to stop. The world went quiet and still, shrinking down to the size of this room.

His eyes snared my focus, his gaze intent on mine. "You've enchanted me, Erica."

Why oh why did he have to speak my name that way? All steamy and alluring. I linked my fingers over my belly and locked my knees together. My toes tapped on the rug.

He strode around the table, lowered his massive body onto the sofa beside me, and captured my hands in his. Lachlan's rough skin warmed mine. I hadn't realized my hands were cold, what with an inferno raging through the rest of me. His touch set off a deep ache between my thighs and a longing to taste him one more time. Twice at most. I moistened my lips. Five was my limit, for sure.

When he spoke, his voice was quiet yet intense. He raised a hand to my cheek and angled my face up to him. "You are the loveliest thing I've ever laid eyes on. You're sexy without even trying to be. You made me laugh and you kiss with all your heart and soul. You've got a passionate heart."

"I shouldn't have kissed you."

"Why not?" His thumb coasted over my bottom lip. "We want each other. No harm in it. We both went there for a fling."

Look away. But I couldn't. His eyes pulled me deeper and deeper into a kind of trance. Oh, how my body ached for his. "I couldn't go through with it."

"Not in those circumstances." The proximity of his body proved headier than the booze I'd downed last night. His other hand came up to my cheek. My face bracketed by his hands, I couldn't stop myself from leaning toward him the slightest bit. He exhaled a ragged breath. "I still want you. And the circumstances are very different today."

"Yes. Different." My words emerged in a dreamy murmur. He smelled delicious, and I yearned to wind myself around his hard body, just to experience him once.

"I've tried relationships. Not interested in them anymore." His nose skirted across mine while his fingers fanned out across my cheek and glided down my throat. "I'm here for four weeks. I've nothing more to give. But I do want you, even more today than last night."

"Mmm." My body came alive at his declaration, my pulse a frantic drumming in my ears. I bent my head back, straining to find his lips. Our mouths passed a breath away from each other. The hunger from last night erupted again, explosive, out of control, undeniable. I sneaked my tongue out to skim his lips. Rewarded by his sharp intake of air, I did it again.

"Tonight," he hissed. "Be mine tonight."

My eyelids fluttered closed and then parted slightly, granting me a hazy view of his smoldering eyes. "What are you suggesting?"

"Spend the night with me."

"What?" My brain, soaked in the liquor of his scent and flavor, fought to make sense of his words.

He raked his lips over mine. "I want you in my bed, for the month.

When I leave, we never see each other again."

The fog lifted with the suddenness of a gust of wind. I blinked rapidly, a cold lump in my gut.

Lachlan dazzled me with his signature smile. "Be my American fling."

Chapter Six

Thoughts whirled in my head, dizzying in their speed, but I couldn't latch onto any single one of them. Be his American fling? He had to be playing a sick joke on me. I angled backward a smidgen and scrunched my lips. My gaze seemed bound to Lachlan's by a magic spell, except I didn't believe in magic any more than I believed in instant attraction. Yeah, that wasn't a good argument against the supernatural. I had experienced instant attraction, of the soul-stirring, breath-stealing variety.

Lust, nothing more. Hormones gone wild. I should see a doctor about it.

Casey bounded off the sofa. He nuzzled Lachlan's hand, gave it a quick slurp, then beseeched me with doggie eyes. No one could refuse the puppy stare. Casey slathered his tongue over Lachlan's hand again and the Scotsman patted the dog's head. Man's best friend glanced at me one more time. I swore Casey was playing matchmaker, urging me to kiss and make up with Lachlan.

Kiss. Yes. I'd love another of those. Like an addict in an opium den, I was. So much for restraint.

His voice was soft and tender. "Think about it, please. We could have an incredible month."

"Then you leave."

"Yes."

I aimed my hardest look at him, the one I usually reserved for clients who fudged their books. "Let me get this straight. I dash over here every night for a quick roll in the hay? Then I skedaddle back to my place, so we don't accidentally develop a relationship."

He opened his mouth, but I silenced him with one raised finger. Casey plopped down in front of Lachlan. *Traitor.*

I scrubbed my palms on my thighs. "Look, I realize my behavior last night might've given you the wrong impression of me. I'm sorry. I had no intention of leading you on. But I am not a casual sex kind of girl."

Lachlan scooted closer. Confronted with his chest, I refused to grant him the pleasure of making me look up at him. Besides, if I glimpsed those eyes again I just might cave.

His words almost purred. "You are a good woman. I can tell, and Gil told me anyhow. Can only imagine what drove you to the club, but it's probably to do with the erse who attacked you earlier."

I decided erse meant ass. Maybe I was getting the hang of this alien tongue of his. The mere thought of the word tongue assailed me with vivid fantasies. *Rats.* So much for setting things straight between us.

He crooked a finger under my chin to ease my head back. I considered closing my eyes, but I'd still feel him near me. "I'm not asking for one night. What I want from you is four weeks of sex and companionship."

"Would this involve conversation? Or strictly wham-bam-thank-you-ma'am?"

He placed a kiss on my cheek near the corner of my mouth. "No wham or bam. Aye, conversation—so long as it doesn't get too personal."

"I see."

One of his hands found my arm, skating up and down my skin with a delicacy that made heat blossom over my skin and delve underneath to suffuse me. His lips moved against my cheek. "What do ye say, neighbor?"

The old warning siren wailed inside me, though muted by a need too strong to deny. Yes, I hungered for him. Yes, a month of sex with this man enticed me like no other offer in my entire life. No one ever offered me a fling before. "I don't know."

Lachlan drew a hand up my arm and over my shoulder to the apex of my neck, cradling it. With a finger crooked under my chin, he slanted my head up until our eyes locked and our lips almost touched. His eyes blazed with a passion so intense it ripped through me too. I fought for breath, for thought, for sanity, but the need erased everything else. His eyes searched mine with sizzling intent. I seized his shirt, the only anchor I could find. His breaths grew heavy. I tugged him closer.

He crushed his lips to mine.

A blast of pure ecstasy shot through my veins, more powerful than any drug, arousing every scandalous desire buried inside me. His mouth was pure pleasure, his body a sinful temptation. When his tongue breached my mouth, I opened to him without hesitation and plunged into his mouth, my senses overpowered by the smoky flavor and silken texture of him. I released his shirt, my hands falling to my sides, and swayed on the molten current of our passion. We possessed and stimulated each other, our tongues tangling, slick and hot and starved for more. His hands groped my back and dragged me into him, our bodies mashed together, my swollen breasts pinned to his chest. I sagged into him.

He broke the kiss, his hands stroking my arms. His lips quivered as if he itched to smile but was too overwhelmed by our lip-lock to manage it. I trembled on the inside, my brain a pool of gray slush in my skull. On the outside, though, I managed a surprising composure. Even my voice was calm. "That was nice."

Both his brows shot up. "Nice?"

He uttered the word as if no woman had ever dared call his kisses nice before. I struggled not to smile at his masculine indignation. "It's a compliment, Lachlan. Accept it graciously."

"Thank you." He enunciated each syllable with care, his tone still stamped with irritation. He screwed up his lips and shook his head at me. "Aye, ye truly are a difficult one."

"You said you liked a challenge." I waved my hands to indicate myself. "Can you handle this?"

"I can."

"Sheesh." I sighed. "You are awfully sensitive for a man who threatened to skelp my ex with a caber."

"Maybe I ought to give ye another kiss, full body this time." He gathered me into his arms, both hands flat on my back. "See if ye think that's *nice*."

Full body kiss? My sex pulsed at the very thought of it. Even though I had no idea what he meant by the term, I could imagine. Man oh man, could I imagine.

He roved his hands over my back. "I need your answer. Please."

Chapter Seven

arning sirens, shut the hell up. Caution, go take a hike. For once in my life, I wanted something *I could have.* With four weeks of freedom left to sow my wild oats, before I lost everything, Lachlan's offer satisfied the need I'd fought since the moment it overtook me a few days ago. Maybe I'd regret this later, but for now, for a few steamy weeks, I wanted this. I wanted him.

I curled my fingers in his hair. "Yes."

He released me and bent forward to snatch up my bag. "To the kitchen for a piece."

"A piece of what?"

"Your brownies." He closed his hand around mine, raising it to his mouth. His lips flitted over my knuckles. "But I'm open to suggestions."

"Later." I bit the inside of my cheek. "Okay?"

He nodded and rose to help me up. "No rush, lass. No rush at all."

I trailed him up the steps out of the living room, down the short hallway into the kitchen. Gil's photographs decorated the walls—scenic images of landmarks, like the Sears Tower, along with portraits of people on the street. Gil was talented with a camera. I understood why customers paid big bucks for his prints.

Lachlan halted. He stared at the wall, head tipped to one side, lips parted and curved with a surprised little smile. He pointed at a framed photo on the wall. "The loveliest of all Gil's works."

I bowed my head and fiddled with my shirt's hem. I knew which photo he was looking at because I'd seen it every time I visited Gil's house. He'd taken the snapshot a few months ago, back when I was happy and oblivious to the calamity ahead.

"Why don't you look at it?" Lachlan asked. "Don't strike me as the shy sort."

He didn't realize he'd lain a gauntlet at my feet. I shuffled closer, sucking in a breath as I lifted my head to gaze at the photo of me. I was laughing, mouth open in a broad smile. Sunlight shimmered on my hair, thrown wild by the wind. My cheeks were pink, my eyes alight with a euphoria I recalled all too well. Bile rose in my throat. In the image, a masculine arm draped around my shoulders. Presley's arm.

"I hate that picture." Pushing past Lachlan, I hurried into the kitchen.

He strode in behind me and Casey gamboled in last. We took seats on opposite sides of the small kitchen table. Lachlan deposited my bag on the tabletop, reaching inside. He withdrew the glass cake dish and set the dish on the table. The still-warm brownies, decadently dark in color, had steamed up the plastic wrap covering them. The tempting aroma seeped out through the wrap, making my mouth water and my stomach grumble.

Lachlan's fingers deftly stripped off the plastic wrap. I imagined him stripping off my clothes in the same manner, with efficient and precise movements, those fingers brushing my skin at every opportunity. Much as the idea excited my body, I wondered if I could go through with our agreement. Sex with no attachments? *I'm not a casual sex kind of girl*, I'd told him, and then I promptly signed on for a month of hot sex, no strings.

I rested my hands on the tabletop, my thumbs twiddling away. "Lachlan, I know I agreed to the sex thing but, um…"

He froze, the plastic wrap in his hand. Without glancing up, he said, "You've changed your mind?"

Was that disappointment in his voice? I spread my hands over the wood surface and zeroed in on the lines of the grain. "I haven't changed my mind. But I don't think I'm ready to get started tonight."

His shoulders flagged. He crumpled the plastic wrap and gave me a closed-mouth smile. "I understand. We could spend time together, so you'll be comfortable with me before we have a poke."

I decided to ignore the poke remark. The context cleared up its meaning, but I didn't appreciate the offhanded nature of the phrase. I was a girl to be poked. *Hmm.* "Doesn't spending time together count as a relationship?"

"Not if we don't discuss anything too personal."

Tapping my nails on the wood, I watched him snag two plates from a cupboard and then ease open a drawer full of silverware. "May I ask what you do for a living? Or is that too personal?"

He grabbed two forks and a knife, then pushed the drawer shut with his hip. "Financial consulting."

Another numbers guy. Why me? He couldn't be a sword-maker or, hell, even a general contractor. Anything but numbers.

Lachlan set the plates and silverware on the table. He studied me for a heartbeat. "Not exciting enough?"

"I'm an accountant. No judgment here." Scratch that. I *had been* an accountant, and I'd receive my judgment sooner than I wanted. "Gil said you have an apartment in Edinburgh. Is that where you've always lived?"

"No, I'm a Highland lad by birth and in my heart." In one long stride, he crossed to the refrigerator. "Spent four years in London after university, working at the stock exchange. Hated it. The traffic, the crime, the frantic pace of everything." He pulled the fridge door open and surveyed the contents. "I quit my job and moved to Inverness to start my own business."

"Wow, I'm impressed. Starting a business is scary."

He shrugged, focused on the fridge's interior, blocked from my view by the door. "Starting it up was the easy part. Fought tooth and nail to win clients, but after a few years things, got rolling. Now I earn enough to live quite comfortably. I've got fifty employees and three offices—Inverness, Glasgow, and Edinburgh."

I gaped at his back. Holy cow. He was rich. *So is Presley. Doesn't mean he's a good guy.* Okay, I'd suffered a momentary lapse, thanks to the innate instinct every human seemed to have that compelled us to be impressed by mountainous piles of dough.

"Alas," Lachlan said, "all I can offer you to drink is water or whisky. Haven't got the messages yet."

What did phone messages have to do with beverages? Deciding not to ask, I changed the subject. "Are you from Inverness?"

"No, I was born and raised in a little village way up in the Highlands called Ballachulish."

"Is that where Gil and Jayne are going? He said you have a place in the Highlands."

"Aye, they'll be staying at my castle." I suspect my chin hit the floor and my eyes bulged wide enough to pop out at the slightest bump. He laughed—a hearty, manly sound. "I'm joking. My house is modest. I don't care for the trappings of wealth and my needs are simple."

"Does that go for sex too?" Oh crap. The question zipped out of my mouth without going through my mental filter. It was him. He turned me into a babbling moron.

He peeked at me over one massive shoulder. "You'll find out soon enough."

Since I'd blundered into this topic, may as well keep going. "I'm not interested in kinky stuff. No whips or chains or anything like that."

"Don't crave excitement?"

"Not that much, no. My needs are simple too."

"Have you tried it? The kinky stuff."

"Ick." I did a fake shudder. "Absolutely not."

Lachlan studied me sideways. "Then how can you be certain—"

"How many times do I have to say it?" Emphasizing each word with a slap of my hands on the table, I said, "I do not want kink."

His lips pursed a little as if he were suppressing a smile, amused by my insistence. "Sorry. We'll drop the subject."

"At last." I looked heavenward and sighed. "Give me brownies now."

Lachlan shut the fridge door and stooped over to haul out the freezer drawer. "Yes, milady. Any other commands for your humble servant?"

"No. Thank you."

"Here to serve." He shifted items in the freezer. "Ah-ha! We may not have much in the way of messages, but we do have one essential item."

He brought out a carton of ice cream and tossed it onto the table. It landed square on its bottom, then slid smack into the brownie dish.

"Perfect." I rubbed my hands together, but then I peeked up at him. "I have to ask. What are messages?"

"Groceries." Lachlan kicked the freezer drawer shut. "Did you decide on whisky or water?"

I chewed the inside of my lip. The old Erica would say water. The new, future-felon Erica had a bagful of wild oats in need of sowing. What the hell. "I'll have whisky."

A slow, sensual grin heated his expression. "My kind of woman."

From a cupboard, he retrieved two glasses and a bottle of what looked to be expensive booze. He clacked it down on the table between us, settled onto his chair, and turned the bottle so I could see the label. I ran a finger down the bottle, from neck to bottom. A cream-colored label curled around its girth, and amber liquid glowed golden in the sunshine filtering into the room. "Scotch?"

"Talisker single malt Scotch whisky." Leaning forward, he spoke in the sultry voice that did wicked things to me. "Distilled on the Isle of Skye, a mysterious place inhabited by the spirits of the ancestors, forever haunting the cairns and standing stones they left behind. It's said the isle has the darkest skies you'll ever find, filled with stars so bright and ancient they might be the spirits themselves. And from this enchanting land is born a single malt as unique as its birthplace." He trailed a finger over the back of my hand. "Talisker is a smoky, seductive whisky."

Why was I breathing hard? I crossed my legs. "You sound like an advertisement."

"Setting you up for the tasting is all." He opened the bottle and poured us both a measure of whisky. His fingers nudged mine when he handed me a glass and a charge arced through me.

I cleared my throat. "Is there a certain way to drink it?"

"For a whisky virgin, I don't recommend guzzling it like you did last night."

"Good advice." I rolled the glass between my hands, admiring the rich, caramel tones revealed by the sunlight glimmering through the whisky. I raised the glass to sniff it. *Oh my lord.* Smoky, sweet, with a hint of earthiness. I shut my eyes and inhaled a longer draft.

"Can you smell the sea and mountains?"

"Yes." I drew out the word, lost in the aromas. "Mmm, that and so much more."

"Have a sip."

I tipped the glass, letting the whisky slide past my lips. A splash of flavors spilled over my tongue. Fruity, toasted, spicy, with a touch of honey. I let the whisky slide down in a languid swallow. A burst of pepper startled my eyes open, but then the spice melted into a warm, sweet finish. I moaned, my eyes drifting half shut.

"You like it then?" Lachlan's voice had gone hoarse.

I parted my lids to drink him in too—the hooded eyes, the stormy heat in his pale irises, and the way his tongue skirted the edge of his upper lip. "I enjoyed it, yes."

His fingers delved between mine, stroking my palm while his thumb rubbed the heel of my hand. "I like the way you enjoy whisky. Makes me imagine that same look on your face when I take your body."

Visions of that moment burst in my mind. I scrutinized the whisky left in my glass, tipping the glass to swish it. "Do you always equate whisky with sex?"

"Only with you." He dragged the brownie dish to him and sank the knife through the flaky top layer, deep into the tender, dark-chocolate flesh beneath. "The sensuality of whisky begs for a decadent partner."

Wow, he should've been a writer—of erotica. I accepted the plate he handed me, laden with an enormous hunk of brownie. He dished out heaping servings of vanilla ice cream. My stomach grumbled just looking at the food. He impaled his own brownie with his fork, piercing the dessert straight through, then plunged the loaded tines into the ice cream. I watched, spellbound, as he took the morsel, now dripping with melting ice cream, into his sensuous mouth. Once he'd devoured the mouthful, he licked crumbs from his lips. "You'll be in my bed tomorrow night at the outside."

I thrust a bite between my lips and as the rush of chocolate and sugar overtook me, I knew I was in deep trouble. Because he was right. Even without the whisky, I couldn't hold out for long. This man understood how to set a bonfire inside me and stoke it until I quaked with anticipation.

He coiled his tongue around another mouthful of the voluptuous confection, chewed it slowly, erotically, and let it glide down his throat. "What are you thinking of?"

"What's to come."

He arched one dark brow, his smirk half suppressed. "You, lass. You're what's to come. In my bed, at my hand, over and over and over."

I shoved a forkful of brownie into my mouth and chomped it. I hungered for him more than the dessert. If he'd asked, I would've fallen into his bed this morning. But just to be contrary, I'd fight the impulse. "Don't get cocky, Mr. MacTaggart."

He surged forward, half his body bent over the table, and claimed my mouth. His tongue tormented me with possessive lashes, twining around mine, then plunging deep. His lips were soft yet demanding, his tongue hot and slick. I slumped, abandoning myself to him, nipping and lapping, letting out little grunts echoed by his own, deeper ones. When he tore his mouth from mine, I wilted into my chair, slack-jawed and breathless.

Lachlan dropped back into his chair. Panting, I struggled to look vexed. He speared a piece of brownie and twirled his fork. I'd wait till tomorrow night, so he wouldn't think I was too easy.

Yes. Tomorrow. I could hold out that long. I *could*.

Chapter Eight

"Y ou owe me eleven hundred dollars." I held my hand palm up, outstretched, waggling my fingers. "Gimme."

Across the coffee table from me, Lachlan sat forward in his armchair, elbows on his knees, and gave me an amused smile. "Do I now."

"You know you do." I tapped the Monopoly board laid out between us. We hadn't left Gil's house all day, and this was our third board game. Lachlan hadn't kissed me since our brownie interlude. Of course, he had suggested strip Monopoly, but the idea struck me as too weird. This was a family game, for crying out loud. "You landed on Park Place, which I own. And I have three houses on it. Your ass is mine, MacTaggart."

"Anytime you want, my sweet wildflower."

I rolled my eyes at his mock-sugary tone. "You have a one-track mind."

"Only when I'm alone with you."

My hand floated up to my throat, my index finger curling around a lock of hair. I didn't realize I'd moved my hand until my fingers tickled my skin. Seated on the sofa while Lachlan lounged in the armchair, I couldn't tear my focus away my Highlander's gaze, the way it simmered at a low boil, whispering steam over my skin. He looked like he was considering whether to throw me down on the sofa and ravish me or drag me onto the coffee table to have his way with me. *Either one's good with me.*

I corralled all my little fake bills and shuffled through them. This was Gil's house. How could I have sex with Lachlan here? My house was no better because it wasn't really my house. If Lachlan knew what a mess my head was, he might reconsider his offer.

"Change, please."

Without raising my head, I looked up at Lachlan. "What's wrong with the way I am?"

I flinched at the tone of my own words. *Defensive much?*

He stared at me, expression blank, for a couple seconds. Then he shook his head, waving orange money at me. "No-no, I said I need change for these five-hundred-dollar bills."

"Right. Of course." I tugged the three bills from his fingers, gnawing my lower lip, and handed him four little hundred-dollar bills as change. Yes, *that* kind of change. "Here ya go."

Lachlan accepted the money, grimacing and scratching his cheek. He opened his mouth as if to speak, then shut it again.

I rolled the dice, and once again, we lost ourselves in the silly battle for the biggest stash of colorful bills. Lachlan gained some headway, but I still had Park Place and three railroads, plus two utilities and various other properties. I began to suspect he was letting me win somehow, since I'd beat him at all the other games too, even the ones I sucked at on a good day. I wasted no time puzzling out how or why he was letting me win because, with this man, the excitement of each roll of the dice took on a new, more electrifying significance.

Especially when he aimed those smoldering eyes at me, blew on the dice, and murmured in a husky voice, "When this game is over, I'll be kissing you for a long, long while."

My body melted, forcing me to slump against the sofa. I meant to slay him with a sarcastic comment, but I managed nothing more coherent than "mmm."

A bit later—I'd stopped checking the time—I rolled and moved my playing piece, a teeny-weeny cat, around the board. When I saw where I'd landed, my fingers clenched into fists, nails sharp on my palms. Four letters taunted me on the game board: J-A-I-L. A sour taste invaded my mouth and my eyes stung. I set to shuffling and reordering my Monopoly money, but acid burned in my chest. Jail. Was the universe mocking me? I shouldn't get this upset about a dopey game, but I couldn't stop the tears collecting in my eyes, about to overflow. I swiped them away with the heel of my hand, fighting back a sniffle. It hiccupped out anyway. Too much stress, that's all this was.

"What's the bother?" Lachlan's voice boomed through the living area and I jumped, a bigger hiccup jolting me. Lachlan pulled at the neck of his T-shirt as his lips twisted. "I'm sorry. Didn't mean to shout, but I asked you twice before and you didn't answer."

"Didn't hear you." A lone tear trickled down my skin, the salty tang invading my mouth.

Lachlan's voice turned softer, almost tender. "Must've been lost in thought, if you didn't hear me ask the first time." He reached across the table to touch my knee. "What's fashed you?"

Even through my jeans, the slight pressure and warmth of his hand on my knee rippled a distracting tingle through me. I gulped. Lachlan studied me with a concern that made me squirm. No emotional entanglements, that was our deal. Yet here he was, acting worried about my change in mood. I fiddled with my Monopoly loot. Crying and making pathetic noises? Sure, that was a simple change in mood. He must wonder if he'd hooked up with a nutcase.

Lachlan caressed my knee, his fingers moving in slow strokes, and all thoughts fled my mind. He massaged a little higher, just above my knee. "Erica?"

I cleared my throat. "What does fashed mean?"

His fingers curved around my knee in a comforting grasp. "Means bothered, which you seem to be at the moment."

"Oh no, not me." I faked a smile, but his scrunched brow told me he didn't buy it. I patted his hand. "Thanks for the concern, but didn't we agree to no personal questions?"

"Yes." He pulled his hand away, his jaw tensing. "I apologize for violating our agreement."

"No biggie." When his face blanked again, I smiled. "That means it's okay."

He exhaled a breath that erased his tension and confusion. "Good."

The relief on his face was so adorably sweet I found myself biting my fingernail to avoid flinging out a hand to clasp his. Instead, I pointed at his playing piece—a Scottish terrier, of course. "Your turn."

My gaze fell to my piece, stuck in jail, and I clamped my lips between my teeth.

Lachlan's lips drew together in a manly pout. He narrowed his gaze on me. "What about a game of Monopoly is too personal to discuss? How can a wee metal cat fash you?"

"It's not the cat." I shut my eyes and pulled in a deep breath, then let it out slowly as I opened my lids. "I landed in jail."

"I can't see the significance."

No, he wouldn't. I shook my head. "It's not important. Can we please move on so I can get the hell out of jail?"

Lachlan snapped up my piece and plunked it down one square forward. With a victorious grin, he announced, "There. Problem solved."

My lips tightened, and I touched two fingertips to them, realizing they'd turned up into a closed-mouth smile. He wanted to make me feel better. If only my problems were so easy to fix. "I would've gotten out on the next move anyway, but thank you."

"What's a jailbreak between fr—companions."

Had he been about to say call us friends? If he uttered the phrase "friends with benefits," I just might vomit. No, first I'd smack him. Then I'd barf in his lap. Why did life have to be so complicated? I gestured at the board. "Still your turn."

Lachlan bent forward, lifted the dice near his mouth, and blew on them. I glimpsed the tip of his pink tongue between his puckered lips. His gaze drilled into me and the room temperature seemed to soar twenty degrees in a matter of seconds. He tossed the dice.

Was I...fanning myself? *Ugh.* Stupid hand. I shoved the offending appendage under my thigh.

Forty-five minutes later, Lachlan raised his big hands in surrender. "The wee lassie is victorious."

"I'd think a financial consultant would be better at Monopoly." I angled my head to squint at him. "You let me win, didn't you?"

With a snort, he waved a dismissive hand.

Springing forward, I jabbed a finger at him. "You did."

"Does it matter?"

I hissed out a breath. "Not very satisfying to win because your opponent gave up."

"A gentleman never bankrupts the woman he plans to seduce."

The chains around my heart loosened the tiniest bit. I longed to kiss him for saying such a thing. Lachlan might've talked me into a fling, but he was apparently old-fashioned at heart. Strange. *Wise up, girl, there's gotta be something wrong with a guy who scorns relationships and won't talk about himself.* Well, for once I didn't care. Really, I didn't. Bring on the hot, meaningless sex.

My stomach roiled.

"Would a prize heal your wounded dignity?" Lachlan asked.

"Depends on what the prize is."

He settled back in the armchair, knees spread wide, and locked his hands behind his head. His admiring gaze traveled over me from head to toe and back again. "I can think of one or two rewards we'd both enjoy."

"I bet you can."

He leaned forward to gather up the paltry bankroll he had left, then stretched out farther to collect up my sizable winnings. With his head inches from my knees, he turned his face up to me. "Time to relinquish your treasure to the banker."

I laid my hand on his, feeling his tendons flex under my palm as he scooped up the toy money. "Not so fast, Scot. Maybe I want a rematch."

"Happy to oblige." His gaze flicked to the hallway, which led to the bedroom, and his tongue slipped out to moisten his sinful lips. When his eyes swiveled to me, the fire burning behind them stole my breath. He dropped the money, flipped his hand over, and clasped his fingers around my wrist. "You're sweeter than Atholl Brose, and I'm aiming to taste ye tonight."

"Uh…" My brain bypassed the unknown phrase—Atholl Brose—and latched onto his final words. *Taste ye.* Tonight. I didn't need a translator to tell me what he meant by that. His tone, deep and erotic, set off a damp ache between my thighs. I clamped my knees together, but couldn't summon the will to pull my hand away. I agreed to this. I told him I could handle it. Wild woman on the loose, wanton through and through. So why did my stomach keep churning? "Um, well, that sounds…What on earth is Atholl Brose? Is that some kind of Gaelic sex slang?"

Yep, I knew how to steer a conversation into a hard U-turn. We needed seat belts for this one.

"No," he chuckled. His free hand came up to cup my cheek. "It's a sweet liqueur made from oatmeal, honey, whisky, and cream."

"Sounds yummy." My heart thudded at the blatant hunger on his face. His chest rose and fell with heavy, shallow breaths—just like mine did. My body went quivery and weak. *This is going to happen.* I fought for some semblance of control, but all I could think of was his mouth on mine. Hot. Greedy. Maddeningly sensual.

Lachlan dragged his fingertips down my cheek, over my jaw, trailing them along my throat to my collarbone. I shivered. Swear to God, I did. And it felt soooo good.

Naturally, I swung us into another conversational U-turn. I squeezed out one breathless question. "Do you speak Gaelic?"

His mouth dropped open.

I hunched my shoulders.

With a kind smile, he skated his thumb across my lower lip. "My mother insisted we all learn."

A single word snapped me out of my stupor. "We? Do you have brothers or sisters?"

"Both." He flopped back in the armchair with a resigned huff. "Two brothers, three sisters."

"Thr—You mean you have five siblings?" I blinked once, in slow motion. Erica Teague, an only child, could not fathom such a brood. "Wow, that's amazing. Do you get along with them?"

"Mostly." He shrugged one shoulder. "With a clan as big as ours, the occasional barnie's to be expected."

"Barnie?"

"A tussle." He tipped his head to the side, studying me again with that unnerving intensity. "Do you have brothers or sisters?"

"Nope. Just me." I picked up the Monopoly board and dumped everything off it. Playing pieces, houses, and hotels scraped across the smooth cardboard to clatter into the box in a landslide. "Do you see your family often?"

A noise, somewhere between a growl and sigh, whooshed out of him. As I tossed the multicolored money into the box, I glanced up at him. His mouth was twisted with a downward slant, his shoulder muscles bunched with tension. "No more talk of family. Agreed?"

I opened my mouth to protest, then remembered with a cold pang that talking about his family might lead him to ask about mine, which might trigger more tears and evasion and general panic on my part. I clapped the Monopoly box shut. "Sure, you got it. No more family talk."

He nodded, shoulders slackening. He pressed his palms to his eyes, then let his hands fall to his lap. "Don't quite understand why, but we've derailed in somber territory. Time to get back on track."

Chapter Nine

With both hands on the chair's arms, he thrust his body up out of the seat and unfolded it to full height. Towering over me, he sauntered around the table to settle in beside me, half on my cushion. His weight forced it to slope toward him, tilting me closer to his brawny chest, so close my shoulder glanced off the hollow of his. He braced one arm on the sofa's back, behind me. Sparks of desire burst under my skin, like matches struck in the dark, flares of heat and incandescent need.

Lachlan slid his hand up my cheek, delving into my hair. With the barest pressure, he urged me to turn my face to his and tip my head back, while he slanted his down until our lips aligned. No more than an inch separated our mouths. His breaths tickled my lips, warm and moist and scented with whisky and chocolate, a ghost of our sensual snack earlier. He teased me with little nips and swift grazes of his mouth across mine. His fingers roamed my scalp, exploring, massaging, driving me wild with the tingly sensations his touch evoked. When he darted his tongue out to trace the seam of my lips, I sagged into him, hands on his firm chest, my throat exposed to him.

"Sweeter than anything," he purred, ducking his head to plant open-mouth kisses on my throat. He drew my earlobe between his lips and suckled with tiny flicks of his slick, velvety tongue. A bolt of lightning shot through me, straight down to my core. He groaned against the shell of my ear. "Forget tasting. Devouring ye is what I'll be doing."

His mouth captured mine in a punishing lip-lock that robbed me of breath and sanity and any awareness of the world around me. Everything telescoped down to us, his lips branding mine, our tongues colliding, the molten passion obliterating my defenses. His five o'clock shadow rasped against my cheek, the rough texture delicious on my sensitized skin. My breasts grew heavy, my nipples went rigid. I flung my arms around his neck as he wrapped his around my back. Bound to his rock-hard body, I moaned into his mouth.

A guttural sound resonated in his chest. He shoved one hand under my buttocks and hoisted me up, then laid me down on my back, spread across the sofa's length with my legs over his lap. His eyes hooded, lips parted, he stretched out alongside me with his body between me and the sofa's back. The erection swelling in his jeans rubbed against me. A wave of dizzying lust swept through me, and I clung to his massive shoulder. He peppered kisses over my forehead, across my temple, down to the tender spot under my ear.

"Lachlan," I murmured, my voice as dazed as I felt. His kisses drugged me. His touch inflamed me. What would the sex be like? Goosebumps erupted all over my skin at the torrid fantasies the thought unleashed.

He grasped my hip, probing the hollow with his thumb, while his lips hovered over mine and those incredible eyes pinned my gaze. His hand skidded off my hip onto my mound, the shield of my jeans no defense against him. The heel of his hand rested there, moving in lazy circles over my clitoris, the caress light but rapturous in its effect. Writhing, I spread my thighs without thinking. His fingers dived between them to pet my sex. His hand kept circling over my clit, and combined with the swipes of his fingers, it had me bucking and gasping as an exquisite pressure mounted deep inside. *More, more,* I yearned to say, but my voice abandoned me. I could do nothing except moan and whimper.

I closed my hand around his swollen cock, trapped inside his jeans.

"Och!" Lachlan pushed my hand away, eyes flashing wide for a heartbeat before sliding almost shut. "Donnae be touching me like that. Yet."

"What if I do?" I brazenly palmed his shaft. Not like me at all, but this man awakened a secret part of me. When I began to stroke him, he batted my hand away again and gave me a half smirk, half frown.

"If ye keep it up," he grumbled, "the train'll derail again."

"Would that be the fun train?"

"Aye." He scraped his lips across mine, his hot breath infiltrating my mouth. His burr thicker than ever, he commanded, "Keep yer wee hand to yerself."

"Or what?"

He tore open the button on my jeans and yanked the zipper down with a loud *scritch.* I swallowed a gasp when he thrust his hand inside my panties to splay it over my drenched sex. With the same motions he'd used before, he circled the heel of his hand over my taut nub, now with nothing separating his rough skin from mine. His powerful fingers swept up and down my slick cleft as his relentless hand rubbed my clit and tormented the tender flesh of my mound. Electric shocks arced through me. My back bowed, my mouth opened on a strangled whimper, and I dug my fingers into his shoulder. His mouth sealed over mine, the kiss brutal and all-consuming. It muffled my cry, set off by his finger dipping inside me, crooked to press into the erogenous spot just inside my opening. My sex clenched in anticipation as fierce pleasure coiled tighter and tighter, a spring about to burst free deep in my body.

A phone rang.

I recognized it with a dim thought, the sound far away and detached from the reality of Lachlan plunging two fingers into me this time, while his tongue lashed mine.

The phone rang again.

Lachlan broke away. Breathing hard, he snagged his phone from the table and glanced at the caller ID. He growled.

He propped himself up with one straight arm and answered the call. Right there, half on top of me with his erection jutting against my belly. Fighting to catch my breath, every inch of my skin flushed, I pushed up onto my elbows. He was taking the blasted call, instead of taking me.

"What?" he barked. His mouth compressed into a grim line. His eyes were ablaze, but this time with anger instead of sexual fire. Spittle sprayed my forehead when he snarled, "Well, bloody find out if it's true, Rory. I want to know now!"

Grinding his teeth, Lachlan listened to the caller. This Rory person could've been a man or woman. I barred my arms over my chest. An old girlfriend?

He gripped the phone tight enough to whiten his knuckles and forced the words out between his teeth. "Sort it out. That's what I pay you for, man."

Rory was a man after all. Good. I smoothed my shirt and linked my hands over my belly.

"It has to be a mistake," Lachlan said. "I can't abide another fight with that bitch—"

Lachlan froze, his gaze swinging down to me. His face blanched, his eyes flashed wide.

I couldn't move, a breath lodged in my throat. My heart raced. *That bitch*, he'd said. Was I a breath away from learning the source of Lachlan's damage?

"Wait, Rory." Lachlan tucked the phone to his chest and said to me, "Personal call."

Before I could respond, he clambered over me to get up off the sofa. My body still thrummed with unquenched need. He hesitated, gazing down on me with lust-darkened eyes and a heaving chest. "Och, I'm sorry. Please forgive me."

"Huh?" Was he leaving me like this, my jeans open, perched on the edge of orgasm?

"Erica—" His chin dropped to his chest. With a rough shake of his head, he turned and stalked down the hallway.

I lay there, exposed and aroused, baffled by his departure. What could be so important? Some "bitch" might cause a fight. Since I knew next to nothing about Lachlan, I had no clue what to make of the incident. I zipped up my jeans and nabbed a magazine to fan my burning cheeks. No amount of fanning would quell the wildfire consuming the rest of me.

My skin felt tight and hot, my body taut with pent-up need. I got up to pace the length of the living room. The sun had descended below the horizon, its rays painting the sky in hues of pink, red, and purple. Even through the city smog, the sunset was beautiful, but nothing short of a divine visitation could've buoyed my spirits. Back and forth, I trudged. Bitch. Personal call. What did it all mean? I itched to interrogate Lachlan about his past. Our agreement thwarted my curiosity, which soon escalated to a real itch that had me scratching at my arms and neck. I hugged myself to keep from scarring my body out of sheer frustration.

When my legs protested the exercise of pacing, I stopped in front of a photo of Gil and Jayne. Both were smiling, their heads pressed together, the epitome of a happy couple. Jayne's auburn hair was cut short enough to curl in artful disarray around her ears. I fingered my shaggy locks, in desperate need of a salon appointment I couldn't afford. Jayne had the kind of plump lips men adored. I lifted my fingers to my much smaller mouth. Maybe that's why I had atrocious luck with men. Yeah, my lack of pouty supermodel lips explained why Presley used and betrayed me and why Lachlan refused to engage in more than a casual affair with me. At least he was upfront about using me.

You agreed to this, remember? Curse that conscience of mine. I wished it would shut the hell up.

"I'm awfully sorry, Erica." Lachlan strode out of the hallway and stopped beside me. His smile was strained, and tension etched lines around his eyes. "Best take you home."

"Now?"

"I'll get your things."

He dashed off to retrieve my coat and the bag I'd brought the brownies in. My forehead pinched, thanks to a surprised crinkling of my brow. The brownies dish was nestled inside the bag. I waved it away. "Keep the brownies."

"They're yours."

"No." I pushed the bag away when he shoved it toward me. "I made them for you. Just return the dish when you're done with it."

He set the bag on the coffee table. Without meeting my gaze, he said, "Thank you."

"No biggie."

We left the house hand in hand, heading across the lawn to my front door. Only the faintest tatters of sunset flickered over the horizon while darkness closed in all around us. The automatic light on my porch clicked on just as we tromped up the steps. I unlocked the door and, facing Lachlan, grasped the knob with my free hand but didn't turn it. My other hand stayed enclosed in his. "Want to come in?"

He threaded his fingers through mine. "Best not."

I suppose I could've been a tad more obvious, like maybe saying *please rip my clothes off and take me right here*. The fire still crackled inside me and his hand around mine felt so right. I didn't want this day to end yet. "Please. I'd like you to come in."

"Not tonight." He released my hand, brushing a kiss on my forehead. "We'll have a picnic tomorrow."

I tried to smile but couldn't muster the requisite emotion. Couldn't be glad he was leaving. After what I'd let him do to me. After he took a call instead of finishing what he started. A forehead kiss? Seriously? I should've rated at least a peck on the lips. I told him none of that, though, instead forcing out an overly cheerful, "Sure, sounds great."

His eyes narrowed, his mouth flattened. "Erica…"

"It's fine, go." I rose onto tiptoes to kiss his cheek. "See you tomorrow."

Without looking back, I stomped into the house and slammed the door. If we'd get on with the sex part of this arrangement, I could stop obsessing over every minuscule clue to his past and his mindset. I wilted against the door. He'd had me at his mercy this evening, achy and wanting, bared to him in body and soul. And what did he do? Took a call. One that upset him and not only derailed our fun train, but blew it to smithereens in the process.

A tapping sounded on the door, inches from my left ear.

"Erica?" Lachlan's voice, muffled by the barrier, carried a thread of anxiety. "Would you open the door, please?"

Sighing, I eased the door open partway.

Lachlan's lips formed a shaky smile. "Thank you."

I closed my fingers around the doorknob. "You wanted something?"

He nodded. "To apologize. I was unkind to you and I regret it deeply."

"No big—"

Two strong hands bracketed my face. He ran his thumbs over the corners of my lips, bending his head until our foreheads touched. "That was no proper goodnight kiss."

I stood paralyzed while his breaths blustered over my face. Claws clicked on the bare floor behind me and, as Lachlan's lips descended toward mine, Casey nudged my hand with his clammy nose. The dog panted and chuffed softly. Lachlan, his lips achingly near mine, paused to reach one hand down to pat Casey's head. I licked my lips, desperate to claim Lachlan's, but I couldn't budge a muscle. Even when Casey slathered my hand with sloppy licks, I held stone-still. My pulse thundered in my ears, my skin sizzled with electric currents, and my mouth watered at the fantasy of what his kiss would be like this time.

Lachlan hooked an arm around my waist, tugging me out of the threshold. He shut the door in Casey's face.

I exhaled a ragged breath through my parted lips.

His lips found mine, pressing into them for a heart-stopping moment. The kiss was tender, deliberate, his lips questing without demanding anything in return. My head and my heart floated on a sultry breeze, whirling and soaring, tethered by his mouth and his hands and that body supporting mine. My lips softened and opened for him, but he merely skated his across mine one last time before raising his head. Bereft of the contact, I blinked up at him.

"Sleep well, bonnie Erica." He tucked a wayward strand of hair behind my ear. "And good night."

He pushed the door open behind me. I shuffled across the threshold backward, my body alive and needy, unsatisfied and yet thrilled beyond measure by his gentle kiss. Casey's tongue slicked across my palm, but I barely registered it.

Lachlan lifted my hand to light a kiss on it. "Until tomorrow."

As he turned to leave, my brain produced one statement. "Apology accepted."

He flashed me a brilliant grin over his shoulder.

I watched him amble back to Gil's house and disappear through the front door. When the living room light switched off, I retreated into my house to feed Casey and go to bed. I wouldn't sleep well, I knew that for sure. Filthy dreams of Lachlan would haunt my slumber.

Tomorrow. Oh, but that word held a promise within it I'd never known before.

Yes, Lachlan, tomorrow.

Chapter Ten

The next day, I sat cross-legged on a fleece blanket on a private beach along Lake Michigan's shore. The secluded spot afforded us a breathtaking view of the blue water unfurling toward the horizon. A dozen feet away, the sand faded into a manicured grass lawn in front of a two-story Tudor house. Trees huddled in a semicircle around the house and the beach, creating a natural privacy screen. A tree-shrouded driveway had led us to the Tudor, but Lachlan bypassed the house on our way to the shore.

I eyed him sideways. "You're sure we have permission to be here?"

Seated beside me, he sighed with mock annoyance. At least I thought it was mock. "Yes, for the third time, we're allowed. Gil knows the owner and comes here often. His friend agreed I could take over beach privileges during Gil's absence." I opened my mouth to speak, but he cut me off with a raised hand. "Relax. We have permission."

Relax? I hadn't accomplished that feat since my arrest. The metallic click of the handcuffs being snapped tight around my wrists echoed in my mind. I shut my eyes for a second, taking a deep breath, and when I opened them Lachlan was studying me. "Does your wrist hurt?"

"Huh?"

He nodded toward my hand. "You're rubbing it."

I glanced down to discover I was rubbing my wrist. The memory of handcuffs affected me more than I'd realized and always seemed to linger at the back of my mind. I set my hands on the blanket. "It's nothing."

"If you say so." He settled his hands on my shoulders and kneaded with his strong fingers, penetrating deep into my tight muscles, coaxing them to loosen. "Has work got you bunched up?"

"Sort of." I leaned back into his ministrations and he glided his hands up to my neck. His thumbs plied my nape while those fingers feathered over my throat. The warmth of his palms skimmed across my skin. I let my head fall back. "That feels so good."

"Maybe later I can give you my full massage."

"Does it involve a full-body kiss?"

"If you like."

"I could go for that."

Casey frolicked nearby, at the end of his retractable leash, which Lachlan held onto by sitting on the thing. No matter how hard Casey pulled, the leash stayed put. Lachlan had some powerful gluteus muscles. I tried to twist around to ogle his ass, but I couldn't get a view of them—so I settled for recalling the hard lines of his buttocks, which I'd glimpsed when he was setting up our little picnic here. While he rubbed my neck, I succumbed to visions of those fantastic glutes flexing as his hips pumped, our bodies entwined, his rhythm relentless, our grunts and moans merging into a passionate chorus. My breasts tightened, my nipples puckered.

Lachlan's lips grazed my ear. "Are you thinking about me?"

"What?" I jerked my head up, torn from my reveries. "Of course, you're right here."

"No." He coasted his hands down my arms to close his fingers around my wrists and raise my hands to my breasts. My fingertips teased my nipples, stoking my fire. He pressed his smooth cheek to mine, and I flashed back to his stubbly cheek rasping against mine last night when he drove me to near climax. He lifted my hand to his face. "You're aroused, and I can't help wondering what you're thinking of."

"Keep wondering." I peeled myself away from him, against my every desire, and batted my eyelashes at him over my shoulder, a sarcastic attempt to be coquettish. "A woman has a right to be mysterious now and then."

Lachlan smiled and shook his head. "Mystery is your forte."

Was that a compliment or a dig? *Beats me.* Well, he'd insisted on no personal talk, and he reaped each and every seed he'd sown. I bent my knee and bumped the picnic basket sitting beside me and my Highland lover. Soon-to-be lover. We hadn't done anything more than sip whisky and share a few scorching kisses—and one thwarted orgasm on my part.

I stretched out my legs, the sun-warmed blanket a soft caress against my bare skin. My shorts and tank top allowed me to soak up the sun's rays. I supported my body with both hands on the blanket behind me. I was not unaware of the way this pose elevated my breasts, attracting Lachlan's attention. Since meeting Lachlan, I'd come to enjoy the way his eyes glazed when I hoisted my breasts like this. No man had ever looked at me with such want in his eyes. I rolled my head to the side and our gazes homed in on each other. "Tell me again why you chose a picnic for today's outing. After the whisky interlude, I expected something more...erotic."

He tsked. "No respectable Highlander beds a woman without proper seduction."

"I didn't realize consuming ant-ridden food while mosquitoes suck us dry counted as seduction."

A chuckle rumbled in his chest. "Do you always look for the negative?" He waved at the surroundings. "Sunshine, blue sky, a warm breeze, and sand between our toes." When he fixed his gaze on me, my belly fluttered. "And the company of a braw, bonnie lass. I'd say this is a perfect moment."

"You're quite braw yourself." He'd moved over to sprawl beside me, propped up on his left arm with one leg bent and his free hand dangling over his raised knee. Shorts covered the bits of him I most wanted to glimpse, but he'd stripped off his T-shirt to expose a torso rippling with defined muscles. A smattering of fine, dark hair over his pecs narrowed down to a titillating wedge that vanished under the waist of his shorts. I'd hoped for the kilt, but he told me it wasn't beach attire.

His brows lifted. "You know what braw means?"

"I also know skelp means to slap and scunner means a nuisance, which fits Presley to a tee."

His mouth dropped open. "How'd you know all that?"

Sinking my head back, I shut my eyes behind my sunglasses. "I did a little Internet search for Scottish slang. By the way, please don't ever again refer to sex with me as having a poke."

"Slip of the tongue."

His fingertips danced along my arm. The tingling they triggered infused every inch of me. I took off my sunglasses to admire his eyes in the pure sunlight. "I still have no clue what you said to me in the club the other night. Since I couldn't figure out how to spell it, I couldn't search for it. I was babbling about the time and you said what sounded like—"

"Your bum's oot the windae."

"Right." I flipped onto my side to face him, mirroring his bent-knee pose. "What on earth does it mean?"

His gaze flew to my groin and his fingers clenched around his knee. He sucked in a breath. Seconds ticked by, and his rapt attention ignited a molten pulse of pleasure in my sex. I sank my fingers into the sand, desperate for anything to grasp in lieu of flinging out a hand to seize his enlarging shaft through his shorts. His hand on his knee tensed and slackened, over and over, as if he were imagining jamming his hand inside my panties like he had last night, this time catapulting me over the edge.

I dropped my knee, thighs clamped together. *Not on the beach.* I flapped a hand in front of his face. "Hey, wake up."

He blinked once, slowly, wetting his lips. Then, at last, his crystalline eyes focused on my face.

"What does it mean?" I asked. "The bum-oot-the-whatever thing."

"Your bum's oot the windae." He draped his arm over his six-pack abs. "It's an old Scottish saying. Means you're talking nonsense, which you were at the time."

"Not if you had been Cliff. He would've known why I was furious." I inched my fingers across the sand until they bumped his. I burned to touch him everywhere, lick him everywhere. "Half of what you say sounds like a foreign language."

"You should visit Scotland. It'll be an adventure for you."

"Maybe I will someday." *When I get paroled.* I tucked my fingers under my palm. "But I'd have to figure out what you're saying first. I wouldn't want to visit a foreign country without learning at least a bit of the language."

"I can teach ye." His hand enveloped mine.

"You're a one-man immersion program already. Feel like I need a passport just to have a whisky with you."

"No need. My borders are completely open to you." He slung an arm around my waist, hauling me to him. My nipples, already rigid, chafed against his chest through my T-shirt and bra. He fanned his fingers out over the small of my back. "Come on over and map me out."

The idea of mapping out his body, it made me wish for more time. Four weeks would fly by too fast. *Don't get attached, remember?* Even if I'd had all the time in the world, I couldn't trust this thing between us, whatever it was. Hot guys always turned into hot messes. I knew this, and yet I'd agreed to a month-long fling with a hot guy who clearly had secrets.

Well, I never promised I wouldn't ask questions. He said we could converse as long as things didn't get "too personal." Time to test the boundaries. I nestled against him with a wriggle of my hips. "So, tell me, why don't you do relationships?"

He sprang to a sitting position, which dumped me on my back. While I heaved myself off the blanket, he flipped open the picnic basket's lid. "Personal questions are off limits."

Wife alert. "When did your last relationship end?"

Lachlan tossed me a plastic-wrapped sandwich and threw me an amused look. "Could we enjoy this bonnie day without an inquisition?"

"Maybe." I unwrapped my sandwich—turkey and Havarti cheese on whole wheat, with lettuce and avocado. A chill trickled through me. I snapped bolt upright and waved the sandwich at him. "This is my favorite.

Are you sure you're not stalking me? Ferreting out all my secrets in order to seduce me into being your sex slave?"

He grinned. "Caught me. I dug through your bins to find the remnants of your food and decipher what your favorites are." He leaned toward me and gave a low, evil cackle. "And I sniffed your underwear."

"A woman's underwear does not smell good, trust me."

"Bet yours would." He nuzzled my cheek. "I got my information from Gil. He said you've had a piece at their house lots of times."

From my research, I knew the term piece meant sandwich or snack. "Why would Gil tell you what kind of food I like?"

"Playing matchmaker, I gather."

He bit off a huge chunk of his sandwich. Vinaigrette dressing dribbled down his chin, and I resisted the impulse to bend over to lick it off. "You've, uh, got something on your chin."

He snatched up a napkin and wiped off the dressing, then returned to eating. Even the way he chewed was sexy. So determined, precise, and yet passionate. Would he apply the same intensity to making love to me? I cringed and ripped off a mouthful of my sandwich. Making love? This was sex, pure and simple. No strings, no complications, no baggage, no hot mess. As if that were possible.

Lachlan ran a finger down my arm. "Care to tell me what's got you frowning again?"

"Not particularly." I reached into the picnic basket to pluck a grape from a bunch cuddled inside a napkin. "Comes under the heading of personal, comma, off limits."

With a bitter smile, he severed our eye contact. "Understood."

His expression went stony. I almost thought he looked...disappointed. These were his stupid rules. I bit back a sarcastic response and munched my grape.

Lachlan swiveled his gaze out to the lake where gentle swells lapped onto the shore. A seagull swooped low overhead, its cry sharp and high. Lachlan's cheerful expression turned unreadable, distant. I had the weirdest urge to pull him into my arms and soothe him with wordless sounds, rocking him until his somber mood passed. *Baggage, moron. Steer clear.*

After scarfing down half my sandwich, I could stand the silence no longer. I grabbed a water bottle from the basket and gulped some of its contents. My fingers coiled around the cool bottle, I circled my thumb over its ridged surface, smoothing out droplets of condensation. A single drop rolled over my thumb. "Scotland always looks beautiful in the movies."

"It is beautiful." He finished off his sandwich in two swift bites. "Can't believe you've never been to Scotland."

"Never been outside the contiguous United States."

"What a shame." He picked a grape and held it near my lips. I parted them so he could set the grape on my tongue, then I sealed my mouth around the fruit. My lips ensnared the tip of his finger by accident. For a long moment, we hung suspended in a bubble of our own making, our gazes burning into one another. An urge overtook me and, helpless to resist, I suckled his finger to savor his skin—salty, flavored with the sweet and tangy nuances of his sandwich. When I released his finger, he skated it around the rim of my mouth. "You'd love Scotland. It's a land of passionate, fiercely independent men and women. A lass like you would fit right in."

I nabbed a napkin to wipe food remnants from my face, anything to distract me from the weight that had settled in my chest. Heartburn, probably. I forced a polite smile. "Maybe someday I will visit Scotland."

Casey yanked on the leash, jerking Lachlan forward. He grunted and pulled the leash's handle out from under his butt to give it a sharp tug. Casey trotted back to us, then lay down between me and Lachlan. I tore off a piece of my sandwich and tossed it to Casey. He caught it with a snap of his jaws.

Lachlan dragged his fingers through the sand. "Where did you grow up?"

"Isn't that off limits?"

"Told you about my background."

"So you did." It was only fair, I supposed. "I was born in Linwood, a small town just outside of Kansas City—on the Kansas side, not Missouri. We were average, middle-class people. Me, the only child, with two loving parents. We moved to Chicago when I was fourteen." I started to take another bite, then realized I was full. Eating as a distraction. A sure way to get fat. *Will a man like Lachlan want you when you're tubby?* I set down the sandwich. "I'm pretty boring, really. Girl accountant, obsessed with facts and figures, friendless, loved by my parents and my dog."

"You have friends. Gil and Jayne, for certain."

"Yeah, but no one else. I'm the invisible woman."

Lachlan paused with a grape near his lips, his gaze intent on me. "I'm sure someone else loves you. A beautiful woman such as yourself must have a horde of admirers."

Are you one of them? I didn't ask, for fear of the answer. "Nope. No adoring admirers. I'm as boring as most of my exes."

"You have had exciting lovers then."

"Not lovers. Boyfriends."

The grape flew into his mouth, as if by its own volition, and I couldn't blame the little fruit for longing to get inside Lachlan MacTaggart. I wanted to crawl in his brain, though, to dig up the reason he eschewed connections. Curiosity. Nothing more.

Finished devouring the hapless grape, he asked, "What's the difference? If you sleep with them, they're your lovers."

"The term implies an arrangement like ours—sex without commitment or attachments. I cared for my boyfriends." I grimaced. "Even the gorgeous ones."

His forehead wrinkled as his brows came close to merging. "Why *even* them?"

I clamped my hands on my knees. "Hot guys always turn out to be hot messes. They've got cargo planes full of their baggage." I scratched the back of my neck, bowing my head. "And then there are the hot guys who use women for their own ends."

Lachlan froze, sandwich midway to his mouth.

I realized with a start what I'd said and what it must've sounded like to him. My throat constricted, but I waved a dismissive hand. "I didn't mean you. Point is, hot guys are dangerous."

"Then I pray you don't think I'm hot."

He was blazing. The hottest of them all. "You're...good-looking and sexy."

"Thank heavens for that." The sparkle in his eyes seemed to fade with his smile. "Who used you for his own ends? Was it the coward who assaulted you?"

"Presley didn't assault me."

Lachlan's jaw tightened, his lips a sharp line. "He was forcing his way into your home."

I hugged myself, rocking in place. Presley's voice haunted my dreams and his betrayal ruined my life. I sucked in a ragged breath.

"What did the bastard do to you?"

"Nothing. You chased him away." And last night I'd dreamed about the incident, except in my dream Lachlan was dressed in his kilt and nothing else, and he wielded a big sword. My Highland knight.

Lachlan grumbled. "You know full well what I was asking."

I straightened and tried for an authoritative tone. "Off limits."

We stared at each other for a long moment. My heart stuttered, the breath was locked in my lungs. Lachlan picked at a stray blade of grass. "Sorry, I forgot my own rules for a spell."

My shoulders flagged, my heart sinking. I think I wanted him to press me for more information. Part of me needed to tell someone, but Lachlan couldn't be my confidante. "It's okay."

He sprang to his feet and offered me his hand. "How about a walk?"

Casey sprang up, all four feet off the ground, and barked his approval of the idea. Lachlan scratched behind Casey's ears, earning a sloppy kiss on his chin.

"Sure," I said. "A walk sounds nice."

I slipped my hand into Lachlan's and twined our fingers. With Casey by his side, Lachlan shepherded me away from the sheltering trees to the open beach at the edge of the lapping waves. I spied the skyscrapers of downtown Chicago, with the Sears Tower looming over the rest, but then we turned left away from the skyline. Hand in hand we strolled, chatting about nothing in particular, careful to avoid personal subjects like Presley Cichon or Lachlan's reasons for giving up on relationships. His hand felt right in mine, comforting, imbuing me with a sense of safety. At the same time, his touch sent low-voltage currents of desire through me. I stopped worrying about the passions he excited and permitted myself to enjoy all the sensations he aroused.

But of course, I couldn't help myself. I lifted our joined hands. "Isn't this against the rules?"

"No."

"That's it? No?"

Lachlan veered us off the beach, under a copse of trees, shaded from the sun. He spun me toward him and dragged my body into his.

Strong arms pinned me there. My heart raced. My every feathery hair awakened to his presence, stirring as if a breeze whispered over my skin. Lachlan bent his head to mine.

The kiss began softly, delicately, but intensified with each brush of his lips, until he plundered my mouth with fierce strokes of his tongue. He had me crazed, pushed beyond the bounds of reason, and I didn't care. He tasted of grapes and sweet Havarti cheese and…Oh God, so many things. His lips held the promise of erotic delights to come, arousing my entire body from the inside out.

His erection swelled inside his shorts, the hard length wedged between us. I ground my hips against him, rewarded by his groan, and rubbed my body into his swollen shaft. He plunged inside my mouth with even more ardor, his tongue more demanding, as his hands clutched at my ass. When he peeled his lips from mine, we both struggled for breath.

One corner of his open mouth turned up in a wry half smile. "It's not against the rules. It's preparation."

I didn't have to ask for what.

We ambled back onto the beach, headed toward our blanket and picnic basket. The sun glared in my eyes and I threw a hand up to shield them. The daystar had sunk low on the horizon, heralding the oncoming night. Where had the afternoon gone?

"It's time to go home," he said, his lips vibrating against my ear. "I've got a surprise for you, and then the real seduction begins." He curled his tongue around my lobe. "If you're ready for it."

Take a risk, be wild. I eased a hand down his firm belly to stroke his shaft through his shorts. So big. So hard. My thumb flicked over his tip and his shaft throbbed in my palm, setting off a shockwave that shuddered through him. I made him shake with desire. The knowledge coursed a hot shiver of my own through me. "I want you tonight, Lachlan."

A breath gusted out of him, his head bowed. "Thank the stars."

Sweat dampened my palms, a squadron of butterflies took flight in my stomach, and my ears rang. *Breathe, idiot.* I sucked in a lungful of steamy summer air, spiced with a hint of Lachlan's natural scent. I swayed a little, intoxicated as never before. I was about to dive headfirst into a deep pool in the pitch dark, not knowing if any water would break my fall. And I didn't give a damn.

Lachlan guided me down the path past a stranger's house, toward home and the impending fulfillment of my Highlander fantasy. He was more than a wet dream come to life, though, and he'd touched something more profound than my libido. Presley wooed me with honeyed words and golden promises, but Lachlan assured me he offered nothing but sex. This time, I'd lock my heart inside an impenetrable vault.

Sure, and pigs flew on the backs of winged unicorns.

Chapter Eleven

set my fork on my empty plate and leaned back in my chair. A breathy moan escaped me as my eyes drifted half closed. The smoky, hearty flavor of the T-bone steak lingered on my tongue, tinged with the fruity undertones of the red wine I'd sipped between bites of meat. Gil's kitchen was so quiet I could hear my breaths hissing and the clock above the stove ticking.

Lachlan cleared his throat. His chair creaked.

Pulling in a deep breath, I looked across the dining room table at him. He shifted in his seat again, and the wooden chair creaked again. His lips were tight, his shoulders bunched. His royal blue shirt stretched snug over his torso while the three unhooked buttons at the top exposed a tantalizing wedge of flesh. I slid my tongue over my lips to lick away the remnants of steak sauce. Lachlan, his attention riveted to my mouth, mimicked the movement of my tongue with his own, darting it out to moisten his lips.

I sat forward, pushing my plate away, and folded my arms on the table-top. The polished wood cooled my arms, except for the circle of warmth where my plate had rested.

My personal chef, aka my Highland hottie, glanced at my breasts. The low-cut blouse I wore exposed their inner slopes, but my folded arms pushed them up, mounding them higher. Lachlan's mouth worked as if he were imagining suckling my nipples. My skin tightened. I'd promised him tonight we'd seal the deal.

He fidgeted, coughing, and swung his gaze up to mine.

I stifled a smile. "Getting sciatica? These wooden chairs do a number on my butt, for sure. Jayne wanted to put some cushions on the seats, but Gil thought it was too girlie."

Lachlan's eyes narrowed. "Could we not talk about Gil and Jayne tonight."

Though he phrased it as a question, his tone transformed it into a command. The set of his jaw and the intensity of his stare set the air between us to sizzling. Now I was wriggling in my chair, besieged by a throbbing between my thighs. "Is there dessert?"

"Oh, aye." He rose, granting me an eye-level view of his raging erection. It strained against his low-slung jeans. As he sauntered around the table to me, the motion of his hips accentuated the bulge in his crotch. Butterflies fluttered in my stomach. He held out a hand to me. "Stand."

"Bossy much?"

He grasped my hand and tugged. "Up. Now."

I swallowed. Damn, but his alpha male act was getting to me. *You don't like pushy guys, remember?* Of course I didn't. I pulled my hand free. "Ask nicely and maybe I'll do it."

Lachlan lunged down, cinched his arms around my waist, and hoisted me off the chair. My feet dangled several inches above the floor. Face to face with his neck, I struggled for words. His rigid cock pressed into my groin. I stopped breathing. My skin grew hot and hypersensitive, the feel of his silky shirt against my bare skin making my nipples go stiff. One of his hands dropped down to clutch my ass. My heart pounded so fast I couldn't catch my breath. I blurted out the first thing that popped into my head. "Dinner was amazing, had no idea you could cook."

Those devious fingers of his kneaded my buttock, slow and deep, plunging into my flesh then withdrawing, over and over.

"I love steak," I said, my idiotic statement punctuated by a squeak. His finger had dipped between my buttocks for the briefest second, and even through my clothes, the sensation tormented me.

Lachlan slid me down his body, inch by glorious inch, until my feet met the floor. My right hand wound up squished between our bodies, smack over his erection. Holy shit, it was hard as granite. A dizzying exhilaration swept through me, and I ran one finger up his shaft to the head. This would be inside me. Tonight. *It's happening.*

I fumbled with the metal button on his jeans.

"Uh-uh." He captured my hands, pinning them behind me. "Not yet."

"Why not?" I craned my neck to see his face.

"Patience," he grated through his teeth.

The way he was holding my hands, I could feel his heartbeat in his wrists, pulsating against my skin, racing almost as fast as mine. "I suck at patience."

He released my hands and backed me up to the table. I gripped its edge. He took hold of my hips, boosting me up onto the table with my legs hanging off the edge. I slapped my palms on his chest, then glided them up and down, up and down, relishing his taut body contrasted with the sleekness of his shirt. I freed one button. My fingers seemed to move of their own volition, slipping beneath the fabric to sketch the outlines of his muscles.

With a hissed intake of air, he dragged me into him, which forced my thighs apart. Wedged between them, he ground his shaft into my groin. "When ye lay yer wee hands on me, I cannae think."

"Stop trying to."

He nuzzled his cheek against mine. His heated breaths blustered through my hair, fanning it out, tickling my skin as each strand floated back down. I wrapped my arms around his shoulders, desperate for an anchor, my head spinning while tiny bursts of fire erupted under my skin. He shoved the dishes out of the way. They clattered to the floor. Silverware chinked. Wine splashed out of the glasses as they toppled.

While he lavished my throat with wet kisses, a single thought surfaced against the onrushing tidal wave of lust. "You're breaking the dishes."

"Buy 'em all new ones." Lachlan hiked my blouse up over my breasts, his hands roughly plumping them through my lacy bra. "Most expensive china on the market, I swear."

His voice had gone hoarse. He thrust one hand inside my bra to liberate my right breast. It sprang out of the cup, caught by his strong hand. His tongue curled around my nipple, spurring the firm tip to harden more. My breasts were swollen and achy, and I arched into his mouth for more. His lips covered my nipple, his teeth scraped the peak. He suckled with fierce hunger, eliciting a throaty moan from me. He nipped at my skin, gentle and teasing.

I cried out. My hips bucked.

Lachlan sucked harder.

Another cry exploded out of me. I bunched his shirt in my fists and yanked it up, but his arms blocked me from tearing it off him.

His head shot up. Panting, he stared down at me, cheeks ruddy.

"What's wrong?" I struggled up onto my elbows, lightheaded from my blistering arousal.

"Cannae do it." He sank down onto the chair. "Not like this."

I pulled my blouse down to cover myself and levered up into a sitting position. My stomach dropped as an ice-cold wave broke over me. "You can't do this to me again. Get me wound up and push me away."

"Not pushing you away." He scrubbed his face with both hands and sighed. "I don't want our first time together to be like this. A quick shag on the kitchen table."

"What makes you think it'd be quick?"

He fixed me with an are-you-kidding-me look. Yeah, it would've been quick. And hot. And earth-shattering. But did I want my first time with Lachlan to be down-and-dirty, over-in-a-heartbeat sex? I slumped, palms on the tabletop. No, I didn't want to start our whatever-it-was like this.

Lachlan pulled me down onto his lap, straddling him. His hands rested on my hips, their weight warm and steadying. His rock-hard shaft prodded my crotch. Still, his expression had softened, and he swept hair from my face with a light touch. "Sweet, I need more time to prepare. You deserve better than this."

"Thought this whole day was preparation."

"For you, yes." He grazed the backs of his fingers over my cheek. "I want it to be an experience. One to remember."

I tilted my head, studying him. "Sounds almost romantic."

"You disapprove?"

"No." I flattened my sweaty palms on my thighs. His fingers were painting a tingling line down my throat, and I had trouble summoning complete thoughts. "You're confusing the hell out of me. First, you dump me for a phone call. Then, you take me on a romantic picnic and cook me a sensual dinner. Your domineering act a minute ago was wicked sexy, but now you're back to being considerate and sweet."

"Sweet?" His lip almost curled when he said it as if the word tasted sour to him.

I gave his chest a playful slap. "What is it with men and the word sweet? It's a compliment, not an affront to your manliness. Trust me, you've got no issues there."

His smile was slow and...sweet, in a sexy way. "I don't?"

"Absolutely not." I leaned in to press my lips to his. Even the brief contact had my body responding, readying. Our faces a breath apart, I whispered, "You are the hottest man on the face of the earth, Mr. MacTaggart."

He caught my bottom lip between his, letting it go with bone-melting slowness. A hint of his taste sneaked into my mouth—masculine, earthy, with a faint spiciness from the steak sauce. He drew me closer until my breasts gave against the strength of his torso. "And you, sweet Erica, are the most enticing lass on earth."

My heart stuttered. If Presley had spoken those words, they would've been a lie, honey for the trap. From Lachlan's lips, they rang with a tender truth. He meant it.

Or maybe I was letting a gorgeous guy bamboozle me again.

Lachlan glided his hands up to my waist, his fingers spanning my back. His words came out stilted as if infused with some deep emotion. *Wishful thinking.* "I know I behaved badly last night. You've no idea how much I regret it."

I fingered the collar of his shirt. "Don't worry about it."

"No chance of that. How can I make it up to you?"

As if his will commanded it, I rolled my gaze up to meet his. Concern clouded his eyes. I shrugged one shoulder. "It was kind of humiliating to be abandoned on the sofa with my pants hanging open."

His face pinched, he gave a tight nod.

Ah jeez, he looked so pitiful. I longed to pull him into my arms and caress his hair. The mere thought trickled ice through my veins. I shouldn't want to comfort him because we weren't anything to each other. But sitting here, with our gazes bound to each other and our bodies entwined, my heart did a little pitter-patter and my hands all but trembled with the need to touch him. *Never learn, do you? Erica the pushover.*

To break the moment, I set my hands on my knees and turned my gaze up to the ceiling as if contemplating a serious issue. When I returned my attention to him, I raised one finger. "I've got it. Tell me something about you. Something embarrassing."

His brow furrowed.

I tapped his nose. "You wanted to make it up to me. This is how you can." I slanted forward a little. "Something really embarrassing."

His lips compressed. After a moment, he sighed and relaxed, though his hands stayed on my waist. "My mother calls me Lachie. Has done all my life. I've told her a thousand times I hate it, but she won't listen. Even called me Lachie in front of girls I dated in school."

"That's mildly humiliating." I crossed my arms over my chest. "I said *really* embarrassing."

Those broad shoulders bunched a little while his jaw worked as if chewing on my request. His fingers tapped an inconstant rhythm on my back. Finally, he tilted his head back and let out a soft groan, his eyes sliding shut. "When I was seventeen, a bonnie girl coaxed me into showing her my, ah..."

He squirmed beneath me, and though his eyes opened, he looked past me toward the refrigerator.

"What'd you show her?" I waved a hand in front of his eyes. "Your porn collection? Your pink bunny tattoo?"

"No." He filled that single syllable with pure mortification, as only a man could do. He rubbed his eyes with one hand, contorted his mouth, and dropped his hands, letting them hang at his sides. Still unwilling to meet my gaze, he muttered something.

"Sorry, I didn't catch that."

With an expression of sheer misery, he aimed his eyes in my general direction. "My dick. I showed the girl my bleeding dokey."

My mind went straight to envisioning a teenage Lachlan undoing his pants for a lustful lassie who'd probably rubbed her hands in anticipation, waiting for the perfect moment to leap on him and—oh hell. What was wrong with me? I couldn't be jealous. Of a girl he knew years ago.

What if she was the one who'd ruined him for relationships?

He lifted his hand to his brow, like a visor to shield his eyes from me. "My whole family walked in on us. We were out in the barn and the family had come home early from a trip into the village. They assumed the girl was about to, ah, give me..."

"A blow job?"

He flinched, and I could picture his wincing face under the shield of his hand. "She wasn't. The girl only wanted to see. Her friends dared her to do it, and apparently, there was a sizable wager involved. But my parents and my sisters and my brothers all saw—and they started laughing their heads off."

Picturing his moment of humiliation, I felt a pang of empathy. He'd been tricked into literally dropping his pants, all so a silly girl could win a bet, while I'd been duped into sleeping with a cretin who stole a quarter million dollars and blamed me for it. Not exactly the same situation. But close enough to pluck my sympathy strings.

I reached out to pry his hand away from his brow. "I'm sorry. I shouldn't have made you tell me that."

At last, he focused on my eyes. "Tell you anything you want to know if it'll help you forgive me."

I cupped his face in both my hands. "Nothing to forgive."

He took my hands and clasped them to his chest—to his heart. With a sheepish grin, he said, "I have a confession. I liked telling you my embarrassing story."

"You did? Why?"

He shrugged. "Now you'll wonder what I've got that lasses would make wagers about."

I glanced down at the stiff line of his erection in his pants. "I can guess."

"No more guessing after tomorrow."

"Good." I curled my fingers against his chest, with his warm hand pancaked atop mine. "Cuz I don't have a barn to lure you into."

"You'll never need to lure me anywhere." So fast a breeze fluffed my hair, he lifted us both up and onto our feet. "I'm yours."

For a few weeks. For sex. But maybe, just maybe, he'd—What? Get to know me, fall head over heels, and vow to stay with me? We could get married in the prison chapel and have conjugal visits every other Tuesday.

Stop torturing yourself with fantasies. There'd be no happily ever after for me. But I could enjoy this time with Lachlan, if I let myself. My troubles had a habit of scurrying into the dark corners, out of sight and mind, whenever I was with him.

I stuffed my hands in my pockets. "If we're not having sex tonight, how about catching a movie? *King Solomon's Mines* is on TV tonight. The good version with Deborah Kerr and Stewart Granger."

"Classic film buff?"

"Grew up watching old movies."

Lachlan enveloped my hand in his and ushered me toward the doorway. "To the living room, it is."

"Wait." I dug my heels in, halting him. "Would you like to come over to my place? I mean, it's not really my place, but I've got a plasma TV. Gil's is LCD, and it has a smaller screen."

He scrunched his forehead. "What do you mean it's not really your place?"

"Well, you see, you're not the only one living in someone else's house." I hugged myself, and my gaze shot to the window above the sink. I glimpsed the bricks of my house. "I live in my parents' house. When my dad retired two years ago, they moved to a retirement community in Florida, but they didn't want to sell the house or leave it empty." I returned my focus to Lachlan—well, to his shirt—and hunched my shoulders. "I don't pay rent, just utilities and taxes and any repairs that need doing."

Lachlan curved his hands around my upper arms, caressing my bare skin with his fingertips. "Why do you seem ashamed of your living arrangements? In Scotland, many grown children live with their parents, grandparents, siblings."

"In America, you're a loser if you live at home. Even if your parents aren't actually present."

He hooked a finger under my chin and raised my face. "I don't care where you live, as long as I'm the only man you're sleeping with for the next four weeks."

My voice had abandoned me. I swallowed against a tightening in my throat, my mouth suddenly dry.

I let him shepherd me out of the house, across the adjoining lawns, and into my home. The constriction in my throat lingered. He didn't care if I lived in my parents' house. Presley had ribbed me about it on a regular basis, and though at the time I dismissed it as good-natured teasing, his comments ate away at my self-assurance like droplets of acid. Now I realized Presley's taunts had been a clue I should've understood much sooner, a clue to his true nature and his real feelings toward me. I figured it out too late.

Lachlan volunteered to make popcorn—a real chore, considering I had the microwave variety—while I turned on the TV and arranged pillows for us on the sofa. By the time African drums began beating out a tribal rhythm, Lachlan had settled in beside me with his much-larger body tucked into the sofa's corner. He draped his arm over my shoulders, cuddling me close.

My gaze wandered to his face, to the smoothness of his cheeks, peppered with a five o'clock shadow, and to the faint crow's feet that fanned out from his eyes when he smiled at something in the movie. I knew so little about him, not even as much as I'd find on a driver's license. The things I did know hinted at the man inside the hot body. He was intelligent. Mature. Steady. Thoughtful. Funny. Sensual.

"How old are you?" I asked.

Lachlan swiveled his head toward me, blue eyes twinkling in the light from the TV screen. "Forty-two. Why the sudden interest in my age?"

"Just filling in your driver's license."

"I don't follow."

"Never mind."

He turned back to the TV, drawing me a little closer, his hand a welcome weight on my shoulder. I loved the solid feel of it, the way it moored me to him. I tried to pay attention to the movie, but a question niggled at me until I could ignore it no longer.

Though I faced the TV, the image blurred, my mental focus squarely on the man beside me even as I fought not to look at him. "Don't you want to know how old I am?"

Don't you want to know anything about me?

"I never ask a woman's age," he said. "Was that a trick question?"

"No." I snagged a handful of popcorn and crammed it in my mouth, then I did something that would've horrified every mother in the world. I talked with my mouth full. "I'm twenty-eight."

His arm around me stiffened. "You're just a bairn. I'm beginning to feel like a dirty old man."

"I am not a bairn. And you're not old." I nudged him with my elbow. "As for dirty...Well, that's what I signed up for, right?"

He laughed, a low and seductive sound, dancing tingles down my spine. "So you did."

I nestled into him, tucking my legs under me, and rested my head on his chest. His heart thump-thumped under my ear. Steady. Strong. When I skimmed my hand down his chest to his waistband, his breath hitched and his heartbeat sped up.

We never touched the popcorn. And the movie...Let's just say it was a good thing I'd seen it a dozen times before. By the time Stewart Granger ordered Deborah Kerr to change into a less stifling outfit to avoid heat stroke, Lachlan had me spread out on the sofa beneath him. His hands groped every inch of me, his mouth ravished mine, and I arched my hips into him in silent pleas for more, more, more. *Take me now*, I begged with greedy thrusts of my fingers into his hair.

He didn't take me, not all the way. Not even halfway. But he left me revved up for a night of sweaty, sheet-twisting dreams that all revolved around him and his powerful, naked body. I knew he'd done this to me on purpose, to make sure I'd remember what was to come.

Me. In his bed, at his hand, over and over and over. That's what he'd promised. If he backed out on me again, I'd die of hunger. He'd gotten me hooked on a nourishment only he could provide, and we hadn't even done the deed yet.

Warning, warning, danger ahead, my brain screamed. Lucky for me, I'd stopped listening to my rational brain right about the time Lachlan called me the most enticing lass on earth.

Forget danger. Screw the future. I was starved for Lachlan, and for once in my life, I'd devour every last decadent bite without a thought for the consequences.

Chapter Twelve

After the blistering fantasies that overpowered my sleep, I woke the next morning in need of a shower. A cold one. Subzero cold. I was so aroused the draft from the central air system stiffened the fine hairs all over my body, prickling my skin with goosebumps and making my nipples shiver erect. Between my thighs, a sultry dampness slicked my swollen flesh. How could a man I'd known for two days do this to me?

From the floor at the foot of the bed, Casey thumped his tail. He'd given up on sleeping on the bed after the umpteenth time I kicked him while half-wakened from a pornographic dream. The poor dog deserved a big breakfast of gizzards, topped off with a pile of Milk-Bones.

"I'm up," I assured Casey, who answered with another tail thump. I disentangled my limbs from the twisted sheets and swung my feet onto the floor. The wood chilled my soles. I cringed, lifted my feet, then placed them on the floor again. Might as well deal with the inevitable.

Casey hopped up, racing around the bed to me. His tail swished. He chuffed, to make sure I got the picture.

With a long groan, I stretched my overworked muscles. "Lemme get in a shower first, 'kay? Walk later."

He whined but plopped his butt on the floor.

I patted his head, receiving a sloppy kiss on my hand in return. My neck ached. I rubbed it until the pain subsided, but then my back decided to join the party. My body suffered the aftermath of a night of epic tossing and turning, brought on by an overdose of insanely erotic dreams. I was addicted, for sure, and I loved it. Never before had I felt so desired, so treasured, so completely alive. The perfect distraction from my problems. If soreness was the price for this experience, I'd take it.

A steaming shower, with my massaging shower head, would iron out the kinks. I scratched Casey's back. "Just a few minutes. Then I promise to feed you lots and lots of icky, slimy gizzards. Yum-yum."

He panted and bobbed his head. Dogs. They were almost as baffling as men.

Just as I dragged my body off the bed, Casey sprang off the floor and onto the mattress, hitting it with a squeak-inducing thud. While the pooch got comfy, I headed for the bathroom. Lachlan had better come through for me this time, or I'd throttle him for corrupting me into a sex-crazed idiot.

I stripped off my satin nightie on the way into the bathroom and cranked up the shower while I brushed my teeth. Steam roiled out of the shower stall around the frosted glass door, which I'd left ajar. Once I'd adjusted the water temperature to the perfect mix of hot and cold, I stepped into the stall and clicked the door shut.

Blessed heat sluiced over me, convincing my muscles to loosen up. I turned my face into the spray. The water cascaded down my skin in warm rivulets that snaked down my belly, exciting every nerve, the sensation reminiscent of fingertips lightly tracing down my body. Visions of Lachlan's delicious muscles flitted through my mind as I massaged shampoo and conditioner into my hair with languid strokes of my fingers. The creamy conditioner drizzled onto my breasts, cool against my heated flesh. My breasts grew heavy, and a memory assailed me. Lachlan's mouth on my nipple. His teeth nipping. The strength of his greedy suckling.

Get a grip, woman.

No chance of that. I lathered up a handful of liquid soap, lavishing the suds over my skin the same way Lachlan roved his hands over me. He'd kiss my neck, squeeze my breasts, murmur "sweet Erica" in my ear. Hunger pulsated through me. *The most enticing lass.* His voice reverberated in my mind, deep and sexy. I feathered my fingers over my breasts, and my nipples pearled.

Dimly, I heard my phone ringing. Oh great. With my luck, it'd be my parents calling and I'd sound drunk—because I was drunk, on lust. I shut off the water and stumbled out of the stall. My phone was still ringing. Snatching up a towel, I wrapped it around my body and rushed to the bedside table. My sodden hair flopped around my head, spritzing water everywhere. I got to the phone one ring before my voicemail would've picked up the call.

"Hello?" Christ. I did sound drunk, my two syllables slurred.

"Good morning, sweet." Lachlan's voice rushed through my veins like whisky, warm and intoxicating. "You sound out of breath. Have you been exercising?"

I cleared my throat. "Just had a shower."

"An exhilarating one, I gather."

"I—" He couldn't know. I was breathless, so he assumed...what? A blush rose in my cheeks, and I tried to squelch it by patting the back of my damp hand on my face.

"Would you do me a favor?" he asked.

"Depends."

"Go to your kitchen, please."

A cold thread wound around my heart. Had he broken into my house? *Jesus, girl, you are so paranoid.* I endeavored to sound nonchalant but likely failed. "May I ask why?"

"I want to see you."

"Um..." My heartbeat accelerated at the idea of him seeing me in nothing but a towel. It was wicked. So not like me. Well, wasn't that my goal these days? Shed the old me and suck life's marrow before I went to the slammer?

Lachlan's voice dropped to a whisper. "Are you in a towel? Or maybe you ran from the shower so fast you're—"

"In a towel. Yes."

"Let me see you. Please."

I bit my lip until it hurt, one hand clutching the towel to keep it from slipping off my naked body. Let him see me? A wild woman did things like this, I supposed. Besides, I was wearing a towel that covered my most private bits. "Okay."

He let out a long breath as if he'd been holding it in. "To the kitchen."

Phone in hand, I sashayed out into the living room and straight through to the kitchen. Lachlan stood in the living room of his house, directly across from the bay window in the breakfast nook. Dressed in jeans and an unbuttoned hunter green shirt, his muscled torso on full display, he was mouthwateringly gorgeous, like a model for a romance novel cover.

I smiled and said into the phone, "Here I am."

"Yes you are." He laid a hand on his bare chest, fingers curling. "You're a vision in the morning, wet and clean, just begging to be sullied."

"Is that your plan? To sully me?"

"And then some." He moved his hand down to his waistband, but his eyes stayed locked on me, his mouth open, tongue tapping the bottoms of his front teeth.

My body tightened, muscles deep within contracting. The air seemed to grow hot and thick, my skin abruptly sensitized to the slightest draft. I couldn't climax from the way he looked at me. Could I?

A crazy impulse reeled through me, to release the towel and let it fall away. My hand holding the sides of the towel together loosened. The fabric slipped just enough to admit a draft that kissed my damp skin.

With one hand, Lachlan covered his enlarging shaft, barely contained by his low-slung jeans. "Any chance of a preview?"

"Preview of what?"

"You." He shimmied his hips, adjusting his length through his jeans. "One glimpse of what you're hiding under the towel."

I scuffled backward a step, my breaths labored. Lord, how I wanted to give it to him. A preview. Considering I'd agreed to sleep with him tonight, what harm was there in playing a little game with him now? My face grew numb, probably because I'd stopped breathing. *Inhale. Exhale.* The numbness faded, but I couldn't tear my gaze from Lachlan's.

What the hell. I took hold of both sides of the towel and spread them open.

Lachlan's eyes flashed wide, his jaw went slack. His voice was a raspy whisper. "Fuck me."

"That's the plan, isn't it?" I closed the towel, unable to restrain my grin.

His hand flew to his head, fingers knotting in his hair. He shook his head slowly. "You are stunning. I cannae wait till I'm buried inside ye."

My gaze landed on the bulge in his jeans. Turnabout time. I tugged the towel around me and tucked one corner inside, between my breasts, to secure it. Leaning back against the kitchen island, I waved at his jeans. "Your turn."

"What?" His face blanked for a second, then a sly grin slid across his features. "Suppose it's only fair."

He unbuttoned his jeans. My gaze was glued to his fingers as they toyed with the dangly part of his zipper. I crossed my ankles, but the pose only exacerbated the ache in my sex. One millimeter at a time, he eased the zipper ever downward. Lower. Lower. The head of his erection emerged, splashed with golden morning sun. With twenty feet and two windows between us, I couldn't make out more details, and besides, shadows blurred the rest of his crotch. The zipper edged down, down, down.

The tip of his index finger coasted along his rigid penis in slow motion. I envisioned my tongue tracking the same path, my fingers following in their wake to encircle his girth. Despite the shadows, with a sharp intake of breath I noted one fact.

My tongue went dry, thanks to the breeze rushing in through my gaping mouth. "No underwear?"

"Why bother? Don't plan on wearing clothes much this month." He unveiled another inch of his shaft. I couldn't get a good enough view from way over here and lunging side to side didn't help. Where had I put the binoculars? His sinful chuckle snapped my focus back to him and shimmied a hot shiver down my spine. "Like what you see?"

I gripped the island for support, suddenly woozy, as the full length and breadth of him surfaced. Shadows shmadows. I knew exactly what I was staring at—the awe-inspiring cock of a wildly aroused Highlander. *Wow.* "Can I come over for a closer look?"

Oh crap. Why had I said that? This man liquefied my brain. Well, he wanted a hot fling with a wanton American. *Strap in, cuz this rollercoaster has no brakes.*

He zipped up his jeans. "This was a preview, remember? We'll both look our fill this evening."

"So, we're on for tonight?"

"Nothing could keep me away." His lips curved up at the corners but remained sealed.

"What about all day? Another picnic or something?"

"Afraid I can't see you today, my plans will take time. But tonight I'll give you a fine meal and a night you won't forget."

Like a last meal for a death-row inmate. I'd lap up every crumb, because hey, it was rude to leave food on your plate. I laid a hand on the towel's top edge, plucking at the fold that bound it. "Until later."

"Counting the minutes."

He hung up, cast me one last scorching look, and strode off into the depths of his house.

I clamped my hands over the sofa's edge, my butt inches from slipping off the cushion. Lachlan had insisted on preparing some kind of surprise for me, and I heard noises from the direction of the bedroom—rustling, thumping, the shooshing of bare feet on carpet, the scritching of…matches? I fidgeted and wiped my sweaty palms on my jeans. Would he ever be done?

The whole day had dragged by, while I tried to distract myself with grocery shopping, bathroom cleaning, dog walking, and even my first attempt at dog bathing. All I accomplished was getting doused with sudsy, filthy water shaken out of a golden retriever's coat. Casey hated baths. Lesson learned.

For my evening with Lachlan, I'd exchanged sweats for a flouncy, sleeveless dress with a pastel floral pattern and a plunging neckline, another Goodwill find. With a bit of safety-pinning, I raised the hem to three inches above my knees. The second I spied myself in the mirror, though, I realized I didn't want Lachlan to see me in another jury-rigged dress. I changed into jeans and a satin blouse instead, with high heels for that bit of oomph.

When Casey spotted me heading for the front door, he'd known, in that doggie psychic way, I was off to see Lachlan and bounced up and down between me and the door, determined to come with me. After two handfuls of crunchy treats and much cajoling, I got the furball to curl up on my bed, stretched out as if he didn't give a hoot whether I ever came home. Okay, he'd start to worry in the morning, if his breakfast was late.

Maybe the dog didn't mind my leaving him because he knew I'd be with Lachlan. Casey had a thing for my Scotsman.

More noises originated from down the hall. What on earth was Lachlan up to? I kicked off my strappy heels—three inches this time, no six-inch stiletto disaster this go-round—and resisted the urge to glance over my shoulder. I'd promised Lachlan I wouldn't peek, but sticking to my vow got harder and harder the longer he made me wait. I drummed my fingers on the cushions and shouted, "Are you done yet?"

Hands slid through my hair from behind. Lachlan's fingertips smoothed over my cheeks, stimulating my senses, his skin warm and slightly rough, scented with that indescribable musk of manliness I'd never experienced with anyone else. He lighted a kiss on the crown of my head, then angled my face up so he could flutter his lips over my forehead. "This is a lesson in patience."

"Already told you I suck at that."

"Shut your eyes."

"Why?"

"Please." He exhaled over my forehead and the rush of heated air stirred the molten need simmering within me. I clenched the sofa cushions, my gaze fixated on his hypnotic eyes, knocked off kilter by the strangeness of his upside-down face. His hands eased my head back a little farther, the masculine scent of his skin flooding over me, inducing a pang of soul-deep pleasure. He moistened his lips and ran them down the bridge of my nose and back up again, a warm, damp trail left behind in their wake. "Trust me, sweet."

Everything inside me went soft. My eyelids drifted shut on their own, weighed down by a delicious relaxation. He peppered kisses on my lids, pressed his mouth to my temple, and—

"Whoa." A chill shimmered over my skin, though I couldn't unwind the slender thread of anxiety from the tapestry of my desire for him. He'd placed a ribbon of silky fabric over my eyes and was tying it behind my head. "A blindfold? I don't know about this."

"I'll take it off if you like, but I was hoping to unveil your surprise after we're in the bedroom." He brushed my hair back from my shoulders. "Can you trust me?"

"Yes." Why didn't I hesitate to answer? Did I trust him, this man I'd met two days ago? It was insane. Yet first responses tended to be the most honest. That would mean I trusted him. *Crazy.*

His hands withdrew. My ears tracked his footfalls, coming around the sofa toward me, and then a breeze whooshed over me. Lachlan must've knelt between me and the coffee table. *How much do you trust him? How much should you?* I shifted in place, pawed at my jeans, and wrung my hands. His mouth sealed over mine, hot and yielding, slamming my pulse into overdrive. My mind shut down. Nerves I didn't know I had flared to life, electrified by his lips slanting over mine, his teeth scraping my lower lip, and yet he held back from touching me with any other part of his body. I slumped forward, aching for more contact, but he moved to stay out of my reach, the gulf between us painfully wide. *Skin, gotta have skin.* I flung a hand up. He evaded me again. I gave an irritated whimper.

He swirled his tongue over my top lip. "Try to relax. This is meant to be fun."

"Take off the blindfold."

"Bit of a control freak, aren't you?"

"Yes." I tried for a scowl but didn't think I achieved it. Adrenaline zinged through my veins with an exquisite burn. "So take off the damn blindfold."

His lips tickled the corner of my mouth. "Why donnae ye remove it yerself?"

For a brief moment, I noted how his accent thickened and his speech grew more casual when he got excited—either by extreme anger or intense arousal. Then he palmed my breast, snatching away my ability to notice anything except what he was doing to me. I stifled a gasp. "Don't know. I guess because letting you blindfold me is a tacit agreement I won't remove the thing until you say so."

"And ye follow orders, even tacit ones?" His tongue curled around my earlobe. "I've trouble believing that."

"I—" Why had I sat here, obedient, unmoving? The answer shot a cold spike through me. I relished not knowing what he was up to, what he had planned for me. I reveled in giving up control. I *liked* it. He blew a steamy breath over the shell of my ear, charting the curve. My chill evaporated. A ghost seemed to have possessed me, because I heard myself saying, "I like the blindfold."

"Let's leave it on then, for a wee bit longer." He lifted me onto my feet, his hands firm on my hips, and crushed my body to his with arms thickly corded with muscles. "But when I take ye, I want yer eyes on me."

So did I. My body sizzled at the idea of it. I wanted to watch him over me, his hips thrusting, plunging into me until I lost my mind from the ecstasy of it.

His tongue darted between my parted lips. Mine met his in a brief touch, a tantalizing sample. He tasted of whisky and chocolate. I slapped his chest, missed, and grazed his arm. "Hey! Have you been eating candy and guzzling booze while I sat here waiting for you?"

"A taste test." He flipped me up into his arms. "It's all for you."

His muscles tightened, and I wobbled as he ferried me across the room. I knew he wouldn't drop me, not with his powerful arms cradling my body. I felt so small in his embrace, yet safe like never before. I guided my fingers up his cheek, into his soft hair. "Are you planning to get me drunk, Mr. MacTaggart?"

"The food and spirits are for after." He pressed his velvety lips to the sensitive skin on the inside of my wrist. "I've no need to ply you with liquor before."

He lowered me onto a plush surface covered with a satiny fabric and with deep cushioning beneath me. My head dropped onto a sumptuous pillow with a *pfft* of air escaping the soft fill, and I rubbed my cheek against the silken cover. The scent of vanilla teased my senses, emanating from elsewhere in the room. My cheeks tightened as a smile curved my lips. I lay on Lachlan's bed. Well, technically, Gil's bed.

My head sprang up. "This is someone else's bed."

"Gil won't mind." Lachlan breathed on the pulse point on my neck, just below my ear. "I asked him."

I tensed. "You asked my friend if he minded you having a poke at me in his bed?"

"No, my sweet, paranoid lass," Lachlan drawled, moving his open mouth down my throat. His lips and tongue painted a damp, hot trail over my skin. "I asked if he minded me entertaining female acquaintances in his home. He said as long as I wash the sheets before he gets back, it was no matter to him."

"How many females have you gotten acquainted with in this bed?"

"None—yet." His lips tickled my throat while his fingers unbuttoned my blouse. The fabric brushed my skin as he spread the blouse open, inch by inch, baring the slopes of my breasts. Cool air shivered over them. "You, my bonnie Erica, will be the first."

Words caught in my throat. The first? His phrasing implied he might bring others here too, during his one-month vacation.

"There willnae be others," he murmured against my collarbone. "I asked ye to be my companion for this month. You and only you."

"What makes you think I care?" I squirmed, partly from discomfort and partly from the heat of his mouth on my skin, his breaths a divine torment shivering over my skin.

He chuckled, the sound vibrating through me. "Ye tensed when I said ye were the first, which means ye care."

"Maybe I'll have other men during the month."

"You won't."

I snorted. "Arrogant much?"

He freed the last button, sweeping aside the halves of my blouse. His hand rested on my bare stomach, his touch light yet possessive. He kissed his way down my breastbone, into the valley between my breasts. I fought the urge to rip off the blindfold. I could. He'd let me. But a reckless part of me relished not knowing, not seeing, simply feeling and listening and experiencing. The blindness heightened every sensation until pain twanged through my ears and down my nerves. But Lachlan's tenderness and his soothing voice eased the pain, replacing it with a keen awareness of his every move, every sound, every scent.

His nose grazed my breast. His lips followed, damp and hot, his breaths ghosting over my skin. My nipples tightened, my breasts swollen and aching for his touch. He slipped a finger under my bra strap and pulled it over my shoulder to hang halfway down my upper arm. Then his big hand stole inside my bra, molding to my breast, and with a quick tug, he popped it free. I arched into his touch. With one flick of his thumb over my nipple, he ricocheted electricity through me. It shot straight down to my core, throbbing through my sex. His ravenous mouth latched onto my nipple, suckling and nipping, making me buck and writhe beneath him. While his mouth tormented my nipple, his hand released my breast and traveled down to the button of my jeans. He unhooked it. I plowed my hands into his hair. He unzipped my jeans with a sharp rip, relinquishing my nipple. I made an irritated noise.

Lachlan laughed and pecked a kiss on my nose. "Patience."

"Told you, not my strong suit."

His fingers dove inside the waistband of my jeans to drag them down my thighs. "I've noticed your impatience. Tonight, I'll teach ye to enjoy waiting."

Chapter Thirteen

hould I be taking notes?"

"Ye won't be thinking clearly enough to jot anything down."

My jeans disappeared. His arm came around me, lifting my torso off the bed just enough so he could strip off my blouse. In nothing but my bra and panties, with one breast spilling out of its cup, I lay there cradled in his arm with my back a hair's breadth above the smooth sheets. The heat of his body radiated over me, exciting every nerve and stiffening every hair. My heartbeat seemed to echo through the room, loud as a sledgehammer, and my breaths came shallow and fast.

Lachlan's weight shifted on the bed.

I raised my head. "Are you leaving?"

"Just grabbing a tool."

A lump congealed in my throat. Tool? I envisioned whips and handcuffs, the imagery dousing cold over me, nearly extinguishing my desire. I didn't like kink, I told him that. He wouldn't—

Something soft and feathery lighted on my skin between my breasts. As he fanned it over one mound, I realized the "tool" was a feather. It tickled my skin in long sweeps, the delicate vanes barely contacting my skin. My arousal surged back to life, so intense I choked back a cry. When he skimmed the feather over the nipple of my exposed breast, I sucked in a breath and threw my head back, my spine arching up toward him. Our bodies met for the briefest second, then I fell back onto the mattress, all but panting for him as the feather traced over my lips.

The feather vanished.

Lachlan reached under me to unhook my bra. His expert hands dispatched the garment in one flick, and my panties went next. A faint breeze from the air conditioning whispered over my naked flesh. Then the feather flirted with my skin again and I stopped breathing. He skirted it over every inch of me, first on my throat, then down my breastbone, wandering ever lower. I shivered when he flicked the feather over belly, just above my mound. As he spread my legs with one hand, the feather prickled the insides of my thighs, down the hypersensitive skin there, and then slowly up again to frisk over my slick folds. The dampness of my arousal burgeoned anew in a liquid rush.

Blistering. Molten. Bone-melting hunger.

It pulsed through me from the epicenter at the core of me, fueled by the feather dancing on my skin and the man hovering over me, both unseen yet tormenting me in equal measure because I couldn't see. And I didn't care. I reveled in the unknown, in the anticipation of what might come next. Doubt, gone. Fear, gone. Control, gone.

The feather was whisked away in a tiny puff of air.

What? *No.* I clenched my hands in the pillow above my head. "Please."

"Please what?"

"Don't stop."

Lachlan planted a kiss on the hollow of my hip. I jolted and clutched at the sheets. His lips forged a path down to my thigh, planting an open-mouth kiss perilously near my downy mound. I grabbed for him, but he snared my wrists in one hand, his grip firm but gentle. I rolled my hips, desperate to get his mouth on me. He restrained my wrists over my belly. His mouth sealed over my sex as his tongue began to swipe back and forth, back and forth. When he licked up and down for one languid stroke, a strangled moan caught in my throat. My knees fell wide open, exposing all of me to him.

He lapped and suckled, I bucked and writhed, he kept up a relentless pace as he alternated up and down, side to side, now circling his tongue around my rigid clitoris and then exhaling heated air over it. I cried out with every lash of his velvety tongue, every wisp of his breaths. His hand cuffed both of mine, but also pinned me to the bed. I struggled against the constraint, wanting free but needing his control over me. He wouldn't hurt me, somehow I knew that. I trusted him to take care of me.

Trusted him? Panic spiked through my chest. "Lachlan, wait, I—"

His tongue raked down my cleft, diving into my entrance, milking all the pleasure my body could offer. I forgot what I'd been about to say, what I'd thought, everything. Pressure built inside me, a pulse-pounding drive to climax that compelled me ever upward against the gravity of Lachlan. Up and up and up, so high my head spun. My entire body went taut, my breaths shortened into sharp gasps.

"Lachlan!" My orgasm catapulted me into the sky, and for one weightless moment ecstasy held me motionless, then released me into a free-fall. Muscles inside my opening pulsated around an emptiness only he could fill. The last wave of pleasure contorted my body, and I sank back into myself. Limp. Chest heaving. Sated, though not completely. A need thrummed inside me.

He let go of my wrists. Breathless, I flailed my hands in search of him. His body settled on top of mine, his erection trapped between us. I buried my face in his neck. "Wow, that was…"

"The beginning." He delved a hand into my hair. "We've got all night."

He peeled his body away from mine. I reached for him, but only grazed his chest. "Where are you going?"

"Nowhere." The bed creaked and rocked as he stood up. He tore off the blindfold. "Nothing could keep me from you tonight."

I squinted at the sudden brightness, but not for long. The illumination was muted, and it flickered. I sat up, nude on the pale green sheets, and started to survey the room, but a solitary sight stole my attention. The golden light from a dozen candles danced on Lachlan's skin, highlighting every muscle. He stood beside the bed, shoulders back, arms slack at his sides—and wearing nothing but his kilt. With my gaze riveted to him, I barely noticed anything else. My mind fixated on his chest, thoughts flaring like fireflies in the dark. I longed to lick his naked skin, skate my palms over his muscles, inch lower and lower until I found his kilt, then rip it off in one swipe.

Lachlan swept an arm wide. "A wee bit of Scotland brought here for you."

I laid a hand on my chest, my thoughts muddled. "What?"

"One day you'll see my country for yourself." He stepped back and spread both arms. "But for now, this is what I can give you."

Paralyzed by the stunning view of his naked chest and kilt-cloaked hips, I could do nothing except nod and stare at the spectacle he'd constructed for me. Candles occupied every available surface, five on the dresser alone, and a single plump one burning on the bedside table. None sat on the windowsill because he'd drawn the curtains. More candles decorated the flat-top wooden chest beside the dresser. Green-and-blue plaid fabric draped over the top of the dresser mirror and served as a valance over the window curtains. Eight-by-ten photographs, each framed in silver, were propped up here and there, in between the candles, so the flickering flames highlighted the images. I absorbed them one by one.

A white castle perched atop an embankment with its spires pricking the blue sky. A row of stone arches curved over a narrow road. Waves crashed against craggy white cliffs.

Lachlan pointed at each photo in turn, seeming to track my focus. "Dunrobin Castle, seat of the Sutherland clan. Glenfinnan Viaduct. The coast of Caithness." His voice entranced me as his bobbing finger drew me from photo to photo and he named each landmark. At last, we reached the final picture. The framed image rested on the bedside table, beside the plump candle. It showed a hilltop view of a quaint village seated at the shore of a small lake, nestled in a valley. Lachlan's voice softened, his expression wistful. "Ballachulish, my home."

"Oh Lachlan." I leaned over to see the photo better. "It's beautiful. I wish I could visit there someday."

He sat down beside me, the bed creaking under his weight. "Why do ye say it as if it's not possible?"

Because felons don't get international furloughs. "When were you last in Bally—Ballakol—"

"Bal-uh-koo-lish." He brushed the back of his hand over my cheek. "I was there Christmas before last."

A year and a half ago. No wonder he seemed homesick. "Work keeps you busy, huh?"

"Aye." He tipped his head to the side. "Speaking of work, do you go back tomorrow?"

Back to work at Cichon, D'Addio & Rothenberg? The firm had fired me three weeks ago. "I'm sort of taking a sabbatical."

"Ah." His lips compressed, his eyes narrowed, and for a moment I thought he'd press the issue. Instead, he ran his hand up my thigh and hit me with his heart-stopping smile. "Back to the fun, eh?"

"Yes please." I shimmied closer, looped my arms around his neck, and skidded my lips over his throat. He cupped my hip, his fingers curled against the backside, his thumb drawing circles on my skin. I swirled my tongue up to his jaw, nibbling there, while I ruffled his silken hair. When he groaned into my ear, passion exploded inside me like a flame doused with gasoline. I pulled his head back to scrape my lips over his collarbone while I mapped out his every muscle with my hands. Toned flesh gave under the light pressure of my hands, his skin warm and soft. Tiny, dark hairs bristled my lips. His skin tasted faintly of salt and spicy soap. I pressed my open mouth to his chest, my teeth gently biting. He groaned again, his thumb kneading my hip hard and fast. I stretched one arm around him to squeeze his ass.

"Och, lass, how ye drive me mad." Before I could take hold of the part of him I craved most, he pushed away to jump to his feet. Scrubbing his face with one hand, he struggled to catch his breath. "Forgot the last stop on our virtual tour of Scotland. The botanical gardens."

"Can't it wait?" His erection bobbed under his kilt, clearly anxious to come out and play. And he stopped to show me garden snapshots?

He hefted up a small wooden crate that had been concealed behind the dresser. Returning to the bed, he settled in opposite me and deposited the crate between us. I tucked my feet under me so I could lean closer. Lachlan shooed me back with a tsk and a wave of his hand. "Patience, *gràidh*, I'm about to show you."

"What did you call me?"

"*Gràidh*." He sifted through the contents of his secret box.

I took hold of the box's edge with both hands. "What does it mean?"

His hands stilled inside the box. His shoulders hunched. "*Gràidh*? It's Gaelic for darling."

He shouldn't be calling me darling. His rules prohibited emotional attachment, which made endearments off limits. But my heart did a funny little flutter when he spoke the word, and I couldn't summon the will to chastise him.

I dropped my hands to my knees. Darling. Why did he have to say sweet things? I hated bewitching words, like the ones Presley used to con me. Yet when Lachlan called me *gràidh*, I ached deep inside, far beyond the level of sexual desire. I ached for affection—his affection. Goddammit, no. I refused to turn into a swooning little moron. *Never again.*

My resolve lasted about thirty seconds. That's when Lachlan lifted a handful of purple flowers, tendering them to me on his upturned palm. A thin white ribbon bound the stalks into a bundle. I accepted the flowers. "They're lovely. Thistle, right?"

"Very good, *gràidh*. You're a canny lass."

Criminy, there he went again. Compliments and endearments. Each one he uttered set off a new pang in my chest.

He brought out another bundle, this one full of bell-shaped purple blossoms that drooped from the stems' tips. Lachlan skated his fingertips over the dainty flowers. "I had to give you this one. It's bell heather, but the Latin name is *Erica cinerea*." He whisked his lips over the blossoms, then clasped his hand behind the back of my head and ravished me with a mind-numbing kiss. When he spoke again, his brogue had thickened, his voice had gone hoarse. "Ye are a bonnie wee flower in yer own right."

I gaped at him, my voice gone, ripped away from me by his earnest, affectionate words. My eyes stung and if I didn't change the mood soon, I might weep right here in front of him. I was naked in body and in soul.

Lachlan handed me a bundle of bright red blooms. "Lastly, Scottish flame flower—for my fiery lass."

Stop calling me yours. I lost the battle, and tears rolled down my cheeks. I longed to be his, but he would leave me in a matter of weeks. How stupid had

I been to think I could handle this arrangement?

Lachlan wiped my tears away with his thumbs, cradling my face in his palms. His brows had scrunched together to etch wrinkles over the bridge of his nose. "Donnae cry, please. They're only flowers."

He didn't get it at all. I let his eyes entrance me, anything to escape the sorrow of my forbidden yearnings. I'd agreed to his limits. I wanted hot sex. Based on how he'd driven me to a mind-blowing orgasm with his mouth, I knew he could give me so much more. Time to get back on track. "I'm okay. Earth-shattering orgasms make me cry. It's a girl thing."

Though his mouth opened, he didn't speak. His eyes narrowed, intent on me. I sighed and stretched, which bounced my breasts up. His gaze zeroed in on my chest, and his tongue darted over his lower lip. Distract Lachlan—check. Recover my composure…a work in progress.

Lachlan collected up the flower bundles, placed them in the box, and set it on the floor. His task gave me a moment to collect myself. My fit of self-pity receded until my attention zeroed in the bulge tenting his kilt. *Want that.* I crawled onto his lap.

His eyes widened. I yanked up his kilt to expose his jutting shaft. It bobbed between us, the head rosy tipped and glistening. I ran my finger along the lines of veins just beneath the skin. Wrapping my hand around his sleek length, I pumped slowly. "No more flowers and pretty words. I want you inside me."

"Donnae have to make yer point so…ahhh." He mashed me to his chest and flipped me onto my back, with him on top of me. I still had my hand around his shaft. He eased my fingers off, then secured my hands above my head with one hand. He was heavy, lying atop me, but it felt wonderful. "Ahmno one to deny a lady, so I'll be fucking ye now."

"About damn time."

His lips curved in a self-satisfied smile.

I rolled my hips up. His erection pressed harder into my belly. I plied his ass with my fingers, locking one ankle around his leg, baring myself to him. He shoved a hand between our bodies, straight into my folds. His deft fingers sank into my drenched, aching flesh. My body bowed up, my mouth opened wide on a strangled cry.

"You're so wet." He dipped two fingers into me while his palm rubbed my clitoris. "Aye, sweet Erica, go on. Show me yer passion."

"Shut up and do something." A cry burst out of me when he bent to devour my nipple. "Please."

Lachlan rose onto his knees and stripped off his kilt, flinging it aside. I lost my breath, awestruck by the sight of his nude body and his erection waving as if beckoning me to partake of its offerings. Couldn't stop myself. I sneaked my tongue out to skate across the undersides of my front teeth while I envisioned coiling it around his—

With swift grace, he nabbed a condom packet from the bedside table, ripped it open, and sheathed himself. He was glorious, towering over me like this. My very own Highlander. I touched a finger to the head of his penis. He fell onto all fours above me, his face hovering over mine. "Tell me what ye want."

"Are you serious?"

"I'm at yer command." He bent down for a quick, rough kiss. "Use yer hands all ye want this time."

"Gee, thanks."

A crooked grin split across his face, but his eyes were wild and blazing. Our gazes converged. He searched my face, his expression dark and lustful, yet tempered by...something. With one knee, he spread my legs wider. Every cell in my body stopped moving. I held my breath, my heartbeats thundering in my ears. He ran his tongue over my lower lip. "Tell me."

"Mm, I want—" Could I say it? Should I? Me, straight-laced Erica Teague.

Poised over me, my Highlander compressed his lips and hauled in a deep breath. His voice rasped. "Anything for you, *gràidh*. Ye need only say it."

"I want you to—" My voice broke off. *Say it, say it, say it.* Oh how I longed to.

Lachlan pinched my clit.

I thrashed under him, shouting wordlessly. *Wild woman, remember?* I met those captivating eyes and told him, "Fuck me."

Chapter Fourteen

Lachlan plunged inside me to the hilt, filling me completely. I clung to him, overwhelmed by the blissful fullness of him consuming me and the power of this moment.

He hesitated, breathing hard, propped up on his straight arms. My legs tight around his hips, I dug my fingers into his back and tugged at him, begging for more, for what I'd demanded from him.

He gasped for air, sweat beading on his forehead. At my rapturous sigh, he growled low in his throat, his eyes contracted into slits.

Hands around his shoulders, I levered my body up to rake my tongue over his sweat-slicked chest.

"Bloody hell, woman." He ground his hips into me, forcing his shaft even deeper.

"More," I pleaded, heedless of whether I sounded pathetic. "Do it, Lachlan. Now."

He withdrew until the tip of his erection nudged my entrance. My senses telescoped down to the vision of him over me, the musky scent of sex, and the delicious friction of his shaft rubbing back and forth, inflaming my flesh until my ears rang and black spots dotted my eyesight. I writhed and beat my fists on the mattress. His tip penetrated me only to slide back out, glide in further, pull out, lunge inside again. Each thrust was more powerful, more intense, plunging in as far as possible, consuming me with a bonfire of need and raw lust. I flailed my head, my hair whipping around my face, strands sticking to my flushed skin, plastered there by the perspiration swiftly sheening my body. My vision blurred, my chest burned.

"Breathe," he commanded, and I drew in one breath, and another. Blessed oxygen revived me, clearing my eyesight. I blinked slowly, dazed by the magnitude of my arousal. He sat back on his heels, took hold of my hips, and lifted them off the mattress, my thighs straddling his. His gaze swept down to my loins. His jaw slackened, and his eyes glazed as he drank in the entirety of my body. "So beautiful. An angel couldnae be as perfect."

Unable to think or speak, I gazed up at him with a kind of reverence, overstimulated from head to toe and more worked up than I'd ever imagined possible, yet touched in a way that had nothing to do with sex.

"I'll be taking you slow, my sweet Erica." His brogue molded my name into an erotic spell, cast by my Highland sorcerer. "Need to savor ye for as long as humanly possible."

Oh. My. God. I gulped back a whimper as my sex tightened, my clitoris so engorged and achy it almost hurt. No man had a right to be this hot. It had to violate the laws of nature.

He widened his stance, wiggling side to side until his knees parted and his cock aligned with my opening. His hands were still locked on my hips, his eyes never wavered from mine. I swore little blue flames flickered in those irises, hints of the inferno he held inside.

He penetrated me inch by maddening inch until his rock-hard, throbbing shaft was lodged all the way in. The fullness of it, the heat and the stiffness of him, overwhelmed my senses. I clawed at his shoulders, my outbursts wordless pleas for more, more, more. His face had gone dark, hard, his concentration complete as he held stone-still. I teetered on the brink, the urgency to tumble over the edge nearly irresistible, but my release was withheld by the incredible man torturing me with his body.

I reared up into him. "Fuck me, you bastard!"

Laughter blasted out of him. "All right, lass. No need for insults."

His arms quivered. Sweat sheathed his entire body, his cheeks reddened with exertion.

Both my hands clamped onto his arms, I clenched my muscles around his girth. "Hurry up."

He sputtered, his face twisted in a mixture of agony and pleasure. "Erica, I cannae—" His eyes flew wide when I tightened those muscles again. "Ah!"

He pounded into me. I shut my eyes to revel in the absolute bliss of him pummeling into me, whipping out, thrusting deep, pumping harder and faster with each stroke. I shouted his name, scratched his back, bucked my hips to meet his thrusts. He lunged into me, his mouth agape, his breaths sharp and quick. My pulse thundered in my ears, every beat banging against my ribs. My body quaked, my muscles went weak, but I prayed he'd never stop.

The vision of him above me and the glorious pressure of him taking me launched me into outer space once more, swimming in the Milky Way, galvanized by the stars. My orgasm detonated like a supernova and I screamed, thrashing from the sheer ecstasy of it, my body milking him for everything he had. Lachlan punched into me again and again until his release squeezed a hoarse, drawn-out cry from him, his lips peeled back over gritted teeth.

A look of pure amazement slackened his features. He gazed at my face, pumping into me once, twice, three more times before collapsing onto the bed beside me. He pulled me into his arms, cradling me against him. The aroma of heather and vanilla still permeated the air beneath the scent of sweat and sex. The sheets lay crumpled and tangled around us.

I rested my chin on his damp chest. "I've never done anything like this before. Having sex with someone I just met."

"Neither have I."

"What?" I popped my head up to scrutinize him, but he didn't look like he was kidding. "Are you serious?"

His mouth twisted into an irritated expression. "I understand why you'd think I'm some sort of a Casanova, given the offer I made, but you've got me wrong."

The notion he wasn't a player set my heart to racing, my thoughts spinning around the axis of a single, forlorn hope. Could he fall for me? *Cut that out this instant, you moron. He wants sex, period.* But he disliked me thinking of him as a Casanova. Maybe…

Apparently, I'd learned nothing whatsoever from my affair with Presley Cichon. I chewed the inside of my cheek for a couple seconds, then I gave in to my curiosity and peeked up at him. "So, you're not an inveterate seducer?"

His entire face relaxed, his lips curving up in a lazy smile. He tugged the sheet up over us. "I've never been called an inveterate anything, much less a seducer."

"How many—" I averted my gaze to his pecs, lips clamped between my teeth. "Sorry, I was about to ask something impertinent and personal."

One big, warm hand came up to stroke my hair. In a tone far too tender for our arrangement, he murmured, "Ask away."

I rolled my eyes up to meet his. "What about the no-personal-questions mandate?"

"Considering everything I've just done to you…" His smile broadened, crinkling the skin around his brilliant eyes. "I think we can temporarily suspend the rules."

My heart leapt. Really. It felt like it might spring out of my chest to do cartwheels on the bed. *Haven't learned a damn thing.* Maybe I was an idiot, but I couldn't pass up this chance. Scrolling my index finger round and round on his chest, my gaze ensnared by the flickering candlelight that danced in his shimmering, jewel-like eyes, I asked my question. "How many women have you slept with?"

"In my life? Six, including you."

My finger froze. I arched my brows and said, in a tone I hoped came out sexily teasing, "Only six? You're so ancient, I figured you must've had fifty or sixty, at least."

Lachlan tapped his fingertip on my nose. "Very funny. I was married for twelve years, and before that, I was selective. I had to care for a woman to take her to my bed."

"And now you're slumming it with me."

His jaw snapped shut with an audible click. He stared at me, hissing a breath out his nostrils, for several long seconds. "Never refer to what we do together as slumming. You're not a prostitute."

"But you don't care about me. You don't even know me."

"I—" He ran a hand over his face, then pressed the heel of his hand to his forehead, his eyes closed. When he looked at me again, his expression was shuttered, unreadable. "I like you, Erica. And I want you. Can that be enough?"

"Well, that was our agreement. Sex only." The odd tension between us had my stomach churning, and the lovely languidness I'd been enjoying began to disintegrate. I had to change the mood, fast. My cheek on his skin, I listened to the rapid beat of his heart. "It's your turn. Ask an impertinent question."

He dragged his fingers down my spine, swiping them across each notch until his hand came to rest over the dimple of my buttocks. "How many men have you been with?"

"Three, counting you."

"One of them would be the bawbag who bullied you."

"Presley? Yes. Unfortunately."

Lachlan's hand stiffened on my backside. "I've no right to feel this way, but I hate thinking of you with him."

"So do I." My shudder was only part fake. I couldn't believe I'd ever let Presley touch me. My skin crawled at the memory of our nights together, though at the time I'd enjoyed being with him. What a fool I'd been. I believed he cared about me, wanted me, needed me. The discomfort faded swiftly, though, as I realized the import of what Lachlan had just told me.

He hated thinking of me with another man. A dangerous little ember of hope sparked inside me.

"Enough personal questions," Lachlan said, sliding his hand down to squeeze my butt. "Shall we get back to the fun?"

"Absolutely." I slung my leg over his, my nipples skating across his chest, hardening from the light friction. He was rousing too, as evidenced by the sheet tenting over his crotch. "Next are you going to tie me up?"

"What?" He gripped my chin, rotating my face toward him. "I would never do anything that might possibly hurt you."

"I just wondered, because you held my wrists earlier. More than once."

His eyes closed for a moment, his lips tight. When he looked at me again, his gaze conveyed tenderness, with a hint of a playful glimmer. "I was trying to keep you from clawing my head."

My heart skipped. "Did I hurt you?"

"No, but it was awfully distracting."

"Oh." I splayed my fingers over his chest. "Thank you."

He squinted at me. "For what?"

"I begged you to fuck me, and you did." I cuddled closer. "It was the best sex of my life."

"First of all," he said, smoothing a hair from my face, "you didn't beg. You commanded. And I must obey the bonniest, sexiest lass I've ever met." He fingers roamed down my arm. "It was the best sex of my life too. No thanks are necessary."

Bonniest. Sexiest. My body responded to those words as if he'd shoved his hand between my thighs again—with a delicious, tingling heat.

A smirk tightened his lips. "Again?"

I gazed up at him through my lashes. "How did you know?"

"Because you're looking at me like you could devour me in one bite." He grabbed my ass in a possessive grip. "I could devour you for sure."

"Then please, feel free. Tonight, think of me as your all-you-can-eat buffet." I nodded at his blossoming arousal. "Don't let that go to waste."

He gave a mock yawn. "Maybe I'm too exhausted. You are a handful."

I grabbed a condom packet from the table. His stiffening erection prodded my backside as he rolled over onto his side behind me. When I lay down on my back, he settled a possessive arm over my belly. His smile was slow and sensual, smoldering with a fire that burned only for me. My skin tightened. I sprang upright, stripped the bed sheet away from his body, and straddled him. His hands settled on my thighs, caressing up and down, exerting more pressure with each pass, his fingers massaging deep into my flesh. Hovering above him, I raised the condom packet to my lips.

Lachlan arched one brow as if dubious, but he'd stopped breathing. His lips parted, his tongue caught between his teeth. His penis bobbed between my spread thighs. My breath hitched, my arousal exploded in a flood of liquid heat.

"Ah Christ," he groaned. "You are going to kill me."

"No." I ran the condom packet over my lower lip. "Just torture you the way you tortured me. Make you beg. Get you so hard you can't think and the only thing you can manage to say is *please, Erica, please.*"

He gripped my thighs, right under my hips, his thumbs nudging my mound. "Please, my sweet Erica, my erotic goddess, please."

"That'll do too." The words came out breathless. I loved it when he said my name that way, all smoky and soft, as if he were whispering an incantation, a love spell woven around the two of us.

I ripped the foil packet with my teeth.

Lachlan's eyed flared wide, then drifted half closed. He pulled gently, urging my knees to bend just enough my sex lowered to within inches of his erection. His shaft jutted against my inner thigh, rubbing a drop of moisture from its reddened tip onto my skin. He eased one hand between my legs, his fingers grazing my mound as his thumb brushed my clitoris with shiver-inducing effect. "Ye are for certain the bonniest, sexiest woman on earth."

"You said that already." I rolled the condom down the rigid length of him, taking my time as I sheathed his velvety flesh. When my fingertips skated over his balls, he hissed in a breath, hips wriggling. He tried to pull me down closer, with his hand on my thigh, but I rose up instead. His look of pure desperation and carnal hunger had my nipples aching and need spiking through my sex. His forehead crimped, his mouth went tight.

I did this to him. I made him crave me so badly he couldn't catch his breath. Excitement electrified my skin, awakening goosebumps that spread up my arms and out over the rest of my body.

"Ah, *gràidh*, ahm begging ye—" He hissed in a breath, scraping his thumb over my clit and down my cleft. When I gasped at the riot of sensations, he gritted his teeth. "Yer killing me."

"Said that before." I curled my fingers around his impressive erection, gliding my hand up and down, the ribbed condom slippery against my palm. "Don't you have anything new to say?"

He swallowed audibly. "The facts bear repeating."

I sank down onto his shaft, taking him all the way. It felt so good I moaned. He grasped my hips, his fingers digging in. He stared at me with the intensity of a cougar eying its prey. I laid my hands on his chest, bracing myself, and rode him with languid strokes, watching his shaft slide in and out. Never in my life had I mounted a man, never had I suggested it, never had I felt so at ease being naked with a lover that I dared do anything so audacious. This was me—Erica the boring, Erica the conservative—in control of a strapping giant of a man, doling out his gratification and wringing every last ounce of mine from his scorching-hot body. I intended to savor this for as long as possible, to make Lachlan as wild for me as I was for him.

He hissed through his teeth. "You're so wet."

"You told me that already too." I threw my head back, drowning in the bliss of our bodies merging, of him buried inside me with each thrust.

He bucked up just as I slammed down and gave a choked shout. "Can't be original when yer driving me mad." He clutched my hips to him as he bucked into me again. "Ah! Faster, lass, faster."

I rose up off of his shaft, gazing down on him, marveling at the gloriously impassioned man beneath me, at my mercy. My strong Highlander darted his gaze over me, eyes feverish. Pained wrinkles cinched tight above his nose. The pleasure escalating within me seared my body, and his blatant urgency turned me on even more. He was crazed for me. I had the upper hand. And I wanted only one thing—to make us both convulse from earth-shattering orgasms.

Swaying my hips, I took my swollen breasts in my palms and pinched the nipples.

Lachlan huffed short breaths, his skin glossy with sweat. His voice was rough, strained. "Erica, have mercy on me."

"Never."

Chapter Fifteen

I impaled myself on his rock-hard shaft, crying out from the blast of pleasure. Our bodies slapped together in a frantic rhythm punctuated by his grunts and my hoarse cries. My hair flapped around me, fanned over my cheeks, tickled my throat. A memory crashed over me, of the feather Lachlan teased me with while I was blindfolded, and my body flashed back to the intensity of that moment, the wild abandon it provoked in me. I ground my sex into him, driving him deeper than ever, my every muscle tensing for the climax.

Lachlan let out an explosive growl, clamping my hips down, and punched into me. Half his body lifted off the bed with the force of his thrust. We slammed back down onto the mattress still joined, the concussion plunging me onto him in the instant he came. He pulsed inside me. His yells echoed through the house. Then his thumb found my clit, rubbing and rolling it, his fingers curled over my mound.

Frantically, I rode him, with his thumb tormenting me, bound to his shaft by his powerful hands. With a power I'd never experienced before, I crashed over the edge. My sex clenched around him, my whole body contracting. The ecstasy of my orgasm unleashed primal, unbridled cries from deep inside me. By the time the final wave ebbed, my throat was dry and I was panting for air.

I slumped onto Lachlan's chest, spent and satisfied beyond description. He glided his hands down my back and up again to comb his fingers through my hair. The gentle sweeping of his fingers on my scalp soothed me into the weightless trance between sleep and wakefulness. I summoned my voice with great effort and whispered against his chest. "Thank you for dinner—and the virtual tour of Scotland."

"You're welcome." Still combing his fingers through my hair, he lifted my hand to his mouth and kissed each knuckle. "I'd be honored to take you to dinner tomorrow night."

"Mmm." Words, and thoughts, fled me. I knew only the joy of this man's body, his touch, his voice.

"A proper dinner." He laced my hair between his fingers. "Nothing like the club the other night."

My mind stirred at the mention of the club and the memories it triggered. Magnificent Lachlan steadying me on my ridiculous stilettos. His amused expression. The whisky. How he'd tasted when I sneaked my tongue into his mouth. In the present, I smiled up at him. "I would love to have dinner with you."

"I'll be honored to escort you."

"Honored? You're being sarcastic, right?"

"Of course not. You are an elegant, captivating woman." He slapped my ass and I yelped. "You're also fantastic in bed. I lucked out when I picked you for my holiday fling. And you lucked out too, since you admit I give you the best orgasms of your life." His mouth stretched taut in a barely restrained grin. "I suppose you ought to thank me after all."

I smacked his chest, though not hard. "Arrogant Scot."

"Cheeky American."

We both laughed.

A moment later, he eased me off him so he could retrieve the bottle of Talisker whisky he'd stashed on the floor beside the wooden chest, along with a round, black box. Lachlan handed it to me. "Highland chocolates from Iain Burnett. These are caramels as rich and silky as you."

I peeled the box open and nearly dropped it when I saw the perfect little chocolate hearts nestled inside. Hearts. Romantic candies. "Uh, thanks. I love caramel."

"You don't look pleased."

Lifting my gaze to his, I mustered a smile for him. "I am pleased. These look yummy."

He pulled me down beside him and we reclined in bed together, the sheets covering us from the hips down. I snagged his shirt from the floor and donned it while he went topless—which was fine with me. I adored his chiseled chest. I adored his body, period. And his eyes. And his smile, his laugh, his affection for my dog, his tenderness with me, the chocolate hearts, the way he called me *gràidh*. That strange heaviness in my chest returned.

Lachlan touched a chocolate to my lips. "Open up."

I complied, and he slipped the candy onto my tongue. I sealed my mouth around it, not chewing, letting the confection warm to my body temperature and dissolve, the succulent sweetness a pleasure almost as satisfying as Lachlan's body. I began to chew with languorous indulgence, releasing the savory, decadent caramel sheltered inside the chocolate shell. It drizzled over my tongue, a sweet and sensuous delight, and I moaned my appreciation.

Lachlan cleared his throat and shifted his hips under the blanket. A suspicious lump had appeared under the covers. I swallowed the remnants of the candy with a rapturous sigh. He licked his lips and poured whisky into a glass, then downed it in one swig. He repeated the process twice more.

"You okay?" I asked.

"If I don't drink myself into a stupor—" He decanted more amber liquid into his glass. "— I'll take you again."

"And that's a bad thing."

He clapped the glass down on the bedside table. "I've never made love to a woman more than twice in one night."

"I've never been made love to more than twice in a night, so we're even." I snagged the whisky bottle from him and gulped it straight from the mouth. When the whisky burn hit, I shook my whole body in an exaggerated shudder, my lips flapping. I wiped my mouth with the back of my hand. "Let's break new ground together. What do you say?"

Eyes stormy, he tore the bottle from my grasp and smacked it onto the table. "I must obey, milady."

"My slave?" I skimmed my hand down his chest to the bulge growing under the sheets. "Oooh, I could get to like this."

I took another gulp from the bottle. He surged toward me, lashing his tongue across my lips to lap up the traces of whisky. In that sultry tone he'd perfected, he said, "Heavenly."

Setting the bottle down, I leaned back against the headboard. "How about tomorrow I give you the grand tour of Chicago? I mean, you're here on vacation, so you should experience the city."

"With you as my tour guide, I'd follow anywhere." His gaze wandered down my body to my behind. "Since tour guides walk in front, I'll get to admire your lovely erse all day long."

"Hate to burst your bubble, but we'll be walking side by side."

"Even better." He shoved a hand under my ass. "I get to hold your lovely erse all day."

I slapped his arm. Reluctantly, he pulled it away. I threaded my fingers through his, loving his firm-yet-gentle grasp when he curled his fingers around my hand. "Tomorrow, I'll show you all my favorite places in the Windy City."

"Can't think of a better way to spend the day." He brushed a kiss across my lips, exciting my skin with the barest touch. "Thank you."

"Wait till you see where I take you before you thank me."

"I appreciate the offer." He lifted my hand to his lips, feathering kisses over my knuckles one by one. "But the taking bit can happen right now."

"Well, get to it, mister."

Lachlan scooped me up in his arms and laid me down on my back, flat on the mattress with the pillow tucked under my head. He slithered up my body, covering me inch by inch with his own body, muscles flexing, skin heated, his erection hard against my yielding flesh. When his mouth reached my ear, his breaths teased my skin. "Time to break new ground."

"Three times in one night?" I raked my tongue over his throat, over that tender spot where jaw met neck. "Are you sure you're up for this, an old man like you?"

"Ye won't be asking me that again." He rocked his hips, grinding his swollen shaft into me. I gasped, and his dark, erotic chuckle rumbled in my ear. "I'm *up* for it, lass."

For the next hour, he proved it.

By the time we finished breaking new ground, I could barely move. An intense, delicious languidness left my muscles slack. I curled up against Lachlan, snuggled under his arm. As I drifted off to sleep, I wondered what the next month might hold for us. Hot sex, for sure. More picnics, maybe. Sightseeing tomorrow, followed by dinner. A couple days ago, I'd wanted to forget my problems by losing myself in one night of passion with a stranger. Instead, I wound up in bed with an intoxicating man who fulfilled my every fantasy—and made me feel safe exploring my deepest desires.

An altogether different urge struck me now. "Gotta pee."

Lachlan, half asleep, mumbled. I made my way into the bathroom, took care of my business, and was washing my hands when I heard the faint twitter of a phone ringing. I dried my hands and sashayed out into the bedroom, but for once my nakedness failed to attract Lachlan's attention. His phone conversation engrossed him.

"Aye," he said, nodding. "She's well. We had a picnic at the beach yesterday—with Casey, of course. Couldn't leave the furry little fellow at home."

I halted at the bed, furrowing my brow at him. Who was he talking to? Gil?

"You are right, Mrs. Teague. She can be stubborn when—"

A breath exploded out of me. I ripped the phone—my phone—from his hand and, with my stomach in my throat, smashed it to my ear. "Mom?"

"Hi, honey. Lachlan was just telling me about your weekend." Her tone veered into that mixture of scolding and teasing only mothers can achieve. "Why didn't you tell us you were seeing someone?"

"I—well—"

Lachlan watched me without expression.

I whumped my butt onto the bed, turning my back on him. "I didn't think about it?" I guessed we were seeing each other in the strictest sense of the word, but I would not under any circumstances tell my mother about our arrangement. "It's a recent development."

"Don't worry about it." She paused, then switched to a conspiratorial whisper. "After hearing Lachlan's voice, I'd jump in the sack with him too."

"Mom!" I nearly sprang off the bed but anchored myself with fingers clamped around the mattress's edge.

She laughed. "I'm not a prude. He seems like a sweetie and I want you to be happy. Is he a hunk? I bet he is."

I angled away from Lachlan to mutter into the phone. "One hundred percent grade-A certified."

"Good for you, honey. I'll let you go. Talk to you soon."

"Bye, Mom." I hung up the phone and turned to Lachlan, my lips pursed. "Why did you answer my phone? It was in my purse."

"I..." He rubbed the back of his neck, shrugging one shoulder. "I was groggy and when I heard a phone ringing, I tracked it down." He flashed me a frown. "You left it on the table by the sofa, not in your purse. Didn't realize it was yours until I answered."

I tilted my head back and grumbled. "Fine, it's not your fault."

He stretched out on the bed behind me, all his muscles rippling. "Your mother says you haven't called in some time. Why is that?"

I threw a hand up. "Off limits."

Lips landed on my back, fluttering soft kisses up my spine to my nape. "I'll make no judgments, you have my word. You can tell me anything."

Now that was absolutely *not* true. But it sounded wonderful, tempting, real. "Forget it."

He nibbled my shoulder and his tongue flicked out to dampen my skin. The air cooled it in the wake of his tongue, eliciting a faint shiver and a soft moan from me. His lips vibrated on my skin when he spoke. "Please tell me."

How I longed to confide in him. I shouldn't. I wouldn't. Even if I told him all my secrets, he'd still scurry back to Scotland in a few weeks. Tension straightened my spine, wrapped its icy talons around my chest, and ached in my jaw. "It's against the rules."

He sat there, unmoving and silent, for a long moment. His mouth rested on my shoulder, his fingertips lingered on my nape. At last, a sigh gusted out of him. "Understood."

A hard lump congealed in my throat as I glanced around the room, considering our non-relationship status. "Do I stay? It's fine if you want me to go. I'm not up on the etiquette of flings."

"Course I want you to stay."

Relief gushed through me, weakening my muscles. I checked my phone for missed calls. There were four—one from my parents and three from Doretta Harper. My skin itched all over at the memory of my last conversation with Doretta. I could sneak into the bathroom to call her. Worms burrowed in my gut at the mere thought of it, though, so I set the phone on the bedside table.

Lachlan coiled an arm around my waist. "Come back to bed."

I nestled back against his brawny body, content in a way I hadn't experienced in years. This feeling, it enticed me more than the incredible sex. It seduced me into believing our "companionship" might not end in one month. Dangerous thoughts. This was a fling for him. He'd made that clear and I agreed to his terms. But maybe...

No. I had to protect my heart, or else my fantasy lover would shatter it into a million pieces. He might not intend to, but if I caved in to my longings, he surely would. Hot guys turned into hot messes. *Remember that, before you fall for him.*

His arm slackened as slumber took him. I shut my eyes and tried to sleep, but my brain refused to turn off for the night. I couldn't fall for a man I met a few days ago. It made no sense and I thrived on logic, on things I could quantify, on the cold detachment of mathematics. Lachlan MacTaggart did not add up. Could I lose my heart to a near stranger? My head shouted no.

My heart screamed *yes, yes, yes.*

Chapter Sixteen

I craned my neck back, staring up at the underside of a huge *Tyrannosaurus rex* skull. Sunlight streamed down from the skylight onto the time-darkened bones of the dinosaur skeleton. Lachlan came up behind me, slipping his arms around my waist to link his hands over my midriff. When he rested his chin on my shoulder, sighing with contentment, I couldn't help leaning into him, into his strength.

"Tell me," he said, nuzzling my cheek, "why do they call this monstrosity Sue?"

"I don't know."

"But you're my tour guide, the one who knows all."

"Are you calling me a know-it-all?" I teased, turning my head to peek at him.

"I wouldn't dare." He straightened, his chin brushing the top of my head. "Are you a dinosaur aficionado?"

"Suppose you could say that." I let my head fall back against his firm body, nestled against his neck. "When I was a kid, I wanted to be a paleontologist."

"Why didn't you do it?"

"Eventually, I realized I needed to be practical. Jobs at universities are hard to come by."

"Do you love accounting?"

The safety of numbers used to comfort me, the way you could rely on them to tell the truth at all times. Until I learned how wrong I was. Numbers could lie when a deceitful human being manipulated them for his own gain. "It was more of a safe choice than a passion."

"What is your passion?"

I swore I could feel his attention on me, his scrutiny and curiosity, like a palpable force willing me to answer. Settling my hands over his, I tried to respond as honestly as possible, though without revealing too much. Keeping the balance between us, secret for secret, seemed vital for some reason. "Well, I've always loved animals. Maybe someday I'll buy a farm, grow my own food and lots of flowers. Raise chickens, cows, horses, whatever."

"On your own?"

"Maybe." I twisted my head around to get a glimpse of his face. "Why do you ask?"

"No reason." He surveyed the *T. rex* in front of us, seeming for all the world to feign an interest in the long-dead creature for my sake. "Tell me more about this charming lass."

I rattled off everything I knew about the dinosaur, which must've bored him, but he acted like I was reciting the most fascinating litany of facts he'd ever heard. He nodded, made "hmm" noises where appropriate, and studied the skeleton with rapt attention. When I'd finished telling him how Sue was the most complete *T. rex* ever found and how replicas of her toured the world, Lachlan stepped up beside me and clasped my hand.

To any onlookers, we were a normal couple enjoying a day at the museum—not two consenting adults engaged in a lascivious affair. I shifted my weight from one foot to the other. "Turnabout time. Is finance your passion?"

He tipped into me, our shoulders bumping. "No, it's not."

"What is your passion?"

"Haven't found it yet."

A family of four wandered past us, the mother and father holding hands, the children scurrying this way and that, their round little faces excited. A lump formed in my throat. I would never have a family. I'd go to prison, a convicted felon, and who'd want me after that?

Lachlan leaned down to plant a kiss on my cheek, smiling sweetly.

My heart ached. This didn't feel lascivious, not even when we were in flagrante. It felt...right. Like more than hot sex, more than a meaningless fling, a way to pass the time until he went home, and I swapped jeans and blouses for prison orange. Would he want me if he knew?

Stop torturing yourself with what can't be.

I realized Lachlan was watching me, head tilted to one side, lips puckered slightly. When he spoke, his tone was uncertain. "Sometimes I think you're not here, you've gone somewhere else in your head. Those lovely eyes are seeing things far away that I can't see. Unhappy things." His hand tightened around mine, and his voice grew more fervent. "I don't like it."

His words enfolded me in warmth. I shuffled closer, my hand floating up to rest on the lapel of his silk dress shirt, my thumb grazing his skin. An electrical current rushed over me, from head to toe. He looked delectable, as usual, like a decadent dessert I knew I shouldn't eat but couldn't resist. My throat went dry as I gazed up at him. "Why do you care what I think about?"

Dark brows squished together, he cast me a quick sidelong glance before averting his gaze again. "Don't know. It just bothers me." His gaze went distant for a moment, then he pulled away the slightest bit. "Is there a gift shop here?"

"Museum store, yeah." The moment, whatever it had been, slipped away. I wanted to get it back, to understand why my unease bothered him, to believe it meant something. But if I tried to steer the conversation back around to the topic, I'd only wind up seeming desperate. Which I was. But why make it obvious? Vulnerability was not my friend.

"I'd like to buy souvenirs for my sisters." He led me away from the display, down the gallery. "Which way?"

"All the way down to the other end."

Lachlan captured my hand in his, and we strolled away from the massive dinosaur, past a re-creation of a mastodon or mammoth—I never could keep them straight—through the meandering crowd, to the far end of the gallery and straight into the museum store. Lachlan freed my hand so he could browse among the store's offerings, his eyes alight, like a little boy elated to see his first toy store. I trailed behind him, marveling at his broad smile and playful mood, so different from moments earlier when he'd confessed my somber mood disturbed him. Now he plucked up a stuffed *T. rex* with mottled green skin and red eyes that somehow managed to be the cutest thing ever. Especially when Lachlan held it up for me, waggling its puffy little arms and said, "Wouldn't you like to hug me? I love to cuddle."

His grin melted my heart. The silly tone of his voice demolished my flimsy defenses, and I snatched the toy from him, seizing the back of his head to drag him in for a firm, lingering lip-lock. A child shrieked in delight behind us. The noise punctured our bubble, and I realized with a start we were in a public place with children all around. I severed the kiss, hopping backward, and fussed with my blouse, focused on the pointless task of smoothing and straightening it.

Lachlan raised his warm palm to cover my cheek. "No need to be embarrassed. I love your impulsive side."

"Not appropriate here." I straightened, rolling my shoulders back. "You said you wanted souvenirs for your sisters. Brothers don't rate gifts?"

"Their tastes aren't this refined." He sounded serious while holding a plush, grinning dinosaur toy. "I'll find gifts for them somewhere else."

For the next twenty minutes, we roamed the store selecting items for each of his three sisters. Catriona got an embroidered purse, Jamie a scarf with bicycles on it—apparently, she loved biking—and Fiona, who collected souvenir spoons, got one featuring Sue's image. On the way out of the museum, Lachlan bought me lunch at the museum's bistro, amid rich wood decor. As we made our way toward the exit, he halted, bringing me up short with him.

"Hold this." He thrust his shopping bag at me. "I need to run a quick errand."

"I'll go with you."

"No." His expression turned a touch pleading. "Won't be long, I swear."

Taking his bag, I shrugged. "Fine, I'll just…stand here."

He trotted off down the gallery, leaving me alone by the entrance doors, behind the imposing skeleton of Sue. I gripped the bag in both hands and pretended to study the exhibit, though my gaze kept flicking to the other end of the gallery. Lachlan had vanished into the crowd, which left me with no clue where his urgent errand had taken him. The restroom, maybe.

"Erica Teague?"

A cheery voice nearly shouted my name, and I jumped. There, having just walked into the building, stood a face from my past. One I'd never imagined I'd see again. My gut clenched, my throat constricted. Oh jeez, why me? Out on the town for the first time since before my arrest, and what happened? I ran into a former coworker from Cichon, D'Addio & Rothenberg.

"It is you!" Danny Liao flung his arms wide as a grin squinted his almond-shaped eyes and surged toward me, clearly determined to corral me into a hug.

No-no-no-no-no. I'd always liked Danny, but I could not handle the topic that would inevitably arise in our conversation. I scoured the museum with my gaze for any sign of Lachlan, or for an escape route, but my fate was sealed. Running would be rude, anyway. "Hi, Danny."

He hauled me into a bear hug, a blessedly brief one, then stepped back to study me. "Where have you been?"

Had he not heard? I assumed everyone at the firm knew.

Maybe my panic and humiliation showed on my face because his grin faded. "Wow, I'm sorry. That sounded weird, didn't it? I mean, I heard what they were saying about you and saw the newspaper article."

Two paragraphs on page four. The headline: ACCOUNTANT ACCUSED OF FLEECING ELDERLY CLIENTS. The sour taste of bile invaded my mouth as acid burned in my gut.

Danny slapped my upper arm. "Never believed a word of it."

I couldn't muster words. My face was hot, on fire, but a deep cold permeated the rest of me. "Thanks. I appreciate that."

"I'm sure you'll beat this bum rap."

Wished I was so sure about that. I couldn't figure out how to respond, though, so I just nodded.

Right then, a pretty Asian woman with two adorable little girls entered the gallery. The kids galloped up to Danny, clinging to his legs and giggling. The woman came up beside him, a genuine smile on her lips.

"Hey Erica," Danny said, "you haven't met my wife Mia, have you?"

Introductions. How would mine go? *Meet Erica, the alleged embezzler who used to work in the cubicle next to mine, until the cops stormed in one day and dragged her off in handcuffs.*

Danny said nothing like it. He laid a protective arm around Mia's shoulders and told her, "This is Erica Teague. She used to work at the firm with me and she is one of the best accountants I've ever met. One of the best people, period."

Tears. Hot. Stinging. About to pour down my face. I blinked them away, gulping against the lump in my throat, but knew blinking wouldn't work for long.

"Ah, there you are."

The sound of Lachlan's deep voice made my knees go weak with relief. I blinked faster as warmth suffused my chest. He'd come back. I all but swooned when Lachlan swung one of his muscular arms around my waist, bolstering me. I looped my arm around him too and clinched him tight. The tiniest wince crimped his face, but he didn't pull away. I forced myself to loosen my death grip on him, but I couldn't bear to let go. I turned my face up to him.

Lachlan kissed the top of my head. "Sorry I took so long, sweet."

He glanced at Danny, then back at me. Oh no. He wanted me to introduce him, I was sure of it. Panic iced through me. Introduce him how? *Here's my Scottish lover, who's giving me hot sex with no strings.* Nope, not saying that. *This is Lachlan, the guy I'm screwing just for the hell of it.* Uh-uh. *This is—*

"Lachlan MacTaggart," he said, proffering a hand to Danny. "Erica's friend."

Friend? Well, it was far less embarrassing than "temporary bedmate."

Danny and Lachlan shook hands, and then he got introduced to Mia with another handshake. I noted the way Mia's gaze roved up and down Lachlan and I didn't like it one bit. But when she met my gaze and winked, flashing me a knowing smile, I decided she wasn't coveting my lover after all.

Lachlan gave me a quick squeeze. "We should be going, don't you think? Plenty to do before our dinner reservation at Everest."

My heart thudded. Everest? Swanky French cuisine. The kind of place where women wore gowns and men wore Armani suits. The kind of place I where I'd stick out like a purple dinosaur. I looked down at my jeans and cotton blouse. I didn't own a gown, and the pantsuits I'd worn to work wouldn't pass muster at an ultra-chic restaurant like Everest.

"Wow," Danny drawled, eyes widening. He slapped Lachlan's arm and grinned. "Pulling out all the stops, eh?"

"Nothing's too good for my Erica." Lachlan nuzzled my hair, and his voice dropped to a murmur. "That's for certain."

A few minutes later, we'd said goodbye to the Liaos and were heading back to Lachlan's rented Mercedes—a convertible, of course. Once I'd climbed into the passenger seat, I frowned at Lachlan. "You could've warned me."

He gave me a look of utter innocence. "About what?"

"Dinner." I enunciated each syllable with hard consonants. "Five-star dining? I have nothing—absolutely nothing—I can wear to a place like Everest. I don't own a skirt, much less an evening gown."

He shrugged. "I'll buy you one."

His matter-of-fact tone rankled. I crossed my arms over my belly, frowning. "I won't be your kept woman."

"Kept?" He opened his mouth but didn't speak, shaking his head. After a few seconds, he spread his hands, palms out. "The dress will be a gift, nothing more."

I eyed him sideways. "Accepting gifts from rich men in exchange for sex is the definition of a kept woman."

He drew back as if I'd slapped him. "It's not in exchange for anything. You're worried about not fitting in at the restaurant, I offered to buy you a new dress." He stretched out an arm to drape it over the back of my seat, pitching toward me. "Stop acting like you're a prostitute. We have nothing to be ashamed of. Do we?"

Looking at him, I couldn't help feeling he wanted—needed—me to reassure him. I supposed this was the norm these days. Casual sex. Pretending we didn't care. Neither of us seemed very good at upholding the charade, or maybe I was indulging in wishful thinking again.

I rested my head against the seat and swiveled my face toward him. "No, we're not doing anything wrong."

He bent closer, erasing the gap between us, his lips within kissing distance. His free hand landed on my thigh, fingers splayed over it. "Let me buy you a dress. Please."

"Are you trying to impress me? With haute cuisine and haute couture to match?" My butt lifted off the seat, my mouth opened on a silent "oh," when his fingers plunged between my thighs and molded to my groin. "Honestly, Lachlan, I'm not impressed by money."

"Not trying to impress you." He repositioned his hand above my head to lazily caress my hair with his fingertips. A tingling started in my scalp, spreading down through my whole body. He inched his fingers up my inner thigh, trapped between my legs. "I want to earn you."

Earn? What on earth did that mean? I couldn't ponder it for long because his hot palm cupped my sex through my jeans, and desire jolted through me. While his hand stoked my fire, his expression was almost pleading. Why, I couldn't fathom, but he needed me to let him do this for me. "I give."

"What?"

"Please buy me a dress." I laid my hand atop his, pushing it tighter into my groin. "If you insist."

He groaned deep in his throat, stroking me with his fingertips. "Thank you."

"Don't thank me yet. You haven't seen the bill."

"Anything for you."

I gripped the edges of my seat as his fingers tormented me through my jeans. So close, yet so far from where I wanted them. "Why are you so determined to have me spend your money?"

His fingers stilled. He watched me for a long moment, then lifted his hand to my cheek, dipping his head closer, until our lips nearly touched. "Because it matters to you, having the right clothing for the restaurant. I want you comfortable, not embarrassed." His gaze skimmed down my body, bouncing over my breasts and hips, pausing at the apex of my thighs, and then back up again to my face. One corner of his mouth curved up. "Though I say you'd stun every man in the place wearing exactly what you've got on now."

I rolled my eyes. "You are so full of it."

"You don't credit yourself enough."

"Nerdy girls don't stun—"

He crushed his mouth to mine, silencing my protest. Silencing the world. I heard nothing except his heavy breaths and the pounding of my heart, felt nothing except his fingers diving into my hair to tilt my head back, granting him deeper access. His tongue plundered my mouth, and I hungrily took of his, my senses overwhelmed by his taste, his scent, his everything.

Lachlan ended the kiss but kept his lips a hair's breadth from mine. "Never call yourself a nerd again. Never." He ghosted his mouth over mine, the faint contact sizzling heat over my skin from head to toe. "You are perfect, *mo leannan.*"

"What are you calling me now?"

He jerked his head up, eyes unblinking. *"Mo leannan."*

"And what does that mean?"

For a few long seconds, he just sat there, motionless. At last, his stony expression crumbled away. He knotted his fingers in my hair, caught my lower lip between his teeth, and let it slide out little by little. His tongue lapped at my lip until it popped free of his teeth, and by then, my body thrummed with desire. He kissed his way up my cheek, leaving a damp, hot trail on my skin. Into my ear, he murmured, "Doesn't matter."

Maybe *mo leannan* was the Gaelic equivalent of "hey, babe." He wouldn't want to admit that, even to his American fling. "You're not going to tell me?"

In lieu of responding, he nibbled on my earlobe, then suckled it until I couldn't remember what on earth we'd been talking about. Without warning, he drew back, facing the steering wheel, and cranked the key in the ignition. "Tell me where to go for this new dress you need."

The nonchalance in his demeanor and tone of voice belied his state of arousal, evidence by the bulge in his pants. Okay, if he wanted to play it cool, so would I. Relaxing into my seat, I let my knees fall open. "You're paying, the choice is yours."

He grinned. "The most expensive shop in town, then."

Chapter Seventeen

I leaned back against the door to my house, inhaling the cool night air, scented with roses. The door chilled my skin, even the parts of me covered by the brand-new, outrageously expensive dress I wore. Lachlan stood poised before me, bathed in the glow of the porch light, his spiffy suit accentuating his muscular build in a subtle way, the charcoal color complementing his skin tone. His eyes glimmered in the low light. The sight of him, all elegance and masculinity, made my fingers curl with the need to fondle and lick him everywhere.

"Dinner was amazing," I said. We'd enjoyed the lushest, most expensive dinner I could've imagined, while ensconced in a shadowy booth. Lachlan plied me with champagne, but I refrained from getting sloshed, despite his insistence I should indulge myself. He'd spoken those words—"indulge yourself, *mo leannan*"—with enough smoky innuendo to set my libido aflame. But getting drunk would dull my senses and I planned to immerse myself in every moment of our arrangement.

He slanted toward me to brace one hand on the door frame beside me. A whiff of Lachlan-scented air whooshed over me. When he ducked his head to my mine, the nearness of him set off a flurry of goosebumps on my arms. His voice was soft and husky, in the way that liquefied my brain and demolished my self-control. "You are so bloody beautiful."

"The dress makes the woman," I said, glancing down at my feet. The only other man who'd flattered me this way had turned out to be conning me. I couldn't believe Lachlan would do that, but I'd lost all confidence in my lie detection skills. And yet, his words never failed to stir my desires, both sexual and emotional.

Just for tonight, I'd let myself bask in his compliments. I'd try to. Try really hard.

"You've got it the wrong way round," he said, coiling a lock of my hair around his finger, sweeping the lock's tip across my lips. The bristly yet soft sensation excited my every nerve. "You make the dress, *gràidh*."

He let go of my hair to slip his finger under the slender strap of my dress, whisking it up and down, his skin on mine like a live wire crackling electricity over me. My breaths grew shallower, faster. I flicked my gaze down to my dress, the deep emerald shade of the silk, the plunging neckline, the slit that extended from the hem just above my knees halfway up the side of my thigh. Designers' names meant nothing to me, since I'd never bought a blouse that cost more than forty dollars, but the sales lady had told me the name as if I should be impressed. Damned if I could remember it now.

"I'm positive," Lachlan murmured, his finger sliding up and down, his flesh hot against mine, "you'd make a paper sack look seductive."

He switched his finger to the neckline, skimming it along the slope of my breast. Heat rushed over me. When my gaze inexorably dropped to follow the track of his finger, as it dipped down into the valley between my breasts, I was shocked to see I wasn't glowing bright red. Fire raced over my flesh and flared hot inside me, but somehow it didn't show.

With a long, sighing groan, he lifted his finger from my breasts to catch my chin with it, encouraging me to meet his gaze. He rubbed his lips over mine, his tongue darted out to taste them, and another, deeper groan rumbled in his throat.

I yawned. Tried to stop it, but my jaw split open and the yawn erupted out of me. *Totally sexy, Erica, you're a real vamp.* I grimaced and clutched my hands over my stomach. "Sorry."

"Don't be." Lachlan cupped my cheek, resting his forehead on mine. "We've had a long day—wonderful, but long—and you're jeeked." He moved away, his shoulder propped against the door frame, and swept a hand over his eyes. "I am too."

Struggling and failing to restrain my smile, I said, "Jeeked means exhausted, I'm guessing."

"Aye." He reached out to caress my cheek, his smile rife with things I shouldn't be seeing, things like affection and—Nope, I would not go any further with that thought. Self-destruction was in my past. Probably.

I dug my keys out of the matching emerald clutch, studded with real emeralds, Lachlan had insisted on buying me. Shoving the key in the lock, I hesitated and peered over my shoulder at him. "Wanna come in?"

He went stone-still, his eyes boring into me. "Are you sure?"

"Uh-huh." I unlocked the door and pushed it inward. "I'm not that tired."

My assertion lacked conviction, thanks to the giant yawn that punctuated it.

Lachlan's big, warm hand settled on my back, between my shoulder blades. Even the innocent touch had my body readying, but instead of offering up his usual carnal enticements, he said, "I would love to come in, but no sex tonight. You're far too tired."

Frankly, I was relieved. My body longed for a good night's rest. But I had to ask. "Losing interest already?"

"Never." His hand skated up to my neck and his fingers gently kneaded my nape, unleashing the weariness I'd fought all the way home, determined not to fall asleep in the car. He kissed my cheek. "I plan on debauching you plenty tomorrow. But for tonight, I'd be honored just to sleep beside you."

Honored? He'd said that last night when he invited me to dinner, but no man had ever told me he'd be honored to take me anywhere or to sleep with me, without sex. While I tried to wrap my brain around his claim, I shuffled into the house. Lachlan followed and shut the door.

A furry body sailed through the air at us.

Casey lunged right past me to tackle Lachlan, who stumbled but stayed upright. He ruffled the dog's hair with vigorous strokes and babbled to Casey like any good dog owner would. Which brought up a question. "Do you have a dog at home?"

"No, but I always had them growing up." He straightened, and Casey finally deigned to greet me with a slap of his slimy tongue on my hand. Lachlan scratched the back of his neck, eyes averted. "My wife did not like animals."

My hands fisted at the mention of a wife. She must be The Bitch, the one who'd ruined my first intimate encounter with Lachlan. I itched to ask more about her, but he didn't want to talk about it. I'd promised not to pry. *Rats.*

Casey nuzzled my hand, whimpering and wagging his tail.

"He wants a snack," I told Lachlan, and headed for the kitchen with man and beast in tow. Lachlan watched with amusement as I fed Casey raw chicken gizzards, to the pooch's delight. When I'd finished, and my fingers were thoroughly slimy and possibly toxic, Lachlan smirked at me.

"Planning to touch me with those hands?" he asked, pointing at my contaminated fingers.

I wiggled them in the air. "Yep. Still want to sleep with me?"

He grinned. "That's why God made antiseptic soap. Besides, I've been all over that body several times, in the most intimate ways."

As the blood rushed to my cheeks, I turned away from him to scrub my hands in the sink. When Presley had witnessed me feeding Casey gizzards, he'd refused to let me get within three feet of him until I'd taken a shower. Seriously. A shower. When I'd pointed out he ate sushi—raw fish—he told me that was different. Raw chicken, raw fish, it all sounded slimy and icky to me.

I heard the shooshing of his footsteps a second before Lachlan came up behind me to take hold of my shoulders. He perched his chin on the crown of my head, while his hands coasted down my arms with deliberate languor, awakening the fine hairs on my skin and triggering a gossamer tingling that spread all over my body. His hands glided down, down, until they encircled my wrists. He paused there with his thumbs on my pulse points, his body firm but yielding against my back. He moved his hands to envelop mine.

Our fingers interlaced, he nuzzled my hair. "We'll risk the germs together. Eh, lass?"

"That's a strange thing to say to a woman you're trying to seduce."

A chuckle vibrated through his chest and into me. "Told you, I only want to sleep together tonight." He rotated our joined hands so the warm tap water sluiced over them, rinsing away the soap. "Besides, I've already seduced you."

The splattering of water on the chrome sink, the gushing of the stream spurting out of the tap, it all had me flashing back to yesterday morning when I'd fantasized about Lachlan in the shower. My breasts tightened, the nipples hardening into taut peaks.

His eyes glazed over as they locked on my breasts. "In the morning, I promise to ravish you with multiple orgasms. Tonight…"

He scooped me up into his arms and strode out of the kitchen, through the living room, straight down the hallway to my bedroom. Since he'd never stepped foot down this hall before, my old paranoia shivered through me on a swift chill.

I raised my head, scrutinizing him. "How did you know where my bedroom is?"

"You mean because this is the first time you've invited me into your bedroom?" He set me down on my feet and I wobbled on my high heels. Sometimes I swore he could read my mind. As another wave of cold broke over me, Lachlan tucked a wild lock of hair behind my ear. "It was common logic, sweet. Your house has one hallway with two doors down it. One of those doors had to be your bedroom."

"Oh." I hunched my shoulders, feeling an utter fool.

"Bit suspicious, aren't you?" He studied me for a moment, without a hint of displeasure, and then started undoing his tie. "Imagine you have your reasons."

The simplicity of the statement, coupled with his apparent disinterest in learning those reasons, served as the verbal equivalent of a bucket of ice water dumped over my head. Back to reality. Back to our agreement. When my mom called, he'd wanted to know more, but tonight he didn't seem to give a hoot. Was he trying to drive me bonkers?

He shed his tie and jacket, beginning to unbutton his shirt. After freeing the second button, he hesitated with his fingers on the third button and swept his gaze over me. "Are you planning to sleep in that dress?"

I blinked several times in quick succession but couldn't shake off my sudden paralysis. My arms hung at my sides, my feet seemed rooted to the spot, and no matter how hard I tried I could not coerce any of my limbs to obey my commands. Watching him casually undressing before me, I'd developed some kind of brain lockout, like when a computer freezes up. A slack-jawed expression was my version of the blue screen of death.

"But, uh, y-y—" I stammered, helpless to keep my focus off his brawny, tanned chest, revealed bit by bit as he unbuttoned his shirt. "Are you going to, um, keep your boxer shorts on or something?"

He tipped his head, his lips ticking up at the corners. "Last night I stripped us both naked and did wicked things to you for hours. Now you're shy about seeing the full monty?"

Still paralyzed, I chewed my lip. Full monty. Okay, I'd seen that movie, I knew what the term meant. "Well, see, nudity feels kind of different tonight. We're not doing anything, and besides, last night you undressed me while I was blindfolded which is kind of different and—"

He surged forward to seal his mouth over mine, squelching my babbling. The firmness of his lips disconnected all the circuits in my brain and any thoughts I'd had splintered into a million pieces. I opened my mouth to him, but he pulled away, severing the kiss.

"If you like," he said in that sultry voice, his brogue a bit thicker, "I'll handle the task of removing your dress from your supple little body myself." He bent to graze his hot lips down my throat, while his fingers trailed down my arms, igniting spark after spark under my sensitized skin. "Would ye like me to?"

"Yes." The word burst from my lips, unhindered by silly things like forethought and sanity. His voice intoxicated me faster than any whisky.

He circled his hands around my waist, reaching for the zipper of my dress. I sucked in a breath when his fingertips tickled my bare skin, already flushed with heat and primed for his touch. He pulled the zipper down in slow motion, his fingers flitting over my flesh in its wake, the drawn-out *zzzzzzt* of the zipper becoming the most erotic thing I'd ever heard. When he'd exposed my entire back, he flattened his palms on my skin and tugged me closer.

"Soft as silk," he purred into my ear, then his hands shifted to spread the dress wide, and cool air kissed my flesh. His sultry breaths whispered over my ear, across the tender skin beneath it.

Still, I couldn't move. My pulse beat so fast it throbbed in my ears. My breasts ached for his hands, his mouth, anything to relieve the agony of wanting.

His shoulders sagged, his body listing toward me as he flicked the straps off my shoulders and the dress tumbled down to pool around my feet. Lachlan took a half step back, raking his gaze over me. I stood motionless, in nothing but a bra and panties—and my heels. His voice was rough and strained when commanded, "Take off the rest."

Just like that, my body roused from its paralysis. As if in a trance, I shed my bra and panties under his scorching gaze. When I kicked off my heels, he licked his lips with the look of a predator intent on consuming his prey. My sex pulsated at the thought, at the desperate hope he would consume me right here, right now.

Faster than I'd ever seen anyone move, he flung off his shirt, slacks, socks, shoes. Everything hit the floor with a clunk or sailed down onto a chair or the dresser. Confronted with his sudden nakedness, and his raging erection, I struggled for breath. My hand rose to my throat, my fingers stroked my skin.

"To bed," he commanded.

Didn't have to tell me twice. I tossed the blanket and top sheet out of the way and dropped onto my back on the bed, one arm bent above my head.

Lachlan crawled over me on hands and knees, settling in beside me on his back. He yanked the covers over us both. "Good night, Erica."

I swiveled my head toward him. Was he freaking kidding? I pushed up on one elbow to glare at him. "How do you expect me to sleep?"

He assumed the appearance of relaxation, despite his rigid length twitching under the covers. "Now you've got something to look forward to in the morning."

I slugged his arm, earning no reaction. "Jackass."

Only then did he turn to gaze at me with faux innocence. "There's no need for insults, *gràidh*."

"You got me all wound up on purpose." I flopped back onto the mattress amid a flutter of sheets and a faint *poof* from my pillow. "You're a tease."

"No, I'm an inveterate seducer. Remember?"

"Hmph."

He lifted one arm, making room for me. "Come here."

As usual, for reasons I couldn't comprehend, I obeyed and cuddled up against his side. My attention deviated to the tented covers, and I squirmed a little.

"Shh," he said, lowering his arm to cradle me close. "I'll help you relax."

I started to ask how, but then he began humming softly. The tune was unfamiliar, yet beautiful and soothing, like a lullaby. I stretched my arm across his chest, snuggling closer, my ear plastered to his muscles right over his heart. Its beats lulled me further, luring me ever downward into slumber.

The instant before my senses shut down, his voice rumbled low and sweet. "Sleep well, *mo leannan*."

Chapter Eighteen

I woke in the morning to the sound of panting and Lachlan muttering nonsense words. Cracking my lids, I squinted at him. Lying on my side facing him, I had a perfect view across his body, since he lay on his back. Casey sprawled between Lachlan's thighs on top of the covers, with his front paws and head on the Scot's exposed belly. Lachlan scratched Casey's head and mumbled more baby-talk gibberish. The dog lapped it up, panting and making little chuffing noises. The sight of the males in my life bonding elicited a funny feeling in my chest.

I cleared my throat. "Am I interrupting?"

"You're awake." Lachlan aimed a playful smile at me. "Thought you'd sleep all day."

"What time is it?"

"After ten."

I glanced at the bedside clock, but it agreed with him. Never in my life had I slept past ten unless I was sick.

Casey leaped up and lunged toward me to slop a kiss on my cheek. Spluttering, I pushed him away. He bounded off the bed, rocking it wildly. Once the aftershocks calmed, Lachlan rolled onto his side to face me.

"Good morning, lass," he said, stealing a quick, soft kiss from me.

"Morning."

"Have a good sleep?" He ran his fingertip along the sheet's edge, where it just covered my breasts.

"Mmm." I flipped onto my stomach. The sheet slipped off my breasts, but still covered my buttocks. When I propped my torso up on both elbows, my breasts dangled beneath me. "Haven't slept that soundly in years."

Lachlan trailed his fingertips up my spine, drawing a tingling line up my flesh. "And all without sex."

I peeked back at him over my shoulder. "You made me a promise last night."

"And I intend to keep it." He placed an open-mouth kiss on my nape. "But first, I have another gift for you, if it won't offend my *gràidh*."

"No, of course not." I splayed my fingers over my pillow, studying the swirling patterns on the fabric. "I'm sorry about last night. I love the dress." When his fingers stilled on my back, I cast him a sideways glance. "I'm just not used to men buying me expensive presents."

"Ah, but you deserve it." He sat up, twisting around to reach down to the floor and retrieve an object. I heard plastic rustling, then he called over his shoulder, "Shut your eyes, please."

I shut them, resting my chin on my linked hands.

A second later, something plush and fuzzy touched down on the skin of my lower back. The thing tiptoed up my spine, vertebra by vertebra, dragging a smaller fuzzy thing behind it. Lachlan's lips grazed my ear. "You can look now."

I opened my eyes and a small, dark-colored object lighted on my shoulder. Lachlan held the stuffed animal there until I took it in one hand. My eyes widened for a heartbeat. The plush *Tyrannosaurus rex* gazed up at me with cat-like amber eyes, its pudgy little arms reaching out to me. The words "Field Museum Chicago" were embroidered on its derriere. Warmth blossomed in my chest, encompassing my heart. He'd gone back to the museum store to buy me a present—this present, the one that proved he'd really listened when I told him about my childhood dream. I bumped my nose into the *T. rex*'s snout. "I love this too. Thank you, Lachlan."

He laid on his side again, one hand resting on my back. "It seemed the perfect gift for a dinosaur enthusiast like yourself."

The words tugged at my heart. Presley had never bought me anything more thoughtful than a bouquet of daisies from the grocery store. Rich as he was, he disliked sharing his wealth—but didn't mind stealing more from the elderly and blaming me for his crimes.

Lachlan traced the backs of his fingers up my cheek, pulling me back to the present. "What troubles you on this bonnie morning?"

"Nothing." Part of me yearned to spill everything to him, but how much did I really know about the man in my bed? Suddenly, the question seemed paramount. I turned my face toward him, and one of his fingers slipped between my lips. He withdrew his hand and sucked it into his mouth, making a little sound of pleasure. I tried to smile, but it faltered. "Don't you ever wonder about me?"

"Wonder?" His brow crinkled.

"Aren't you curious about me? About my life? My past?" Somehow, my simmering curiosity about him drove me to ponder whether he cared to know anything about me. How could he not wonder when I burned with a need to know more about him?

"Of course," he answered, with a half-hearted shrug. "But it's against the rules. You reminded me of that when your mother called the other evening."

So I had. *Rats*. In my panic to steer him away from subjects too close to my legal problems, I'd accidentally put him off asking any personal questions of me.

I kicked my feet out from under the sheet, so it covered only my buttocks, and bent my knees to swing my feet in the air. Fingering the tubby arms of the stuffed *T. rex*, struggling to hit a nonchalant tone of my own, I told him, "You could, you know, ask me a few questions. If you want."

"Ah…" He turned onto his back, linking his hands under his head. "That would be violating our agreement."

Despite his casual posture, his mouth had tightened. Probably didn't want me asking him questions in return. *Ugh*. What had I expected? I agreed to this insane arrangement, which meant I had to deal with the consequences of it and tamp down my curiosity. Easy to say, not so easy to accomplish.

I sprang up into a sitting position, rotating my legs off the bed to sit at the edge of the mattress, my hands clamped over it. Shoulders slumped, I stared at my bare feet.

Lachlan's hand found my back, gliding up it in slow circles. I couldn't help leaning into the touch.

As usual, my mouth got the better of me. "Don't you want to know anything about me? I don't know that much about you. You have brothers and sisters and once showed a girl your penis in a barn, that's about it." I yanked the sheet around my waist to shield my privates. "I don't know your favorite color, your favorite song, anything."

He groaned, his hand falling away from my back. He plucked at the sheet and grumbled, "My favorite color is blue. I don't have a favorite song. What else would you like to know?"

I covered my eyes with my hands. Ugh, what was I doing? Trying to force emotional intimacy with a man who wanted none of it.

Lachlan sighed, then slipped an arm around my waist, urging me back down onto the bed. I went with him, landing on my back with him straddling me, his face hovering over mine. He braced himself on his elbows, with his hands at either side of my face. He combed his fingers through my hair, his eyes glowing an otherworldly blue in the morning light. "I want to know everything about you, but I'll be leaving soon. Can we not just enjoy this time together?"

He wanted to know me. Though he still wouldn't act on that desire, the realization he did care buoyed my spirits. "Yeah. Sure."

"Good."

He nibbled my lower lip, his tongue darting out to sneak between my lips, tantalizing me with a taste of him. I moaned, shoved my hand into his hair, desperate to tug him closer. He resisted, scraping his mouth over mine until I opened for him. He seized the chance to plaster his lips to mine, while his tongue forged deep, lashing against mine in a wild dance. I sucked on his tongue, earning a groan from him.

He peeled his mouth away and shifted off me, his leg pressed to mine, his erection jutting over my belly. He swooped down between my thighs. I spread them wide, granting him full access, and he parted my folds with his thumb and forefinger, sliding his middle finger down to stroke me. I choked back a throaty cry, my hands fisted in the sheets, heels planted in the mattress. His thumb and forefinger petted my folds while his middle finger swept up and down my slick flesh. The tip of his finger swirled around my clitoris, round and round, harder and harder, until he thrust his fingertip into the head of my clit. Pleasure shot through me, pulsed in my sex, and I bucked into his fingers, thrashing my hips in a desperate plea for more.

"You like this," he rumbled, pressing his cheek to mine. "What else do you like?"

"Oh," I breathed, as his finger toyed with my nub. I clutched at his shoulders, clawing and whimpering with wanton disregard for my composure or what he might think of me like this. "I like e-everything you do to me."

His finger dove down to plunge inside me. My back arched, a gasp frozen in my throat. His breaths rasped near my ear, ragged and heavy, sexy as hell.

"Erica." His rough voice morphed my name into an entreaty, his voice deeper, his accent thicker and hotter than ever. "Do ye want mah hand or mah mouth?"

I writhed and dug my nails into his shoulders as he twirled his finger around my clit. "Mouth, please."

He lunged down to kneel between my thighs. I raised my knees, letting them fall wide apart, and my body hummed with a pent-up hunger. He gazed down at my sex with that odd reverence, licking his lips in a long, languorous sweep of his tongue. "I need to feast on ye. Now."

"Yes, please, yes."

My eyelids sealed shut as his mouth found my clitoris, his tongue laving it with gentle strokes that swiftly intensified into ravenous lashes. I thrust my hands into his hair, clawing at his scalp, whimpering from the intensity of the sensations he provoked in me.

Far away in the background, the doorbell chimed. I struggled to remember what that meant, but then Lachlan plunged one finger inside me, then two, curving them into the sweet spot just inside my opening. My whole body convulsed. I flung my hands up to clench them in my pillow, lost to the ecstasy of his clever fingers.

The doorbell chimed again. Casey began barking, and something in the tone of his barks snapped me out of the spell Lachlan had woven around me. I sprang up, pushing Lachlan away. On his knees, off kilter with one hand on the bed, he gaped at me.

"I have to see who's at the door," I said and jumped off the bed to snag my robe from the back of the door and yank it on.

"Ye've gotta be kidding me." Lachlan's jaw had fallen open. His wide eyes tracked my movements, and his shoulders wilted when I rushed out the bedroom door.

I flashed him an apologetic smile. "Sorry."

Casey stood sentry at the front door, his barks now interspersed with sharp snarls. He bounced on his front feet, though not with the glee he reserved for Lachlan. No, the dog was disturbed. And I could think of only one person who evoked this response in Casey. My heart thudded. A chill raced over my skin, eradicating the heat Lachlan had so easily stoked in me. Goosebumps prickled my arms. I shooed Casey away from the door and grasped the knob, then hesitated. I did not want to see who was on the other side. I hauled in a deep breath and swung the door open.

Presley Cichon beamed his trademark laser-white smile at me, the one that used to make my stomach flutter. These days, it made my stomach roil. He leaned one shoulder on the door jamb. "Morning, babe. Are those pink cheeks for me?"

I stared at him. Pink cheeks? Oh crap. I was still flushed from Lachlan's ministrations. I glanced over my shoulder, but Lachlan hadn't emerged from the bedroom. Squaring my shoulders, I glared at Presley. "What do you want this time?"

"To come in and talk."

"Why?"

He rolled his eyes. Dressed in a T-shirt and skin-tight jeans—designer, no doubt—he looked like a typical trust-funder out slumming it in the burbs. "About all the stuff we haven't talked about. Let's clear the air, babe."

"Clear the air?" I shook my head, amazed at his audacity. "You set me up and now you want to play nice? Gimme a break."

He moved as if to step through the doorway. I slapped a palm on the jamb and grasped the door's edge in my other hand, effectively blocking him. He frowned for a split second, but then cranked his lips into a smile again. "Come on, Erica. Maybe I want to apologize."

Maybe he wanted to? I snorted. "Go peddle your bullshit somewhere else."

Presley compressed his lips, grinding his teeth. A dark emotion flashed in his eyes. "Why you gotta be such a bitch all the time?"

A sharp retort popped into my mind, but I bit it back. He wanted to get a rise out of me, for some reason, and I wouldn't give him the satisfaction. "Go home, Presley."

"Let me in first."

"No."

He stepped a foot over the threshold, his body inches from mine. I kicked at his designer sneaker. He chortled, but then something past my shoulder caught his attention and he froze. His eyebrows lifted. "So, you are banging Scotch Tape."

I glanced back to see Lachlan at the entrance to the hallway, dressed in nothing but his low-slung jeans, with the button unhooked. He stood with his feet wide, hands coiled at his sides, yet his expression remained impassive. His eyes, however, were locked on Presley.

My ex-lover glowered at my current lover. "What's your game, Scottie?"

Lachlan arched one brow but said nothing.

"Go away," I hissed at Presley, shoving against his chest. "No way in hell you're ever getting inside my house."

Presley bored his gaze into me for a second, then spun on his heels and stomped away from the house to his obnoxious-yellow sports car. As I shut the door, tires squealed on the street. I rested my forehead on the door. When I'd been with Presley, he'd barely set foot in my house because he couldn't fathom why I'd want to spend time here when I could be in his luxurious penthouse. It never occurred to him I wanted to share my world with him. He scoffed at the suburbs. Now that we'd broken up, and he'd framed me for embezzlement, all he wanted was to get inside my house. Bizarre.

A hand gripped my shoulder. I jumped.

"Easy," Lachlan said. "He's gone."

I raised my head, shuffling around to face him. "You didn't throttle Presley this time."

Lachlan closed in, backing me up to the door, planting his hands at either side of my shoulders, surrounding me with his body. "You seemed to have things in hand and I didn't want to barge in where I'm not wanted, like last time."

"You were wanted then." I placed a palm on his bare chest, absorbing the heat of him, relishing the firmness of his muscles. "And you're wanted now."

"Am I?" He pinned me to the door, sweeping aside the folds of my robe to rub his groin into mine, his erection hard and thick.

"Oh, yes." I rolled my hips into him.

"Well then." He picked me up and rushed down the hallway into the bedroom, plopped me onto the bed, and stripped off his jeans. "Best take advantage of the moment, eh?"

I grinned, flipping my robe open to expose my nakedness. "Take advantage of me anytime, for as long as you want."

He pounced on me, and soon I'd forgotten all about my unwanted visitor.

Chapter Nineteen

*P*lease," Lachlan murmured against my neck. He dragged his lips down my throat to place a damp kiss in a spot right at the base, the one that made me shiver. His skillful tongue stimulated and taunted my skin. I shivered. *Damn him.* When I arched my back, the silky cotton sheets of what I'd come to think of as Lachlan's bed coasted over my skin.

"Why do you want it?" My words emerged on a soft moan, thanks to his tongue flicking over the mound of my breast. My low-cut T-shirt was no defense against Lachlan MacTaggart and his devious tongue.

His hand sneaked under my shirt, gliding up my side. "I want unfettered access to you, my sweet rose."

"You mean you want me to be your twenty-four-hour love slave."

His hand bumped into the band of my bra. The barrier didn't stop him and after a millisecond pause, he tracked the band behind me to the clasp. Before I knew it, my bra hung loose and his hand was inside the cup, on my skin, his thumb and forefinger pinching my nipple. His voice had strayed into husky territory, an untamed land I rushed into without reservation. "Lass, I like surprising you and I have proof you like it too. Give me a key, and I'll surprise you more often. In many and varied ways."

Goosebumps prickled my skin, chased by a slow-building heat and a burgeoning dampness between my thighs. *Double damn him.* But he was right. I loved his "surprises." They always ended with me screaming his name while thrashing beneath him.

I'd spent three weeks with Lachlan. *Three weeks.* My body sang at the mere thought of seeing him every day and my heart did reckless things when he aimed his killer smile at me. After our dinner outing at Everest, I'd laid down my own rule for our whatever-this-was. One afternoon, while we were sharing another picnic lunch with Casey—in the park this time—I'd set down my sandwich and announced, "No more fancy-shmancy dinners at places where I couldn't even afford a glass of water."

Lachlan had swung his head up, doing that adorable dimpled-between-the-eyebrows thing. "You didn't like Everest?"

"No, it was great." I took a sip from my can of root beer, needing a couple seconds to phrase my explanation. "You told me once you don't care about the trappings of wealth and your needs are simple. I let you know mine are simple too." I tapped my fingernail on the can. *Tick, tick, tick.* "Which is why I don't get the Everest thing. It was sweet and all, but you know you don't have to try so hard to impress me."

"Don't I?" He scratched his cheek, staring down at the sandwich perched on his thigh, seeming genuinely nonplussed.

"No," I'd said with deliberate emphasis. Then I did a Lachlan thing to Lachlan, hooking my finger under his chin to urge him to look at me. "Trust me, money does not impress this girl."

"What does?" He fiddled with the collar of his shirt and cleared his throat. I tickled him with the finger still rooted under his chin, winning a faint smile from him, but he quickly turned serious again. "I'd like to know."

He wanted to know what impressed me? Maybe I should've lied. But Casey chose that moment to hop up from where he'd been lounging on the grass to nuzzle Lachlan's hand. My dog adored him, so I told the truth. "You impress me, Lachlan. You're a good man. The best."

And a fantastic kisser. An exciting lover. Fun to talk to, to hang out with, to laugh with.

He'd captured my hand with his then, my finger sticking up between his thumb and forefinger. "Good, bad, I don't know. But you make me feel like a man, Erica."

Stunned, I'd floundered for a response. He drew my finger into his mouth, sucking lightly until I forgot everything we'd just said to each other. Now, back in the present, I gazed into his gorgeous eyes and wondered what he'd meant when he said I made him feel like a man. I considered asking him for about a millisecond before he ducked his head under my shirt to latch onto my nipple with his mouth. His tongue swirled around the taut tip, erasing all my questions.

After our discussion in the park, we'd eaten at home more often than we'd eaten out, and when we did go out, it was to informal restaurants. Sometimes he would cook for me and other days I cooked for him. This morning, he'd fed me a feast of sausage links, bacon, scrambled eggs, tattie scones—which I learned were made with potatoes—and black pudding.

Only after I'd eaten the pudding did he confide it was made with pig's blood. I recalled gagging at his revelation and smacking his arm. "How could you let me eat that?"

He'd shrugged. "I eat it all the time."

"Yuck." I'd rushed to the kitchen sink to cleanse my tongue with the sprayer. "It's disgusting, Lachlan."

"Sorry." His lip curled with a repressed smirk. "You were wolfing it down until I mentioned the key ingredient."

That was all he'd offered as penance—that and a round of "who comes first" played on the sofa, this time with no interruptions, because he'd switched off his phone. Before the black pudding incident, I'd declined his repeated offers of haggis. A girl must have her limits and sheep stomachs were mine. He assured me most modern Scots made their haggis with synthetic casing instead of stomach, but I still said no thank you. I decided the black pudding was his revenge for my shunning of his country's national dish.

Lachlan shoved my shirt and bra up over my breasts in one swift motion. His lips clamped over my nipple and sucked so hard I cried out. I scraped my nails down his back. Without detaching his mouth from my nipple, he muttered, "Key."

What the hell. I wanted to give it to him anyway, though I couldn't fathom why. A breathless rush of syllables escaped my lips. "Okayfineyes."

Eyes alight, he took my nipple between his teeth and tugged gently, elongating it while his tongue laved the swollen peak. I dug my nails into his scalp. He released my nipple, and it popped back. "I'll give you mine too."

I let a slow smile spread over me. "Then *I* can surprise *you*."

"Hmm." He feigned concern, lips compressed. "Should I worry? You might steal into my bedroom to massage my...account ledgers."

I slapped his shoulder. "Better be nicer to the woman who gives you the best sex of your life. Especially after you tricked me into eating pig's blood."

"Point taken. Though I really didn't think the black pudding would be a problem." He tore off my sweatpants and panties as one and hurled them to the floor. I writhed when his mouth sealed over my sex. Just as I mounted the heights of ecstasy, about to fly off the cliff, he pulled away. "Is this nice enough?"

"Bastard."

His grin stirred an odd sensation in my chest. Light. Fluttery. Perfect.

"Give me the key," he said, "and I'll be even nicer to you. So nice you'll forgive me for the black pudding debacle."

"There was no debacle."

"You shrieked and punched me."

"I smacked you on the arm. And I did not shriek."

He coiled his tongue around my hardened clit. "Key."

"It's in my house." My sex thrummed with unquenched need, still simmering on high heat. I gestured at my body, attempting nonchalance, though my heavy breathing may have ruined the effort. "I can't go get the key. You've taken away my clothes."

"You've got a key in your pants pocket." He held up a warning finger when I opened my mouth to protest. "And there's a spare under the potted plant beside your back door."

"How do you know about that?"

"Gil told me."

I'd told Gil in case of emergency. So much for neighborly confidentiality. Bending over the bed's edge, I fished my key out of my pants pocket.

Lachlan patted my ass. "I rather like this view."

My breasts dangling, I rolled my eyes at him. He snared me around the waist and hauled me back up to sit facing him. I wagged the key in his face. He reached for it, but I locked my fist around it. "Uh-uh-uh. Yours first, you sneaky Scot."

He yanked open a drawer in the bedside table, nabbed a key, and proffered it to me. When I plucked the key from his open palm, he closed his hand around my wrist. I spread my fingers. He took my key, but his hand still restrained mine.

I tugged. "Let go."

"A kiss first."

"Sure."

With my hand locked in his, I scrambled around until I was on my knees, braced with one hand. Then I lowered my head to plant a kiss on his hard shaft. He grumbled something unintelligible.

"What was that?" I cupped my hand over my ear. "Couldn't quite make it out."

"A real kiss."

"Coming right up." I lavished his glistening head with a full-tongue kiss. A strangled noise caught in his throat. He let go of my hand, relinquishing the key.

I dropped onto my elbows, my ass high in the air, and took his shaft deep into my mouth. A gasp broke his groan as I withdrew and circled my tongue around his tip. He grasped my ass in both hands. I thrust in and out, over and over, emboldened by his throaty noises and the way his fingers sank into my backside. My breasts grazed his thighs, shooting electricity through my nipples and straight down to my core. His body went rigid, a sure sign he was about to lose it.

"Erica!" Lachlan cried.

I released his shaft and sat back on my heels. His hands fell away from my ass. I stretched my body, making sure to hoist my breasts before his face. "I could go for some brownies."

He leaned in, his eyes boring into me, his cheeks ruddy with need. "You stopped."

Struggling not to smile, I shrugged one shoulder. "So?"

His chest heaved with each breath. "You're in for it now...Erica."

The way he growled my name sent a hot shudder through me. "Bring it on...Lachlan."

I imbued his name with all the salacious desire I could muster. Never in my life had I tried to sound sexy. But this man made me feel desirable, every second of every moment we spent together.

Lachlan seized my hips and jerked my butt out from under me. I flipped onto the bed flat on my back, with a highly aroused Highlander poised above me. He brushed his nose against mine. "Thank you for the key."

"Ditto."

"I'm already planning my surprise for you." He grabbed a condom from the table. "What have you got in mind for me?"

"Something wicked your way comes."

"A Shakespearean girl, eh?"

I wrapped my arms around him and held on like the world would fly away if I let go. He slid inside me with aching slowness, his every movement a delicious torment. And that's when I knew I was lost. One more week and then...His voracious mouth stole my thoughts, chasing away the worries for a long, blessed interlude.

For the next three days, I barely saw Lachlan, even at night. He'd stop by to say good night, but declined to stay the night—with or without sex. I couldn't help worrying he'd lost interest in me, but when I asked what he was up to, he insisted he had "video calls" to take care of and it had nothing to do with me. He'd cursed and muttered that he didn't "have a bloody clue how to use Skype." His irritation over the calls showed in his tight expression and the tension in his voice, but I kept my questions to myself.

Yeah, I was boiling over with curiosity. Somehow, I contained it—but just.

On the third day, I wandered over to Lachlan's house. The day before,

I'd seen him pacing in his living room, arguing with someone only he could see on his laptop screen. Today, I'd decided to surprise him with a visit, whether he liked it or not. Being his fling did not mean he got to take me for granted. But as I lifted my hand to knock on the front door, I heard his voice, loud yet muffled by the door and walls.

"The bitch gets nothing," he hollered. "Nothing. Ye hear me, Rory?"

Ah, it was Rory again—and The Bitch to boot. Who the hell was this woman that she could get Lachlan so riled up? She must be the reason why he shunned relationships.

Don't go there, I warned myself. *You can't save a man who doesn't want to be saved.*

I scuttled back to my house without knocking.

The day dragged by, more boring than any day had a right to be. Nothing kept my interest and my thoughts inevitably circled back around to Lachlan, again and again. By evening, after a laborious day of fretting in front of the TV, I shuffled into my bedroom alone. Though I itched to interrogate Lachlan, I reminded myself yet again I'd agreed to no entanglements, which meant his "video calls" were none of my concern.

Casey leaped onto the bed to slop a kiss on my chin. I just dodged a similar smack on the lips by rotating my head at the last second. I hugged the pooch and scratched behind his ears. His tongue lolled, his lips curled in what resembled a smile. I liked to think Casey did smile, and it meant he loved me. The dog chuffed.

"I know." I scratched his back. "I wish Lachlan was here too. Maybe we'll see him tomorrow."

With a snuffle and a toss of his head, Casey settled in at the foot of the bed. While I untied my shoelaces, I glanced at the clock on the bedside table. Eight-thirty. The sun had set an hour ago and night drenched the world outside. My little lamp, situated on the table, bathed the room in a soft, bronze-y glow. For the third night in a row, I wouldn't sleep in Lachlan's arms. I'd gotten dangerously accustomed to the warmth and solidity of his body cocooning mine.

I kicked off my tennies. They hit the floor with a *thunk-thunk*. I missed him. Okay, I could admit that without endangering my heart. Couldn't I?

With that thought bouncing around in my brain, I tore off my clothes and marched straight into the shower. Maybe a good pummeling with hot water would melt away my worries. The steaming water jetted down on my body, hard and powerful, plying my flesh much the way Lachlan's fingers did whenever he massaged my neck and shoulders, or when his hands drifted lower to knead my breasts. Now, alone in my shower, my breasts grew swollen and achy, starved for his touch. *No feast tonight.*

Visions of Lachlan's delicious muscles flitted through my mind as I rotated under the pelting streams. My hand roamed up to my throat, my fingers teasing the tender flesh there just the way Lachlan would've done with his mouth. He'd kiss my neck, plump my breasts, rumble *gràidh* in my ear.

Hunger pulsated through me. *Gràidh*. His voice echoed in my mind, deep and sultry, rife with an intense hunger. I feathered my fingers over my breasts and my nipples shot hard. Liquid heat gathered between my thighs, along with the familiar tingling tension that infused my entire body.

Lachlan. Naked. Our bodies entangled.

I snatched the shower head out of its holder. Switching the lever to the massage setting, I let my head fall back as water pounded into my flesh. I aimed it at my neck to beat out the soreness, but the memory of Lachlan's mouth moved me to lower the shower head to my breasts, where it pounded on my nipples. I gasped at the power of the sensation.

Lachlan. Inside me. Thrusting. His hips pistoning into me, my back bowing, his face wrenched with mind-blowing pleasure. I widened my stance and dipped the shower head until it pummeled my aching sex. Pleasure rocketed through me so hard and fast I slapped my free hand on the wall, whimpering. "Oh shit."

My mind was obsessed with fantasies of rippling muscles as my orgasm blasted through me in wave after euphoric wave, doubling me over, my sex clenching tight but empty inside, my legs quaking from the power of my release. "Lachlan, yes!"

The shower door swung open.

I yelped, dropping the shower head. It clattered to the tile floor. Lachlan's gaze flicked to my hand positioned inches from my sex, down to the discarded shower head, and then gravitated back to my face. Clad in nothing but a condom, he angled his head, those thoroughly lickable lips ticking up at the corners. "Screaming my name, and I haven't even touched you yet."

Heart racing, I fumbled to hook the shower head back in its clip but missed. "W-what are you doing here?"

"Surprising you."

Chapter Twenty

H> sauntered into the shower, backing me up to the wall, and raised my hand to hold the shower head at his shoulder level. Hot water drizzled down our bodies, between our bodies, beading on his pecs and spraying up to glimmer on his hair. The shower head slipped from my fingers. Lachlan caught it. "I see ye started without me."

"What happened to your all-important Skype stuff?"

"Hell with it." He grasped my hip with one palm, the shower head clasped in his other hand. "I'd ask what ye were thinking of just now, but ye gave me a good clue when ye shouted my name."

Crap. I ducked my chin to my chest, unable to meet his gaze. *Crap, crap, crap.*

He brushed his cheek against mine, his evening stubble a sensual roughness on my skin. "Don't be embarrassed. I've climaxed while daydreaming of you too."

I peeked up at him. "Really?"

"Aye."

"I like that." When his thumb glanced over the sweet spot just next to my hip bone, I tipped my head up. His stubble chafed my throat, but it was a blissful friction. "I'm glad you're here."

"Cannae stay away." His Adam's apple jounced against my neck. "I donnae know why, it's never happened to me before. I…missed you."

I lunged my fingers into his hair, reveling in this perfect moment with him, and he made a rough sound deep in his throat. He *missed* me. My heart soared at the confession. "I missed you too."

Lachlan snapped the shower head into its clip on the wall. "Ye won't be needing this anymore."

He flipped me around, mashed me to the wall with his body, and nudged my feet apart. My breaths shallowed, my skin tightened, my every nerve came alive with anticipation. He sneaked one hand in front of me to work my nub, already swollen and slick for him. I rocked into his caress, slapping my palms on the tile wall as the need fired up inside me once again, hotter and harder than before. His fingers pinched my clitoris, arcing pleasure through me like an electrical jolt, rending a loud moan from me.

"I need you, Erica."

He rocked his hips back, then drove his shaft deep inside, overwhelming me with the euphoric fullness of him.

I threw my head back, a scream caught in my throat.

He growled, "Ye've got to be mine, only mine."

Before the meaning of his words could sink in, he slammed into me again and my brain shut down. He pumped with relentless force and speed, I gouged my nails into the tile walls, our sharp breaths reverberated, wet skin slapped against wet skin, and even through the steam and water, I scented my own arousal. His heels smacked on the floor with each powerful thrust of his hips, flattening me against the wall. I balanced on the brink of a climax so intense it would blow away the one I'd achieved on my own. Somehow, through the haze of ecstasy, his words flashed through my mind.

Ye've got to be mine, only mine. He couldn't mean—

"Erica." His chin dropped to my shoulder and words burst out of him, punctuated by grunts. "Ah God, *mo leannan*, yer so soft and sweet and— och!"

"Don't stop, please."

"I willnae." He pounded harder, faster, a frantic melding of our bodies. "Come fer me now, *gràidh*."

As if by his command, pleasure erupted inside me, stunning a whimpering scream out of me. "Lachlan, yes!"

The pace of his thrusts quickened even more, his balls slapping on my ass. His release pulsed inside me, his feral cries resonating off the walls. He sagged against my back, his lips on my shoulder. Between pants, he said, "Now that's how you scream my name."

"A shower was supposed to relax me."

He lifted my hand to kiss my palm. "Are you saying I haven't relaxed you?"

"Oh, you sure did. Just not in the way I'd planned." I wriggled around to face him. "We probably scared Casey half to death with our caterwauling."

"Men don't caterwaul. We give masculine shouts of appreciation."

I held his face in my hands and ravaged his mouth with all the passion he'd just incited in me. The afterglow hadn't yet faded, and I longed to stay close to him. He kissed me back with an ardor rivaling mine, his hands groping my body. I loved the way he kissed. It melted me from the inside out and branded me with his passion. *I'm yours, Lachlan.*

We peeled our lips apart. I thanked the universe Lachlan didn't have the power to read my mind. *I need you,* he'd said. *Ye've got to be mine, only mine.* He'd spoken those words too, I hadn't imagined them, but did he mean any of it? Or were the declarations fueled by lust? He was leaving a week. Plus, he'd made it clear he wanted no relationships. I had to stop searching for what wasn't there.

Barking erupted in the bedroom.

A chill stiffened the hairs on my neck.

The hunger vacated Lachlan's features. He shut off the water and hustled to the bathroom door. "Casey, what's the bother?"

I secured a towel around myself, joining a nude Lachlan at the doorway. Casey stood at the window, front paws on the ledge. His growling turned into snarls. His lips, flapping from the ferocity of his snarls, pulled back from his sharp canine teeth. Lachlan raced to the window. He jerked the curtains aside and his body went rock-still.

"What is it?" I asked, hurrying to his side.

A shocked face gaped back at us from the other side of the glass. Presley Cichon spun around and bolted.

Lachlan yanked on his pants and sprinted out of the house. I pulled on my sweats and T-shirt, tripping on my way to the door. With both hands, I propelled my body off the floor.

"Wait!" I yelled, in pursuit. Casey beat me to the front door, which wobbled on its hinges after Lachlan's departure, and galloped into the night. The hairs on my arms prickled. I froze at the top of the concrete steps. Casey had latched onto Presley's pants leg, snarling and preventing my ex-boyfriend from fleeing. Presley tried to kick at the dog, but lost his balance and stumbled. Lachlan seized Presley's shirt and hoisted him off the ground.

"Casey!" I clapped so hard my palms hurt and didn't stop until Casey detached his teeth from Presley's pants leg. The dog scampered to me.

Lachlan shook Presley, who sputtered and flailed his fists at Lachlan but landed punches on nothing more sensitive than Lachlan's iron biceps. I pushed Casey into the house, shutting the door after him. Lachlan's voice boomed off the houses.

"What the hell do ye think yer doing?" He rattled Presley again. "Spying on a wee lass? I'm gonnae skite mah fist on yer face till yer spitting teeth."

"I was looking for Erica, that's all," Presley whined.

"Haud yer wheesht, ye bloody bawbag!" Lachlan's brogue had thickened, and his face had gone scarlet. Spittle spattered Presley's face. "Ye've been rummeled this time and ye willnae get away with it."

"With what?" Presley's voice squeaked the tiniest bit. "I haven't done anything. You're the one going ape shit and hollering nonsense. I came to see Erica, heard a weird noise, and checked it out."

"And then yer erse fell off." Lachlan's breaths huffed through his nose. His eyes were wild, his lips curled on every word. "Means yer a liar, ye eejit."

I sprinted to Lachlan and slapped my hands on the bulging bicep of his left arm. "Put him down, Lachlan. Please." His gaze rotated to me. A muscle twitched in his jaw, but he maintained his grip on Presley. I squeezed Lachlan's arm. "Do it for me."

Lachlan unlatched his fingers from Presley's shirt. My ex crumpled to the ground in a jumble of legs and arms. Lachlan swiped his palms across each other and tipped his chin up, his gaze flinty. Presley scrambled to his feet and floundered to straighten out his disheveled clothes. Lachlan held his ground, his fingers working as if he typed on a keyboard—or itched to throttle my prowler ex. I stepped sideways between him and Presley.

The "bawbag" glared at me. "Still screwing Scotch Tape, huh? Shouldn't he get back to the zoo? Bet the girl gorillas miss him real bad."

"Shut up." I lodged my hands on my hips and scowled at him. "What on earth is wrong with you? I know you're the lowest level of scum in the pond, but I never pegged you for a peeping tom. What, you haven't ruined my life enough?"

"I did nothing." He set his lips in a defiant line. "You did it all to yourself."

"You know what? You're right. I did do this to myself." I jabbed a finger at him. "I trusted you."

He rolled his eyes.

Lachlan bared his teeth, cracking his knuckles. He bent forward, and I sensed he was about to launch his massive body at Presley. I edged closer to Lachlan, splaying my hands on his chest. "Let me handle this, okay? Trust me."

Lachlan's gaze landed on mine and his expression softened a touch. He took one step back. "If he makes a move toward ye, I willnae be responsible fer what I do."

"If he makes a move, you have my permission to skelp him till he's road-kill."

"Hey!" Presley waved his arms. "I'm still here, ya know."

I whirled on him. "I'm aware of that. Maybe I should call the cops to report a prowler."

"Who do you think they'll believe?"

Him, of course. The Cichons had connections everywhere. One call from Presley's daddy and the whole incident would get swept under the rug with an industrial blower. I stared into the eyes of the man who'd abused my affections, all in the name of covering up his own greed and criminal tendencies. How could I have cared for Presley, for even one second?

My gaze swiveled to Lachlan. Jaw set, eyes squinted, he drilled his gaze into Presley's. As if perceiving my attention, Lachlan focused on me and his lips formed a faint smile. My heartbeat sped up. How could I stop myself from caring for Lachlan? I couldn't, and I didn't want to, anyway.

Turning to Presley, I pointed at his Alfa Romeo parked at the curb. He hadn't bothered with stealth any of the three times he'd come here. *Arrogant ass.* "Get out of here."

He sneered at Lachlan, whose hands knotted into fists. Lachlan squinted his eyes and flared his nostrils. I'd never seen anyone's nostrils do that, and whoa, it was scary-sexy. Presley's face paled, his smirk faltering. He scurried to the Alfa Romeo. Neither Lachlan nor I spoke or moved until the sports car zoomed out of sight, the purring of its engine fading into the night.

The adrenaline that kept me upright through our little confrontation flooded out of me. My knees buckled. Black spots dotted my vision and my ears rang, but Lachlan gathered me up in his steady arms.

"Easy." He pressed a kiss to my forehead. "Slow, deep breaths."

He opened the door without setting me down. Casey tailed us into the bedroom where Lachlan laid me on the bed. The sheets were already pulled back and my body crushed the soft, slippery petals of—

I pushed onto one elbow, blinking slowly. Pale pink rose petals lay strewn across the bed and on the pillows. I hadn't noticed them earlier when we discovered Presley the Peeping Cichon. Now, I noticed everything. Candles flickered on the dresser and the bedside table. A silver tray on the table held a plate of strawberries and a fondue bowl brimming with liquid chocolate, alongside a bottle of Cristal champagne.

Lachlan sat down beside me. The bed jostled, the mattress sinking under his weight. He swept his fingers down my cheek and let his thumb fall on my lips. "This was the other part of your surprise."

"It's amazing." I picked up a rose petal and buried my nose in it, inhaling the sweet aroma. I skated the silky petal over my lips, then used it to tickle Lachlan's mouth, which made his lips twitch. I twirled the petal in the air. "Thank you. I love all of my surprise."

"You're exhausted." He blew out the candles on the table. Shadows engulfed us. "I can recreate this for you tomorrow night."

"I'm okay."

He nodded at the arm propping me up. "Your arm's shaking."

It was. *Ah, man.* "I'm still okay to—"

"No." He patted the mattress behind me. "Lie down. We're going to sleep."

"We?"

Lachlan tapped a finger on my forehead. "Lie back."

I sprawled on my back amid the roses. Lachlan crawled over my body to stretch out alongside me. He curled an arm around my shoulders and drew me close. I turned onto my side, head tucked against his shoulder, one hand on his chest. My palm rose and fell with his breaths and his heartbeat thumped under my ear, slowing second by second. I felt my own pulse decelerate, my breathing falling into sync with his as if we were tuned in to the same wavelength.

He wouldn't even tell me why he fled Scotland, yet he assaulted my scumbag ex in my defense. And he cuddled up with me afterward, soothing me with his warm, solid body.

"Tell me," I said, "why do you get so angry at Presley?"

Lachlan snorted. "He harasses you, spies on you, upsets you so much you shake. And you wonder why I'm angry?"

"Good point." I sighed. "Truthfully, I kind of like it when you throttle him. Does that make me a bad person?"

"Truthfully..." His fingers slid into my hair, combing through the locks. "I rather enjoy throttling him. Am I bad, then, too?"

"No." I wriggled to cozy up even closer to him, entranced by the feel of his body cradling mine. "You're not bad. You're very, very good."

Lachlan exhaled a groaning sigh. "Never been a violent man, but that—that—"

"Scunner?"

"I was going to say 'asshole,' but scunner works too." Lachlan wrapped his arm tighter around me. "He's a bully, and I hate bullies. No one should try to bend another to their will just for the sake of control."

"Mm." My brain had already begun the shutdown process, thoughts disintegrating, and I couldn't focus on the meaning of his words. So tired. So relaxed.

"Sleep now, sweet."

His fingers threaded through my hair again in a hypnotizing rhythm. My eyelids fluttered shut on their own, despite my best efforts to prop them open through sheer willpower. Couldn't sleep. Too much to say. Semi-wakefulness granted me the courage to speak forbidden words, but the heat of his body, the gentle motion of his fingers—these things eased me ever downward into slumber.

The words I yearned to say bombarded my mind. *What happened to you, Lachlan? Why can't you let me in?* I suffered an aching need to know more about him, but in the instant before sleep claimed me, a final question taunted me.

Did I care too much?

Chapter Twenty-One

*I*n the morning, I cuddled on the sofa with Lachlan, sharing a totally healthy breakfast—chocolate chip pancakes slathered in maple syrup, with whipped cream on top and crispy bacon on the side. *Mmmm.* My senses were in ecstasy. But no food, however scrumptious, not even chocolate, could compare to the decadence of making love with Lachlan MacTaggart. Making love? I pulverized a piece of bacon between my fingers. I had to stop thinking of it in those terms. This was sex. Sizzling, amazing, and mind-altering, but sex nonetheless. He was leaving in seven days. I would never see him again once he got on that plane.

My eyes stung. I squeezed them shut. He told me he wanted to know all about me, but he never suggested he might stay to find out.

"All right?" Lachlan asked, caressing my cheek with one finger.

"Fine." I put on a halfway decent smile, I thought. "Dust in my eye."

His brows knit together, etching that adorable crease above his nose. I skimmed my palm down his cheek and he sighed, staking a slab of pancake from our joint plate, balanced on his knee. I forked a whopping chunk and stuffed it in my mouth.

No one should try to bend another to their will just for the sake of control. My sleepy brain managed to hang onto those words, the ones Lachlan offered last night as an explanation for his throttling of Presley. What did bending someone to your will have to do with Presley being a creep? More importantly, what did it have to do with Lachlan and his ex-wife? Maybe nothing.

Maybe everything.

How could I have agreed to this idiotic arrangement? Sex and companionship. Nothing personal. No relationship. I'd wanted him so badly I ignored a basic truth about myself. I did not do casual. Panic about my future drove me to arrange a tryst with Cliff, but I now understood I couldn't have gone through with it. One kiss with Lachlan sent me running from the club, horrified at what I'd done. Yet here I was, enmeshed in a "fling" with a man I'd fallen for but who wanted no part in a relationship. Despite holding me all night. Despite his rage at Presley's stalking. Despite feeding me pancakes and introducing me to Scotch whisky. He felt something. He must.

Lachlan wiped syrup from my chin with his thumb. "You've gone serious all of a sudden."

"Have I?"

"Don't pretend you've no idea what I'm talking about." He leaned in, his body a wall of muscle surrounding me. "I can see the cloud over your head. It's gray and heavy with rain about to pour onto you." His lips twisted in a crooked smirk. "I like you wet, not drowned."

"There's no cloud. I was thinking, that's all."

"About what?"

How much I'll miss you. I slouched, avoiding his gaze. "You'll be gone in a week. There must things you'd like to do before you go."

"Besides you?"

I nudged him with my elbow. "Yes, besides me."

"Yes." He set our plate on the coffee table. "I would like to experience this country a bit more. And I've got an idea of how to do that."

"What kind of idea?"

His expression pinched, he eyed me sideways. "You probably won't like it."

I folded my arms over my breasts. "Tell me."

He scrubbed a hand over his face, then he fixed his sharp gaze on me. "I want you to take a trip with me, to drive around as much of the country as we can in the time I've got left."

"You make it sound like you're dying."

"I'm not dying." He settled a hand on my thigh. "Will you come with me, Erica?"

Words died on my tongue. Excitement zinged through me and my heartbeats quickened. A road trip with Lachlan? More time with him. Alone. More time for me to fall head over heels in love with him, right before he zipped back to Scotland and forgot all about his American fling. My stomach churned. I couldn't go, anyway. I was legally bound to remain in the state.

He propped one ankle atop the other knee, dropped it again, and drummed his foot on the floor. His hand stroked up and down my thigh. "Say something, please."

"Um…" Though my heart screamed *yes-yes-yes*, ready to leap into Lachlan's arms, my head took a step back. "I can't."

"But you're on sabbatical from your work."

"Yeah, but I can't just pick up and go. I have—" *A criminal trial I'm going to lose.* "—obligations."

"Such as?"

I gripped my knees hard. "Off limits."

Yeah, I realized I was being a hypocrite—wanting him to confide in me while I kept my own secrets. I longed to confess my problems to him, to be enfolded in his arms while he vowed everything would be okay, but I couldn't. Too many barriers stood between us. The Great Wall of China stood between us.

His shoulders sagged, along with his expression. "If you don't want to go, it's fine."

A car horn beeped outside, and I jumped. Lachlan stared at me, his foot drumming faster. I wrung my hands. The urge to pull him into my arms was overpowering, but I beat it back with all my self-control. "I want to go with you, Lachlan. But I just can't. My life is way more complicated than you realize and I know you have zero interest in hearing about it. Which leaves me with no way to explain." I caved my shoulders in as if I might shield myself with them. Fat chance of that. "I can't—" How the hell could I explain without explaining? "I can't leave the area. My reasons are personal."

"Ah." He angled away from me the tiniest bit.

Though he wouldn't meet my gaze, I rested one hand on his arm and pored over every detail of his features, memorizing the faint scar near his right ear, the single gray hair in his left brow, and the tiny, dark flecks in his arctic-blue irises. "Why is this so important to you?"

His gaze shifted to the window, which overlooked the backyard and the park beyond it. Children climbed around on a jungle gym while their mothers watched from a park bench nearby. Lachlan's eyes clouded, his face an impassive mask. When he turned back to me, I couldn't decipher his expression.

Like a firework bursting, his smile returned—*the* smile. The one that disintegrated panties and brought women to orgasm in an instant. Okay, maybe that was an exaggeration, but his smile did awaken my nether regions and encourage my breasts to tighten.

"I enjoy your company." His gave my hand a quick squeeze. "Nothing more."

The room temperature seemed to plummet at his impersonal gesture and tone. A pang started in my chest, dull at first, but intensifying into a throbbing pain. "Right, no personal involvement. I needed the reminder, thanks."

Lachlan rubbed his forehead with his thumb and forefinger. "I'm sorry. It came out all wrong." He dropped his head back and groaned. "Och, you make me lose my mind. I can't drum up the right words when I'm with you." With a rueful smile, he tilted his head toward me until our gazes locked. "My bum's oot the windae now."

I laughed. His smile demolished the pang in my chest and the pitiful wall I'd tried to build around my heart. I leaned my head on his shoulder. "I can't leave the state, but I could go for a little road trip. Get away from the city for a few days." I propped my chin on his shoulder. "How's that sound?"

"Perfect. We've had the main course—these weeks together here. It's time for dessert."

"A road trip sundae with sex and a cherry on top?"

His brows knit together. "There are times when I think Americans speak an alien language."

"Right back atcha, Mr. Highland Sex God."

His eyes glittered with amusement. "Sex god?"

"Don't let it go to your head. If your ego swells any bigger, you'll never fit on an airliner."

He hauled me onto his lap, straddling his hips, our faces level. His hands roved up and down my back, grazing the silky fabric of my shirt across my skin. "Tell me one thing?"

"Okay." *Anything in the world for you.*

Lachlan's hands came to rest on my hips. He tensed and cleared his throat. "Am I a substitute for Cliff? The eejit you were meant to meet at the club."

His question made that pang come back, under my ribs, right over my heart. "I don't understand what you're asking me. Cliff was a jerk who stood me up."

"But you wanted to meet him. He…excited you."

There he went with the excitement stuff again. What was his deal with it? I scrunched my lips, exhaling through my nose. He wanted to sneak into the forbidden zone of conversation, but I couldn't tread anywhere near it. Still, he watched me with that pitiful-puppy look, expectant and fearful at the same time. How could any woman resist a needy, hunky Highlander? I sure couldn't.

You're hopeless, Erica, falling for another numbers guy with secrets. I was a hopeless romantic, which I decided I could live with for the moment.

I splayed my hands on Lachlan's chest, exploring the muscles concealed under his T-shirt. "It wasn't Cliff that excited me. It was the idea of a fling, of chucking all my inhibitions and letting my inner wild child come out to play. I needed to feel alive."

"You chose me because I was the first man to approach you."

My hands rushed up his chest to his broad shoulders. "Actually, a rather enticing specimen bumped into me before you showed up. He smelled like beer and vomit, and he said I was hot but my breasts are too small for his taste. He staggered out of my life forever. I was devastated."

Lachlan almost smiled, but his dark mood seemed deeply rooted. "I'd no right to ask you about that."

"The topic is borderline off limits." I pushed my hands up behind his ears to bracket his head. His lips parted, his chest still with a breath held inside. I slid my mouth over his, sweeping back and forth, our breaths mingling. "From the second you spoke my name that night, I wanted you. Cliff could take a flying leap. Every other man in the club disappeared. I saw only you. I wanted only you."

"The same for me, lass." His voice had gone hoarse. "You excite me like no other."

Did he mean no other in the club that night? Or no other, period? My heart pounded at the possibility, and I brushed my tongue over his bottom lip. "You're no substitute, Lachlan."

He cupped my nape in one big hand and pulled me in for a scintillating kiss. My body tingled from the tip of my skull to the nails of my toes. He tasted of maple syrup and whipped cream, with a tantalizing hint of chocolate. His tongue danced with mine, coaxing me to delve deeper into his mouth as I wrapped my arms around his neck. My toes curled, and I moaned into his mouth.

"Lachlan," I said, when our kiss finally ended, "do me one favor."

"Anything you want."

I rested my forehead on his. "Never stop surprising me."

"Wouldn't dream of it."

The natural scent of him wafted over me and I rubbed my cheek against his, oblivious to the scruffy texture of his morning stubble as it scraped over my skin. "I'm sorry I keep calling you a bastard while we're having sex."

"I am a bastard. Just ask my wife."

I lifted my head to study him. "You're divorced, right?"

He shrugged one shoulder. Not a yes, not a no. He had to be divorced. I would not have an affair with a married man.

As if he'd read my thoughts, Lachlan smiled tenderly. "My wife is out of my life, permanently."

"Oh. Good." The Bitch was gone. *Yay.* "Did you have any children?"

The unreadable look overtook him again. I slid my hands out from behind his neck, down onto his chest. Chewing the inside of my cheek, I counted the folds of my knuckles. "Sorry, that was too personal a question, wasn't it?"

He exhaled a long sigh. "I've no bairns, though I want them very much."

"So do I." Lachlan perked up, though I had no idea why. The familial desires of his American fling shouldn't be of any interest to him. But I kept babbling. "I didn't have any siblings, and I guess that made me want a family of my own. Lots of kids scampering around the house. And of course, a husband who loves me as much as I love him."

"A lovely dream." He sank his fingers into my hair, his palm on my cheek, and I leaned into his touch. "I hope you get it someday."

"I hope you get yours too."

A silence settled between us, not exactly uncomfortable, but echoing with questions unasked and declarations unspoken. Maybe I was indulging in wishful thinking and I was the only one holding back unspoken things. I nestled my head on his shoulder, my face against his neck. He did the same, his heated breaths tickling my skin. For the longest time, we just held each other. Seven days. This all would end, and he'd be gone from my life. Part of me believed he wanted to stay or ask me to go with him, but something held him back. The sensible part of me understood he'd meant what he said about no relationships. And yet he held me, his embrace firm, as if he never wanted to let me go.

But I'd have to let him go. He was going home, and I was going to prison. What a pair we made—him locked up in fears I couldn't understand and me framed for a crime my asshole ex-boyfriend committed. Both of us imprisoned in our own ways. Given time, maybe we could find a way out of our bonds and be together. I tightened my arms around his neck. *Don't you dare let go of me, Lachlan MacTaggart, because I won't let go of you.*

Chapter Twenty-Two

M y tailbone hurt, and a spot up against my right shoulder blade had begun to pinch. Bright sunlight stabbed into my eyes and, despite wiggling my butt every which way possible, I could not find a comfortable position in the metal folding chair. On the corroded metal desk in front of me, a bobblehead leprechaun made clicking noises, its motions activated by tiny solar panels on the figurine's base. To the left of the desk, a window air conditioner blustered moderately cool air into the room.

I drummed my fingers on my thighs, forcing myself not to clench my teeth. Waiting was not my strong suit. To avoid insanity, I let my thoughts travel back to my wake-up call this morning. Lachlan had called my cell phone and, still drowsy, I'd forgotten I was in his bed until I rolled over and the whisper-soft sheets slipped over my skin. Lachlan purred sweet words to me through the phone, rousing my body faster than my mind could shake off sleep. I recalled mumbling something dirty, about what I wanted him to do to me. Then I'd realized he'd called me, which meant he'd left me, and I bolted upright. "Lachlan, where are you?"

"Right here," he'd said, as the bathroom door swung open and he ambled out. "I'd never leave you, especially when you're naked and wet."

"I'm not wet. Haven't taken a shower yet."

He'd crawled onto the bed then and inched up my body, licking my skin as he moved. "Not that kind of wet."

In the present, I allowed my eyelids to close, lost in the beautiful memory. Anything to evade the reality in front of me.

"Erica." Doretta Harper's voice cut through my reverie. She snapped her fingers. "Wake up, girl. I need your full attention."

My attorney bent in front of me, her concerned eyes focused on my face. Having just walked into the office, Doretta held a stack of file folders to her chest. With a shake of her head and a disapproving cluck, she retreated around her desk and took a seat in her cracked and creased executive chair.

I rubbed my eyes, straightened, and folded my hands on my lap. My conservative skirt suit was black, to match the somber mood of this meeting. "I'm here. What's going on?"

"Are you awake now?" Doretta's mouth quirked in a half smile. "Seemed like you were daydreaming a minute ago."

"I'm fine." I cleared my throat and looked straight at her. "I'm listening."

"Good." Doretta leaned her elbows on the desk, atop two piles of file folders, one higher than the other. Her pantsuit, a lovely shade of salmon, complemented her cocoa skin. Her close-cropped hair glistened honey blonde in the sunshine. Her coffee-colored eyes probed into me. "The DA's made an offer."

"I told you no plea deals."

"Hear it before you shoot it down, hon. Please."

"Fine." I slumped in my chair.

Doretta tapped her red-painted fingernails on the file folders. "DA's offering probation plus restitution."

I clenched my teeth and pangs shot through my jaw. Restitution? Like I had a quarter million bucks stashed in my sofa. "No."

"Erica." Her tone reminded me of a teacher scolding her student. "No jail time. You hear me? *No jail time.*"

"I get it." My stomach churned, bile rising in my throat as my chest tightened. A thousand curses popped into my mind, but swearing wouldn't help. I had no choices left. No way out. If I went to trial, I'd surely lose. Who would believe me over the powerful and connected Cichon family? The entire clan had rallied around Presley, labeling me a gold-digging, senior-citizen-robbing slut.

Weariness plunged down on me, heavy as an iron blanket. I buried my face in my hands. God, I wished Lachlan were here. Stupid, but I couldn't help it. He soothed me. In this moment, I needed that more than anything. But this was my mess, not Lachlan's.

"I know this isn't perfect," Doretta said, her voice full of sympathy, "but the evidence all points to you. A deal's your safest bet."

Nausea roiled in my gut anew, pressing up into my throat until I could taste the bitterness of it. I drew in a deep breath, exhaled, and lowered my hands. "I appreciate you taking me on pro bono and I know you're doing the best you can, but no. I cannot and will not accept any deal that requires me to plead guilty." The anger I'd repressed for so long erupted, scorching my soul and hardening my voice. I spat the words. "I did not steal the money. I am innocent. If I plead guilty, it's over, no second chances. If I'm convicted and go to prison, at least I might appeal."

"Oh hon." Doretta shook her head, her dark eyes filled with sympathy. "I believe you. Presley Cichon is a jackass and a scam artist to boot, but neither of us has the resources to prove it. I don't want to see you go to prison. Someone like you…"

Can't handle prison. That's what she intended to say. I was a stupid girl, easily duped by a charming con man. How could I hope to survive behind bars? Baloney. I was stronger than anyone gave me credit for and I would get through this. About time I started acting like it.

"No deal." I rose and offered Doretta my hand. "Thank you for all your help. You'll never know how grateful I am."

She clasped my hand but didn't shake it. "Baby, I hope you know what you're doing."

So do I. "I'll see you at trial. Goodbye, Doretta."

When I reached my car, I collapsed into the driver's seat, overcome by the need to weep out my fears and frustrations. I fought back the urge, though, and twisted the key in the ignition. My throat tight, I steered the car in the direction of the one place I swore I'd never visit again.

Presley Cichon's apartment.

The doorbell chimed inside the apartment, muted by the massive wooden door. Scratching my arm, I glanced left and right. I half expected security guards to surge out of the shadows and tackle me to the floor, but nothing happened. After a minute, maybe more, ticked by without any sign of life in Presley's apartment, I punched the doorbell button again. *Bing-bong-bing* sang the chime.

Footsteps. Inside. Coming closer.

My gut clenched. My mouth went dry. This had sounded like a good idea, to assert myself and be the strong woman, but as I watched the pinpoint of light in the peephole vanish, my pulse accelerated. He was looking at me. Calculating. Assessing. He wouldn't hurt me physically, I was sure of that. Cowards like him blustered but didn't have the nerve to follow through.

I straightened, grasped my purse strap tighter to my shoulder, and lifted my chin. Let the creep look.

The door pivoted inward, and there stood Presley Cichon. Half naked.

I felt my lips tighten as I compressed them. Yeah, he was leaning against the door wearing nothing but a low-slung pair of short-shorts. Muscles on display. Toned thighs exposed. A smirk distorting his pretty face. Gaze sweeping up and down the length of me. He licked his lips and cranked up his playboy smile.

Once upon a time that smile would've set my belly aflutter. Now, it gave me acid indigestion and made my fingers twitch with the urge to smack him.

"Hey babe." He tilted one hip, making the shorts dip a little lower on the opposite side. "What can I do you for?"

"Cut the act, Presley. I don't fall for it anymore."

"Act?" His shoulders lifted, and he glanced around in confusion—the totally fake and sarcastic version of it. "Don't know what you mean."

The breath hissed out of me. "We need to talk."

"Sure thing." He swung the door wide, gesturing for me to enter. "Always a pleasure. For both of us."

His innuendo rankled, but I'd made a decision on the way over here. No matter what he said, I would not give him the satisfaction of unsettling me.

I stalked past him into the spacious apartment, which could've fit my entire house and then some. Stark glass windows spanned one wall, floor to ceiling, for the whole length of the studio layout. Modern furniture— all glass and metal, with the occasional sterile white trim—sat in strategic places throughout the apartment. Unfortunately, I knew this place very well. I made a beeline for the only semi-comfortable chair around, a chrome number with white leather upholstery and minimal cushioning. My tailbone smarted the second I perched on the chair.

Presley ambled to the nearest window, braced one hand on the metal frame, and crossed one ankle over the other. His shrewd gaze landed on me. "Ready to dump Scotch Tape and come back to America?"

"Come off it, Presley. You don't want me back any more than I want to get back together with you. I was your scapegoat, nothing more."

"Huh." He rapped his fingers on the metal window frame. "Can't imagine what you mean."

"Why did you steal the money in the first place? You're rich, you sure as hell don't need it."

"Don't know what you're talking about."

Okay, I hadn't expected him to confess his guilt and vow to straighten out the whole mess, but I had at least hoped...I don't know. Some kind of hint he might actually feel bad about what he'd done, deep down, on a subconscious level. We had dated for three months. Was a smidgen of remorse too much to ask for? Not that I wanted him back. No way, not ever. But I needed closure.

I just managed to keep my shoulders from deflating. "Did you ever even like me? Just a teeny bit? Or was it all one long con?"

He eyed me sideways, that calculating gleam in his eyes. "Don't know—"

"Oh please." I sprang to my feet, every muscle tensed as if for a fight, and glowered at him. "Quit pretending you're clueless. We both know what you did. You seduced me so you could set me up as your patsy, and holy mackerel, you did a bang-up job of it."

Those lips, the ones I'd kissed so many times—*ew*—ticked down at one corner for the briefest moment. He turned his gaze to the vista outside, the skyscrapers and Lake Michigan in the distance. His fingers rapped on the glass like a drum roll. When he spoke, his voice was taut as a high-tension wire. "It wasn't personal."

A harsh laugh exploded out of me. "You have got to be kidding me. Sex is as personal as it gets."

The memory of Lachlan flashed in my mind right then, in a montage of every time we'd been together. Nothing personal, that was our agreement. Yet I'd told Presley the truth. For me, sex was intensely personal. I swallowed a groan. What a time for an epiphany about my current, er, situation. The realization pierced me deep, right in the heart. Lachlan was more than my casual lover, at least to me.

Next stop, self-destruction station. Disembarking in ten minutes.

Presley frowned at me, his gaze flicking over my purse. "What you got in there? You're holding onto it like the thing's gonna fly away."

I loosened my fingers, which I still had clamped around the purse strap. "Answer me one question. Why me?"

He stared at me like I'd spoken Swahili.

"Why me?" I repeated. "Lots of girls to choose from in the office. You could've found a perky ditz who wears miniskirts to work—you know, your usual type."

Eyes narrowing, he glanced at my purse again. His lips puckered.

I hugged the purse closer. "What is your problem?"

He stomped to me, lunged down into a squat, and spoke directly to my purse. "In case Erica's recording this, anything I say from here on is under duress because my crazy ex—Erica Teague, the embezzler—is behaving in a threatening way. I had no knowledge of her stealing money from moldy old farts."

Presley looked up at me with a self-satisfied smile.

I scuffled backward a couple steps. "My purse is not a surveillance device, you moron."

He rose, stretching and yawning. "Just covering my ass. Since you won't do that for me anymore."

"Grow up." I shook my head, jaw so tense it hurt. "Answer my question. Why me?"

"Isn't it obvious?"

"No."

He ran a hand across the back of his neck. "I needed somebody uptight and anal, the A-type personality everyone would believe could snap and commit a crime out of spite."

Though I had a sinking feeling I knew the answer, I had to ask. "Spite for what?"

"Me dumping you."

My jaw fell open. I clapped it shut. He dumped me after I was arrested and released on bond, and he'd done it on the courthouse steps with his hoity-toity parents watching from ten feet away. They had glared at me so hard I thought they might spit on me as they passed by on their way down the steps. Instead, Presley's father had lobbed a final insult at me.

"We'll be suing you for defamation," he'd snarled. "Accusing our son of complicity in your crimes is despicable."

Complicity. The bastard was completely and solely responsible.

Presley moved toward me, reaching out a hand to grasp my upper arm. "Since you're here, how about we hook up one more time, just for fun?"

Words, gone. Like a sheet yanked away by a hurricane wind.

"No?" He shrugged, sighing. "What should we do, then? I'm not giving you what you want and you're not giving me what I want."

"What do you want from me?"

"Nothing."

"So, stalking is your new hobby." I shut my eyes for a heartbeat, then added, "Stop pestering me. Just leave me alone to go to prison in peace."

Though his face was turned to the window, he rolled his eyes to stare at me. The intensity of his gaze set my skin to crawling. I glanced at the front door, but I'd have to sidle past him to get there. He wouldn't hurt me physically, that's what I'd told myself when I rang the doorbell. Now I wasn't so sure.

Presley bent at the waist, leaning in to get closer to my face. His expression had gone blank, but his voice was all syrupy sarcasm. "Did I bweak yo wittle heart?"

I could not stop myself. I swung my leg up, planted my foot in his gut, and shoved him away. He staggered backward and burst into laughter. His guffaws echoed off the glass, and the effort made his eyes tear up. As he calmed down, he swiped at his eyes with the back of his hand.

"Well?" he said. "Did I?"

"Break my heart?" I shook my head, frowning. "Hardly. I would've had to love you for that to happen."

His eyes flew wide for a second before he tamped down the reaction, his expression once again full of disdain. "Come on, you fell for me. Admit it."

"Even I am not that gullible."

My phone warbled. I jumped and fumbled to dig it out of my purse. Presley watched me with a bemused look on his face while I picked up the call, without even glancing at the caller ID.

"Where are you?" Lachlan's voice rumbled through the speaker, straight into my ear. "I knocked on your door, but you weren't there. Thought you might be getting ready."

"Um, getting ready for what?"

"Our trip. I hoped we might start it today."

"Oh, right, the trip." I wanted to turn my back to Presley, but the thought of him doing who-knew-what behind me made my skin itch again. Instead, I edged toward the windows. "I'll be home soon."

"Are you all right, *gràidh*?"

Despite having my ex staring at me, I started to melt inside when Lachlan called me *gràidh*. My cheeks heated. And so did...other places. I murmured into the phone, "Yes, I'm fine. I'll see you in a bit, okay?"

"I'll be waiting." His voice sank into sultry territory. "I've been imagining all the things I want to do to you. I'll strip you naked and—"

A frantic laugh hiccupped out of me. "Uh, sure, sounds great. See you later."

I disconnected the call before Lachlan could say another word. My cheeks were already on fire, and Presley was smirking at me as if he'd heard what Lachlan said. He couldn't have. But my embarrassment probably gave him a clue.

"So," Presley said, folding his arms over his bare chest, "are you moving to Nessie-land to have little Scotchie babies? Bet you look hot in plaid."

Enough of this. I'd get no closure here, and I was sick of his taunts. I stomped past him, and as I grasped the doorknob, I called over my shoulder, "Stay away from me or I'll throttle you myself next time—then I'll let Lachlan beat the crap out of you while I eat popcorn and cheer."

I stalked out into the corridor and slammed the door.

Chapter Twenty-Three

Lachlan swooped me up in his arms and whirled us both around. My feet sailed through the air, but my heart soared even higher. He stepped backward and kicked the door shut behind us. I'd knocked on Lachlan's door a mere minute earlier, barely getting out my words before he grabbed me. He deposited me on the wood floor of the entryway, though he kept his arms around me.

"It's true?" he asked, his lopsided grin widening.

"Yes." I pecked a kiss on his mouth. I'd made my decision on the drive home from Presley's. "I want our road trip to start today. I thought about it all night and this morning and then in the car I realized—"

His lips cut off my ramblings. When we came up for air, he said, "How soon can you be ready?"

"Already packed. Got ready last night."

He looked entirely too overjoyed for a man who considered me his American fling.

Don't hope, don't do it.

He crushed me to him. "You're a miracle, *gràidh*."

The entire English language vanished from my brain. I opened my mouth, but no words came out. Lachlan took my parted lips as an invitation for a deep, ravishing kiss that left my knees wobbly and my body humming. I breathed one word. "Casey."

"I asked Mrs. Abernathy. She'll take him while we're gone." He ducked his head. "Where we're going, they don't allow pets. I'm sorry, I tried to find a pet-friendly place."

"It's okay. Casey loves Mrs. Abernathy."

"Gave her my key to your house. Was that all right?"

"Yes." My lips enveloped his, my tongue thrusting into his mouth, rasping over his, ever starved for more of him. "Thank you for taking care of all the arrangements."

He nibbled my lower lip. "Welcome. Shall we go?"

A week on the road with my Lachlan MacTaggart. I was in so over my head, but I couldn't have cared less. I grinned. "Absolutely. Let's get on the road."

Lachlan painted kisses on my temple, my cheek, the corner of my mouth. "Got my bags in the car. Let's go grab yours, my sweet lass, and get on the road."

His sweet lass. His *gràidh*. Why did he have to keep saying things like that, leading me on? I stifled a groan. I was leading him on too. Pretending I could spend one week with him, say goodbye, and go on with my life, happy and content. But I wouldn't do any of it. My life was in the tank, the deepest, darkest tank on earth.

Lachlan grazed a hand over my cheek. Concern tightened his forehead. "Feeling unwell?"

"Uh-uh."

He slipped his hand around my nape, drawing me in for a sweet, sensual kiss. My body craved him more than ever and my heart longed for things I couldn't have. A man like Lachlan would stand by me, no matter what. He'd fight for me, anytime, anywhere. Except he wouldn't. Not for me. Another woman, one lucky enough to meet him after he'd recovered from whatever wounded him, would get the parts of him I only glimpsed.

I reciprocated his kiss, imbuing it with every ounce of desire and yearning I possessed, praying he might feel my need for him, the man, and not just my sexual need for his body. *Feel it, Lachlan, please.*

He pulled away. "You still seem unhappy. Where did you go this morning?"

I opened my mouth to tell him it was none of his business, but a wave of weariness and resignation crashed over me. My shoulders drooped. I shut my eyes, exhaling a long breath. Might as well tell him. Staring at his chest, masked by a T-shirt, I let the words tumble out. "I went to see Presley."

"The erse who's been harassing you? Why?"

Every ounce of energy flooded out of me as I replayed my conversation with Presley, and my throat constricted. I wrapped my arms around Lachlan, burying my face against his chest.

He stroked my hair, threading his fingers through it. "What happened?"

"Sure you wanna know?"

"Positive." He curled one arm around me, pressing me close.

I turned my head so my cheek rested on his chest. With his fingers in my hair, soothing me, I lost any will to remind him of our agreement. How I needed him to care. "I thought I needed to confront him, to get some kind of closure. But he just made fun of me. Can't believe I was ever involved with him. Can't believe I actually thought he might—" I squeezed my eyes shut, desperate to stem the tears gathering in them. "Guess I needed to believe he wasn't a total slimeball. But he is."

Lachlan enfolded me in both his strong arms and kissed the top of my head. "What did he do to you?"

"Today? Not much. He was sarcastic and dismissive."

"I meant in the past."

"Don't think you really want to hear about it."

He rested his chin atop my head, his voice taking on a hint of something resembling regret. "Whatever he did—and I won't push you to tell me, since I have no right to—but whatever he did, I hope it's over now. I hate seeing you like this."

"It is over. Way over." I wriggled out of his embrace, rubbing my arms. "Couldn't even get him to tell me why he keeps coming to my house." I eased my hands into his, holding on tight. "Let's forget the serious talk. I want to go away with you and have fun."

"That I can give you."

Keeping hold of one of my hands, he led me out of his house and across the lawns to my front door. We collected my bags, piling into Lachlan's rented Mercedes convertible. He'd put the top down. The plush seat cradled me, much the way Lachlan did after we made love. I treasured those moments, the safety I found while cuddling with him, for a brief time.

The car rocked as Lachlan yanked his door shut. The engine rumbled to life, so soft I barely heard it over the classical music emanating from the stereo. Vivaldi's *The Four Seasons*. The MP3 player plugged into the stereo picked up in the middle of the fourth concerto—"Spring." A time of new beginnings, hope, promise. We should've listened to "Winter." It suited my future best. I sensed Lachlan's gaze on me, a warm caress of his undivided attention. The cold inside me thawed a smidgen.

He rested his hand over mine on the center console. "I won't ask what's been eating at you these weeks, but I want you to know you can tell me if you like. Maybe I can help."

Lend me a bank vault's worth of money, so I can hire detectives to ferret out evidence of Presley's guilt. As if I would ever ask him such a thing. He couldn't do anything to save my future, but he helped my present more than he knew. I twined our fingers and gave him the best smile I could muster, which wasn't much. "Let's get on the road and have fun. That's all I want to think about right now."

He nodded, though he looked less than convinced. I'd learned enough about him to realize he wanted to fix my problems. He had no idea what they were, or how impossible fixing them would be, but he itched to dive in there and set things right. God, I loved him.

My heart thudded. A chill swept over me, though a deep and gentle warmth washed it away in a matter of seconds. I loved him. Holy mackerel, when did that happen? I slumped in my seat, the warmth fading away. Didn't matter what I felt. He'd leave anyway, even if I told him. Hearing and seeing his reaction to phone calls about his ex-wife confirmed it for me. He was damaged beyond anything I could repair.

So, here I was. Erica Teague, wild woman. *Hah*. I was a complete and total mess, sinking ever deeper into the abyss.

I tried to focus on the scenery, to block out my melancholy thoughts. The streets of my neighborhood gave way to the urban roadways, packed with cars. My vision retreated into the recesses of my mind, the roads a blur of motion and color. Mozart had taken over for Vivaldi by the time we hit the freeway. The concrete roadway buzzed under us as if a beehive cradled our car's wheels. Our car. I shouldn't think of it that way. Beginning in this moment, I had to separate myself from Lachlan, emotionally, and stop hoping for a future with him. Pull back. For both our sakes.

A police car passed us on the left. I watched it recede ahead of us and for a moment I indulged in a fantasy that Lachlan had broken me out of jail and we were on the run together, a pair of romantic fugitives, our love too strong to be severed by anything. Even if Lachlan wanted to break me out, I would never let him. So I'd do what I'd advised Lachlan we should do. I'd enjoy this time with him. And deal with the future later.

I crossed my legs and massaged his thigh. "Where are we going, Sex God?"

His face scrunched, he shifted position as I slid my hand higher. "Our destination is a surprise."

"Oh?" I edged my fingers closer to the enlarging bulge in his pants.

He grasped my hand, settling it on the center console beneath his. "You'll like it, I promise."

"Will it be sexy?"

He flashed me a secret smile. "Patience, *mo leannan*. Patience."

On our drive south from Chicago, I discovered my companion had a fetish for cheesy tourist traps. We stopped at the Paul Bunyan statue in University Park, where the ginormous lumberman slumped as if too wiped out to hold himself up, his axe dragging on the ground. My cheery mood waned a bit looking at that statue because I could identify with poor Paul's weariness. Life was dragging me down too.

Way to dive into the fun, eh? I chewed the inside of my lip and tried to shake off the malaise. Lachlan seemed to notice my mood change, because he rushed at Paul's giant axe, pretending to strain to lift it, his face contorting with mock effort. He fell on the huge blade with a death scene deserving of a Shakespearean tragedy—if not for the wildly overblown horror on his face.

I couldn't help it. I laughed, so hard my sides hurt.

Lachlan gave up the stage show and marched back to my side. He laid a hand on my cheek, running his thumb over the upturned corner of my mouth. "That's better. I'll humiliate myself anytime to see that beautiful smile."

All I could do was gaze up at him with what must've been idiotic adoration. How could I not love him? He'd make a fool of himself just to cheer me up.

After that, our tour of tacky monuments revved into high gear with a water tower emblazoned with a smiley face, a statue of Abe Lincoln holding a "Go Bears" sign, and a Nazi buzz bomb. Roadside attractions had never intrigued me, but Lachlan's boyish enthusiasm for them infected me. Before I knew it, I was getting excited at the prospect of taking a detour off the interstate to see the first Dairy Queen franchise.

We kept traveling south down Interstate 45, with the scenery whizzing past our windows. In the town of Loda, Lachlan exited the freeway to head for another attraction, though when I asked what it was, he simply told me, "You'll see."

When we pulled up to the village park, and the attraction came into view, the blood fled my brain. A chill raced through me, prickling my skin. There, on the grassy lawn of the park, stood a large metal cage marked with a sign identifying it as the Loda Jail.

Lachlan pointed at the cage. "A hundred years ago, they kept prisoners in that contraption. Must've been a pleasant experience, eh?"

His tone was casual, his expression was interested. I gulped against a lump in my throat, but it remained stuck. Fidgeting, I struggled to sound unaffected. "Yeah, I'm sure it was a pajama party."

My voice cracked, just a bit. I hoped Lachlan hadn't noticed, but no such luck. His head swung around, his gaze homing in on mine. "What's wrong?"

"Nothing." I tried to relax back into my seat in a casual way, but even I realized I looked awkward and tense. "Jails aren't fun, that's all."

A vision flared in my mind, of me locked in the Loda Jail for four to fourteen years. In my nightmare fantasy, Presley stood nearby snickering while Lachlan led a parade of tourists past me. In a disinterested tone, he informed them, "And for our last attraction, here's the world's dumbest girl, who let a scunner con her into taking the fall for him."

The real Lachlan cupped my face in both his warm hands, leaning in until his breaths tickled my skin. The intensity of his gaze made the hairs on my neck and arms stand up at attention.

"Erica," he murmured, "please don't cry."

Oh no. I *was* about to cry. Tears welled in my eyes, stinging and threatening to spill out. I blinked them away.

He brushed his lips over mine, his kiss soft and tender. "I never meant to upset you, but clearly I have. I'm sorry."

"You didn't do anything." I fought the impulse to crawl into his lap and curl up there. "Can we just go somewhere else, please?"

He nodded and released me so he could steer the car back toward the freeway. We made no more stops to gawk at odd monuments. And I stared straight ahead at the freeway unreeling before us, a gray strip extending beyond the horizon. Gray. Colorless. Lifeless.

My future, embodied in asphalt.

Chapter Twenty-Four

*J*ust outside of Champaign, we pulled into the semicircular, brick-lined drive of a historic mansion. Sky blue trimmed the white mansion and slender Corinthian columns buttressed the wraparound porch while lacy railing lined the porch and the second-floor balcony. Lachlan opened my door for me and took my hand as we mounted the brick steps toward the mansion's front door.

A sparrow landed on the brick steps to my left, fluttered its wings, and flew away. I wished my anxieties could flit away as easily.

Hand in hand, we strolled into the bed-and-breakfast. Though the place was gorgeous, with hardwood floors and wall paneling and a crystal chandelier suspended over the entryway, it didn't suit Lachlan. He should've slept in a stone castle with ancient weapons on the walls instead of Victorian paintings. A pretty gray-haired woman signed us in, regaling us with tales of ye olden days, which flew right through my distracted brain. The countdown clock in my head banged with jackhammer strength. A handful of days to go.

"Have a wonderful stay, Mrs. MacTaggart."

I startled at our host's statement. "I'm not—"

"Thank you, Mrs. Wilkins," Lachlan said, tossing an arm around my shoulders. "I'm sure we'll both love it here."

He hauled me away from the desk toward the sprawling staircase upholstered in crimson carpeting. Constrained by Lachlan's arm, I performed a little contortionist act to twist around so I could wave at Mrs. Wilkins. I elbowed Lachlan, muttering out the corner of my mouth, "Why'd you let her think we're married?"

"It made her happy. She adores newlyweds." He spoke the last two words in a ridiculous imitation of Mrs. Wilkins's voice. "Where's the harm in letting her believe it?"

A spark of hope flickered into a tiny flame inside me. Maybe he wanted to believe it, or play at being married to see if it wasn't as bad as he remembered. Right, and Presley wanted to fall on his knees and beg my forgiveness right before turning himself in to the police.

When we reached our room on the second floor—with balcony access, naturally, and picture windows granting views of both the tree-shrouded drive in front and the lush gardens behind the mansion—he unlocked the door and cracked it open a few inches. I scrunched my eyebrows. Before I realized his intention, he picked me up and, kicking the door inward, carried me over the threshold. I held my breath, my body weightless in his arms. Men carried their wives over thresholds, not their concubines. *Get real, Erica.*

He set me down beside the bed. Our bags already awaited us, tucked in between the dresser and the wall, across from the four-poster bed. The male half of the husband-and-wife team who owned the bed-and-breakfast had brought up our luggage while we signed in and got our room key. I shuffled toward my wheeled suitcase, glancing out the windows. Ivy surrounded the panes while flowering trees and bushes painted a colorful vista below. The b&b boasted a magnificent garden, with tables for dining outside. So romantic.

Lachlan hooked an arm around my waist to turn me toward him, pulling me tight against him. "Like the surprise?"

"I love it." Linking my hands behind his neck, I rested my cheek on his chest. "I wish we could stay here forever, on a never-ending honeymoon."

He flinched from head to toe. His entire body went rigid.

Cripes. Had I said that out loud? I jerked my head up and clamped my lips between my teeth. I stopped blinking, afraid to move the tiniest muscle for fear of what I'd blurt out next. When I dared to speak again, I cleared my throat and gave a nervous laugh. "I meant a fake honeymoon. You know, like Mrs. Wilkins thinks we're doing now."

Lachlan's gaze had gone inscrutable again, his emotions and thoughts shuttered behind a mask. His arms fell to his sides. Sheesh, it wasn't like I'd said I loved him. He backed away a couple steps, eyes unblinking. I opened my mouth to make a sarcastic quip but stopped. His hands were trembling, his jaw too. Our gazes converged, and for a few seconds, I swore I could read his mind, experience his true feelings for me. Those blue eyes pleaded with me. *Just say it, Lachlan, promise to stay with me.* But then his gaze darted away, snapping the thread that united us.

He scrubbed his hands over his face. "You know I'm leaving in a matter of days."

A sigh deflated my shoulders and my spirit. Apparently, I'd never learn.

"What's your point?"

"You said…" He burst into motion, pacing between the door and the opposite wall. "Have I given you reason to think I won't go?"

"No." Well yeah, he kind of had. Not in explicit terms, but in his actions and in his Gaelic endearments. How long would I let him go on screwing with my feelings? I grated my teeth, lava-hot fury boiling in my gut. One thing I knew about myself—when cornered, I resorted to anger. "Don't worry, I won't chase you to the airport and throw myself at your feet, begging you to stay. I can find another sex partner at Dance Ardor."

He reeled around, seizing my arms. "Donnae ever go back to that club again!"

I punched his chest. "Let go of me, you—you—*Homo heidelbergensis.*"

His face went blank. "What'd you call me?"

"*Homo heidelbergensis.*" I wrested free of his grasp. "It's an ancient species of prehuman hominid. I was going to call you a Neanderthal, but then I remembered they didn't live in the U.K., but *heidelbergensis* did."

His closed lips stretched taut, one corner curved up. "A timekeeper, an accountant, and an anthropologist. My, you are a Renaissance woman."

I scowled and stuffed my hands in my jeans pockets. "I read a lot."

"Sorry." He reached out to touch my cheek but pulled his hand away. "I shouldn't have shouted at you. But I can't stand the thought of you going back to that…den of iniquity. Men would take advantage of you."

"Oh, you mean like you've done?"

He grimaced, shoving a hand through his hair. "Is that what you think I'm doing? I told you honestly what I could give you and left the decision in your hands."

Right, it was all my fault. Hell, maybe he was right. I'd leaped into his bed with all the dignity and forethought of a dog pouncing on a fresh bone. I squeezed my eyes shut as a knot cinched tight in my stomach. I'd mutated into a desperate slut. Me. The girl Presley had called goody two shoes because I wouldn't hop into bed with him until five weeks after we started dating. And I'd thought that was fast.

"I've upset you again," Lachlan said, his voice thickened with emotions I didn't care to figure out anymore. "Forgive me, *gràidh*?"

I grunted, opening my eyes, and went suddenly breathless at the sight of his pleading expression. When he knelt and raised his clasped hands to me, I waved for him to get up. "Fine, I forgive you."

He bowed his head, a breath rushing out of him. "Thank heaven for that."

Rising, he stumbled backward a step, then regained his usual grace as he strode to an antique chair next to the bedside table and draped his immense body onto it. I sank onto the bed. My feet dangled six inches off the wood floor. The bedside table separated us, but I knew more than furniture kept us apart. Lachlan braced his elbow on the chair's arm, his forehead in his palm. His fingers tunneled into his hair, spread wide as if he battled to restrain the thoughts in his head.

I bent my legs to sit cross-legged on the floral bedspread. Hands on my knees, I tapped my fingers in a staccato rhythm and stared at the floorboards. "Are you okay?"

He made a noncommittal noise.

Rocking on my butt, I counted the seconds until I reached a hundred and twenty-four. Tired of waiting, I snatched a brochure about the historic house from the table and read the life story of the lumber magnate who'd built the mansion for his wife. Fascinating. I couldn't remember a word of it after I finished perusing the brochure. I slapped it down on the table.

Lachlan peeked at me around his palm, which still propped up his forehead. "You're fashed, but I don't know why."

"Really." I unzipped my boot and kicked it off. The boot ricocheted off his shin, making him wince. When I kicked off the other boot, he bolted upright with his hands latched onto the chair's arms, but my boot flew wide. It clopped down near the bathroom door. "All I said was I wished we could stay here forever—which is, by the way, a common thing Americans say when we're happy—and you freaked out."

Lachlan crossed his ankles, uncrossed them, linked his hands, fastened them on his thighs. "I did not freak out."

"Right. I imagine there's a masculine Scottish word for it."

"Erica—"

"Chill out." I tore off my socks, lobbing them toward the dresser. One caught on a drawer handle while the other plopped to the floor. "I am fully aware of the rules, Lachlan."

He heaved his body off the chair and scuffled to me. As he knelt before me, he settled his hands on my thighs and the familiar warmth tingled through me. Sometimes I hated my body for responding so easily to him. He slid his hands up and down until his palms cupped my knees. "I am sorry, for whatever I've done to upset you this time. I seem to have a knack for it." His hands lay still, his earnest gaze locked on mine, and my traitorous body softened even more. "*Gràidh*, what can I do to make it up to you?"

"Stop calling me that."

His forehead crinkled.

"I'm not your *gràidh*. I'm your American fling."

He braced his hands on the bed at either side of my hips, straightening them to raise himself up, his eyes now level with mine. "I know what you are, *mo leannan*." He raked his mouth up my jawline, from my chin to my ear, his lips parted just enough to moisten my skin with the heat of his body. As he forged a trail down my throat, his feather-light kisses punctuated the words he purred against my flesh. "Sweet. Kind. Strong. Stubborn. Clever."

His lips glanced across the slope of one breast and followed it down. My head fell back as I instinctively arched my back, my body buzzing with an electric hunger radiating out from the apex of my thighs. He slipped his tongue under the edge of my bra, drawing a gasp from me.

"Beautiful," he whispered, nuzzling the valley between my breasts. "Sensual. Soft. Irresistible."

"I—" Everything I'd intended to say, angry words borne of hurt and dashed hopes, disintegrated under the onslaught of his mouth and hands.

"The bonniest of all." He dived one hand inside my jeans to cup my behind. I sucked in a breath, my thighs opening of their own volition. He tilted his head back, those arctic-blue eyes on fire. "Are ye ready for me?"

Be strong. Push him away. He was my weakness and he damn well knew it. Only one other man had tried to placate me with sex and Presley had failed. Lachlan would succeed. *Dumb, desperate slut.*

With lazy strokes, his fingers inside my jeans plied my flesh. He rubbed his chin over the mound of my breast. "Find out for myself."

He held me close as he eased me down onto the bedspread. He dispatched my clothing while I lay dazed, overdosed on hormones, then shed his own clothes. I stared at his naked body, my mouth watering at all those hard muscles and softer spots, the ones I'd explored with my hands and tasted, over and over, during these weeks. He was glorious. The epitome of masculine beauty. And the things he could do with those powerful muscles and expert hands...not to mention his expert tongue.

Lachlan knelt at my feet, closing his fingers around my ankles in a light hold, barely grazing my skin. When he skimmed his hands up my calves, I shivered from the exquisite bliss of the contact. So gentle, so deliberate, almost reverent in the painstaking care he took to arouse me in the sweetest way. My breathing turned labored, my breasts bouncing from the heavy rise and fall of my chest. My taut, rosy-red nipples bobbed in front of me and caught Lachlan's eye. Instead of giving me his wicked grin, he gazed at my breasts as if they held the mysteries of the universe.

Then his tongue sneaked out to moisten his lips in a leisurely sweep until his mouth glistened.

I lifted my head, braced on my elbows. "Wha—"

He glided his hands over my knees, up the insides of my thighs. I let out a long, shaky breath, my skin sizzling with excitement. His hands eased my legs apart. I was frozen, my belly quivering, my breasts swollen and so sensitive the faint whisper of my own exhalations sent pleasure zinging down to my core. Lachlan pressed his damp lips to my inner thigh, kissed his way up to the apex, and hesitated there. With his fingertips, he lazily stroked the curly hairs on my mound. He planted a wet kiss on my hip, and a ragged moan emerged from my lips.

I stretched a hand down to comb my fingers through his silky hair.

He turned his face into my palm, flicking his tongue out to taste my skin. He moved his head squarely between my thighs, his mouth a literal breath away from my sex. His eyes locked on mine, and they seemed to glow an incandescent blue in the sunlight. I glimpsed something in them, something different, something like...longing. But then he sealed his mouth over my clit, suckling it, and I was helpless to notice anything except his mouth, hot on my slick flesh. His tongue, velvety and questing. He stimulated me little by little, with slow and intensely sensual laps, as if he wanted nothing more in the world than to bring me pleasure.

My throat tightened. I couldn't take my eyes off him, and that old pang in my chest returned, stronger than ever.

Lifting his head, he crawled up my body—hands skating over my skin, caressing every inch of me, licking and nibbling his way over my belly and breasts—until his face hovered over mine. His hands curved around my breasts, his thumbs drawing circles around my nipples. The whole time, his gaze stayed fixed on me, setting off a deep shiver that quivered in my breaths.

I swallowed hard, but the tightness in my throat refused to lessen. "What are you doing?"

"Worshiping you."

Need pulsed through me as his thumbs flicked over my nipples. "Lachlan—"

"Shh." He slanted his mouth over mine with firm pressure, then softened the kiss, rubbing his lips back and forth, running his tongue along the seam of my lips. I parted them for him, and he murmured into my mouth. "Let me show you."

"Show me?" Barely a whisper.

In the instant his tongue thrust into my mouth, he plunged his shaft inside me, lowering his hard body to cover mine. His head was buried in my hair, his lips danced over my skin, his breaths fanned my hair across my cheek and neck with a tickling sensation that had me writhing and moaning into his mouth. His tongue thrust deep, in time with each stroke of his shaft. Strong hands roved my body with a tender need. He took me slow and sweet, like a man who loved me with all his heart, and when he came with one long, powerful thrust, my climax broke through me with a rapture that overflowed my soul. Wave after wave of ecstasy gripped my body as every muscle inside me fastened around him. Even my body couldn't bear to let him go. Tears blurred my vision and slid down my cheeks. My heart ached for what I could never have, for what he'd shown me but refused to give me.

Love.

Panting, still snug inside me, he swept hair away from my face and touched his lips to mine for an all-too-brief moment. The severing of the contact tore at my heart, pulling more tears from my eyes. He kissed away the drops, his fingers stroking my cheeks. "Why are you crying, love?"

More tears rolled down my cheeks. *Love*. He shouldn't call me that, not when he planned to leave me in a few days. I rubbed away the tears, drew in a deep breath, and cleared my throat. "It's nothing."

Jaw set, he stared at me.

I feigned a laugh, which came out sounding totally phony. "Guess you're such a great lover, I cry from the pure ecstasy of it."

A frown tensed his whole face. "You aren't going to tell me, are you?"

"No."

He rolled off me, flopping onto his back. "You can't keep crying and not tell me why."

"You don't want to know."

"Stop saying that." He jumped off the bed and swept me up into his arms, kicked the covers aside with his foot, and plopped me back onto the mattress. I squeaked as my ass bounced. Lachlan leaped over my body to lie down alongside me. Tugging the covers over us both, he pulled me against him, our chests smashed together, my breasts mounded against him. "I'll be holding you until you tell me the truth."

"Oh darn."

His lips twitched in a near smile. "If we're not talking, then go to sleep, woman."

"Woman?" I tried to kick him but couldn't get leverage. "I'm not your chattel."

"I know. I have no claim on you."

"Do you want to? Have a claim, I mean." The second I asked the question, I wished I could take it back.

"Go to sleep," he said.

Okay. There was my answer.

I rolled over, turning my back to him to get some space, but he pulled me into him again. We snuggled under the sheets, spooning with his hand over my womb, while the heat of him permeated my entire body. Cocooned in his embrace, I couldn't fight my exhaustion anymore and my lids sank shut. When his body slackened against me, I knew he was falling asleep.

Voice groggy, he mumbled, "Stay with you forever."

I laid my palm over his hand where it still rested across my womb.

Sleep never came.

Chapter Twenty-Five

*I*n the last glimmer of daylight, our convertible rolled down the street toward our adjacent houses. In a matter of minutes, we'd be home—and in a matter of days, Lachlan would fly out of my life forever. I blinked back tears, though their burn lingered. We'd spent two more blissful days at the bed-and-breakfast. I concluded Lachlan had no memory of the vow he'd made while drifting off to sleep, so I opted not to mention it. I hadn't brought up his freak-out attack again either, instead choosing to savor my time with him. And yet my soul ached every time he kissed me.

Lachlan navigated the car into the driveway of Gil's house. I'd forced myself to begin thinking of it as Gil's house again in a vain effort to prepare my heart for Lachlan's departure. Who was the eejit now?

A few minutes later, we walked across the lawn to the concrete path that connected my driveway to my front steps. Lachlan laced his fingers with mine as we approached the stoop.

We both stopped. His fingers clinched mine.

My front door hung ajar. The interior was dark, silent.

A chill crashed over me, bearing down on my chest like a massive weight. Everything seemed to screech to a halt, and even my heart thumped slower as if burdened by the pressure in my chest. I could do nothing except stare at the open door. *Someone broke in. They could still be inside.*

Lachlan let go of my hand. In a crouch, he crept toward the doorway.

I tugged his sleeve. When he glanced back, I mouthed, "9-1-1."

He nodded and mouthed, "You call."

Before I could coerce my muscles to move, to grab him and stop him, he pushed the door inward further and sidled through the opening.

My legs refused to budge, caught in phantom cement. I struggled to swallow, my mouth dry as sand. I dug my nails into my palms, desperate for the clarifying pain. I could not lose it. Lachlan was taking a reckless risk for me, and I had to call the police. I ripped open the zipper of my purse to excavate my phone from the depths. Why the hell did I have such a huge purse? Everything got lost in its bottomless depths. My fingers began to shake, and just as I found the phone, it tumbled from my grasp. I bit back a curse. The tremors spread throughout my body. *Suck it up, girl.* I hauled in a fortifying breath and yanked out the phone, moving a finger to press the 9 button.

"Och!"

I froze. That agonized cry had come from Lachlan. Had the intruder hurt him? The phone tumbled to the ground as I flung my hand up to cover my mouth. No, no, not Lachlan.

Scuffling erupted inside the house. A guttural yell cracked the air.

I cursed under my breath. I would not stand here like a stupid damsel in distress while the man I loved battled who-knew-what. I charged through the front door. My purse slid off my shoulder to splat on the concrete stoop. Nothing could've stopped me in that moment. Lachlan shouted again, followed by more thumps and grunts. I raced down the entryway, veering toward the living room, where the sounds had originated. Visions of Lachlan bloody and crumpled on the floor exploded in my mind, but I shoved aside the panic. Shouts meant he was alive. Noises of a struggle meant he could still move. I burst through the doorway into the living room and stumbled to a stop.

Lachlan had Presley in a choke hold. Presley thrashed but couldn't break free. Lachlan fisted his hand in Presley's hair, keeping his free arm collared around the other man's neck. With a growl, Lachlan yanked Presley's head back and glared into his bulging eyes. "What the hell are ye doing in mah woman's house?"

His woman. My hand flew to my chest, over my heart. Had he really called me his woman? Sure, that's what I needed to focus on right now, not the fact my current lover was choking my former lover.

"Tell me!" Lachlan roared, ringing my eardrums. Presley gagged.

I pointed at Lachlan's arm around Presley's neck. "I don't think he can speak."

Lachlan's eyebrows drew together, then realization relaxed his features. He released the choke hold, but in the same instant, he used his hands to cuff Presley's behind his back. Pinned to Lachlan's taller, brawnier body, Presley spat blood. The skin along his jaw and around his left eye had begun to purple. Ohhh, Lachlan got in a good shot. A similar bruise was darkening Lachlan's jaw.

Presley glowered at me, probably because he couldn't turn around enough to aim his hatred at Lachlan. "Scotch Tape attacked me for no reason. Your pit bull's out of control, babe."

I anchored my hands on my hips, despite the faint trembling in my limbs. "Answer Lachlan's question, or I'll cut the leash and let my pit bull tear your throat out."

Lachlan's lips hitched up at the corners. His gaze leveled on me, and an altogether different shiver raced through me. He yanked Presley's hands, making the twerp bellow. "Once more, ye filthy bawbag. What are ye doing in mah woman's house?"

A warm exhilaration chased out the last of my shakes. Every time he called me his woman, I forgot what was happening around me.

"Door was open when I got here," Presley said. He struggled against Lachlan's hold, then sagged his shoulders, brows pulled down by his deep scowl. "I came in to check on Erica."

"Gimme a break," I said. "First, you try to force me to let you inside. Then, we catch you spying through my bedroom window. And to cap things off, you've broken into my house."

"Did not."

"Stop lying. I don't swallow your crap anymore." I stalked up to him. "I know you broke in."

He jutted his chin up, nose high in the air. "Prove it."

What pissed me off the most was that he was right. I couldn't prove it. If I called the cops, his family would call in a team of lawyers as twisted and scummy as Presley. They'd make me out to be the villain. After all, I was an embezzler who stole from the elderly.

Lachlan aimed a questioning look at me. "Did ye call the police?"

I rubbed my arm, shoulders hunched. "No."

Presley sniggered. "She knows."

Lachlan wrenched Presley's hands so hard the worm whimpered, his face contorted in pain. "What do ye mean she knows?"

I sidled closer to Lachlan and laid a hand on his bicep. "Let him go."

"What?" Lachlan shook his head and huffed out sharp little breaths. "Ye cannae mean it. This bastard is tormenting ye."

"Yeah, I know, but you have to let him go." The words left a sour taste in my mouth. I squeezed his arm. "Please, Lachlan. I'll explain everything later."

He stared at me for a long moment, his expression hardening. I kept my hand on his arm and my gaze locked on his, willing him to trust me. He shoved Presley away. The golden boy of the Cichon dynasty sprinted out of the house.

Lachlan pulled me into his arms. Tears welled in my eyes, but I summoned all my self-control to banish them. The back of my throat hurt. I expected to see blood pouring out of a hole in my chest where my heart should've been. His hands warmed my face, his thumbs tracing circles on my cheekbones. "Why, lass? What hold does he have on you?"

"There's a lot to explain." Spots on my cream-colored sofa snagged my attention. Blood stains. I scratched my arm, besieged by a sudden itch deep under my skin. "Would you mind if we continued this conversation in the bedroom?"

Lachlan ushered me down the hallway, shutting the front door along the way. The time had come to divulge everything to him.

Chapter Twenty-Six

Lachlan slouched on the bed, his back to the headboard, his long legs stretched out before him. I huddled beside him, inches away, though it felt like a vast and fathomless canyon separated us. My feet tucked under me, I sat angled toward him. My fingers moved of their own volition, tapping and rubbing against each other. I shoved them under my legs. I leaned one shoulder against the headboard.

Lachlan settled a hand on my knee. "You owe me no explanations."

"Yes I do." The impulse to push his hand away surged inside me, but I fought it back. His touch both comforted and unsettled me and I couldn't reconcile the warring emotions that boiled inside me. If he'd opened his arms to me, I would've climbed onto his lap and drowned myself in his kiss one more time. *Stay strong. He deserves to know the truth.*

"Lachlan—" My throat seized up and cut off my words. Why was this so hard?

He squeezed my knee. In the depths of his luminous eyes, I glimpsed an understanding I'd never witnessed before, from anyone. The words flowed out of me.

"I'm in trouble. It's bad, and I don't see any way out of it." I shifted my weight and then realized I'd unconsciously edged closer to him. He ran his hand up to my thigh, and the sight of it snared my focus, robbing me of words for a long moment before the trance evaporated. "I trusted the wrong man. He was one of those hot guys who turn into hot messes. He charmed me, and I fell for it hook, line, and sinker—except this hook ripped me apart from the inside out."

Lachlan clasped my hands. His gaze never wavered from me.

"I was involved with Presley Cichon. He seduced me, and I believed every honeyed word he fed me." I shook my head. "I should've known he was using me. Chicago's most eligible bachelor wouldn't date an accounting nerd."

"Nerd?" he spat, then pressed his lips to the back of my hand. "I told you never to call yourself that again. You are a stunning, sensual woman. The kind any man would be fortunate to take as a wife."

My heart stuttered. He'd said—*Forget it.* "Anyway, Presley comes from a rich family. Old money, the kind that buys anything and anyone, and I guess I let myself be seduced by the luxury of wealth too. I slept with him, gave him all my trust, let myself be happy with this amazing guy. Only he wasn't amazing." My shoulders crumpled. I listed forward and caught my forehead in my palm. My throat had thickened, agitating my words. "He was a goddamn fucking liar."

Stock-still, radiating tension, Lachlan cinched his mouth into a line. He said carefully, "What did he do to you?"

"I worked for his family's accounting firm, one of many businesses they own. His mother put him in charge of the firm after he got his MBA because she thought the job would force him to grow up. That's where I met him." I brought the other hand up to bolster my head with both hands, overcome by the sudden sensation of heaviness, as if my head had morphed into a bowling ball. "I should've known better than to date my boss."

"You did nothing wrong."

"That's not what everyone else thinks." I wrested my hands free of his and gripped my upper arms. He settled a hand on my thigh, a comforting gesture I needed badly. "Presley embezzled a quarter of a million dollars from a dozen of the firm's clients, all of them senior citizens. He framed me for the crime. The day after I was arrested, when I got out on bond, Presley tracked me down and bragged about how he set me up. It was my word against his and the Cichon family is connected everywhere. I'm screwed." I hugged myself hard to ward off a soul-deep chill, but to no avail. "And it's my own fault."

Lachlan ground his teeth. His hand on my thigh curled into a fist.

"Presley kept asking to use my computer, said his was glitching, and I...I am such an idiot. I gave him the password for my work computer." Tears scorched my eyes, the hot liquid seeping through my lids. I sniffled and swiped at my eyes with the back of my hand. "About a month ago, someone gave the police an anonymous tip that I was embezzling funds from the firm. Since Presley used my computer, it looked like I was guilty. I told the DA my suspicions about Presley, but there was no evidence. All of it pointed to me. When the shit hit the fan, Presley came out smelling like fresh linen and I stank of guilt." I sniffled, gulping down the bile that kept surging up into my throat. "I was fired. They're pursuing criminal charges. I found a lawyer to take me on pro bono, but she doesn't have the resources to investigate Presley. Odds are, I'll go to prison—unless I take a plea deal, which I will not do because it means admitting I'm guilty. So, it's off to the big house for me."

Lachlan dragged me onto his lap, enfolding me in his brawny arms. He cradled me against his chest, my legs tucked under me. The tears spilled out. I buried my face in his neck and clung to him as if he were the last thread holding me together. He stroked my hair, murmuring words I couldn't understand because my brain had shut down. I knew nothing except the strength of this man's body and the scent of his aftershave, the salty taste of my tears, and the beating of his pulse in his neck, throbbing under my lips.

"You're staying with me tonight, not here," he said, his tone decisive. "Then I'm hiring you the best bloody solicitor in the world."

I popped my head up, gazing at him through a blur of tears. "Solicitor?"

"A lawyer. To defend you."

Sniffling, I shook my head. "I like Doretta. I'm not firing her. And besides, I can't let you do that, I didn't tell you about this so you'd give me money. Considering you attacked Presley to protect me—three times—I needed to tell you the truth. But this is my mess, not yours."

"Wrong." He swaddled me in his arms, slanting his head to mine, our noses touching. "This is Presley Cichon's mess. And he will pay for what he's done. I'll make damn sure of it."

I rubbed out the tears and pushed off his lap. "You're leaving in four days."

"No." He swung his legs off the bed, his back to me, and snatched his phone off the table. "I won't leave until you're settled."

But he would still leave. What had I thought would happen? He'd profess his love and vow never to leave me? He said things like that only when he was half asleep and wouldn't remember it later.

While Lachlan made his call, I retreated into the bathroom. His voice rumbled through the door, his words inaudible but his determination clear. He was taking care of me. Fixing my mess. Why? I sagged against the door and slid to the floor, my butt striking the vinyl flooring, my palms flat on the cold surface. He needed to fix me so he could go home with a clear conscience, knowing he hadn't left me in the lurch. But he would abandon me. In four days or four months, it made no difference. A chunk of me would go with him, tearing out a bloody wound nothing could heal.

Head in my hands, I succumbed to sobs.

Presley destroyed my life. Why shouldn't Lachlan have the honor of shredding my heart and soul?

Ten minutes later, I slunk out of the bathroom, after splashing cold water on my face until my eyes were no longer red and puffy. The splashing had smeared my makeup, so I took another few minutes to repair the damage. Lachlan had witnessed enough of my weakness. From here on out, I would be stronger.

Lachlan wasn't in the bedroom. I wandered down the hallway into the living room. Not there either. I scanned the vicinity and spotted him in the kitchen, perched on a stool at the island with my laptop in front of him. His attention was riveted to the screen, his eyes darting side to side, his expression stern and focused. The bruise on his jaw had grown a lump. I crossed into the kitchen and nabbed a bag of frozen peas from the freezer. Lachlan glanced at me only when I pressed the peas to his jaw.

He placed his hand over the bag as his focus swerved back to the computer. "Thank you."

I climbed onto the stool across from him. "What are you doing with my computer?"

"Not framing you for a crime, that's for certain."

The disgust in his voice summoned a memory of his muscles rippling when he clamped his arms around Presley's neck. Then there was the time he hoisted Presley off his feet. I sat up straighter, folding my arms on the island.

Lachlan arched an eyebrow. "What are you smiling for?"

Was I smiling? Well yes, I was. Thoughts of Lachlan pummeling Presley made me smile. Go figure. I broadened my smile into a grin. "I was remembering all the times you beat on Presley."

"And that makes you happy?"

"Mm-hm." I rotated my hips to swivel my stool back and forth. "Nobody's ever tackled anyone for me before. A chivalrous, attack-ready man like you must be very popular with the lasses in Scotland. No matter what we might say, women all fantasize about men who'll skelp scunners for us."

Lachlan rubbed his neck, averting his eyes. "I don't make a habit of it."

"Still, you must have to beat the ladies off with a caber."

He grimaced, then spun my laptop so the screen faced me. "I know what the bawbag was doing here."

I squinted at the screen. The web browser was open, displaying a travel booking website. "I don't get it."

"Look." He pointed at the middle of the screen. "Either you were planning a trip to Switzerland and paused in the midst of making the reservations to go on a road trip with me, or that filthy snake was making your travel arrangements for you."

By "filthy snake" I assumed he meant Presley. I couldn't recall Lachlan ever using my ex-lover's name, since he clearly preferred other epithets. I leaned forward to study the computer screen. It showed that not only had I opened an account on the travel website, but I'd started the process of booking a flight to Switzerland for tomorrow afternoon. "What's the point of this? I doubt he was surprising me with a free trip to Geneva."

"I found something else too." He held up a flash drive no bigger than his thumbnail. "I interrupted him before he could get this back. It was still plugged into your computer. The files on here would've made it look like you had a Swiss bank account with a quarter million dollars in it. I checked, but he didn't get a chance to transfer the files to your computer."

"That sneaky, conniving little scumbag." I stomped my foot on the stool rung. "Gah! No wonder he was so intent on getting into my house. He's not done framing me." I gripped the edge of the island. "I bet he was planning another anonymous tip to the police. Hey guys, she's about to bolt for a neutral country." I kicked the island. Pain shot through my foot. "My bail would be revoked. I'd have no chance of finding any evidence to implicate him."

"That will not happen." Lachlan stretched his arms across the island to cover my hands with his. "You have my word."

"Lachlan, I can't let you—"

"Aye, you can and you will." He pushed his shoulders back, his gaze pinned on me. "This is not charity. I help my friends when they're in need."

"Thought I was your fling."

He sandwiched my hands between his, overpowering my chill with his heat. "You are my *gràidh*, Erica. And I will help you whether you like it or not."

His authoritative tone brooked no argument and sent a charge through me. Whether I liked it or not? In that case..."Okay. I accept your money and your investigators and whatever you give me. I do want to keep Doretta as my lawyer, though."

"Fine."

"Thank you, Lachlan."

He strode around the island to pull me into his arms. Nestled against his chest, I felt my lips curving into a new smile as he combed his fingers through my hair. "Anything for you, *mo leannan*."

I shut my eyes, my arms padlocked around him, entranced by his firm body against mine and the way he'd murmured his Gaelic endearment. "Don't leave me, Lachlan. I love you."

Chapter Twenty-Seven

His fingers in my hair stilled. His breaths ceased, though his heartbeat pounded beneath my ear. How could I have been so stupid? I shook my head, hair flapping around my face. "I-I didn't mean to say that. Forget it. I'm still in shock from all the Presley stuff and I—"

"Hush, Erica." His soft words belied his physical tension. Faint lines creased his forehead. "I won't hold you to anything you say tonight."

A frenzy of fear and passion and need whirled inside me. The embarrassment of blurting out my feelings disintegrated as a realization stunned me like a spotlight in the pitch black. I wanted him to hold me to what I'd said. I wanted him to repeat what he'd said while falling asleep the other night. I wanted him with me always. I loved him, and I no longer gave a flying fig about his stupid rules.

Grabbing fistfuls of his shirt, I shook him. "You know what? Forget what I said about forgetting what I said."

"Your bum's oot the windae again."

"No." I raised onto tiptoes to level our gazes. "I love you, Lachlan. I don't want you to go home unless I can go with you. Stay with me, or take me with you."

He stared at me, face blank, for so long I thought he'd died standing upright. His eyes slid closed. His shoulders sagged, seeming to drag his chin down with them. He stumbled backward, arms raised partway as if he needed to steady himself. He'd retreated so abruptly I lost my balance and careened into the island.

Lachlan hoisted his head up, his blue eyes bleak and glassy. He took a tentative step toward me, reaching out, but let his hand fall before he touched me. Both arms hung limp at his sides. "I'm sorry, Erica. I can't stay with you."

I shoved away from the island and rolled my shoulders back, chin lifted. "Yes, you can. If you want to." I rubbed my clammy palms on my jeans. The entire world seemed to stop, awaiting his answer to my next question. "Do you *want* to stay with me?"

He shifted his weight from one foot to the other and back again, almost rocking on his feet, and rubbed the back of his neck. His features crimped, but his eyes still had that bleakness in them. The sight of him so distraught made me want to hug him, which ticked me off. After the way he'd pestered me to tell him the truth, now he refused to grant me the same courtesy. I'd bared my heart and soul to him and he seemed on the verge of bolting.

"Well?" I demanded. "Do you want to be with me? Do you love me?"

Though he ceased moving his body, his gaze swiveled toward me. His voice was rough, unsteady. "I cannae stay."

"Yes. You. Can."

"Aye." He dropped his chin to his chest, locking his hands behind his head. "I owe you no explanations, just as you owed me none."

The room tilted around me. Of course. That had been his preparation for avoiding any questions I asked. *I will not cry.* "Very clever. By telling me I owed you no explanations, you freed yourself from any similar obligations to me. Presley Cichon would approve."

A muscle leaped in his jaw. "I am nothing like him."

"Really." I rested a hand on the island's rim, tapping one finger on the surface. Nausea swelled in my gut and rose into my throat. "Why did you call me your woman? Why tell me I'm more than a fling, I'm your *gràidh*? What the hell was all that about?"

"You are more."

"I'm beginning to understand why your ex-wife thinks you're a bastard."

He flinched. "Donnae talk about things ye cannae understand."

"Then explain it. I just poured my heart out to you and got skelped with a caber for it."

"Forget the bleeding caber and skelping." His eyes wild, he rushed toward me and pinned me between his body and the island. He rooted his hands on the countertop at either side of me. "Listen, because I'll tell you this only once. Aisley, my wife, was a posh lass from the day I met her. Not wealthy, but elegant. Her hair had to be perfect and if the wind touched it, she had to fix it. She pursued me, a flattering event for any man. But after we were married, she stopped flattering me."

I had to crane my neck to meet his gaze—and then wished I hadn't. Never in my life had I witnessed such despair and anguish.

He bent his head near my ear. "On our first anniversary, she told me I was a bore, and I wasn't delivering the excitement she needed. I'd suspected she was unhappy for some time, but whenever I tried to talk to her about it, she laughed it off as nothing." He braced his forehead on my shoulder for the space of two slow breaths, then raised his head, leveling his gaze on mine. "That's when it started. The little jibes, the constant complaints, the endless demands for more, no matter how much I gave her. A man can only take so much. I..." He turned his head away. "Before Aisley, I was what Americans might call a macho man. I won the caber toss often. I'm not saying this to impress you, but to help you understand. Aisley turned me into a weakling. I began to believe her complaints about me and I tried to be what she wanted, but I never could please her. The last strong act I managed was moving us to Inverness. She hated the Highlands, so things only got worse after that."

Now I understood why he'd told me he despised bullies who bend others to their will just for the sake of control. I yearned to touch him, but it felt wrong somehow. He was confiding in me at last and I would do nothing to break this moment. But I would've given both my kidneys for a chance to skelp the tar out of his wife.

He leaned into the island, head down, his lips achingly close to mine. "One day, Aisley announced she'd had enough and was leaving. I asked why. She told me I was a right bastard because I'd failed to give her the excitement she needed, in bed and in life in general. She wanted to travel to exotic places, make love in public, drink and smoke and experiment with shamans' drugs." He gave a harsh laugh. "I'd no clue she craved such things. For pity's sake, I thought we had a good life together. And now she tells me she wants a hedonistic life of traipsing around the world. We didn't have the money for that, not yet, and besides—" He shut his eyes and shook his head, then tipped his head forward. "I like my simple life in the Highlands."

My heart swelled, aching for him, for what he'd endured. A simple life. Children. Turkey sandwiches with Havarti cheese. Chocolate chip pancakes. He cherished all the same things I did, shared my taste in food, and I fit so nicely on his lap and in his arms.

No. I could not afford to entertain the thought.

"Aisley changed her mind about leaving when she realized my financial consulting business was becoming successful. She seduced me into taking her back for another three years." His nose bumped mine. "It was hell. I will never go down that road again."

"Oh Lachlan." I looped my arms around his neck, caressing his skin with my fingertips. "I'm so sorry for what you went through."

His breaths grew heavier, blowing over my skin. Awareness of him shimmered through me, liquid and delicious. His left hand sneaked onto my back to pull me closer to him. "Erica, don't ye see." His lips grazed mine. "I cannae be with ye in the way ye want. I told ye no relationships."

"I don't—"

He crushed his mouth to mine in a bruising kiss. His tongue lashed against mine, demanding a response that my body gave without reservation. *He's going to say it.* My head swam. He deepened the kiss with a fervor I'd never known from him before, a desperation so intense he ravaged me with it. When he pulled away, I couldn't breathe. "Ye know the rules, Erica."

Something inside me snapped. The force of it propelled me to shove him away. "The rules? Are you kidding me? Screw your rules, just tell me what you feel."

"I told you."

The sadness and certainty in his eyes triggered a slow, cold understanding in me. "You think I'm like her. Your bitch ex-wife."

"She's not my ex-wife. We're still married."

I went numb, slack-jawed. "You said you were divorced."

"You assumed I was. I never said it."

"But…you let me go on believing it. It's the same as lying."

"No, Erica. It was the rules. Nothing personal, remember? You agreed to it."

I clapped my gaping mouth shut. Who was this man standing before me? I didn't recognize him at all. "I'm surprised you didn't make me sign a contract. A formal tryst agreement. Then again, you would've included all your loopholes in that too. You're a liar."

"I didn't lie." He took a shuffling step toward me. I raised a warning hand, and he halted. "I thought we were divorced but there was a clerical error. Aisley's taking advantage of it to renegotiate our divorce settlement. She wants everything."

To fund her worldwide slut tour, no doubt. "If she's taking you to the cleaners, how did you plan on paying for top-notch investigators to clear my name?"

"I said Aisley wanted everything. She's not getting it."

"Congratulations. You screwed over another woman." I moved toward the doorway, but he latched onto my arm. I did not glance at him. "If you think I'm like her, why are you helping me?"

"You are nothing like her. I know it."

I couldn't keep the pain out of my voice. "You talked me into a fling. You said all those sweet things to me. And the first night at the bed-and-breakfast, you made love to me." I cast him a sidelong look. "It wasn't just hot sex. You made *love* to me."

His fingers tightened on my arm ever so slightly.

I searched his face for some sign he wanted to work this out between us. All I found was fear. "You led me on, Lachlan. You used my body and broke my heart."

He let go of my arm to brush the backs of his fingers over my cheek. "These weeks with you were the best of my life. But you're better off without me." His hand dropped to his side. "I've nothing left to give, except money."

"You are a bastard."

"Aye."

Lachlan brushed past me, walking out of the kitchen. Seconds later, I heard the front door shut. I didn't cry. What was the point? His wife screwed him up so bad he couldn't shake off her influence. No other woman had a chance in hell with Lachlan.

I retrieved Casey from Mrs. Abernathy's house and curled up in bed with the one male who never let me down.

Chapter Twenty-Eight

Two days. They elapsed second by second, each tick of the clock piercing me like a nail driven straight into my heart. Every time the phone rang or a car drove by, my idiotic heart sped up with the futile hope it was Lachlan. By the second morning after his departure, I'd given up. I was slouched in a chair at the kitchen table, staring out the bay window at the house next door without really seeing anything, when the doorbell chimed.

Casey woofed.

I jumped up so fast my chair toppled over backward. Tripping over the legs, I bolted out of the kitchen and down the hallway. Excitement rushed through me on a dizzying wave. My heart pounded harder than my physical exertion warranted. I flung the door open, breathing too hard to speak. My entire body wilted.

Not Lachlan.

My parents stood on the stoop, suitcases at their feet, smiles beaming at me. Their smiles faltered when their gazes landed on my face.

"Oh honey." My mom grasped my upper arms and hauled me in for a hug. "It's not that bad, is it?"

"Course it is," Dad said, his familiar gruff voice breaking the dam. My tears flowed then, uncontrolled, and sobs shook me from head to toe. Dad coughed. "Maybe we should get her inside, Deb."

My mother tsked. "When she's ready, Frank."

I extricated myself from Mom's hug and swiped at my tear-stained face. Sniffling, I assured them, "I'm okay."

She shook her head, her expression full of motherly knowing and compassion. "We got here just in time."

"In time for what?" That's when it hit me. I blinked slowly at the pair of them. "Why aren't you in Florida?"

"Lachlan called."

My chest throbbed at the mere mention of him. What the hell was he doing calling my parents? A chill raised goosebumps on my arms. With exquisite care, because the words pained me with near-physical effect, I asked, "What did he tell you?"

"Not much," Dad said, shrugging. "Just that you're in some kinda trouble."

Mom dug a tissue out of her cavernous purse and stuffed it in my hand. "Lachlan said he wished he could be here to see you through your troubles, but you two had a falling out and he was sure you wouldn't want him around right now. We should come, that's what he said."

"But—he—" *I can't stay with you.* Didn't matter what I wanted, he'd made the decision for me. I blew my nose, backing into the house to let my parents come inside. Casey attacked them with paws on their stomachs and tongue lashing out at any exposed skin. His tail wagged fast enough to power a tornado. Two years had gone by since my parents moved to Florida, more than a year elapsed since their last visit, and in the meantime, everything rocketed down into hell on a high-speed train. I wiped at my eyes as the tears slowed to a trickle and pushed the door shut. "I'm not with Lachlan anymore. Why would he call you?"

"He's got it bad," my father pronounced.

I couldn't help the faint smile that tugged at my lips. My dad using modern slang always made me laugh. Well, not always. I didn't laugh now, and my weak smile faded within seconds. "I think you're mistaken, Dad."

"Nope." He shoved his thumbs under his waistband and rocked back on his heels. "That boy's got it bad for our little girl."

Mom nodded. "He sure does. Lachlan wouldn't hang up the phone until we agreed to come back to Chicago. He even paid for our plane tickets."

"He—what?" The man who'd abandoned me paid for my parents to come home and take care of me. He made love to me then kicked me to the curb. He called me *gràidh* but implied I was like his wife. The contradictions piled up higher and higher until I couldn't see the sky. On top of everything else I didn't understand about him, I still had no clue what *mo leannan* meant, which somehow hurt worse than anything else. He called me something in Gaelic but wouldn't tell me what it meant. It was either an insult or...

Mom hooked an arm around my shoulders, tugging me close. "Now, sweetie, I think it's time you tell us what in heaven's name is going on around here."

I leaned into her, grateful for the support since I had the disconcerting sensation of plummeting through the floor. My chin quivered when I said, "Can we sit down first? This is gonna take awhile."

The trouble with retired people is they have no jobs to call them back to where they belong, so they can stick around to pester you forever. Okay, that's not fair. The elder Teagues hung around mostly because of my legal problems. But sheesh, they kept staring at me like I'd dyed my hair purple and gotten six piercings in each ear, with a nice big tattoo on my forehead for good measure. Maybe I just looked that messed up.

A few days after they arrived via Lachlan Airways, the doorbell rang. Mom and Dad had insisted on going to the grocery store without me—ordering me to "take it easy," though the very idea made me itch all over—and I was sprawled on the sofa flipping channels on the TV, punching buttons on the remote so fast I glimpsed nothing more than flashes of each show. When the doorbell sounded, I sprang upright. My pulse slammed into overdrive. That stupid little voice in the back of my mind asked, *Is it him?*

Casey barked, but not with the unabashed enthusiasm he reserved for people he loved—like a certain foreign national. Despite knowing it wasn't *him*, I hurried to the door and swung it open, breathless with anticipation.

A FedEx delivery man aimed a polite smile at me, proffering a digital thingy for signing for packages, along with a blue-and-white, letter-size envelope emblazoned with the FedEx logo. "Erica Teague?"

I nodded.

The delivery man pushed the envelope and digital tablet a few inches closer to me. "Gotta sign for this."

After scribbling my signature, I took the envelope. The FedEx guy trotted back to his truck, parked at the curb. I eased the door shut, holding the envelope with my thumb and forefinger as if it might latch onto me and suck the life from my body. Anticipation had mutated into a stomach-churning mix of anxiety and curiosity. I stared at the address label, at my name in big letters and, above that in smaller lettering, a name in the return address that made my chest tighten.

Lachlan MacTaggart.

I dangled the envelope by my thumb and forefinger, letting it swing back and forth like the pendulum on a grandfather clock. Tick-tock, tick-tock.

"Oh get a grip," I chastised myself, groaning with exasperation. Jeez, I could be such a coward sometimes. I ripped open the envelope and snagged the single sheet of paper inside it. The floor seemed to drop out from under me. The empty envelope slipped from my fingers and rustled as it hit the floor. The sheet of paper contained two words, written in a familiar hand: *I'm sorry.*

My jaw clenched and trembling, I squinted at the letters scrawled on the off-white paper, which looked and felt expensive. After a week, all he could manage was two frigging words? He hadn't even bothered to sign the note. Three syllables, that was all I rated.

Casey whimpered, pawing at the empty envelope on the floor. He snuffled, his nose pressed to the torn edge of the envelope.

"What is it?" I bent beside him to pluck up the envelope and spread it open with two fingers. There, at the bottom, lay a crushed sprig adorned with small, bell-shaped purple flowers. I picked it up, holding it gingerly at eye level. The blossoms were squished flat, but still recognizable as bell heather—*Erica cinerea.*

I sank back on my heels, clasping the sprig to my breast, and closed my eyes as I inhaled a shaky breath. He sent me my flower. *Ye are a bonnie wee flower in yer own right,* he'd told me, right before he made love to me, awakening uninhibited passions I never knew I possessed.

Casey slathered my cheek with his slimy tongue. I scratched his head and, brushing tears from my eyes, pushed up onto my feet to head for the bedroom. The stuffed dinosaur Lachlan had given me sat on the dresser. I tucked the heather sprig between its stubby little arms. The letter I slipped into a drawer, on top of a pile of bras and panties. It seemed appropriate somehow to have Lachlan inside my underwear drawer, since he'd always enjoyed stripping my undergarments off me.

After that morning, the days blurred into each other. Meetings with investigators and forensic accountants, all hired by Lachlan and overseen by Doretta Harper. At my final hearing about Doretta's motion to dismiss the charges, she gave a command performance worthy of Perry Mason, laying out all the evidence Lachlan's team had uncovered, all of which proved Presley had set me up. After the judge had announced his decision to dismiss all the charges against me, I'd stood motionless, unable to breathe or think, just gaping at the Illinois state seal on the front of the judge's dais. All charges dismissed. No more felon Erica. A sense of unreality swirled around me as if I'd tripped into a rabbit hole and, like Alice, stumbled into a strange fantasy land.

Doretta had grabbed my shoulders to turn me toward her and give me a quick shake. "Snap out of it, girl. It's over. You're free."

She dragged me into a bear hug and we both burst out laughing. Tears streamed down my cheeks—tears of joy this time—while I grinned at

Doretta. She grinned right back. My life was mine again.

Movement at the back of the courtroom drew my attention. I caught sight of a figure exiting the courtroom. Tall. Broad shoulders. Short, dark hair. My heart jumped into my throat, my stomach fluttered.

Doretta hauled me in for another hug. When I glanced at the doorway again, the figure was gone. I must've imagined it. I wished Lachlan were here, to share in the victory he'd facilitated, so I hallucinated seeing him. Man, I had to get a grip.

A few hours later, after a boisterous party at a nice—but not super-expensive—restaurant, I arrived home to find a glass vase seated on my front stoop, inches from the door. Pink roses nestled among a splash of bell heather that overflowed the vase, and though no note had been attached, I knew who'd sent them. No one but Lachlan gifted me with heather.

The next day, the FedEx guy returned with a box from Scotland. It held a bottle of Talisker single-malt Scotch whisky and a brief note. It read simply, "To celebrate your freedom. Congratulations, *gràidh*."

I set the bottle on the dresser, next to the dinosaur and her armful of wilting heather. The bottle remained unopened.

Weeks drifted by, and Lachlan took to calling my parents to ask how I was. My parents, of course, told me every time he called. He must've known they would. Meanwhile I, apparently, became a bit obsessed with talking about a certain Scotsman. I learned this one morning at break-fast with my parents. Dad was reading the sports pages while munching on Fruit Loops—yeah, a senior citizen really eats those—and Mom had paused in eating her oatmeal to ask me if I wanted to go to the beach that afternoon.

Of course, the beach made me think of...stuff. I poked at the bowl of Cheerios in front of me, my appetite dwindling. "Maybe. I don't know. Kinda tired today."

"Fresh air'll do ya good," Dad said, without looking up from the sports pages.

I swirled the little O's in my milk with my spoon. That's when it hap-pened. I blurted out, "Does Lachlan always call at the same time every day?"

Dad slapped his newspaper on the table, dug his money clip out of his hip pocket, plucked out a five-dollar bill, and handed it to Mom. Smirk-ing, she accepted the money. Dad sighed. "I should know better than to second-guess you, Deb."

I glanced from one parent to the other, flummoxed. "What's going on?"

Dad stuffed the money clip back in his pocket. "We had a little bet go-ing. Your mother said you couldn't make it five minutes after sitting down to breakfast before you started talking about Lachlan. I told her it'd be ten, at least." He glanced at his watch, then shook his head, eying me with a rueful smile. "Four minutes."

Head bowed, I rubbed a hand over my cheek, which was hot from the blush rising under my skin. "Am I that bad?"

"No, honey," Mom said, though amusement sparkled in her eyes. She leaned toward me across the table and whispered in a conspiratorial tone. "Why don't you call him?"

"Yeah," Dad chimed in, "we're getting sick of hearing you moon over him."

"I don't—it's not—" *Aw hell.* I gave up arguing the point, but I couldn't bring myself to dial his number. More days blurred by until one Monday morning I got a call from a big accounting firm, one of the top competitors of Cichon, D'Addio & Rothenberg. They offered me a job interview. The next day, I had the best interview of my life—no hard questions, lots of compliments from the bosses, and a job offer at the end. A knot coiled tight in my stomach when someone mentioned in passing that "Mr. MacTaggart was right about her, she is smart as a whip."

Mr. MacTaggart. I'd gotten a job because of Lachlan. I could've lived with that, but after considering the offer for a day, I realized I didn't want to be an accountant anymore. Like I'd told Lachlan, accounting had been the safe career choice and not something I loved to do. I still needed a job, but after everything I'd endured these past months, the idea of going back to accounting made a cold ball congeal in my gut. My parents told me I should take my time deciding what to do with my life now. Since I had no clue what I wanted, in any facet of my life, I took their advice.

Week eight post-Lachlan, I got another unexpected call, this time from Presley's lawyer. I almost hung up when the gentleman introduced himself that way, but a morbid curiosity kept me on the line.

"He wants to see you," the man told me matter-of-factly.

"Excuse me?"

"Presley. He's been asking for you." He hesitated, the line silent for a long second. "I'm just relaying the message. Go or don't, the decision's yours."

I spiraled a lock of my hair around one finger, pulling it taut until the pressure cut off the circulation. Releasing the hair, I stared at the white lines it had left in my skin. Though impressions on my finger would fade away, Presley would never disappear from the world. Maybe I should face that demon one last time, but nausea rocked my stomach at the thought of it. "I'll think about it."

"He's out on bond, back at home."

I thanked him and hung up.

The next day, after tossing and turning all night while stewing about the situation, I drove to Presley's apartment. Last time, he'd been all smirks and half-naked assumptions. This time, he answered the door wearing faded blue jeans and a black T-shirt, his socked feet shooshing on the wood flooring. Shoulders slumped, dark smudges under his eyes, he gave me a weary half smile and ushered me into the living room. I sat on the ultra-modern sofa, while he collapsed into the metal-and-leather chair across the glass coffee table from me. I set my purse on my lap and folded my hands atop it, fingers tapping.

"Thanks for coming," he said, as he rested his head on the chair's back. "Wasn't sure you would."

"I almost didn't." Biting the inside of my cheek, I studied him for several seconds. Gone was the arrogance. His head drooped forward, and he avoided my gaze. I drew in a deep breath. "What do you want, Presley?"

"To tell you—" He squirmed, clearing his throat, then raised his head to look at me with red-rimmed eyes. "I'm sorry."

Shock iced through me. My mouth fell open, but I clamped it shut. I had no clue how to respond because he sounded and looked…sincere. But I still had questions. "Why did you embezzle from your family's own company? You're not exactly wanting for cash."

"I don't know." He scratched his neck, screwing up his face. "My trust fund gave me a monthly stipend, but I…wanted more. It seemed so easy to just take the money and make it look like somebody else did it. I didn't think anyone would really catch on."

"So, what, you framed me as a backup plan, just in case?"

"Kinda. Somebody did notice, though. Some little nobody, an assistant to an assistant or something. They reported it, and one of the partners called the cops."

Huh. I'd assumed he called the police on me. "So maybe you didn't get me arrested, but you still set me up and never did a blessed thing to clear my name. And what about your scummy little attempt to make it look like I was fleeing to Switzerland?"

"I didn't…That wasn't what you think."

"Oh, you mean you weren't going to call the cops after planting the evidence on my computer."

"No." He cast his gaze down at my feet. "I wasn't."

My jaw dropped open again, and I shook my head. "Then what was the point?"

"I, uh, thought I could break up you and your new boyfriend. If I got him mad enough, maybe you'd get sick of him and dump his ass." Presley shrank back in his chair, his shoulders caving in. "Stupid, I know. But I was—" He swallowed visibly. "Jealous."

Oh. Dear. God. How had I not seen that coming? Because I never believed he really wanted me, convinced I was just a randomly selected pawn. I had no idea what to make of his confession.

Presley sat forward, elbows on his knees, hands dangling. "I betrayed you and I get that you'll never trust me again or want anything to do with me."

"Duh."

He winced, but then nodded. "I deserve that. You hate me for good reason, and the irony is…" He dropped his head, cradling it in both hands and groaning. "The irony is I fell for you, Erica. For real."

I drew back, not blinking or breathing for a moment that felt like eternity. Head down, he gazed up at me through his eyelashes. I fiddled with the metal snaps on my purse and finally said, "You have a funny way of showing it."

He slumped back in the chair, a breath gusting out of him. "Yeah, I'm a dick. Everybody knows it."

"Explain to me why you set me up if you, uh, cared for me." Even speaking the words made my skin crawl. I could not fathom the concept of Presley Cichon—the bane of my existence, the man who ruined my life— harboring feelings for me. I could believe the moon was a ball of cheese easier than I could accept this revelation.

Presley shrugged. "I'd already set things in motion before we started dating. You seemed like the perfect—" His face pinched into a pained expression. "The perfect patsy. I was in too deep to turn back, and by the time I realized I was in love with you, it was too late."

I snorted. "Please. I don't think you know the meaning of the word love."

Nausea roiled in my gut. Acid crept up my throat, scorching it. The acrid taste of bile infiltrated my mouth. I understood the word's meaning all too well, but the knowledge came in vain. The memory of Lachlan's first note flashed in my mind. *I'm sorry*, it had said, and I'd nearly had a meltdown reading it. Now Presley was saying the same words, but I felt nothing. Just an empty resignation. Closure, I supposed. Thing was, I didn't need it anymore.

"Erica, I really am sorry." He rubbed his eyes with his thumb and middle finger. "My parents left me in county lockup for a week before they bailed me out. Then they took away my trust fund, so, uh, I'm broke. At the end of the month, I lose this place and I'll have to move in with my sister and her three screaming brats."

"I feel sorry for the kids."

"Not asking you to feel bad for me."

"Then what do you want?" I scooted forward to stare straight into his eyes. "You ruined my life. I can't forgive you and I'll never forget what you did to me."

"Yeah. I figured." He turned his face toward the windows and his gaze went distant. "I asked my parents to pay you a settlement, to cover your legal expenses and your—" He swallowed visibly. "Pain and suffering."

"Am I supposed to be grateful?"

"No. Just wanted to tell you myself." He swung his gaze back to me and his jaw trembled ever so slightly. The tremors leeched into his voice too. "I'll be going away for a long time, Erica."

He laughed, but it sounded hollow and devoid of mirth. The anger simmering inside me, scalding my chest, cooled a bit. *Ugh.* I refused to feel sorry for him. The son of a bitch had happily consigned me to the future he now faced. Justice had come back around to him at last. Still, he looked the way I'd felt for all those months. Hopeless.

"Well," he said, pushing up out of the chair with a sigh, "I'm sure you wanna get out of here. Thanks for coming."

I trailed him to the door, uncertain of what to say, so I said nothing.

As I walked out the door, Presley spoke. "I hope you and Scotch T—the guy you've been seeing are happy. It's obvious he's totally into you, and you deserve a good life."

Pausing just past the threshold, I glanced back at him over my shoulder. "I hope your attitude reversal is sincere, for your sake. But frankly, it doesn't matter to me anymore."

"Yeah." He rubbed a hand over his cheek, shoulders drooping. "I know."

I walked away without looking back.

Chapter Twenty-Nine

The next morning, my doorbell rang at ten a.m. on the dot. Casey started barking and hopping up and down on his front feet, the way he'd always done when—I halted halfway to the door, my heart racing. This was how Casey had reacted whenever Lachlan showed up. But it couldn't be him.

The dog whimpered, scratching at the door. He gave a little chuff.

I shooed him away, wrapping my hand around the knob. One deep breath. Two. Three. My pulse slowed a bit, yet I couldn't shake the fluttery anticipation in my stomach. *It's not him.* Fingers clenching around the metal knob, I shut my eyes for a heartbeat. Somehow, I knew before I opened the door. I recognized...something beyond explanation.

Plastering on a bland expression, ratcheting my spine straight, I drew the door inward.

Lachlan towered there, shoulders back, his entire body a picture of steel-reinforced tension. Both hands were balled into fists. His wary gaze settled on my face, and he flexed his fingers as if coercing them to relax. "Good morning."

Even his voice rang with tension, like a cast-iron bell tapped with a hammer.

I couldn't move. My mouth went dry. I struggled to maintain my feigned composure, but inside a tornado of pain and desperate hope ravaged me, throwing my stomach into a nauseating lurch. I gulped down my gorge. "What do you want?"

Was that icy voice mine?

His shoulders slumped. He shoved a hand through his hair. "Please, Erica, let me talk to you. Please."

My gut lurched again at the bald pleading in his tone. My hands itched to reach out, take his face in my palms, draw him in for a kiss imbued with all the fear and anguish and longing I'd repressed for two long months. The pain he'd caused. With his rejection. With his harsh words that skewered my soul like arrows to the chest.

I wrenched the doorknob, fingers tight, the knob clicking with each half revolution, back and forth, back and forth. *Click, click, click.* I gnawed the inside of my lip, the tang of blood on my tongue.

Casey pushed between us to leap up on Lachlan.

Still I gnawed. I wrenched. *Click, click.*

Lachlan scratched Casey's ears, the action seeming half-hearted, and murmured something to the dog. Casey scampered back into the house and straight to the sofa where he jumped onto the cushions and planted his chin on the sofa's back, observing us.

My unwanted guest furrowed his brow, reaching out to touch my lip. His thumb came away spotted with red. His eyes widened the slightest bit. "You're bleeding."

"It's nothing."

He ran his thumb over my lip, and that little spot between his eyebrows cinched into a dimple. "Why are you chewing on your lip like this?" Understanding dawned, and his face fell. "It's me."

Frozen, I stared up at him, at the face I'd kissed and held and adored for four weeks. Unwanted? As much as I wished I'd gotten over him, I couldn't lie to myself anymore. I wanted him, even now, after everything he'd done. Despite the hole inside me he'd carved out. Despite my best efforts. But I could not give in to my own weakness. Not this time. "Go away, Lachlan."

His thumb still touched my lip, and heaven help me, a thread of desire unfurled within me, warm and liquid and so beautiful. I ached for this feeling. For him.

"Please, *gràidh*." His voice was rough but tender. He stroked his thumb over my lip once, twice. "Don't hurt yourself because of me."

I couldn't stop the harsh laugh that barked out of me. "Hurt myself? I don't need to. You've done a rather spectacular job of it for me."

My heart clenched at the sound of my own voice, so hard and frosty, not at all a reflection of my confused emotions. Every attempt I made to control my anguish resulted in a colder, sharper edge to my words, and I hated it. I hated him. *Liar.* I squeezed my eyes shut to stave off the tears pooling in my eyes as my lip trembled under his thumb. Maybe I could fool him, but I understood what this was. I didn't hate him. I couldn't hate him, though he'd ripped my heart out and tossed it in the trash compacter. I hated myself, for one simple reason.

I still loved him.

"Don't cry," he whispered, his breath drafting over my face. I cracked my eyes open to find him inches away, his hands cupping my face, those jewel eyes glittering with a pain matching my own. He slid his hands into my hair, his fingers massaging my scalp with irresistible tenderness. "I made a horrible mistake and I've regretted it every day since, more than you could possibly know." His voice cracked, his eyes glistened with…tears? "I know I broke your heart but—"

"Broke my heart?" I sniffled, my voice melting from ice to a puddle of searing agony. "You destroyed me, Lachlan."

His chin dropped to his chest. His dark hair grazed my face. I sucked in a breath, inhaling the spicy, masculine scent of him. My body slanted toward him of its own volition, softening, yearning. He bent closer, his mouth exquisitely close to my ear. "Please give me a few minutes to explain why I treated you so terribly. I need you to understand."

"Your ex-wife's a raging bitch. I get it." Gone was the sharpness. It took all my willpower to iron out the worst of the quavering from my voice.

His blue eyes seared into mine with a hot desperation. "I was afraid, I admit it. What I feel for you is so strong, I can't control it." His hands found my upper arms, his fingers kneaded my flesh gently. "I thought I needed control, to protect myself from being tricked again. But I was wrong. I don't want to be without you anymore, you're everything that's good in my life. I need you, *gràidh*."

"Stop calling me that." I shook free of his hands, stumbling back a step. "It's too late. Go back to Scotland and move on."

"I can't do that." He rolled his shoulders back, straightening, and fixed his clear gaze on me. "I won't pester you, but I'm not leaving town without you. I'll be staying at The Langham. You can reach me there or call my mobile."

"Don't hold your breath." Of course he was staying at a swanky hotel, probably in the presidential suite or whatever they called the most expensive, opulent room in the joint. "The Langham, huh? Guess you're done slumming it out here in the burbs."

A muscle ticked in his jaw. "I would've preferred to stay with Gil and Jayne, my good friends, but I didn't want to crowd you."

"Instead, you're hanging around to stalk me."

"Erica." He scrubbed a hand over his face, sighing. "I told you I won't bother you."

"But you're not leaving town without me." I tried to ignore the excitement that raced through me at the idea of him sticking around in an effort to win me back. *Remember when he walked out on you.* The memory washed over me on a chill, but his proximity and the earnest, determined look on his face made my breath catch. "Go home, Lachlan."

"I am home." He captured a loose lock of my hair between his fingers, tucking it behind my ear. "You are my home. I'll spend the rest of my life making up for what I did, making you happy—if you'll let me."

A pang throbbed in my chest. If he'd spoken those words the last time I saw him, back when it mattered and could've fixed everything...but he hadn't.

He trailed a fingertip down my cheek, the faint contact a delicious tickle on my skin. "I've waited two months, *mo leannan*, the worst months of my entire life. I'm not leaving you again. Not ever."

I couldn't get enough air. My chest heaved with the pressure of an enormous, invisible weight bearing down on it. "It's not enough. I can't—I won't—"

Lachlan fell to his knees, his head tipping forward until his forehead met my belly, right over my womb. Stunned, I gripped the door's edge in one hand and the jamb in the other. The world tilted around me. Lachlan grasped my hips, his face crushed into me. Tears welled anew, my throat burned, my breath hitched.

"Give me one more chance," he said, his voice muffled. "I don't deserve it, but I'm begging you, please. I won't bollocks it up this time. I swear to God, I will be the kind of man you need, the kind you deserve."

What I deserved. Presley mentioned that too, and both men seemed convinced they knew what I wanted, what I needed. I had no frigging idea what I wanted. Tears spilled down my cheeks. My breaths came fast and shallow, almost hyperventilating. I covered my mouth with one hand, desperate to stifle my hiccupping noises. He tilted his head back and our eyes met. Electricity zinged between us, but it wasn't desire this time. Pain crackled around us, inside us, between us, through us. I swallowed a sob.

He rose then, pulled me into his embrace, and buried his face in my hair. I sagged into him for a moment, the comfort and safety I'd experienced with him before returning, sweet and welcome and so badly needed. But memories assailed me, of him telling me again and again that he couldn't do relationships. Of that day in my kitchen when he refused to express his true feelings. When he abandoned me.

I wrestled free of him, swiping tears from my face. "No."

He nodded, shoulders drooping, and rubbed the heel of his hand on his chest. Expression remote, he spoke in a monotone. "If you want me, you know where I am."

Lachlan turned to leave, and I shut the door, unwilling to watch him walk away from me again—even though I'd forced him to this time. I sank to the floor, limp against the door, and unleashed the tears. They sluiced out of me like a downpour from the heavens, wetting my cheeks, burning in my eyes, dripping off my chin onto my T-shirt. Salty liquid, hot and tangy, seeped between my lips to taint my tongue.

The back door slammed shut.

I jerked, frozen mid sob.

My parents trundled in from the kitchen, carrying plastic sacks of groceries. I'd forgotten they were still staying here. Seeing Lachlan erased my memory. Mom and Dad had gone out to buy groceries, and I bowed out of the excursion, too exhausted to stomach a public outing.

Plunking her bags on the floor fast enough to make them tip over and spill their contents, my mother raced over to me with worried eyes. She knelt beside me, settling a hand on my shoulder as she examined me with her gaze. "Honey, what's wrong?"

Dad dropped an eighteen-roll pack of toilet paper on the floor by the sofa. His gaze narrowed on me, he asked, "Was that Lachlan we saw leaving just now? Did he make you cry?"

"Yes. No." I shook my head as if that might clear my thoughts. It didn't. "I mean, he was here, yes. Don't really want to talk about it, okay?"

At least I'd stopped crying. But slumped against the door, my hair disheveled and my shirt damp, I must've looked god-awful. Dad, never one to delve into emotions, rocked back on his heels and clasped a hand on the back of his neck, head bowed. Mom helped me up off the floor, then encased me in a suffocating hug.

"Want I should shoot him?" Dad said.

My lips twitched, not quite a smile but as close as I'd get right now. "No, but thanks for the offer."

"Your father's joking," Mom said, casting him an exasperated glance. I took the tissue she produced from her pocket. It was wrinkled but clean, and I blew my nose with an unladylike snort.

Dad huffed. "If he's upsetting her this much, I will shoot him—right where it counts."

He pointed at his groin.

Still surrounded by my mother's arms, I rolled my eyes. "Please don't. Lachlan didn't do anything. He was very sweet, actually."

"That's why you were in a heap on the floor balling your eyes out."

"I'm exhausted, that's all." I shuffled to the sofa to pet Casey, who was watching me with doggie concern. "I think all these months of stress have finally caught up to me. Besides, I thought you guys liked Lachlan. You have been talking to him almost every day."

My parents exchanged a look, one only they understood, then Mom said, "We do like him, but we love you. Do you want to work things out with him? We'll support you, whatever you decide."

"What do I want? Good question." I shrugged. "No fucking idea."

She eyed me up and down, her forehead wrinkling. I suspected this was the first time either of my parents had heard me use the F-word. Dad raised his eyebrows, but Mom gave me a tight smile.

"Well," she said, "you are in a pickle then, aren't you?"

"You could say that."

Mom pursed her lips. "Deep down, you know what you want to do."

If I did, the knowledge was submerged far under the waters of my mind. Lachlan had been so sincere, so anxious and worried. But if I forgave him and let him back into my life, I had no guarantees he wouldn't have another freak-out attack. I understood the reasons for his behavior, but understanding gave me no security. I trusted Presley, he used and betrayed me. I trusted Lachlan, he threw me away. Of course, he'd told me he'd leave, and I stupidly fell in love with him anyway. What was I supposed to do now? He paid for my legal defense, he called every day to check on me, he flew here from Scotland for the sole purpose of winning me back. And still, I couldn't shake the memory of that day in my kitchen.

His final words that day stung worse now than ever before. *I've nothing left to give, except money.* Minutes ago, he'd claimed he wanted more, implied he could give me more than his bank account. What did I want? What did I need?

My head hurt, my stomach too. I clutched my gut as a wave of nausea broke over me. Groaning, I leaned against the sofa.

"Still feeling sick?" Mom asked.

"Just the flu."

"Hmm. That's what you said two weeks ago, but it's not getting any better, is it?"

"I'm fine." I scuffled in a half circle to head for my bedroom. "Need a nap, then I'll feel better."

Without waiting for a response, I shambled into my room with Casey in tow. I shut the door and collapsed onto the bed, on top of the covers. Casey whumped onto the foot of the bed, resting his head on my ankles. As I spiraled down into a restless sleep, one thought bounced around in my brain like a pinball.

What do I want? What do I want?

Chapter Thirty

Two days later, a powerful impulse possessed me, as if an alien entity took over my body and compelled me to act. I'd wasted countless hours chewing my nails, guzzling pop, and chowing down on chocolate—all in a futile attempt to avoid thinking about Lachlan. In Chicago. Ensconced in a luxury hotel. Waiting for me.

Sleep? No, not for me, not since the nap I took right after he threw himself at my feet begging me to forgive him. Tossing and turning, interspersed with crying jags, consumed my nighttime hours. I still didn't trust Lachlan not to toss me aside again, but I couldn't go on this way. With no other recourse than to confront my ex-lover, I gave in to the impulse.

Which was how I wound up standing inside the most opulent hotel room imaginable—the Infinity Suite at The Langham. Of course he was staying in the Infinity Suite. Presidential suite wouldn't be good enough. He just had to find something called an Infinity Suite. I'd heard The Langham was ritzy, but holy mackerel. The living room spread out around me, cavernous and yet bright with sunshine pouring in through the floor-to-ceiling windows, beyond which the skyscrapers of Chicago towered. Here on the twelfth floor, the view was spectacular. I scuffled past two glossy black tables, one nested under the other, and between the plush, curved sofas. A baby grand piano nestled in one corner of the room. I halted, staring up at the chandelier above the sofas and tables. It glimmered gold in the light of its own bulbs.

When I'd marched into The Langham and told the desk clerk I was here to see Lachlan MacTaggart, the young man had summoned the concierge who promptly ushered me up the elevator and straight to the twelfth floor. Taking me into the luxurious suite, the concierge had led me through the grand foyer and into the living room. Lachlan had left instructions, the concierge told me, that if I showed up someone should bring me right to his suite. Whether he was overconfident or desperately hopeful, I didn't know yet. But after his performance the other day, I leaned toward the latter.

Performance? No, it hadn't been an act. He'd begged me to give him another chance. Got down on his knees and *begged*. Lachlan. The man who exuded masculine confidence. My self-assured, wickedly creative lover. Oh, but he wasn't mine, not anymore. Unless I…

Bile rose in my throat and I dug out the bottle of Tums I'd stuffed in my purse, chewing up two of the tablets. I must've caught a bug, because my stomach had turned into my worst enemy for the past two weeks.

I leaned against one sofa, too weirded out to sit. The concierge swore Lachlan was here, somewhere inside this mansion-size suite. I glanced around, catching sight of the dining room, past the doorway to the foyer.

"Lachlan?" I called out, my voice echoing faintly off glass and marble. "Are you in here?"

A door shut elsewhere in the suite. Footsteps clapped, drawing nearer. I tried to straighten my blouse, but it refused to do anything except be wrinkled. At last, Lachlan emerged from the foyer, dressed in gray slacks and a crisp white shirt, long-sleeved with gold cuff links. The top button of his shirt hung open. His hair looked damp as if he'd just showered.

Oh great. My mind went straight to envisioning him in the shower, naked and wet, steam billowing around him. Of course, that image segued into a memory of our time in the shower together, a different shower, one far less luxurious than the one here must be, but no less erotic. *Oh, come on.* I was angry and nauseous. I should not be fantasizing. Steeling my resolve, I pushed away from the sofa. Angry. Hurt. That's what I should project. I barred my arms over my chest, lifting my chin.

He smiled. The brilliant, heart-melting smile that made everything inside me go all gooey. Why did he have to go and do that?

"Erica," he said, imbuing my name with so much emotion it set off a pang in my chest. "I'm so glad you're here."

He took a step toward me.

I stumbled backward, holding up a hand, palm out. "No. You stay over there."

And of course, his brow crinkled. The spot between his brows dimpled, making him look so adorably confused and needy, like a puppy in a rainstorm. Hugging myself, backing up another step, I swallowed against a swell of nausea in my throat. My hands were freezing, so I stuffed them under my arms.

Lachlan fastened his gaze on me, his mouth tight. "Are you ill?"

"No." Lightheaded, yes, but not ill. It must've been the altitude. Way up here on the twelfth floor? My legs quivered. "I'm f—"

He started to move toward me, but halted with one hand outstretched, suspended in midair between us. "Erica?"

Regaining my balance, I locked my knees and tried for a breezy tone as I waved at the surroundings. "Thought you had simple tastes."

"I do." He lowered his hand slowly, in fits and starts. "There are two conventions in town and baseball games too. This was the only room I could get."

"Poor you, stuck in this hovel."

His lips curved up at the corners and the sun glittered in his eyes. "You almost smiled. Teasing me is a good sign, I hope."

I hunched my shoulders, focusing on the buttons in his shirt instead of his face, certain I'd never get through this conversation if I kept gazing into his eyes. Change of subject. Pronto. "I saw Presley a few days ago."

He locked his thick arms over his chest and frowned at me. "Why the bloody hell would you do that? After what he did to you."

My mind traveled back to the day two months ago when he'd told me all about his ex-wife. The explanation clarified why he hated bullies and why he made the comment about bullies bending others to their will for the sake of control. But now, with the suddenness of a spark flaring into a bonfire, I grasped why he despised Presley so much.

My scalp tingled, my eyes went dry from lack of blinking. I fluttered my lids, unable to shake the certainty of my revelation. "You thought Presley was doing to me what your wife did to you. That's why you attacked him repeatedly, why you would never speak his name, and why you're so upset I went to see him."

"Aye." He gave me an exasperated look. "Wasn't it obvious months ago?"

I flapped my arms once, huffing. "No, not to me. If you wanted me to understand that, you should've told me, for heaven's sake. I'm not telepathic."

He bit into his upper lip as his shoulders flagged. "Aye, you're right. My fault."

"Good. We agree on one thing, anyway."

Shoulders bunched, he said, "I would like to know why you went to him. If you'll tell me. Please."

I swung my arms, trying to figure out what to do with them besides scratching my face or picking at my hair. I opted for stuffing my hands in my jeans pockets. "He asked to see me, and I decided I should put that demon to rest." I kicked the floor with the toe of my sneaker, pretending to study the weave of the beige carpeting. "He's out on bond and his parents have taken away all his toys. He's broke." I hauled in a long breath, releasing it slowly as I raised my gaze to Lachlan. "He apologized for framing me. Says he always loved me and he hopes I have a good life."

Lachlan's lips thinned, his body tensing. "Does he."

"Yep." I rubbed my arms, suddenly cold. "Men are apologizing to me right and left these days."

He parked his taut ass on the opposite end of the sofa from me, slouching forward to brace his elbows on his knees, but he never broke eye contact. "You must think I'm just like him. Insincere, lying, uncaring."

"Actually, I think Presley was being genuine."

"What about me?"

"I'm sure you mean everything you've said."

"But?"

I swiveled on my heels to face the wall of windows, the action setting off a tilting sensation that had me sucking in a breath until it settled down. Hands shoved in my jeans pockets, I regarded the cityscape before me. "I've never thought you were like Presley. He abused my trust and didn't see the error of his ways until he got caught. You figured out you'd screwed up without needing to be arrested. Plus, you told me from the start you couldn't give me more than a fling."

His footsteps shooshed on the carpeting as he approached behind me. I caught his ghostly reflection in the window but couldn't make out his expression. His voice sounded close behind me. "From the moment I saw you in the club, I wanted to give you more, give you everything. The second I left your house that day, I realized what a terrible mistake I'd made, but I hurt you too badly to run back inside and beg your forgiveness. Giving you time seemed like the best choice, the only choice."

The sincerity in his voice made me long to lean back into him, let his arms close around me, let his strength and kindness wash away all my fears. I couldn't do it.

"Erica, you are *mo leannan*."

I turned around—and came face to chest with his massive body, no more than an arm's length away. The man exuded sensuality, even while engaged in a serious conversation. He couldn't help it. My line of sight fell directly on the swathe of skin exposed by his open collar. Skin I'd touched, kissed, licked. I'd memorized every inch of him, from his firm pecs to the sinuous lines of his muscular thighs, all the way down to his long toes and back up to the lush, dark lashes framing his eyes. I'd kissed those too. Hell, I'd run my lips over most every part of him.

My cheeks heated. The fire spread out, rushing through my entire body, sensitizing my skin until the barest draft from the ventilation system excited my nerves and stiffened the tiny hairs all over me.

I coughed, backed up, smacked into the glass. Fumbling for anything to say, I laid a hand over my collarbone. "You never told me what *mo leannan* means."

He reached out, his fingers hovering near my cheek, but withdrew his hand, curling his fingers into his palm. "It means my sweetheart."

A tingling swept through me, part chill from the cold glass at my back, part thrill from the realization of what he'd just confessed. My gaze swung up to his instinctively. The raw emotion there, his rapt attention glued to me, it had my heart pounding and my body softening. My voice came out higher pitched than usual. "All this time you've been calling me your sweetheart? Why wouldn't you tell me?"

He lifted a hand to my face, trailing his fingertips down the line of my jaw. "Didn't intend to call you *mo leannan*, or *gràidh*. Those words came out before I realized what I'd said. By then it was too late, and I couldn't keep from saying them over and over." His fingertips feathered over my lips for a heartbeat before he pulled them away. "I want to give you more than sweet words, though. I want to give you everything."

My ears had begun to ring, and I realized I'd stopped breathing. Still, I couldn't catch my breath. "I just...not sure..."

The room whirled around me. My knees buckled.

Lachlan caught me in his brawny arms before I hit the floor. My purse tumbled off my shoulder to plop onto the carpeting. Blackness spotted my vision as I spun down, down, down. He swept me up in his arms, carrying me out of the living room. I let my eyes drift shut, since they insisted on doing it anyway, and the gentle swaying of his movements lulled me into a trance. Warm, he was so warm and strong and soft in the right places, like where my head rested against his shoulder. The scent of his cologne wafted over me, redolent with musk and spice and a hint of the outdoors.

When he laid me down on a plush surface, I was too far gone to care. Sleep, yes, that's what I needed. Dimly, I heard him walk away, then return a moment later. The bed—oh yeah, this *was* a bed—jostled as he settled onto the mattress. I sensed him leaning over me, his scent all around me, and he placed a hand on my forehead as if checking for a fever. Apparently satisfied, he replaced his hand with a cool cloth. The chill of it roused my mind. Peeling my eyelids apart, I gazed up at eyes as pale and incandescent as blue topaz. Concern tempered their brilliance, though, and strained his features.

Lachlan brushed the back of his hand across my cheek. "Erica, sweet, how do you feel? I should call for a doctor."

"Uh-uh." I pulled in a long, cleansing breath. "I'm fine. Besides, doctors don't come running when you call."

"If I pay enough, one will."

"Please don't. I didn't eat enough breakfast, that's all."

He adjusted the cloth on my forehead, then combed his fingers through my hair. "Passing out is not the sign of a well woman."

"I must have the flu."

"Hmm." He frowned at me, his hip pressed against my thigh, and braced himself with one arm on the opposite side of me. "You don't have a fever."

"Stop fussing, I'm perfectly fine." Pleasure threaded through me at his fussing, at the way he was tending to me, caring for me. I wouldn't tell him that, though.

"Fine?" He shook his head, one corner of his mouth quirking up. "Is that why you're flat on your back in bed?"

In his bed. I glanced around at the huge mattress and the four-poster bed that housed it. The sheets were crumpled, the pillows indented with the shape of Lachlan's head. A hot shiver coursed through me. I lay in Lachlan's bed, where he'd slept all night. His skin had touched the same fabric mine touched now. The sheets were slick, like silk.

"How much does a suite like this go for?" I asked, just for something to say, to avoid considering the storm of emotions his tenderness provoked in me.

"Six a night," he said, averting his gaze, screwing up his lips.

I blinked slowly. "Six hundred?"

He gave a curt shake of his head, his features pinched.

My forehead stretched as my eyebrows shot up. "Six thousand? Dollars?"

"Ah…yes."

This suite cost more than I'd ever made in a month, or two months, or six. "You said you had enough money to be comfortable, but you neglected to mention you're filthy rich."

He rubbed the back of his neck, watching me. "Does it matter?"

"No. I'm surprised, that's all." The first stab of a headache pierced my eyes. My muscles longed to give out, to flop me back onto the bed. The luxuriant bed that felt like a cloud under me. Yeah, if I had six thousand dollars a night to spend on a hotel room, I might stay here too. Through a yawn, I said, "Money doesn't impress me."

"You told me that before."

"Did I?"

"Aye, but never mind." He leveled his gaze on me, his expression turning inscrutable. "Not that I'm complaining, but why are you here? I thought you wanted me gone."

"I came here to—" *Smell you, touch you, kiss you.* "Talk."

"Let's talk, then."

Did he have to hover so close? The heat of him penetrated my clothes, warming my skin, warming parts of me I didn't want warmed up right now.

He arched one brow. "What did you want to discuss?"

"Uh…" I had no idea. My head still felt a bit swimmy, my mind was unfocused, my stomach was still unsettled. I groaned, pressing a hand to the cloth on my forehead. "Can't think."

"Rest here for a bit." He dragged the blanket over me, his hand lingering on my arm, fingers caressing my flesh in slow circles. My eyelids grew heavy again, and this time I didn't know if I could keep from falling asleep.

He moved to stand.

"Wait," I said, pushing up as he sat back down and angled toward me. The washcloth slid off my forehead onto the bed. My face bumped into his chest. The wonderful scent and heat of him flooded over me, surrounded me, triggering an ache in my chest. A yearning I'd fought for so long. I felt too awful now to care about being strong. Tilting my head back, I met his questioning gaze. "Stay with me. Please."

His lips curved up in a shaky smile, and he let out the breath I hadn't realized he was holding. "Of course I will."

Without another word, he climbed over my body to lie down beside me. He didn't try to put his arm around me or nuzzle against me. He just lay there, a couple inches away, and folded his hands over his six-pack abs, concealed beneath his dress shirt. I was grateful beyond words, and besides, I had no clue what to say to him. Talk? Sure, I'd thought I wanted to do that. But once I got here, I couldn't remember any of the things I'd planned to tell him. Cutting things. Definitive things. Unimportant things.

I tossed the washcloth onto the sleek, modern bedside table—surely it was waterproof, right?—and settled into the cushy mattress, underneath the silky-soft blanket. Sleep seduced me, luring me down into its shadowy, weightless depths. No dreams haunted my slumber, no thoughts, no worries, just a deep and peaceful sleep the likes of which I hadn't known in months, maybe years. I woke bleary-eyed and fuzzy-brained, rising out of a fog into the bright sunshine, squinting until my eyes adjusted.

Where was I? Huge windows, view of the city, and…My heart did a little hop-skip. Right next to me, turned on his side to face me, slept Lachlan. Everything rushed back to me with a heady abruptness. The Infinity Suite. Almost passing out. Lachlan catching me. Caring for me. Lying with me.

Raising up on one arm, I took in the sight of him there, eyes closed, a slight smile on his lips as if sleeping beside me gave him all the pleasure in the world. As if he belonged with me. As if he loved me. But he'd never said the words, which left too much room for doubt. And yet, I yearned to curl up against him, to feel his strong arms encircle me, drawing me tight against him. To hear him call me *gràidh* and *mo leannan*. I stretched a hand out to touch his face, then pulled it back, fisting it over my belly. He'd vowed he wouldn't leave town without me, but he hadn't asked me to go with him to Scotland—or anywhere. Though I understood why he hesitated, why he'd walked out on me two months ago, my heart and soul were tapped out, sapped of the strength to argue or watch him break down again. If he woke up and started murmuring sweet words to me again, I'd melt. Problem was, I couldn't shake the bone-deep fear he'd lose his nerve and run back home to Scotland like before.

You are my home, he'd vowed.

Pain cramped the back of my throat. Despite the fear, despite everything, I needed to speak the truth, even if he couldn't hear it. Maybe it was best he never hear the words. I whispered them into the air, so hushed I scarcely heard it.

"I forgive you."

Sliding out of the bed, I tiptoed into the living room, found a paper and pen, and left him a note so he wouldn't wonder what became of me. I hurried out of the suite and down the elevator, but the concierge intercepted me on my way through the lobby. He insisted on hailing a taxi for me and I didn't argue. By the time I got home, all I wanted to do was crawl into bed, huddle under the covers, and sleep more.

But when I walked through the front door, my parents were waiting in the living room. They leaped off the sofa with a spryness even Casey couldn't match. The dog bounded up to me but refrained from accosting me, instead choosing to lick my hands. Mom and Dad lingered near the sofa, though they came around the backside to scrutinize me with parental concern.

"Where have you been?" Dad asked.

"I went to see Lachlan."

They glanced at each other, Dad smirked, and Mom dug a ten-dollar bill out of her pocket, handing it to Dad.

I frowned. "What are you betting on now?"

"You," Mom said, as if betting on their daughter was a common parental pastime. "Your father said you must've gone to talk to Lachlan, but I said no, you're much too stubborn to go to him until at least tomorrow."

Dad pocketed the money, still smirking.

My frown deepened into a scowl that I felt cinching my face tight. "I'm agonizing over a very personal decision and you guys are making wagers about it?"

"What else have we got to do?" Dad said. "Retirement's kinda boring, and we got used to all the activity at the village."

The village meaning the retirement community they'd moved to after he quit working. I was beginning to think life in swampy Florida had saturated their brains and turned them into loons. But, I supposed, betting on my love life was their way of showing they cared about the outcome. Cared about me. And, in a weird way, cared about Lachlan too. I still couldn't decide how I felt about their strange camaraderie with him.

Of course, they were better judges of character than I was. After meeting Presley once, they couldn't disguise their dislike of him, though they never told me they didn't like him. Completely taken in by his act, I'd ignored their attitude toward him, dismissing it as a sign of overprotective parents. With Lachlan, in spite of knowing he'd dumped me and hurt me badly, they still liked him. I withheld the gory details of our breakup, but they'd seen me weeping over him. For them to like him anyway...I wasn't sure what to make of it.

My mother marched up to me and planted her palm on my forehead.

I swatted her hand away, probably making a petulant face. "I don't have a fever."

"No, but you are pale."

A phone warbled. Mom excavated it out of her purse and answered, a smile lightening her expression. "Hello, Lachlan. How are you?"

I jerked my hand to reach for her phone but reeled it back an instant later. Talk to him, don't talk to him. Yell at him, kiss him. My heart and mind couldn't agree on what I should do about Lachlan.

"Yes, she's here," Mom told Lachlan. She paused between each phrase she spoke, listening to his responses. "No, she didn't mention it. We'll take care of her, don't worry. I'll tell her."

She hung up, dumped the phone in her purse, and shook her head at me. "Lachlan says you passed out earlier."

I gazed heavenward but found no answers there. "He's overreacting. I *almost* passed out, that's all."

"Hmm." She watched me for a moment, then said, "Lachlan wants you to know he heard what you said this morning right before you left. I don't know what that means, but he thought you would."

Right before I left? He'd been asleep—or so I thought. No, he couldn't have heard me when I told him I forgave him. But what else could he have meant?

"Erica was bound to get sick," Dad said, "after all the stress she went through the past few months."

Mom tsked. "That's not why she's sick, Frank."

"Really. Then what's your diagnosis, Dr. Deb?"

She surveyed me with a neutral expression, but her gaze hesitated over my belly before she looked at my face again. "You're going to a doctor, even if we have to hogtie you and drag you there on our backs. I already called and made you an appointment for three o'clock."

"You what?" I sputtered, executing an honest-to-goodness double take.

My mother sighed. "I knew you wouldn't go on your own."

"Should've heard her," Dad said. "She pretended to be you and whined real good until they squeezed you in this afternoon."

Well, I supposed I couldn't really blame them. I'd been nauseous and exhausted for two weeks, hadn't eaten much lately, and had resorted to napping in the daytime to make up for lost sleep. Maybe I did need to see a doctor. Resigned to my fate, I rubbed my forehead and let my shoulders sag. "Okay. I'll go."

Mom clapped a hand on my shoulder. "Good girl."

Dad glanced at me, then Mom. "Should we call Lachlan and let him know?"

"No!" The syllable exploded out of me, harsher than I'd intended. I flung a hand up to cover my mouth. "I'm sorry, that came out wrong. But please don't call him. I'll deal with him later."

An odd expression flickered over my mother's face. "I have a feeling you'll need to see him sooner rather than later."

A prickling started on my scalp and rushed over my whole body, not quite cold, not exactly warm. It was more an awareness just below the surface of my mind. I couldn't grab onto it, and I had a sinking feeling I'd regret it if I did latch onto the knowledge.

I seized a lock of my hair, twining it around my finger. My lip curled at the grimy feel of my hair. I dropped the lock. "Need a nap and a shower before my appointment."

But in the back of my mind that slippery little fragment of knowing taunted me.

Chapter Thirty-One

I balanced atop a stool at the bar inside Dance Ardor, my heels lodged on one of the rungs. The bartender brought me my second glass of sparkling water. Yesterday, I'd visited the doctor's office and received my diagnosis. I still felt numb, unable to process what I'd learned. Yet even before my doctor's visit, I'd made my decision about Lachlan. After the appointment, I worried about what he'd think when I told him about my condition. Would it be too much for him? Would he hop on the next flight home?

You are my home, he'd said. I shut my eyes, my mind reeling back to yesterday in his hotel room. His sweet concern. The way he'd tended to me. How he'd lain beside me while I slept. My throat burned, and a coldness blanketed me. Why did the thought of him still affect me this way? I should've been inured to his presence by now.

I swigged my sparkling water. The carbonation tickled the back of my throat, making me cough. I'd never get inured to Lachlan MacTaggart.

Scanning the club, wincing at the bright flashes of the strobe lights, I searched for my guest. I'd sent Lachlan a text message—yes, I was a coward—inviting him to meet me here. Why here, my parents had asked. Good question. I couldn't really explain it, but this was where I'd first met Lachlan and somehow it seemed appropriate to experience the critical moment in our relationship in the place where it all began.

No Lachlan yet, though.

I turned back to the bar, sipping my drink. A gorgeous guy dressed in an expensive suit, without the jacket, sat down on the stool beside me. His hair had that ultra-chic rumpled style. He flicked me a quick, appraising look. His gaze heated when he spotted my breasts, highlighted by the low neckline of the emerald dress Lachlan had bought me way back during our one month together. Mr. Fashion Victim stroked his shadow beard and smiled—at my boobs. "Hey, beautiful. Can I buy you a real drink?"

A real drink. I choked on air, sputtering. Lachlan had offered me the same thing the first time I saw him, here in this club. My first taste of Scotch whisky had hit me hard, though not as hard as the Scotsman who introduced me to it. When he offered me Talisker whisky and described the Isle of Skye to me, oh my…

"Well?" the gorgeous boob-talker said. To his credit, he'd shifted his focus to my face. His eyes were a scorching shade of caramel brown. Most women would've swooned at his attention. His moves left me cold, with a familiar emptiness yawning inside my heart.

"Thank you," I told him, cradling my glass in both hands, "but I'm not drinking alcohol these days."

"What, are you Mormon or something?"

"No." *I'm…No, don't think about it, not here, not now.* "I'm a health nut." I tipped my glass to him. "My body is a temple."

The sedate song that had been playing faded away. Hard-driving electronic music pulsated through the club, vibrating my stool and grating on my nerves. I rubbed my temples and tossed back the rest of my sparkling water, gesturing to the bartender for more. The last time I'd visited this establishment, a certain Scotsman strode up to me in a blue-and-green kilt, his demeanor all gentle confidence and easy sensuality.

"May I worship at your temple, *gràidh?*"

My heart thumped so hard pain stabbed through my ribs, stealing my breath. My rational brain shouted at me to get hold of myself first, but a reckless heat rushed through me, overpowering my reason. Elation shot adrenaline straight into my veins, heightening every one of my senses, awakening the hairs on my arms and the back of my neck. I spun around on my stool. My dress snagged on it and rode up my thigh, but I barely noticed the chill of air teasing my flesh.

Lachlan grinned. He wore the kilt and the black T-shirt—and those damn combat boots.

The gorgeous guy beside me bristled. "She's with me, jackass."

"No, I'm not." I fought the impulse to hurl myself at Lachlan. This meeting was supposed to be mature and serious, not wild and fevered like our first encounter. A nagging voice in my head asked why I'd arranged to meet him here, then, if I didn't want the same outcome. Okay, okay, maybe a part of me did want that. Our first kiss had been life-altering, and I craved the pure, mindless pleasure of succumbing to my desires, succumbing to him.

I intended to hop off my stool gracefully, but I'd made the fatal mistake of wearing the same stilettos as before, the second time ever I'd worn sky-scraper heels. I'd eaten three good meals today, but the dizziness lingered in the background. The second my stilettos touched down on the shiny floor, vertigo twirled my head for a split second and I lost my balance. My right heel slipped out from under me, careening me toward Lachlan.

He caught me in those powerful yet gentle arms. Pinned to his body, I tipped my head back to drink in the sight of him. Worry creased his brow.

"Relax, I'm just clumsy," I said, making zero effort to disentangle myself. He was warm and solid and more tempting than ever, and my mutinous body seemed intent on dissolving into him. A bit too breathlessly, I added, "Feeling much better today, actually."

"Glad to hear it." One corner of his mouth ticked up. "You do have a tendency to swoon into my arms."

Ah yes, our first meeting. Had my subconscious arranged for me to tumble into him again? *Stay focused, woman.* I flattened my palms on his chest, swirling my fingertips over the ridges of muscles hidden under his shirt. So much for staying focused.

Mr. Fashion Victim jumped off his stool. "This douche bothering you?"

"Not at all." I gazed up at Lachlan, unblinking, seduced by his smolder-ing blue eyes. Dimly, I realized I was moistening my lips, but I couldn't concentrate on anything except his eyes. "I'm with the Highlander."

Lachlan's smile lit the entire world and shot liquid heat through my body. Reason and intentions disintegrated, blown away by the winds of an all-consuming need. I wrapped my arms around his neck and flung my legs up to encircle his waist and lock my ankles behind him. Heedless of the crowd around us, I crushed my mouth to his. Our lips fused in a messy and desperate kiss, his lips grinding against mine with a fervor beyond anything we'd shared before. Two months without his kiss, his touch, his—

He thrust his tongue inside my mouth and I moaned, clawing my fin-gers into his hair. Oh, he tasted divine. I couldn't get enough, though I lashed my tongue in greedy strokes, crazed with the need to devour him.

The boob-talker muttered, "You weren't the hottest chick in here, any-way."

My Highlander set me down on my feet. His eyes were glossy and hooded, his lips moist from our kiss. He blinked rapidly, and I noticed wetness gathering in his eyes. Tears? My strong Scot wouldn't shed them, no way. But the fact he teared up launched my heart into orbit, weightless and free, spinning out into a universe that was hollow and vacant without him in it.

Lachlan placed one big hand on my cheek. "That eejit's wrong. You are the hottest chick in this place."

Still soaring, I clasped my hand over his. "I was afraid you might not come. I mean, I know how much you hate this place."

"I will always come for you." He shifted his hand, cupping my nape. "Always."

Yesterday, when I reached my decision, I'd promised myself from here on out I'd be honest with him, no matter what. *Okay, here goes.* "I miss you. I want to make this work, but we need to talk about a few things first."

His expression blanked, his mouth went slack. He spoke slowly, his tone measured. "Are you sure that's what you want?"

"Positive." I brushed my lips over his, murmuring against them. "Can't deny the truth anymore. I love you. I want to be with you, for as long as you'll have me."

"As long as I'll have you?" He shook his head, eyebrows squished together. His accent thickened with an emotion that roughened his voice. "I'll be having ye for the rest of our lives and whatever comes after. Ye'll not be getting away from me again."

"I wasn't sure if you were sick of my angst."

Lachlan shook his head again, his lips parting. "Don't be daft, lass. I'll never get sick of you."

His hand on my hip glided up my back, over my shoulder, grazing across my collarbone to flutter over my throat and settle on cheek. His blue eyes, glinting in the flashing strobe lights, enthralled me. I could've gazed into those eyes forever, but I needed an unequivocal answer from him. "The real question is, are you sure?"

He wound his arms around me and held on like he'd never let go. "I've let go of the past, once and for all. Losing you woke me up and forced me to see what I'd done to myself—to you. All I know is I can't abide a future without you in it."

My breaths grew labored as the import of his statement sunk in. He ducked his head close to mine, but just when he spoke, the music crescendoed to deafening levels and drowned out his words. I cupped a hand over my ear, shouting to be heard. "What? I can't hear you."

He pulled in a deep breath and, in the instant the song ended, he hollered, "I love you."

Everyone in the club turned to stare at us. Some looked baffled, others amused, and still more glared at us like we'd committed a heinous crime by interrupting their dancing. Who cared what they thought? Lachlan had spoken the words. Well okay, he yelled them so loud his voice reverberated off the club's walls and rattled my eardrums, but yeah. He'd said it.

Tears streamed down my face. *Stupid hormones.*

I staggered backward, turning away from him, my heart in my throat.

It was time to tell him everything. Time to face the consequences and put his commitment to the ultimate test.

Lachlan came up behind me, stroking his hands over my shoulders. "I love you, Erica. Did ye not hear me?"

"People on Jupiter heard you." My fingers clenched in the fabric of my dress, I gnawed the inside of my cheek. My heart was racing, my thoughts were spinning. He slid his hands down my inner arms. When his skin grazed the insides of my elbows, I shuddered. His hands skated down, past my wrists, and he fitted his palms into mine, lacing our fingers together, tugging me into him.

When he bent to whisper in my ear, I shut my eyes and sagged into him. His lips fluttered over my earlobe. "What's wrong, *gràidh*? You said you wanted to talk, but now you're pulling away."

"Sorry. I do want to talk, but I'm—" *Honesty from now on, remember?* "I'm afraid you won't like what I have to say."

His fingers tightened around my hands. "Nothing you might say will change how I feel. I love you and I swear I will never leave you again."

How did he infuse those simple words with so much passion and certainty? I squeezed his fingers, my heart swelling with a dizzying whirlpool of emotions. I yearned to believe him. No...I did believe him. The truth of his declaration rang in my soul.

The music started up again. Bass thumped through the floor as a woman's sensual voice purred about desire unheeded. Lachlan slipped one arm around my waist to hug me close, his cheek pressed to mine. When his hand drifted down to shield my womb, his fingers swirling over the fabric of my dress, I swallowed hard. I'd missed him so much.

"Please, Erica." His sultry plea sent another shiver through me. He raised our joined hands to his lips, fluttering kisses over my knuckles. "Trust me to love you no matter what."

I nodded, my insides quivering. Fear. Anticipation. Desire. They all coalesced into a ball in my stomach. I croaked, "I reserved a private booth."

He hustled me around the dance floor's perimeter, past couples entwined in each other's arms, cloaked in shadowy corners, engaged in kisses so erotic and intense they might've been illegal in public. More couples flowed off the dance floor, still linked in hip-grinding action, twirling around us like participants in a pagan ceremony of fertility. Lachlan grasped my hand tighter, tugged me close to him, and placed a protective arm around my shoulders. He shot a dark glare at a man whose gaze flew to my half-exposed cleavage as we passed him. The man cringed and swung his attention to the dance floor.

Lachlan ushered me out of the main club area, around a half wall, down the hallway that housed the private booths, each hidden behind plum-colored velvet curtains. Lavender light showered down from bulbs recessed in the ceiling, painting our skin in otherworldly shades. The walls dulled the urgent beat of the music, but my urgent need for Lachlan only escalated into a deep throbbing between my thighs. Two months plus raging hormones equaled one horny accountant—er, unemployed *former* accountant. I had to get a handle on my lust, though, because we really did have important matters to discuss.

I pointed toward the third booth. "That one."

Halting in front of it, Lachlan swept the curtains aside with one hand. His other hand landed on the small of my back, urging me inside. A U-shaped sofa sat tucked behind an oval table, with a single lamp on the tabletop, its light bathing the space in a creamy, intimate glow. When I scooted across the sofa, my dress caught on the purple velvet upholstery and rode up my thighs.

Lachlan stifled a groan.

I glanced up to find him engrossed by my exposed thigh, his lips parted, tongue flicking out to moisten them. I tried to yank the hem down, but it wouldn't budge. The velvet held it fast, and unless I stood up, no way was it moving. I gave up.

He lowered his body onto the sofa beside me, one arm draped across the back behind my shoulders. His other hand lighted on my bare thigh. "You still drive me mad, without even trying to."

"Ditto." I gulped down a gasp when he pressed his palm onto my leg, his fingers delving down to stroke my inner thigh. "I should be more circumspect about this, but I lose my mind whenever I'm close to you."

"I know the feeling."

Fingers. Petting. Igniting. The blaze erupted in my core and flashed through my entire body. Off kilter, again. But it felt wonderful.

He slanted toward me, his lips within kissing distance. "What did you need to say?"

"Guh…" Nothing else would come out of my mouth. My lips tingled with the need to taste him again—and this time, let the fire consume us both until nothing existed except our limbs entangled and our bodies merged in rhythmic hunger.

"Still afraid?" He feathered kisses along my jaw, light and teasing. "You can tell me anything, Erica."

Could I? My hand rose to cover my belly. If he freaked out on me again, I didn't know what I'd do. Hit him. Burst into tears. My heart would be shattered for sure this time, with no chance of repairing the damage.

"I'll go first," he said, pulling back a little, though he stayed close enough the scent of his cologne enveloped me. "I'm divorced, finally and forever. I made certain of that."

"Congratulations." I wriggled in place when his fingers began stroking the exposed skin of my shoulder. I rested my hands on my knees, but his fingers on my thigh wrecked my attempt at composure.

"Not looking for congratulations."

"What, then?"

"I want what you promised me yesterday when you thought I couldn't hear. I want—I need for you to say it now."

No point denying I understood what he meant. "Okay."

His hand on my thigh tensed, his fingers curled.

"I forgive you, Lachlan."

Chapter Thirty-Two

He leaned in again, his breaths tickling my lips. "I took the last two months to clear out my life. Finalize the divorce. Sell my company." He withdrew his hand from my thigh, clenching it on his lap. "And to work out my, uh…fears."

I turned my face to his without thinking and wound up eye to eye with him, our mouths grazing each other. My heart stuttered, my stomach flip-flopped. For a man's man like Lachlan to admit he'd been afraid took guts. But I didn't understand why he'd made such drastic changes in his life. "Why sell your business?"

"Because I don't need the income anymore, and I've lost my taste for helping avaricious elites stuff their coffers with more money than they'll ever spend."

My brows lifted. "Were all your clients that bad?"

"No, most were good folk. But I'd had enough of the few greedy ones." He scratched his jaw, his lips contorting. "I want a better life. I want to build a family, but I'm missing the keystone."

"And what's that?"

His voice was soft, almost a whisper. "You, Erica. You are the keystone, and the life I want will fall down around me without you."

"Oh." The blood must've evacuated my face because my cheeks no longer sizzled. I opened my mouth to speak again but clapped it shut. I had no clue what on earth to say.

His pulse throbbed in his neck and he took slow, controlled breaths as he watched me with wary eyes. He scooted closer until our bodies collided and his mouth hovered so near mine I could taste his breath. "I made a mistake. I will spend the rest of my life making it up to you. I love you, lass, with all that I am. My life will be meaningless without you in it."

Surprised by the steady, deep pitch of his voice, I searched his face, noting the determined set of his jaw and the clarity in his eyes.

He reached into the breast pocket of his T-shirt and took hold of a small object I couldn't see. With it concealed in his palm, fingers closed over it, he offered his hand to me. "This is yours, whether you take me back or not. It's a token of my love and respect for you, both of which will never die. I'm yours forever, my sweet Erica, my *gràidh*, the bonniest, sexiest lass ever to grace this earth and the cleverest, strongest woman I've ever known."

His words burrowed deep into my soul, fanning a flame that had never quite died, no matter what he might've done. I couldn't let the flame sputter out because that meant I'd given up on him.

Lachlan spread his fingers, revealing the object in his palm. A diamond ring.

I stared at the ring, at its gold band topped by a glittering diamond. Tasteful. Beautiful. Not so large I'd feel weird wearing it, but not too small either. *Perfect.* I jerked my head up and our gazes intersected, locked together as if a steel cable had snapped taut between us and nothing could sever the connection. The air around us seemed to crackle with the energy of our passion and adoration for each other.

He crooked a finger under my chin. "Will you marry me?"

My gaze flitted to the ring. *Tell him now.* My trembling hand flew to my throat, but I could not break eye contact with him. Staring into the depths of his topaz-blue eyes, a certainty resonated through my soul. I trusted him. So, I confessed—in a roundabout way. "Remember on our road trip, the first night we stayed in the bed-and-breakfast?"

"Yes. I upset you, though I didn't understand why at the time."

"Now you do?"

He nodded. "I was still pretending I could walk away from you and feel nothing about it."

"It's all in the past." I folded my arms over my belly. Telling him the whole truth suddenly seemed vitally important, for reasons I couldn't fathom. "Do you remember what happened after I threw my boots at you?"

He flashed me a grin. "I made love to you, and after, you were very relaxed."

"Uh-huh." I watched his profile, losing myself for a moment in the rugged beauty of his features and the knowledge he was mine, for good. I cleared my throat and forged ahead. "We forgot something."

"I don't follow you, sweet. You'll need to be a wee bit more specific in what you're trying to say."

My instinct was to look away, but I made myself meet his gaze head-on. "No condom."

He arched one eyebrow at me, then his gaze went distant as if he were mentally rewinding to the night in question. He relaxed, brushing his lips over my cheek as he patted my naked thigh. The casual touch segued into a long, sensual caress that had me squirming. His voice flowed through me like the warmth of whisky in my veins. "Hardly matters now."

"You don't understand." I winced, wringing my hands on my lap. "I'm pregnant."

His eyes bulged. A fragile smile tugged at his lips, faltering in repeated attempts to take hold, until at last a grin overpowered his face, tightening lines of joy around his eyes. "We're having a bairn?"

My brain could produce nothing more meaningful than a grunt and a nod. Maybe he hadn't yet realized what I'd been fumbling to say. "It's my fault."

His hand stilled, but his voice stayed sexy and sweet, with a hint of pleasure in his tone. "Your fault?" He shook his head. "Is this what you were afraid to tell me? Did you think I'd be angry?"

I hunched my shoulders and hugged myself. "Should've reminded you. About, you know, the condom."

"I seduced you that night." He sighed, nuzzling my neck. "It was my responsibility to remember a condom. I got so caught up in needing to wipe that frown off your face, I forgot everything else. It's my fault."

"Are you sorry it happened?"

"I'm sorry I was so careless with you." His hand started moving again, drifting higher, perilously close to my mound. He dragged his lips down my throat, then angled his face up to mine. "But I could never regret making a bairn with you."

The anxiety flooded out of me so suddenly I sagged into the sofa back, relief freeing me to gaze at him with loving admiration. "Neither could I."

I nodded, helpless to speak anymore. Tears filled my eyes—tears of elation this time.

Something metallic pressed into my cheek, and I realized he had the ring hooked over one finger. I grasped his hand, drawing it down to my chest, holding it over my heart. I plucked the ring off his fingertip. "Yes."

"What?"

"Are you deaf? The answer is yes. I would love to marry you, Lachlan."

His laughter, deep and throaty, resonated in his chest. A reckless grin spread his lips wide, making him resemble a child who'd just gotten the most expensive toy ever for Christmas. "Thank you, *gràidh*. Thank God for creating a treasure like you and, heaven almighty, thank *you* for giving me another chance." He peppered kisses over my cheeks, my jaw, my chin. "You will never regret it, I swear on my life."

I soared through the stratosphere again, lightened of a burden I hadn't realized had weighed me down until this moment. The diamond sparkled in the muted light, held between my thumb and forefinger. Half crying, half giggling like a schoolgirl, I said, "Are you going to put this thing on my finger or what?"

"Och, yes." He hauled me onto his lap and shimmied down the sofa to its end. Rising, he deposited me on the sofa with my feet hanging off it. My dress had ridden up even higher to crumple around my waist, and my black lace panties peeked out from under the fabric.

Lachlan knelt before me on one knee. His gaze flicked down to my panties. He scrubbed a hand over his mouth, blinked furiously, and lifted his gaze to my face. The familiar hunger simmered in his eyes and roughened his voice. He took the ring, raising it between us. "You are the center of my universe, Erica Teague, and I'm blessed to have you for my wife."

"My goodness, I've never heard you babble before tonight." I grinned despite the tears flowing down my cheeks because they were borne of pure, unadulterated bliss. "You really are a changed man."

He slipped the ring onto my finger, head bowed, and turned his eyes up to look at me. "Don't care if I sound like an eejit. Best get used to my babbling because I intend to let you know every single day how much I cherish you." He dropped his head, pressing his puckered lips to my belly. "And our bairn. Which I'm certain will be a bonnie wee lassie just like you."

When he tilted his head back to smile at me, I bent to rest my forehead on his. "I think it'll be a boy. Braw and handsome like his father."

"Hmm. Maybe we should have several bairns, to make sure we get a boy and a girl."

"How about dozens of little MacTaggarts running around in the heather?"

"Dozens, aye." A smile of unrestrained joy broke across his beautiful face. With half-closed eyes, he drank me in from top to bottom as if he were plotting which lascivious acts he would lure me into tonight. His gaze hiccupped at my breasts, but then he met my eyes and captured my face in his hands once more. His lips teased mine, his tongue sketching the outline of my mouth with short, erotic licks. I thrust my hands into his hair to drag him in for a bone-melting kiss, our hot tongues wrestling, our moans and groans muffled by each other's mouths. When I was on fire from head to toe, inside and out, I broke away.

Lachlan pulled me tight against his hard, aroused body. "Not done with you."

My breasts were crushed to his chest, aching for his touch. The hard ridge of his erection pressed into my belly, and my sex began to throb. "Oh Lachlan."

He shoved his fingers inside my panties, down into my cleft. "You're so wet."

"Please, wait—" His fingers stroked my sex in slow, powerful circles. I shuddered with a hunger so intense it derailed my train of thought. I threw my head back, exposing my throat to him. He licked and nipped and kissed his way up from my collarbone to my ear, suckling the lobe while his fingers tormented my clit. I gasped. "Not here. Please."

He stopped. Just like that. His fingers rested on my mound, not moving. "Where?"

"Can't go to my place. My parents are there."

"My hotel," he growled, and swept me up into his arms as he stood. "Hurry."

Lachlan yanked my dress down to cover my thighs. I managed to snag my small purse off the table before he strode out of the booth, the curtains billowing around us, and down the hallway to the club proper. I padlocked my arms around his neck, certain nothing I said would halt him. He marched straight across the dance floor, and couples scattered to get out of our way. The set of his jaw told me anyone who got in our way would get mowed down by my Highlander. People stared at us in disbelief, but everyone stepped aside for the Scotsman lugging his bride-to-be out of the club.

Once outside, he paused. "Where's your car?"

"There." I pointed across the parking lot. The cool night air raised goosebumps all over me. I wrapped my arms around him more snugly as he rushed across the pavement to my car and set me on my feet beside the passenger door.

"Keys," he commanded.

I dug them out of my purse, lightheaded from the hormones raging inside me, and handed over the keys. "I see we're back to monosyllabic Lachlan."

He grunted, unlocked the door, and hurled it open. "Not capable of conversation right now. All I can think about is stripping you naked and ravishing you until sunrise."

"Well, in that case…" I climbed into the car and, on purpose this time, let my skirt hike up. "Get a move on."

Chapter Thirty-Three

Three Weeks Later

On a sunny Wednesday morning, I stood in a field of heather, hand in hand with Lachlan as we spoke our vows before our gathered families. Lachlan wore—what else?—a kilt fashioned from the MacTaggart clan tartan, the blue and green I'd seen when I met him in Dance Ardor. I had chosen a simple dress, somewhat old-fashioned in style, with plenty of lace and a flowy skirt, that made me feel like a Highland princess. A breeze ruffled the dress and my hair, but I noticed nothing except him. My hot Scot.

A tree-cloaked hillside sloped up behind us, while before us a gentle grade extended down to our new house, and beyond that lay the glassy waters of Loch Leven with its smattering of islands. The village of Ballachulish nestled along the loch's shores, quaint and small and beautiful, surrounded by the shadows of the mountains but seated smack in a disk of golden sunshine. Not a single cloud marred the azure sky, though a certain golden retriever danced around amid the guests, as far as his retractable leash would allow. My dad held tight to the leash's handle, but no one seemed to mind Casey's exuberance. Just as the ceremony started, the dog sat down and fell silent as if he understood the importance of the moment.

When Lachlan slipped the wedding band onto my finger, tears rolled down my cheeks—which I blamed on hormones, of course. Never mind that my heart swelled with joy and I couldn't stop gazing adoringly at my new husband. Lachlan's smile trembled as I placed the ring on his finger, and his eyes glistened—though, being a caber-tossing, hammer-throwing Highland man's man, he didn't cry.

After the ceremony, my father clapped Lachlan on the shoulder and said, "Glad I didn't have to shoot you."

Lachlan arched an eyebrow at me.

With a sheepish shrug, I told him, "The possibility may have been discussed at one point. Weeks ago."

Dad grinned. "I offered, but Erica said 'nah, don't bother.' "

"Frank," my mom said in her best indulgent tone, "don't scare the poor boy. We decided we like him, remember? Offing your new son-in-law is rude."

"I'd only wing him," Dad insisted.

Both my parents had a teasing gleam in their eyes. I'd warned Lachlan he'd have to get used to the Teague family pastime of harassing our friends and relatives with odd sarcasm. I'd patted his cheek and assured him, "It means we love you, honey."

Now, as my mom enveloped him in a bear hug while my dad simultaneously gave his hand a powerful shake, Lachlan aimed a bemused smile at me.

"Okay, okay," I said, pushing my parents away from my husband and linking my hands around his arm. "There will be no winging Lachlan today."

"Today?" Lachlan asked, eying me askance, with a slight smirk.

"I need some way to keep you in line." I rose onto tiptoes to peck a kiss on his lips. "Can I have my own sword?"

"We'll see."

Lachlan's brothers approached us then, sly grins lighting up their faces, both as gorgeous as their elder sibling, my sexy-as-hell husband. Aidan and Rory—yes, I'd finally met the infamous Rory, Lachlan's solicitor and brother—slapped Lachlan on the back.

Aidan winked at me. "Picked a hot one there, Lachie. When do I get to kiss the bride?"

"Never," Lachlan replied in a dead-calm voice. "Don Juan MacTaggart does not get to practice on my wife. And don't call me Lachie unless you're wanting to get skelped."

"So sensitive," Rory said, sidling around Aidan to get closer to me. "Welcome to the family, Erica. Best get used to Lachie being a humbug. He's a boring, humorless man."

I didn't miss the glint in his eyes or the upward twitch of his lips. Yes, the Teagues and the MacTaggarts would get along fine, thanks to their shared love of teasing each other without mercy.

"Oh don't worry," I assured Rory, snuggling closer to Lachlan. "My husband is exciting and entertaining for me. Maybe he just doesn't like you two scunners."

Aidan and Rory burst out laughing. Lachlan watched them while shaking his head, a slight smile curving his mouth, until Rory managed to say, "She's already taking to our language. Better watch your wife, Lachlan, or she'll be a true Scottish lassie before you know it, cursing at you in Gaelic."

"Let me help her along," Aidan said, his expression all innocence as he clasped my shoulder in one hand. "Now just say *an toir thu dhomh pòg.*"

Lachlan slapped a hand on Aidan's chest and shoved him away. His brother stumbled backward, laughing so hard his eyes watered.

"What?" I asked, glancing between Lachlan and Aidan.

My husband's mouth twisted into a half-restrained smile. *"An toir thu dhomh pòg* means will you give me a kiss."

Note to self: Never repeat a Gaelic phrase told to you by Aidan MacTaggart.

I met Lachlan's sisters too—Catriona, Jamie, and Fiona. They'd declared me "the fourth sister" while helping me get ready for the wedding this morning, and I already felt like one of the family, thanks to the MacTaggarts' kindness and humor. Though they'd just met me a week ago, they treated me like their long-lost daughter. And both sets of parents had become fast friends as well. Niall MacTaggart was teaching Frank Teague how to play shinty. The game looked kind of like field hockey, but it confused the heck out of me.

Gradually, the wedding party headed down the hill to their cars parked in front of our house, to drive into the village for the reception. My brilliant husband had arranged to hold the party in the village, so we could sneak off to our house for a private party. Our parents, the last guests to leave, stopped to say goodbye before the MacTaggarts drove the Teagues into town for what promised to be a hell of a shindig. Casey bounded around the group of us, his tongue lolling and flapping.

As my mother hugged me, she whispered, "I hope you tested his engines already. Doesn't look like he'd have any trouble, but you don't want a nasty surprise on your wedding night."

"Mom!" I hissed, my cheeks flaring hot. "Honestly. It's a bit late to worry about it, don't you think?"

She pulled back just enough to hit me with a mother-knows-best look. "Well, did you?"

"Take him for a test drive?" Had I ever. She did not need to know the details. "Yes, he's...well equipped."

Thankfully, she left it at that, seeming satisfied with my response. Mothers.

Not long after that, our parents and Casey piled into a vehicle and departed. Casey would return to our homestead in the morning to settle into his new life as a Scottish farm dog. For tonight, Lachlan and I needed privacy.

As the last taillights receded into the night, my husband hoisted me into his arms and carried me over the threshold of our new home—our farm in the Highlands, where we'd raise our bairns. I'd thought my life was over when Presley Cichon framed me for embezzlement. Instead, I'd found everything I ever wanted.

Lachlan set me down, shut the door, and smiled that smile. "Welcome home, Erica MacTaggart."

"It's so beautiful, Lachlan."

He held up a finger. "Got another surprise for you."

"You know how I love your surprises."

He trotted into another room, which I thought was the living room, and returned with his prize. My hand flew to my chest. "I thought you were kidding when you said—"

"A Scotsman doesn't joke about these things." He spread his legs wide, chest high, looking every bit the Highland hero in his kilt and white, long-sleeved shirt. "Like my claymore?"

"Oh yes."

The sword must've been five feet long, its blade glinting in the light. He swung the claymore through the air in broad swipes. Right then and there I knew life with Lachlan MacTaggart would never be boring, but it would be sweet and fulfilling and full of wonder.

Lachlan brandished the sword in both hands. "Better run for yer life, lassie, 'cause ahm coming fer ye."

I sprinted for the bedroom, giggling all the way like an idiot, with my husband in hot pursuit. When we got to the bedroom, I let him catch me. He tossed the sword on the floor and scooped me up in his strong arms. "Time to pay the tithe."

"Tithe?"

"Aye," he said, with overly done solemnity. "Every Highland wife must pay her husband a tax on the wedding night."

I rolled my eyes. "You've got way more money than I do. Want the five bucks I still have in my purse?"

"Not money, *gràidh*." Lachlan heaved me onto the bed, and I yelped as I plopped onto the lush bedding, my butt sinking into it. His grin was wicked and promised many, many things. "I had another kind of tithe in mind."

"Hmm, in that case..." I stretched my entire body, which boosted my breasts high enough they almost spilled out of the dress. "I'll pay up gladly."

Lachlan stripped off his clothes faster than I'd ever imagined a man could disrobe, then sprawled over me, his hard body a blissful weight atop me. He thrust a hand under me, fumbling for the buttons of my dress. His lips pinched, his jaw clenched, and the spot just above his nose crinkled. After about ten seconds of jostling and struggling, he sprang to his knees and threw his arms up. "Bloody hell, woman, what kind of contraption have you got holding you in that thing?"

"Buttons." I pushed up into a sitting position, my face aligned with his waving erection. My mouth watered at the sight of his acres of muscle, his washboard abs, and oh yeah, his stiff shaft. I batted my eyelashes at him, putting on my best innocent face. "Is there a problem, my lord and master?"

His mouth puckered again, but this time because he was trying so hard not to laugh. "Careful. I might take you up on the lord-and-master bit."

I got to my knees, shuffling around so my back faced him, and glanced at him over my shoulder. "Surely a powerful warrior such as yourself can handle a few buttons."

Lachlan growled low in his throat, seized my dress, and ripped the buttons open in one jerk of his hands. Cool air wafted over my now-bare skin, but before I could shiver, his hot hands flattened on my back. He unhooked my bra, and his tongue touched down on my skin, tracing a slick path down my spine, dancing over each vertebra, igniting sparks that set my whole body on fire. He shoved the dress off my shoulders. With his mouth now on my neck, he murmured, "*Tha gaol agam ort.*"

"I don't speak Gaelic yet."

He pushed the fabric over my hips. It pooled around my knees as he dispatched my bra, sending it fluttering to the floor. I reached back to slide my fingers into his hair. He clasped my waist in both hands and, with stunning grace, hefted me up and out of the dress, spun me around, and laid me out on the bed, flat on my back.

Lachlan tore off my panties. "*Tha gaol agam ort* means I love you." He lowered his body onto mine once again, his erection trapped between our bodies. "Forever, *mo leannan.*"

"I love you too. Forever and ever." I wriggled, and he sucked in a breath. "You're mine, Lachlan MacTaggart. *Gràidh.*"

He cradled my head in his hands, gazing deeply into my eyes. "I love the way you say *gràidh*. You pronounce it perfectly."

"Is it my pronunciation you're interested in at the moment?" I locked one leg around his, rubbing parts of him into slick, swollen parts of me.

He made a choking sound. "Couldnae give a fuck about yer pronunciation right now."

Wrapping my arms around him, I raked my nails up and down his back. "Show me what you are thinking about."

He slanted his mouth over mine in a hard kiss, full of heat and tangling tongues. He groaned into my mouth, and my sex pulsed, my core aching with emptiness only he could fill. When he pulled away, his eyes burned with a bonfire of hunger matching my own.

"Now," I begged, arching my hips into him. "Please."

"Anything for you, *gràidh*." He drove into me with one long, powerful thrust. I cried out, my back bowing from the sheer ecstasy of him consuming me. He took me with leisurely strokes, driving me to the brink of madness, until I clawed at his back and pleaded for release, only to beg him with my very next breath never to stop. He braced his body on straight arms, grunting and shouting my name, his chest heaving, pumping harder and faster into my inflamed flesh. Sweat sheathed his body and dripped off his chest onto mine where it mingled with my own sheen of perspiration. The smell of sweat and sex permeated the air, the scent of my own arousal so strong I might've been embarrassed, if not for my husband obliterating my every thought with his throbbing shaft.

My body convulsed as I came with a whimpering scream, clutching at Lachlan until my fingers dug into his upper arms. He exploded inside me with a sharp yell. I spiraled down from the heavens back into my body as he thrust a few more times, then collapsed beside me, breathing hard. I fought to catch my breath, my body humming from the inside out like a guitar string plucked hard. But oh, how I loved the way Lachlan plucked my strings.

He pulled me onto my side, tucked against his body, my head pillowed against his shoulder. "Are you happy, sweet?"

I propped my chin on his chest so I could meet his gaze. "You know I am. A few months ago, I thought I was going to prison. Just a few weeks ago, I thought I'd never have what I really want." I snuggled into him, brushing my fingers over his cheek. "Now I have everything. With you."

He captured my hand, enclosing it in his. "You've given me more than I ever dreamed I'd have. Nothing will ever take me away from you, Erica."

"I'm not going anywhere. This is where I belong." I cleared my throat and prayed I'd pronounce the next part right. "*An toir thu dhomh pòg?*"

A breath rushed out of his nostrils. He hugged me tighter, his voice fierce with passion. "Keep speaking Gaelic."

"Why?"

He flipped us both over, with me beneath him and his quickly rousing shaft. "Because hearing you speak Gaelic will keep me going all night."

"Promises, promises."

"A guarantee."

For the rest of the night, he demonstrated that he would always keep his promises. Sometime in the wee hours of the night, we curled up under the sheets, exhausted in the best way, and fell asleep in each other's arms, content in our life together.

Forever.

LOVE THE

HOT SCOTS

SERIES?

VISIT
AnnaDurand.com

TO SUBSCRIBE TO HER NEWSLETTER

FOR UPDATES ON FORTHCOMING BOOKS IN THIS SERIES.

Anna Durand is an award-winning, bestselling author of sizzling romances, including the Hot Scots series. She loves writing about spunky heroines and hunky heroes, in settings as diverse as modern Chicago and the fairy realm. Making use of her master's in library science, she owns a cataloging services company that caters to indie authors and publishers. In her free time, you'll find her binge-listening to audiobooks, playing with puppies, or crafting jewelry.

She'd love to hear from you! Contact Anna via her website at AnnaDurand.com.